The Forbidden Forest

By

Joan Byrd

Deep Indigo Books

Published by Indigo Sea Press
Winston-Salem

Deep Indigo Books
Indigo Sea Press
302 Ricks Drive
Winston-Salem, NC 27103

This book is a work of fiction. Names, characters, locations and events are either a product of the author's imagination, fictitious or used fictitiously. Any resemblance to any event, locale or person, living or dead, is purely coincidental.

For information regarding bulk purchases of this book, digital purchase and special discounts, please contact the publisher at indigoseapress@gmail.com

Cover Design by Pan Morelli
Manufactured in the United States of America
ISBN 978-1-63066-557-9

I dedicate *The Forbidden Forest* to all my loyal readers who enjoy a page turner.

As you read, try to picture yourself among the scouts as they grow quiet and nervously walk single-file, down the middle of the Old Wagon Road as a dense fog crept in around them.

The sudden thunderstorm didn't help their jitters concerning the danger lurking on their right. One wrong step might find you being sucked inside the deadly tree line of The Forbidden Forest!!!

—Joan Byrd

CHAPTER 1

Reverend Jack Spencer sat quietly in his church office writing his sermon for the following Sunday. To start his next sermon on Sunday afternoon felt unusual for the thirty-year-old minister, but leaving on Monday on a five-day youth retreat had come unexpectedly.

The church budget had been tight for the summer months, due to half the congregation choosing to go on long vacations instead of working summer jobs. Over half the members of Grace Moravian were either schoolteachers or school staff. The small town of Graceland, North Carolina, employed almost 1/3rd of its citizens at one of three local schools. Graceland Elementary, Graceland Middle, and Graceland High School. That left the other 2,400 adult citizens employed at shops, cafés, the town bank, Marty's Food Market, the local library and many fine folks, conversed back and forth to the next town to work at Maxwell Furniture factory. Several mothers with younger children chose to stay home to raise their brood.

With only two churches in the small town, Grace Moravian and Shady Grove Baptist, both churches had almost equal membership. Grace had ten high school youth in the group that went on summer retreats each year, but their plans had been canceled this year due to the covid virus keeping families in their homes the previous year. All their parents were anxious about making family vacations plans since restrictions had been lifted, leaving no money for the youth retreat.

The students had reluctantly decided this year's youth retreat was not going to happen and had made plans to go with their parents on vacation instead. Not only were the teenagers disappointed over not being with their friends for a week, but their parents had gotten use to having this time to themselves, to rest, relax and have a little romantic getaway.

Jack closed his laptop then shut his eyes, recalling what had changed at the last minute to make it possible for the youth to go away on their youth retreat. Absentmindedly, Jack reached for his ruler and started tapping the end on his desk and his thoughts went back to hearing that same sound twenty-years ago when he was only ten, and on the same camping retreat the church teens had excitedly excepted from Tom Bruster.

"Why couldn't I tell Tom the complete truth about remembering my experience? Maybe, it's because if I said it out loud, no one would believe me and what actually happened in those woods."

TWO WEEKS PIOR:

"Reverend Spencer, Mr. Bruster is here to see you sir." Debra Morgan, the church secretary had rung his office to announce the wealthy banker.

"Please show Tom in Debra." Jack got up to greet his wealthiest church member and shake his extended hand. "Please have a seat Tom and tell me what has you so excited you needed to see me in person?"

"Helen and I just returned from our cruse and heard the church budget report about the youth funds being too low to send them on their annual summer retreat." The banker looked around the tidy office, then smiled down at his young preacher.

"You heard correctly Tom. This has been the first time since covid shut down the country, most of our members decided to make family vacation plans, so the church funds have dropped considerably. I realize the young people are unhappy about spending their summer vacation with their parents this year instead of their friends, but I can only assume their parents aren't happy over having to give up their usual romantic getaway with their mate, either."

"Exactly my point Jack!" Tom Bruster folded his arms and leaned back in the big chair. "The youth at Grace Moravian have had to wait two years for their next retreat and who are we to take it away for a third year? Many are seniors and this will be their last chance to make the trip with their fine group."

"Tom, is there a reason for discussing this subject?" The young minister glanced up at the clock and felt relieved to know he still had forty-five more minutes before his meeting with the church board.

"There is a very good reason for this conversation Jack and its why I left work long enough to come here and discuss it with you. My granddaughter Amy. She has had her heart sat on one more retreat with her church friends before heading off to college!" Mr. Bruster sat up on the edge of his seat, determination written on his robust face. "Helen and I had another European trip planned at the end of August and after talking it over we decided to give that money

8

to the church youth fund, on one condition."

"Strings Tom?" The young minister raised his eyebrow.

"Nothing that you wouldn't approve of, I assure you." The well-dressed man removed his jacket and pulled out a brochure, then handed it to his minister. "Recognized the place, Jack?"

Jack Spencer stared down at the familiar cabins, nestled in the tall trees. He could tell they had not changed in twenty years. The preacher couldn't control the shivers that ran down his spine, as the stout banker watched his reactions closely and gave Jack a cocky smile.

"You do recognize the place, don't you Jack?"

"Camp Eagle's Nest, in the Black Forest! It's hard to forget a camp like that one when you are a ten-year-old scout who loved camping in the woods." Eyes still glued on the photo of Camp Eagle's Nest. Jack couldn't take his attention off the end cabin, the one closest to the strange forest, his cabin and where he had heard its tapping before getting a last glimpse of him before leaving the following morning.

"Jack, I want to send all ten of our youth to Camp Eagle's Nest, for a one week, all expenses paid." Tom Bruster smiled broadly when Jack glanced up. "I will pay for as many counselors as you need, with you being their leader."

"That's very generous of you Tom" Jack felt as though time had caught up with him as he recalled the girls last words to him and the anxious look from the thing. "A week? Make it five days Tom, then I can go with the youth. I need to get back for Sunday's sermon. We've got to keep a group of teenagers busy in the compounds of Black Forest. Besides the campground pool and tennis court, all that's left is the hiking trails. Can Eagle's Nest be the right choice for our group, Tom? We were scouts, ready for the rugged outdoors, teenagers today might find the camp boring."

"The full day hike on Old Wagon Road is anything but boring Jack. You, of all people, should know that." The banker gave his young minister a knowing smile. "Remember how intriguing and excited you scouts were hunting for treasure at Saylor's landing? How the travelers would bring their wagons in for the night. Especially the six-mile walk next to the Forbidden Forest and how quiet the group of usually noise boys were following their scout leader and avoiding the scary woods too close for comfort."

"I'm sure the youth would enjoy the history that went on down

9

that road, but teenagers are not like scouts Tom. It is built in a serious scout that what the scout leader says is gospel, but some teens, especially the boys, want to make fun of 'ghost stories' and act brave around the nervous girls. It will take all the counselors spaced out between the group of teens to keep them on the road and keep any showoffs from wandering close to those woods. We will all have our work cut out for us Tom on that six-mile track beside the Forbidden Forest. To lose one child in there is not excepted!"

"Jack, with you in the lead to give them warning to stay on the road and counselors in between and on the end, I know our smart group will heed your warning. Since you know from personal experience what it's like to get too curios and disobey your scout leader's order to keep on the road and not stray inside the Forbidden Forest." The rich banker smiled up over his black-rim glasses.

"That happened twenty-years ago Tom, but either you are making a joke for my benefit or you simply forgot the facts!" Jack raised his eyebrow when he heard Mr. Bruster give a soft laugh. "I know you remember how foggy it got that day as we made our way quickly in a straight line due to the road narrowing. Reverend Preston was anxious because he heard thunder and knew the Old Wagon Road was not a safe place to be in a storm. I was keeping my attention on my friend's back, like our leader asked when out of the blue I felt hands grabbing me while holding my mouth so I couldn't shout out. I explained all that to my scout leader when I finally made it back to camp."

"Yes, I recall your story about getting pushed inside the forest Jack, but you couldn't point out your attacker, so it sounded like an outgoing scout after a new adventure to solve the long mystery behind the lost people who had went in and never came out." Tom Bruster just laughed when the young preacher shook his head. "I recall how ambitious you were Jack, gaining all your badges and rewards in your first two years as a boy scout, every cub scout badge given. In the summer of 2001, you were determined to get the biggest scout award and you did. On the last day of camp, Jack Spencer was the only scout to receive the prestigious Eagle Scout Award!"

"You should know Tom, being the Scout Master's assistance and standing next to him handing him each badge or reward." Glancing up at the clock, Jack knew his time was growing close to the board meeting. "Tom, I have a meeting with the church board in less than twenty-minutes, so if we can move this one on?"

"Why certainly pastor. We can reminisce the good-old-days later." The banker crossed his legs. "Like I was saying, everything will be paid for so the church can save the pitiful amount youth fund until next summer, when giving picks up. Trip, there and back, Campsite rented for the second week in July, boat rentals for Lake Swan, food for the entire trip, enough cabin rentals for youth and staff, having their own private cabin. I did request to have you placed in cabin seventeen since you seemed to enjoy it at ten. Maybe those strange things you heard in the woods next to that end cabin, return to welcome you back." He snickered. "Just joking about the welcoming committee preacher, but I did think you might like your old cabin again. As for my request, I must be one of your counselors, Jack."

"You want to be one of the counselors Tom? You seriously want to go on a five-day youth retreat with ten active teenagers and leave all the comforts of home and office?" Jack couldn't resist the obvious.

Tom Bruster had never volunteered for any committee or job, connected to Grace Moravian and now the busy businessman and wealthy homeowner, equipped with a butler, two maids and a chef, insisted on going to a camp retreat with ten teenagers.

"I admit my time does not usually allow me to do any volunteering at church, Brother Jack, but since my granddaughter ask me to help the youth and I have had experience with Eagle Nest, Saylor's Landing and the Forbidden Forest, I felt obligated to go along. Besides, I need to keep watch over Amy while we're walking those long six miles beside that evil forest." Tom Bruster stood up, a serious expression on his face. He slipped on his jacket, never taking his eyes off the young preacher. "Jack, you never really explained to your leaders what happened inside that forest the two days you were lost there, nor how you managed to get out when no one else could for over 800 years."

"Tom, I got lost in those woods and strange things happened that I cannot recall. Maybe whatever it was had powers to block my memory of what I witnessed." Jack Spencer started packing up a stack of papers, needed for the meeting in five minutes. "Brother Tom, I was only ten years old when I got lost and since then, my mind has been filled with Holy Scriptures, embedded within my memory after college and divinity university. Since I have become the pastor here at Grace Moravian, I have written hundreds of sermons and learned each one from memory and heart." Jack stood up and stretched before giving the rich banker his winning smile. "Tom, plan a committee meeting with the ones I choose for counselors, two adult men and one lady, for the girls, along with yourself. Two weeks will fly by so we need to get the word out. I will share the retreat plans with the board members, who are gathering as we speak, in the meeting room, unless you would like to present it to them now."

"No need Jack, you'll do fine. I will set the meeting for next Tuesday at our home around 7:00p.m., if that suits." Tom Bruster walked to the door, feeling happy with his generous gift. "Anything else before I rush off?"

"Just so you'll know, after the meeting on Tuesday Tom, we will let the youth know about their summer retreat Sunday afternoon when they meet for M Y F.at six." Jack was glad his meeting with Tom Bruster was over and telling the young people next Sunday at Moravian Youth Fellowship, made the young pastor happy as well, as he made his way to the board meeting, ten minutes late.

THE PRESENT:

"I didn't exactly tell you everything Tom Bruster." Jack stood staring out his office window into the empty parking lot, his mind drifting back to that summer he could never forget. "Yes, I was only ten years old, but I can remember every single thing that happened that day as we walked down that narrow Wagon Road, passing by the dark forest for six long miles. How the fog came in so dense and thick I could hardly see my friend LeRoy's back in front of me. Then feeling Billy Haskell grab my arm, cover my mouth and drag me away from the safety of the road's middle and next to those dangerous woods, speaking those deep-mean words next to my ear before giving me a shove, sending me through the never-to-return tree line into a world of unbelief."

CHAPTER 2

THE SUMMER OF 2001

"Alright gang, we're going to take a hike down the Old Wagon Road, just off the Black Forest Road that brought you to Eagle Nest Campground." Howard Preston, the Scout leader, had patiently waited for the boys to finish eating their breakfast in the rustic chow-hall. After getting their attention, he had stood up to tell them about the long hike that would consume most of their day. "Up until now, all the hikes we've taken have been through the Black Forest's wood's trails and the longest trail was a three-mile circle that made its way back to camp. The Old Wagon Road is exactly twelve miles, from end to end, starting just three miles from camp on Black Forest Road. Buster Reaves will take us to the starting point in the church bus so we can spend all our time on the old historic road which will just come to a stop near the camp." The scout master and group leader smiled out over all the excited faces of the boys. "We will take a packed lunch in our backpacks and stop for lunch halfway down wagon Road. I'll let brother Tom tell you about what you will be seeing and doing today."

"Six miles into our hike, we will arrive at a place call Saylor's Landing, S-a-y-l-o-r, not S-a-i-l-o-r, don't expect water, a dock, or ships. There is a big clearing that only exists in that area and we will show you where the old timers drove their wagons in for the night after traveling over the Blue Ridge. As you walk around the wide space where many different families stayed over many different years, you might just find a hidden treasure from the past. What boy doesn't like to search for lost treasure?" Tom Bruster watched several hands go up, anxious expressions on each boy's face. "Let's go with Johnny! What's on your mind, John?"

"What kind of hidden treasures are out there Mr. Bruster?" Johnny asked excitedly.

"A few things I recall reading about were wagon rings and pins, broken china pieces, coins, some dating back to the 1700's and a few pieces of jewelry, tarnished and rusted, not being made from gold or pure silver. Once we arrive at Saylor's Landing, we will fill you in on all the state park's rules for treasure hunting, what you can and cannot do to hunt for your treasure. This is also where we plan to break for lunch, due to it being the only clearing on Wagon Road. After our lunch break, we will resume our walk down the old road and this is where things get interesting. As we make our six-mile journey back to camp we will be traveling alongside the mysterious Forbidden Forest." Tom noticed young Jack Spencer's hand waving anxiously waving. "Jack, you have a question or do you need to go to the toilet?" the Scout counselor laughed along with the other boys, but noticed Jack remained serious.

"I do have a question Mr. Bruster and if your speech is not too much longer, I can hold out going to the toilet when we are excused to prepare ourselves for today's adventure, sir." This time it was Jack getting claps and laughs on Tom Bruster. "My question is, why is this stretch of the Black Forest called the Forbidden Forest when the rest of this park reserve is called the Black Forest?" Jack's imagination was building due to other strange things that had already happened near his cabin. There was a rumble from other scouts, wondering the same thing as Jack, why is it called Forbidden?

"Fellows, the thick and spooky forest that runs down the right side of Old Wagon Road for six miles got its gruesome name many years ago. The dark forest should be avoided and you must 'never' wonder too close to it, and God forbid, wonder inside its web. I can tell you plainly scouts, those who have gone in have never come out! So, before you ask the obvious Jack, let me plainly say, since there has never been a personal witness to report what is inside those woods, we simply don't know how they can go in but cannot get out."

"How long have people been disappearing inside the Forbidden Forest, Mr. Bruster?" Jack had sat up on the end of his bench, his curiosity building stronger by the minute.

"No one knows for sure Jack, although passed down legend claims some evil force was trapped inside a substantial amount of woodlands in the Black Forest and the reports of the missing goes back as far as the first American Indians Nation, before the first settlers sailed across the ocean in search of the new land." Tom Bruster did enjoy keeping a group of scouts wide-eyed with interest.

"Mr. Bruster and I will fill you in with more details as we make our walk down the old road. I promise you will hear more about the Forbidden Forest, boys, when we stop for lunch. But now, we need all of you to go back to your cabins and prepare for the twelve-mile

14

walk. Like your brother scout Jack, remember to use the toilet before you leave the cabin because you won't get another chance until we reach Saylor's Landing, six miles in. The kitchen staff will have our lunches packed along with plenty of water, fruit and snacks. Remember, a scout does not liter! Keep any used paper or plastic in the small trash bag tucked inside your backpack." The scout leader dismissed the boys and they ran to their cabins, yipping and shouting with excitement over their new adventure.

As the group of scouts and leaders started out down the Old Wagon Road, the boys noticed how well the dirt road had been packed down and was told it came from many years of wagon wheels and lots of horses, that had traveled this very road since the early 1700's. With excitement, the scouts listen to either Reverend Howard Preston, their scout leader or Tom Bruster, the volunteer scout counselor who had a flare for dramatics, point out and describe various plant life or an occasional small animal, living in the high country.

"I'm sure by now, all of you have noticed the tall, majestic trees that nominates these woodlands and why it was thought fitting to name the forest after." Tom Bruster had stopped the boys before sweeping his hands on either side of the old road, where the tall, dark leaf trees grew plentiful. "One can see why this tree is called the Black Oak. Its leaves are so dark green they could easily pass as black." Feeling sure of his knowledge on the subject, the big man sucked in his chest and stuck out his lips in pride. "Perhaps there are some of you who have some knowledge of trees growing in our state and may even be aware that the Black Oak grows plentifully in the piedmont and surrounding areas in North Carolina. Yet, there is a big difference in those Black Oaks and the ones growing up here in the Black Forest Reserve. This is the only spot in our lovely state, where the leaves actually appear black and almost mystical. The ones growing in the piedmont could past for a white oak easily enough." Tom gave a cocky smirk. "No one knows why these trees are so different on this 1000-acre reserve. No one except, our Lord, of course."

"It is an unexplainable mystery scouts, but that's just one reason we find this old forest so interesting." The scout leader smiled out at the serious faces. "It's also the reason the miles simply pass us by. If you look up ahead, you will see the broad clearing known as Saylor's Landing and that is our half-way mark boys! We shall first hunt for

15

would-be treasures, then sat down for lunch. Let's move scouts and rest where the old timers rested many years before us."

The group of active scouts stood looking around at the barren smooth landing, that appeared strange surrounded by the tall black oak trees. "Reverend Preston, did someone, say a settler, clear this big track of land so, tired travelers could stop and find rest for the night?" Jack Spencer's interest in everything that went on in years past, had brought out his curiosity.

"Jack, you ask some really good questions son." The scout leader smiled back at the handsome youth. "Again, no one really knows why this large area is almost barren as it has been for as long as records have been kept, dating to the 1700's. It could have been like this well before then, but there were no other records found to claim it. Soil chemist have taken samples of the dirt here, digging down layers to match years, trying to catch any trace of harsh chemicals that could destroy the soils nutrients and balance, but they could only find traces of ashes and dried embers, thought most likely left behind by campfires. The experts had no logical explanation as to why this barren land could not grow plant life."

"May I Preston?" Tom Bruster stepped up and once again waved his hand in a dramatic fashion over the bare ground in front of every scout. "Legends have been passed down through the Cherokee Indians that once roamed these hills before the white man came, and they speak of the reason why, land sitting in deep dark forest sets bare! The legend states the devil, Satan, himself, stood on this very spot and curst one of his rebelling fallen angels. In his anger, Lucifer cast Lazar, the angel turned demon, inside the long dark woods just coming into view on our right. The Cherokee speak of how their ancestors stood in frozen fear as they witnessed the great fire that surrounded the evil one as he lifted his hand, speaking in words that could not be understood. In a flash, they looked on in horror as the guilty Lazar simply disappeared and a great noise was heard near the forest's edge. On their knees and trembling in great fear, the Indians could hear the screams coming from the devil as well as the demon who was now trapped inside the forest. The fires grew hotter around the wicked one as his great scream echoed throughout the mountains. The fires around Satan, in his anger, destroyed all the nutrients in the soil so far down, it became useless for growing plant life." Still showing his spirit for drama, Tom added. "Since that horrible night, many people who have camped on these grounds, swear they can smell fire and sulfur at the stroke of midnight, followed by one creepy satanic laugh and one painful scream inside the Forbidden Forest, that echoes through the mountains."

"Gosh, Mr. Bruster, who in their right mind would ever think of camping on this spot for the night sir?" Chubby Teddy Crawford asked wide-eyed and shaking.

"Sir, it doesn't make any sense. If a person can walk inside that forest, what keeps them from just stepping back out?" Once again, Jack was thinking with common sense.

"Jack, again, no one who has crossed the line and gone inside that forest, has come back out. So, we can only assume there is some kind of force that holds them inside, much like a Venus Fly Trap or the new rodent box trap, where both victims go in but cannot get out." The scout leader was cut off by Billy Haskell when he burst out laughing.

"I get it! They can check in but they can't check out!" he continued to make fun by using the famous commercial on roach traps. "I'm not afraid of no stupid forest! I bet grownups just made up all that bull to scare their helpless little young'uns from sneaking out of camp. Those dumb old timers were probably just afraid the Cherokee would steal 'em!"

Jack stared over at the big-mouth troublemaker, then turned his attention on his leader. "Sir, how close is the Forbidden Forest to our camp? Earlier, you said it came out near the Eagle Nest." Jack's interest was for an obvious reason and staying in the end cabin next to very dense woods suddenly concerned him.

"What's wrong Spencer? Afraid you'll go sleep walking and end up in that fallen angel's trap?" Billy Haskell punched his friend's arm and they both had a good laugh at Jack's expense. "All alone in that scary end cabin, setting just a few feet away from that dangerous forest."

"Billy, you and Joel may not think it's too funny if you're the ones trapped inside those woods with no way out!" Tom Bruster never liked a smart mouth kid and these two were good at being irritating.

Jack Spencer knew Billy Haskell and Joel Mason were nothing but bullies and the bright young boy couldn't understand why Reverend Preston allowed them to join the scouts in the first place. All they ever did was throw off on what a scout stood for and brag about never receiving a stupid looking patch to ruin their neat

17

uniform with. Jack assumed the good man was trying to help make them better Christians, but Jack thought his preacher was fighting a losing battle. Jack turned to face the two snickering boys.

"Billy, I did not ask about the forest being near Camp Eagle Nest because I was afraid!"

"Alright Spencer, if you're not afraid, then why do you care if the Forbidden Forest sets right beside your cabin?" Joel nudged his friend's arm and got a chuckle.

"Yeh Spencer! Good old cabin 17 sits right on the very end of Eagle Nest! Why, some of those spooky old trees come out over your dark cabin! Boo!" Billy Haskell wagged his finger in front of Jack's face. "Does Jackie boy want to change cabins, chicken?"

"No Haskell, I do not! I like my cabin just fine! You can keep your dirty, stinky cabin on the other end, far from me!" Jack Spencer gave the laughing boys a serious look as the other scouts gathered around their hero. "If you want to know the real reason I asked the distance of the Forbidden Forest, it is because of the strange sounds I hear at midnight coming from the woods beside my cabin!"

"Strange sounds?" Tom Bruster perked up, tired of the boys bickering back and forth, but now young Spencer had said something that made him curious. "Jack, did you really hear strange sounds or did you just say it to shut Haskell up?"

"I'm glad it got him quiet sir and made him and his shadow walk away, but I really have heard unusual sounds coming from that forest and it would make you hair stand up on end sir." Jack could tell by the gathering scouts and Tom Bruster's sudden interest, they all wanted to hear what he had to say. Johnny Wilson asked wide-eyed.

"Did it sound like some kind of big bird Jack? You know, an owl or some other kind of screeching sound?"

"It was defiantly not any kind of bird Johnny. The thing I heard sounded more like a big cat screaming, only with echo's that carried over the mountains." Jack could not control the cold chills that raced down his spine like it did whenever he heard the beast screaming out, but apparently just for him to hear. "It appears every night at midnight, while everyone else is sound asleep and I have come to the conclusion that it only intends for me to hear its cry." Jack looked over those listening and could read concern on his minister's face. "It started the very first night we arrived and I just knew everyone would be abuzz with the thing that screamed in the darkness, but no one mentioned it, so I kept it to myself until now.

18

Knowing there's a demon inside those woods, this thing I been hearing could be him, threating me for being so close, but he cannot reach me."

"Jack, is that the only thing you hear from those woods son?" Howard Preston wanted to make sure all his scouts were safe at night and hearing this was disturbing to the minister, thinking a wild cat or a mountain lion could be on the prowl. They were in the high mountains after all.

"There is one other sound I hear Reverend Preston and that one bothers me the most." Jack swallowed, his attention looking toward the dark forest looming up on their right.

"Jack, does this other thing sound more dangerous than the screaming cat?" Tom Bruster was suddenly grateful that his cabin was in the middle of camp. "Does this other animal frighten you the most Jack?"

"It's not an animal I hear sir. If it had been another animal fighting for domain, I would have assumed the strongest would have survived or drove the other one away." Jack looked up at both his leaders. "For starters, neither of these things I heard frighten me. The last one I spoke of merely bothers me the most!"

"Then, what is it Jack and why does it bother you so much?" The scout leader needed to hear what had this brilliant boy so upset before the scouts started their treasure hunt.

"It bothers me because I don't know how I'm supposed to help someone who calls out my name to save them and when I looked out into the darkness, there's no one there!"

CHAPTER 3

After the scout leader told Jack he would stay the night with him, all the other scouts relaxed, knowing their friend wouldn't be along when the things returned. Billy Haskell and Joel Mason only made jokes about Jack's story and said he should have saved it for the campfire's spooky story time after dark.

Howard and Tom called the scouts around to start the treasure hunt. "Alright boys, we are standing on Saylor's Landing and before I let you search for lost treasures, there's a few rules you must follow. You are all aware the Black Forest is a state park and we cannot have any scout breaking any of the park's rules. Once we tell you what they are, we trust each scout to obey them or they will get three demerits and sat out the remainder of the hunt. Tom will read the rules out for you, so listen closely."

With the rules in his hand, Tom Bruster looked out over the listening boys. "You may not do any digging."

"Wow! It's a good thing I forgot my pick and shovel then!" Billy Haskell laughed out as Mr. Bruster stared angrily over his glasses.

"One more cute remark Haskell, and you can sit the hunt out!" he watched the rude boy make a face before continuing with the rules. "You may brush dirt away with your hand if you spot any items protruding up from the ground. What few small trees and plant life you see growing here must not be disturbed. You may look under small rocks but remember no throwing. Do not move any rocks bigger than a basketball. If you have any question, please ask now. You will have thirty minutes to search before a warning bell goes off, leaving only five minutes, then your scout leader will count down the last minute and you must stop and be standing in front of us. The scout that finds the best treasure will be rewarded with a special badge. Good luck fellows! Start now!"

The boys scattered out on the three-acre property, carefully searching for anything of interest and hoping they would find the best treasure, then be awarded the special badge to add to their uniform shirt. Occasionally you would hear an excited yep, when a scout spotted an old relict or a happy, I found a treasure, shouted out among the group. The boys knew they could not share their finds until after the thirty minutes were up, so each scout continued to search, hoping they might find something even better.

Jack was about to give up with the hunt when he thought he heard the familiar sound of the girl that called his name at midnight. Following the soft voice, Jack wondered down to the edge of Saylor's Landing and after looking around at the uneven ground, realized no wagons could set on such a slanted hill. So why had the mysterious girl lead him there? Jack looked around and behind him and realized he was alone in the unusual spot. Jack could see some trees growing behind the slopping hill so he moved a little further out, stopping abruptly when he heard the girl's soft voice again, this time closer.

"Jack, look under the white rock! You will find where I hid my neckless!"

Jack Spencer swirled his head around, hoping to get a glimpse of the mysterious girl who knew who he was. Looking down, he could only see lot of brown and black stones laying all around him. "Look under the 'white rock'!" gazing down at the many dark rocks, the young scout lifted his shoulders in question. "There is nothing on this ground but black and brown rocks! I must be hearing things, White rock! Yeah, right!"

"That's right Jack, I said the white rock, not one of the many black or brown rocks! Look under the Flower Tree!" Once again, the anxious voice of a young girl.

"Flower Tree? On this barren ground?" Jack narrowed his eyes, thinking this 'spirit' was playing some kind of joke on him. "Where are you?"

"Open your eyes, Jack! The Flower Tree stands right behind you!"

Jack twirled around and looked up at a giant Formosa tree. "The Tree of Flowers!" Jack scurried up the slope and almost tripped over the solid white stone when he heard the scout leader blow his whistle, the warning signal. He had only five minutes left to find the girl's neckless and get back to the troop before Reverend Preston called stop!

"The necklace is under the rock Jack! Hurry!" The sweet voice drove Jack down on his knees. He carefully lifted up the perfect rock, a treasure all by itself here on this strange spot, and instantly saw a lady's white silk handkerchief, with lace around its border. He took it and slowly opened the soft cloth to reveal a golden locket that dangled from a solid gold chain. Jack's head perked up when he heard Reverend Preston slowly counting backward.

"60, 59, 58, 57, 56, 55, 54, 53, 52, 51, 50" the minute countdown had started and Jack jumped to his feet, gently holding on to the delicate treasure and hearing the young lady's voice anxiously say, hurry, Jack sprinted back to the troop and slid to a stop just as his scout leader called out, EVERYONE STOP!

Jack could see several scouts proudly holding tight to their found treasures and several drooped heads, indicating those boys hadn't found anything. The scout leader smiled out at the obvious lucky finders and motioned to the boys with empty hands to take a seat on the ground. "Let me start with LeRoy. Show us what you found son."

When LeRoy James held out his small treasure, Tom Bruster tried to hide his smile as the leader tried to stay professional and ask the smiling scout to describe his treasure. "I found this really old bottle cap sir. Gosh! I just bet it dates backs to the civil war!"

Billy Haskell and Joel Mason burst out laughing. "Boy, you are one stupid dumb ass James!" Haskell continued to laugh as he made fun of the boy wearing glasses. "Hey, four-eyes, maybe you better get some new glasses!"

"Yeah, Bill is right dumb-dumb! Them civil war Rebels didn't have bottle Pepsi's!" Joel Mason continued to rib the shy boy, making Jack Spencer grow angry at their ribbing his good friend, LeRoy. "Billy found that Pepsi cap this morning in the chow hall trash can and we tossed it down for some dumb cluck to find!"

"Yeah, I bet it's not even worth 1/10th of a penny!" Billy Haskell howled. "Loser!"

"Haskell, you and Mason can just stop with the bulling abuse right now!" The scout leader stared down at the two troublemakers. "What did I tell you about littering around here?"

"A good scout does not litter! So, what, who needs to be a 'good' scout anyway? It ain't any fun!" Billy Haskell narrowed his eyes at the pastor. "Being a stupid scout stinks! As soon as we get back home, I quit this pure organization."

"That is fine with me Haskell! But until we return, you are still a scout under my command, so, I'm warning you, behave for the remainder of this trip or I will have a word with both your parents!" Reverend Preston noticed the sudden change on their face and the preacher knew instantly these two troublemakers were afraid of their parents and acted tough when they weren't around them. After they had settled down, the scout leader watched LeRoy James, now red in the face from embarrassment, drop his head and fall down with his troop.

Feeling sorry for his friend, Jack stood back waiting his turn, knowing deep inside, he had to have the very best find of the day.

Johnny Wilson proudly showed off his rusty horseshoe he had found buried just below the ground. With excitement, the scout shared his search. "When I spotted the end sticking out, I got down on my knees and started scratching away the dirt with my claws. The horseshoe wasn't very deep, so I knew I was within the park rules. Isn't it neat? An old horseshoe from the past!"

"That is a great find, Johnny! It will be hard to beat!" Reverend Preston called on Randy Russell, who found an old nail and Jake Williams would lift up a broken piece of china. Everyone had assumed Johnny would be the big winner until Jack stepped up holding the white silk handkerchief. Howard and Tom stepped closer, staring down at the old handkerchief, obviously belonging to a young lady around the early 1800's.

"Jack, this old handkerchief is in really good condition. Where on earth did you find it?" The scout leader asked, impressed with the youth's great find. Even Johnny Wilson was so fascinated with the exquisite treasure, he wasn't upset he had lost the number one spot.

"I found this handkerchief safely hiding under a perfect white rock which rested under the shade of a massive Formosa tree, in full bloom!" Jack smiled as a roar of applause came from the happy scout troop, now circling their hero. That is, all the scouts except Billy Haskell and Joel Mason, who watched with envy and hate. Billy stood up, motioning for his friend to follow, then walked over to stare at Jack's find. He gave a snicker.

"Sure Spencer, like you really found this white handkerchief, which should be yellowed and wrinkle from age, lying under some stupid WHITE rock?" Billy stared up, no trust for Jack's ridiculous statement. "You know what I think Spencer? I think you knew about this treasure hunt, so you brought one of your mama's brand-new handkerchiefs from home and hid it in your pocket, then pretended to find it under a WHITE rock, just to get another stupid badge!"

"Yeah! Billy is right Reverend Preston!" Joel Mason narrowed his eyes at the young genus with mistrust. "We all know there are no Formosa trees around here and there sure as hell isn't any white rocks! Look around Spencer! Plenty of black rocks! Plenty of brown rocks, but not one little biddy white rock in sight on this cursed land!"

"Jack, would you care to respond to your fellow scout's charges?" The scout leader motioned all the scouts back down, except Jack, then he sat down, joined by Tom and Max Carver, the other two leaders.

Watching Jack closely, all the scouts waited for the highly decorated scout to answer. "Yes sir, I most certainly do. My parents have always taught me to obey all rules, especially those made by God. To make up a story just to get an award is one thing I have 'never' done. Telling lies is following the devil's rules. I did find this girl's handkerchief under a white rock sir and the rock was laying directly under the flower tree, where the voice said she put it."

"Are you saying the voice you have been hearing at midnight in the woods by your cabin, spoke to you here, at Saylor's Landing? A girl, who confided in you where she had hidden her handkerchief years ago?" Tom Bruster stood up to have another look at the beautiful find.

Billy Haskell started laughing again, trying to entice all the other scouts to join him and his friend over their hero's ridiculous story, but found the remaining scouts keep their loyalty for their brave hero, Jack Spencer. "Mr. Bruster, don't fall for Jack's stupid story sir! Have you seen this so-call flower tree standing tall around the barren ground? I say Spencer is lying!"

"Billy Haskell, keep still! I can tell if that handkerchief is old or recently purchased at a department store!" Tom Bruster held out his hand for the silk handkerchief.

"Please do check out the handkerchief Mr. Bruster, but it was only used as a wrap for the young lady's real treasure." Jack pulled out the golden locket and held it up by the gold chain. The noonday sun reflected off the pure gold, causing the locket and chain to glisten and sparkle with a thousand lights. Once again, the excited scouts surrounded Jack, hooping and shouting while Billy Haskell and Joel Mason could only look on with envy and pure jealousy.

All three leaders checked out Jack's treasure and were astonished to find a date engraved on the locket, but were unable to open the locket cover to see if it had a picture inside. Jack watched and waited anxiously. The need to know who this mysterious girl was. Whoever she was, Jack thought, she had to be a ghost, perhaps left behind by mistake or worse, with the taunting Forbidden Forest so close by. Maybe the forest had lured her parents inside its forbidden boundary, leaving the girl alone. Afraid she would die there and no one find her, she would hide her most precious procession, the locket holding her portrait so she might be identified. Deep in thought, Jack considered the fact that neither Leader could find the locket's secret opening and it may be left up to him to discover it. Jack whispered his thoughts softly, thinking he was alone. "Perhaps the girl will help me learn its secret."

"Jack, did you say something son?" Reverend Preston smiled down, gently holding the prized locket on the white handkerchief.

"No sir, I was merely thinking out loud." Jack's attention was on the golden locket and he wondered what they found out about it. "Did either of you figure out how old these things were, Reverend Preston?"

"We can tell you the exact date on the locket Jack, so the handkerchief should date back to around the same period." The scout leader glanced over at the other scouts, still seated and chatting about Jack's great find and wondering exactly where he had found them. "Scouts, you may gather around so Mr. Bruster and I can tell you all what we found out about Jack's treasure find! Then we will break for lunch."

The group of boys ran over with excitement to hear the results, but never doubting their hero's words. They listened with eagerness.

"Scouts, your fellow scout, Jack Spencer, has found the very best treasure ever discovered on Saylor's Landing. The locket and chain it was attached to was solid gold and it was engraved with the month and year it was given to this mysterious invisible girl that speaks to Jack, December 25th 1800, between the Revolutionary War and the Civil War. Knowing a lot about antiques, Tom Bruster is certain it will have a high price value, as well as the silk handkerchief, embroidered with a Formosa tree, which is described in gold thread as the Flowering Tree."

"As for Jack's other story that brought questions from two of our scouts, while Reverend Preston and I were examining the neckless and hanky, Mr. Carver, our fine helper, walked back to the direction Jack came running from to do his own investigation. True to young Spencer's remarks, Max found a large Formosa tree in full bloom and underneath lay one perfect white rock."

"To be honest young man, I was quite surprised to find exactly what you had described to all of us, except of course the young lady's whispers, guiding you to her locket. I was skeptical over you finding a white handkerchief that had not faded with the many years it rested under that white rock, that looked out of place, as did the tree. The locket and chain were not tarnished at all and appeared brand-new, so I admit I was lending toward the same blame as Billy and Joel. The truth is Jack, even if you managed to sneak a priceless locket and old handkerchief with you on this camping retreat, you could have never brought in a seventy-foot Formosa tree and the perfect oval white rock without our knowledge or having the strength of superman." Max Carver received a round of laughter from most of the scouts and their leaders. "I should have known better to ever doubt the most respected and highly decorated scout in our troop. I hope you can forgive my doubt, scout of the year!"

"Of course, I forgive you Mr. Carver and I can understand your doubting my story. It's not every day a scout reports seeing a large Formosa growing where nothing else can grow, or finding a young lady's priceless treasure under a white oval rock, when all other rocks are dark shades." Jack smiled up at the 5'6" man with thinning brown hair. "And, although this mysterious girl speaks only to me and even calls me by my given name, she is as real as the tree, the rock, and the locket wrapped up neatly in her handkerchief."

"Wow! Can we see the big tree and white rock before we leave Saylor's Landing, Reverend Preston?" Red faced from all the excitement, Teddy Crawford was dying to see the famous flowering tree for himself as well as a white stone among so many black and brown stones. He grabbed his round stomach when it growled, bringing out several giggles. "Oh gosh fellows, a boy has to eat!" he laughed out and gave a snort. "I think we better eat our lunch first though boys, like the scout leader said cause I'm real hungry!" Once again the obese boy's stomach rumbled loudly as Billy Haskell got up and moved up beside Teddy and rudely spoke up.

"Fatty Teddy, you could curl up into hibernation and skip eating for a solid year and survive off that fat belly you carry around with you!" He punched his friend as they laughed at the embarrassed overweight young boy.

Jack had taken about all he could from this obnoxious boy's bad behavior, so he struck back. "Silly Billy, you could learn your Bible a lot better if you started reading it and then start following the golden rule, treating others the way you like to be treated, Haskell-Rascal!"

26

"Keep your no-count sermons to yourself Spencer!" Billy narrowed his eyes on Jack. "I still say you cheated! Probably stole those girly things from old lady Martins Antique Shop downtown Graceland!"

"Bill's right smart mouth! I bet when we get back home, we're going to see want-ad's hanging on every light pole in town and read about it in the Graceland newspaper about your fingerprints being found on that old lady's doorknob! Mable Martin's Antique Shop, robbed by a highly decorated boy scout." Joel Mason gave a sarcastic laugh. "Then old Jack Spencer will be put in the slammer until he's too old to find a girl!"

"Haskell, Mason, you boys hear me and good! Jack is right!" The scout leader had taken all he could from these two rude bullies. "Start reading your Bibles! Begin with the ten commandments and start praying about your attitude!" He walked over and got in their faces. "Hear my warning boys and take it serious! One more rude remark from either one of you and I 'will send you back home'! Do you understand boys?" the usually calm man almost shouted. "I would rather lose one of my leaders for taking you home out of my hair than having to put up with any more of your mean comments! What's it going to be Haskell! Mason, do I have you word to keep quiet from now on?"

Billy Haskell glanced over at Jack Spencer, who was obviously pleased over the scout leader's demands, then he turned to give his friend a nod before answering. "Alright sir, we both know when to keep still!" as the bully watched the minister walk away to gather the scouts for lunch, he turned to get eye contact with Jack, whom he considered his main arch-enemy and he thought "When the time is right Spencer, I will get even and have my revenge!"

CHAPTER 4

Jack Spencer had finished eating his lunch and sat waiting for his leaders to break away and resume the day's adventure. His mind was on the treasure he had found earlier and the invisible girl that led him to it. Feeling anxious over getting the locket and handkerchief back from his scout leader, Jack realized his minister was holding it for him to keep it safe, due to its rarity and cost. The young scout felt sure he would find out soon enough what was to become of his treasure. He remembered whatever any scout found, they could keep it for themselves, so Jack Spencer trusted Reverend Howard Preston, the minister of Grace Moravian Church and knew he would return the handkerchief and locket when the time was right.

As Jack remembered the girl's soft voice guiding him to her personal belongings, he knew in his heart she trusted him to keep it for her. So, there was no doubt in Jack's young heart what he would do with these trusted gifts given him to protect. He would keep them always and never be tempted to sale them, no matter their great value. Their sentimental value weighed far more to the young scout because they belonged to the young mysterious girl who knew his name and had asked him to save her.

"Save you from what?" Jack thought. "From that thing that screams out with echoes through the woods? The girl was in the forest at midnight, yet beyond the Forbidden Forest today when she spoke to me right here at Saylor's Landing. Can she escape those woods in spirit? Save her how? Save her soul and help her get to heaven to find peace and rest?" Jack leaned on his chin, his forehead wrinkled in wondering. "How does she know me? And how did she and that thing know I would be in cabin 17?" Jack never realized he had spoken his last words out softly until he heard a man say his name and noticed the man's shoes directly in front of him. Jack gave a startled jump and looked up to see his scout leader smiling down.

"Deep in thought Jack? I am very proud of you son! I know you have a lot of questions running through that smart head of yours right now and I'm not sure if I have all the answers, even what lies under the locket cover, but it seems to have some sort of secret latch that neither I nor Mr. Bruster can figure out. But, maybe you can unravel the hidden secret when I give it back to you Jack." Reverend Preston held out his hand to help the ten-year-old boy up from the ground. "Who knows, perhaps the young lady's spirit will aid you in learning her secret."

"We don't have many more days left to camp here sir, so I'm not sure if I can uncover what's behind this strange mystery in that short time." Jack noticed the other scouts were busy strapping on their backpacks, so he quickly reached for his and slung it over his shoulders. "Are we going to leave Saylor's Landing now sir? Did my daydreaming make me miss you telling the other guys about how the wagons lined up when the old timers stayed here overnight?"

"I could tell you were preoccupied Jack. That's why I came over to get you so you wouldn't miss anything we have to say about the wagon rest. That's what they called it back then." The friendly pastor patted the young boy's head. "The troop is ready to hear about the wagon rest, then after we go see your flower tree and white rock, we're off for the last six miles down the Old Wagon Road.

As they walked over toward the scouts, Jack noticed how quiet the group of boys were and he smiled up at his minister. "Look how quiet my fellow scouts are sir. You think they're afraid of the ghost left behind when the wagons pulled away?"

"My young friend, I'm afraid the only souls left behind around here are still haunting inside the Forbidden Forest." Reverend Preston placed a fatherly hand on Jack's back and led him in front of the troop of scouts. "Thank you for waiting on Jack, boys. We don't want any scout to miss out on what we are about to tell you."

Tom Bruster stood up and waved at the flat ground in front of the scouts. "The land directly in front of you could hold up to twenty-large wagons with plenty of room for their team of horses or mules, in some cases. When the earliest travelers park here, they would circle their wagons, due to the Cherokee Indians that roamed practically all the Blue Ridge. Today's Cherokee tribe has grown considerably smaller and now resign in the Cherokee Indian Reservation, where we took you last summer on retreat. Some of the first records, if there was any kept, have been lost or destroyed but making a study of the Black Forest State Park, I discovered there were a few records dating from the late 1700's through the 1800's left behind by the last tenants here at Saylor's Landing. They recorded names, dates, and the number of adults and children traveling in their wagon. Frank Saylor was recorded as the first keeper of the Wagon Rest, so in 1721, the state name this three-acre parcel after Mr. Saylor. It was just assumed Mr. Saylor must have built a one room log cabin to live here, but the next couple to take over the job as Keeper of the Wagon Rest, became known as the tenants and they updated the record book as well building a two-room log cabin with an upstairs loft, for visiting relatives or friends in need of a bed for the night. Kenneth and Doris Todd, the middle-aged couple were thought to have built their fine cabin just over the ridge."

"Excuse me Mr. Bruster, but did you say their cabin was near that ridge over there?" Jack was pointing toward the hill he had disappeared behind after following the girl's voice. "Did the Todd's records mention them having any children sir? A daughter, perhaps?"

"Jack, there were no children mentioned in the late 1700's or early 1800's records, made by the Todd's." Reverend Preston gazed down at the brilliant young boy and could see his disappointment. "You were hoping the records would mention the Todd's having a young daughter, weren't you son? The young lady who led you to her, perhaps favorite, Christmas gift? One of great value, perhaps a family heirloom, dating back even further than the personal engraving place there just for her. The young lady that had in her procession a very expensive hand-knit lace handkerchief with what appears to be silk threads woven as artwork creating a beautiful-colorful Formosa tree and described underneath the flower tree in pure-gold thread. Lace was hard to come by in the late 1700's and one had to be highly skilled in the art of weaving to create a piece such as the one left by your mysterious young lady."

"Reverend Preston, I am aware the treasure this young lady has left in my procession has great value and there are some who would put it on the market immediately, hoping to get rich, but that is not who I am. She gave me her priceless gift because she has put her trust in me to help save her, somehow, someway?" Jack studied the scout leader's face and only saw compassion and understanding, not one who just sees him as a misguided child with daydreams. "I admit, I was hoping for a name to go with her voice, same as I was hoping the locket would open and reveal a portrait of her face." Jack noticed for the first time since Tom Bruster started his report on the Wagon Rest, that his scout leader had placed the girl's items in his buttoned shirt pocket. The young scout's sharp eyes spotted a corner of the white handkerchief sticking up out of the pocket. Hearing everything grow quiet, Jack realized he was alone with his minister so he turned to find the last scouts going over the ridge to check out the flower tree and white rock. Jack felt the preacher touch his arm and say his name, so he looked up.

"You noticed I have put your great treasure away in a safe place, haven't you son? You can trust me Jack, can't you?"

"With my life sir!" Jack gave his scout leader a big smile. "You intend to hold on to my treasure to make sure it gets back safely with us." Yes, Jack trusted the good Christian leader, same as he did his father and same as he did his Lord.

"Under the circumstances, I thought it best Jack, for several reasons." The minister smiled as he patted the boy's thick black hair. "First, I remember what it's like to be a ten-year-old scout Jack, believe it or not. I was just like you when I belonged to troop #7, under Walter Wilks, my scout leader, who worried about my love for great adventures and wellbeing on many a camping trip. Like you, I worked hard at getting every badge a boy scout could earn, and the eagle scout award was my biggest challenge, but I achieved it and I have no doubt you will receive yours this year, son. Ambitious scouts like us are known to bend, stoop, climb, jump, run and dive into any safe body of water, whether we're wearing swim trunks or a dress uniform when out hiking on a hot day and need a fast cool down!" Preston laughed along with Jack Spencer. "Second, you have made enemies with Haskell and Mason and I wouldn't put it pass those two-misguided youth to try and steal the girl's locket and handkerchief from you. And last, the high price value placed on your find could exceed well over a few million dollars. Do you see why I am holding on to this great treasure you found Jack?"

"Yes sir! First, sometimes a scout's quick responses and sudden actions could prove a scout's misfortune and the very rare procession he has found and meant to be protected and kept safe is suddenly lost and the beautiful young lady who trusted him will become downtrodden and sad. Second, you are absolutely correct about Haskell and Mason sir! I could tell by the way Billy Haskell was giving me the evil eye, he was planning something bad." Jack went from serious to his bright smile. "As for the girl's gifts, they hold a different kind of value to me sir. They are special to her and she is special to me, so until I can return her Christmas gift back to her hands, I will keep them with me always, safe and sound."

31

"Jack Spencer, you do have a way with words son and that is exactly why I will save your gift from that beautiful young lady." The scout leader gave a happy chuckle. "Tell me son, what makes you think this mysterious girl's spirit is beautiful when you've never even had a glimpse of her?"

"I just know sir." Reverend Preston had never seen ten-year-old Jack, so serious. "I hear her soft voice speak my name, as though she knows me well and I can picture a vision of her great beauty in my head. A sweet sixteen-year-old with incredible long blonde hair and eyes the color of a cloudless sky right after the rain. I can see her running through the dense forest, her long white dress blowing out behind her bare feet. I cannot explain it sir, but I know this is exactly the way she looks as she runs happily and unafraid inside the evil Forbidden Forest."

"It is truly a mystery Jack." Both scout and his leader looked up when Tom Bruster blew a loud whistle and started lining up the other scouts, while waving them over and calling out the time. "Son, if you can get her locket to open, you just might see that blue-eyed blonde smiling back." The respected leader patted the young scout's back and started leading him forward. "We can speak of this later son, but for now, we are about to hike passed the most dangerous stretch on the Old Wagon Road that any man has traveled!"

CHAPTER 5

"Listen up scouts, I need you boys to start walking in twos. A buddy system, to make sure each scout stays on the road and isn't tempted to wander off toward the Forbidden Forest, that long stretch of dark-thick woods that lie on you right. You might wish to just admire the left side on your long six-mile walk and enjoy its peaceful-tranquil beauty." The serious scout leader didn't take his eyes off the group of excited boys. "Choose a partner, then line up for inspection. I will be leading this troop for the entire six-miles, Mr. Carver will take the middle and Mr. Bruster will have your back." Howard Preston waited patiently as he watched the boys grabbing best friends beside them before facing forward, while every young face stood staring at the woods to their right. There was a frightful stillness surrounding the dense-dark forest that seemed to terrorize the nervous boys while just across the old road, the Black Forest was alive with nature sounds. Happy-chirping birds of all kinds, Katydids, crickets and tree frogs filled the afternoon air with their joyful music. Teddy Crawford's hand flew up, as sweat trickled down his cherry-red cheeks. "Teddy, you have a question son?" the scout leader could tell most of the boys were afraid of the strange forest setting just a few yards away.

"Sir?" His voice cracked causing Billy Haskell and Joel Mason to snicker in their hands. "Why is that scary forest so quiet? Do you think the birds and all the other critters know to keep out?"

"Well son, God did place a seventh sense in all his animals, birds and critters, to help them know good from bad, right from wrong." Reverend Preston had been checking out the scout's positions and noticed Billy Haskell and Joel Mason had managed to get behind Jack Spencer and LeRoy James, but he was relieved to know Tom Bruster was directly behind them, should they try to pull a prank on Jack. Not wishing to call out their names, the scout leader worded his next statement carefully. "Boys, there are some of you who are prone to play jokes on your fellow scouts, so I am warning you, this is not the place to misbehave! There is serious trouble waiting beyond that tree line to our right, so no pushing or shoving! Your leader will take strong actions against you if you try! So, stay with you buddy on the road and do not stray off for any reason! Scouts, do you all understand?"

"YES SIR!" could be heard loud and clear from every scout waiting in line, although the two bullies watching their leader had smiled and called out mockingly.

The troop had walked three miles when their scout leader held up his hand for them to stop and turned to face them. "Water break boys and some new instructions for the last three miles. Take you bottle out where you stand, drink whatever you need then place it back inside your backpack." Howard Preston drank some water while he waited until the last scout had finished with his water. "Boys, you have followed the rules great so far, so please, keep it up. You will notice for the last three miles, this old wagon road gets very narrow, due to the extra growth coming from both sides of the dirt road. Being a historic landmark, the Old Wagon Road has been left the way it was when the old timers drove their wagon down it. Trust me boys when I say this road is the only safe place here. You all know the dangers coming from the Forbidden Forest and even though the Black Forest cannot trap you inside it boundary, it can and will get you lost if you venture inside it and get turned around.

It has been reported that Mr. Saylor cleared out the trees from the Black Forest side to make this road for would be travelers. He knew the dangers coming from the Forbidden Forest, stories had been passed down from generation to generation. The smart man knew to stay clear of the dangerous woods, due to its reputation for sucking in people who got too close and where never seen again. So, what I am saying is, the road is safe to walk on because no part of the Forbidden Forest was used to make it. Due to your safety scouts, we must start walking in a single line and keep in the middle of the narrow road. From here on out until we reached the end and are back on the Black Forest Road near the campground, I advise every scout to look forward and never let your attention wonder toward the right. Fellows, no one knows what makes people walk past the border and into those woods of no return. Do they see something just inside the trees that draws their victim in too close? Is it the trapped demon, seeking out lost souls to lure into his lair? Could it be some force of nature that pulls you in like a strong magnet?" Preston's attention never strayed toward the strange forest but remained focused on each boy, especially Jack Spencer and Billy Haskell.

"Sir?" Jack's hand lifted calmly, the only boy scout not afraid.

34

"Go ahead Jack, what do you want to share with us?" the preacher knew this clever young man didn't need an answer to any question, he felt the need to share something important with the group.

"For the first three miles as we passed the Forbidden Forest, there were no sounds of nature, only a death-like stillness. Correct?" A positive nod came from the scout leader. "Listen closely sir, the faint cry of the raven, somewhere deep inside the dense forest. The mournful howl of a wolf, a far distance away. And the scream from the wild thing, that echoes through the mountain." Jack watched Howard Preston lift his head, giving it a tilt to listen. His eyes fell on the young boy staring back at him. "You can hear the same strange sounds coming from within the forbidden forest. Now listen to the deathly quiet forest to your left sir, where once the happy sounds could be heard by all of us. The singing birds, the katydids, crickets and thousands of little tree frogs, have all grow silent."

"Jack, what does it mean?" LeRoy James swallowed back his fear as he heard the other scouts echo his words to the brave leader who seemed to know something they didn't.

"It's only a guess, fellow scouts, but I believe whatever causes people to stay and never get out once inside its boundaries, has it dwelling place somewhere through this section of the Forbidden Forest. Most likely a rock cave or underground place of inhabitant, deep inside the forest, well hidden from everyone."

"Dang! What an imagination!" Tom Bruster couldn't control his laughter. "Jack, I do believe you have a future, writing science-fiction novels, young man!"

Howard Preston wasn't as critical toward the young scout's theory. "Tom, don't be too quick to judge our young genus. We both know Satan exist and if his anger was kindled toward one of his disloyal fallen angels, he was capable of punishing him inside a boundary, never to leave until Christ's return." Reverend Preston stared down at Jack. "Jack, I guess we will never know if what you think is correct, but this beast you hear you refer to as the thing, could very well be a disturbed demon, fill with hate and solitude, who collects people for purposes unknown, so he won't ever be alone trapped inside the forest forever.

"Hey, what about that girl Jack hears?" Teddy Crawford shivered at the thought of being trapped by a disturbed Demon. "If the locket and handkerchief belong to her and Jack heard her speaking to him outside that forest today at Saylor's Landing, does she possess some kind of power that helped her escape the closed boundary trapping all those others inside?"

"Darn if old chubby Teddy don't have a great point!" Billy Haskell smiled up at Jack Spencer. "What's your theory on that one Spencer?"

"Actually, the same thing had accrued to me earlier Haskell, when I heard her speaking directly behind me. If she had been visible, the mysterious girl would have been only an arm's length way from me when she spoke." Jack looked thoughtful for a few seconds. "I can honestly say, I don't know the answer right now, but if I hear her speaking to me again tonight, I will ask her."

"I'm glad to hear you say you will ask her tonight, Jack." Reverend Preston checked his watch and noticed they were behind schedule by thirty-minutes. He smiled back at Jack. "I was hoping you didn't hear her call you from the dark forest before we get off this road. You might have gotten tempted to move over closer in hopes of catching a glimpse of her."

"No sir, I would never disobey your orders to stay in the middle of the road." Jack looked around the long line of scouts to see his scout leader. "I have no desires to be lost forever Reverend Preston. If I can help save this girl outside that forest, I'd gladly do it, but I've got my life all planned out and by the grace of God, I shall fulfill those dreams."

"You are a smart boy, Jack! I know you will succeed!" The scout leader glanced up and noticed dark clouds in the western sky, just over the distant mountains. "We best get moving scouts and let's pick up the pace. The weather forecast is calling for the possibility of storms late this evening, but they could come in sooner over the mountains. We don't need to get caught out in a thunderstorm, especially on Old Wagon Road with woods looming up on both of our flanks! Remember, keep in a straight line, boys, one behind the other, keep moving and all eyes straight ahead!"

There was an echo of "Yes Sir" coming down the line of nervous scouts as they started moving swiftly down the narrow road. With only one mile left, Reverend Preston stopped his troop of scouts after hearing distant thunder. He noticed the clouds had grown darker in the western sky and several streaks of lightning could be seen clearly. It was obvious to the minister the storm was headed straight for the Old Wagon Road.

"Listen up fellows, now is the time for every good scout to show their bravery and the skills you've been trained for when facing an approaching thunderstorm. We must stay calm and pick up our pace, moving as quickly as conditions allow." The scout leader had to speak out loudly so his voice could be heard to the back of the long line due to the sudden wind that blew down the dirt road. "Studying the quickly changing conditions to the weather, we may find ourselves in a heavy fog up ahead, so keep your attention on the scout walking it front of you! I never leave without being prepared for anything, so each leader has a fog light with them in case of a fog. It makes seeing the middle of the road easier, so stay focused on the scout ahead of you. Remember where you are boys! If you lose focus, it could prove dangerous, should you stray off to the right. Just stay alert, I need to get all my boys back safely!" Reverend Preston glanced around at the other two men. "Tom, Max, keep the fellows in line! Let's move!"

The group picked up their speed and just as the leader had warned, a dense fog fell over Old Wagon Road, making it difficult to see the one walking in front. Then, as the sky grew darker and more threating, both the boy scouts and their three leaders had to strain their eyes to see where they were going. Within the thick fog, the two scouts in the rear managed to get together, making plans that would alter Jack Spencer's course. With the rushing wind and distant thunder growing louder, Billy Haskell and Joel Mason's voices could not be heard. They reviewed their evil plan to get even with the perfect scout who had made a fool out of them.

"So, Joel you stay in line so dumb LeRoy will think Jack is still there." Billy narrowed his eyes on the ten-year-old scout walking straight down the middle behind Max Carver. "When the times right, I'll grab Spencer and drag him over to the Forbidden Forest."

Eyes wide with fright, Joel grabbed his friend's arm. "What if he pulls you in with him?" being nervous, the twelve-year-old's voice sounded high.

"Relax will you, I'm no fool pal! I'll not give pretty boy the chance to drag me in! The perfect little scout will be confused as to where he's at, so after I shove him inside, I'll get back with you guys!" The big bully sounded sure of himself.

Voice still pitched higher due to his nervous fear, Joel questioned his friend. "How the heck will you find your way back in this fog, Bill? You might get yourself lost out there and get turned around, then wind up inside those scary woods too!" the scared friend glanced back up at Jack Spencer moving on quickly. "Couldn't we just wait until tonight, sneak in his cabin and steal his expensive treasure and leave him tied up or something?"

"Nothing doing buddy!" Billy Haskell stared up at Jack with pure hate in his eyes. "I'm going to rid myself of Jack Spencer once and for all!" He gave a snicker and smiled over at his nervous companion. "As for finding my way back friend, I got myself a fine fog light, compliments of Mr. Bruster, who somehow lost his from his back pocket earlier." Billy held up the green flashlight, designed to cut through thick fog and made for scout leaders.

"You stole old man's Bruster's fog light?" Joel swallowed.

"Not exactly pal, I simply borrowed it for this emergency!" The thirteen-year-old troublemaker gave his friend a cunning smile. "I, for one, don't wish to get trapped by that evil demon!"

Up ahead, Jack kept moving forward, calling back ever so often, to make sure his friend was following close behind him. "LeRoy, how are you doing buddy?"

"I'm keeping up with you Jack, thanks!" LeRoy felt safe with his best friend walking in front of him. "Do you think we're about at the end of this scary road, Jack?"

"Sure friend, just a little bit further!" he called loudly, over the wind. "Just keep your eyes on my shirt! We'll be back at camp laughing about this day in no time!"

"Sounds good Jack!" LeRoy took a deep breath, knowing the dangerous woods were so close he could almost feel them closing in. He whispered to himself. "I'm ready for a good laugh."

Jack had not taken his eyes off of Max Carver, so he never noticed the bigger boy sliding in beside him until he had him in a tight grip with one strong arm and his hand plastered over his mouth. Knowing his friend Joel was ready to slip in Jack's place to keep LeRoy from missing his friend, Billy Haskell dragged a fighting Jack Spencer away from the road and toward the right, next to the scary tree line. Lowering his voice to disguise it, Billy whispered close in the young scout's ear.

"Alright Spencer, you have made a fool out of me for the last time! Go and find that mysterious girl Jack! Maybe she can save you!" he gave a sarcastic laugh. "She must be real lonely Jack if she wants you to save her!" With those words, Billy Haskell gave Jack a hard shove and sent the young scout across the boundary line and into the Forbidden Forest.

CHAPTER 6

Unable to stop himself from falling after getting shoved through the dark tree line, Jack fell flat on the moss-covered ground. Usually calm, the young scout jumped to his feet, panic overtaking him as he looked around and saw only trees. Jack could feel his heart racing with fear of the unknown and his first thought was to escape. He knew he had to be near the edge of the forest so letting his scout training kick in, he stood perfectly still to get his barrens. He took a relief breath when he noticed the opening next to the old road, so he moved swiftly toward the fading light and when he tried to step back out, some kind of invisible force held him back. Jack knew he was trapped inside the Forbidden Forest, but a good scout never gave up. Looking through the tree line for any glimpse of his fellow scouts on the old road, Jack could only see an empty road. Breaking the stillness, Jack spoke up softly.

"I guess the fog and treating storm made it impossible for anyone to miss me yet." Jack instantly remembered his friend and the thoughts of him not being there to keep him calm made the loving boy feel bad. "LeRoy will wonder why I haven't spoken to him. Maybe he will find me missing and report it to Reverend Preston. I can stay right here and they might come back and find a way to get me out of here." Jack's thoughts went to his scout leader who had trusted him to obey the rules and not stray toward the evil forest. "I hope Reverend Preston don't think I betrayed his trust in me. I know it was Billy Haskell that pushed me in here! Why would he pretend it was someone else by lowering his voice? Surely the big bully would assume I would never get out of here!" Jack stared out as the storm raged outside the woods. "I could walk through the woods along the old road and see if it comes near the campground." Jack studied the situation. "Or, I can remain here and hope my scout leader comes in search of me. Either place, I could call out to them when I spot someone."

"No one will hear you, Jack." Came the soft feminine voice somewhere nearby. "I saw that mean boy Jack, the one who pushed you in here."

"You don't even know Billy Haskell friend, but you have him

plugged right." Jack looked around the empty forest for any sight of her.

"Plugged? I don't understand Jack. What is plugged?

"It means you recognized his bad behavior." Even in his predicament, Jack laughed. "Billy Haskell is a very mean fellow."

"Mean, is he?" She spoke softly. "If he ever crossed the forbidden line to this forest, Lazar would make this Billy Haskell one of his slaves, for his entire life." Jack noticed the girl spoke unafraid of this one called Lazar.

"Lazar? Is he the demon Satan placed here, to dwell inside this forest forever, until Christ returns?" Jack wondered if Lazar was the 'thing' that screamed and its sound echoed throughout the forest.

"Yes and no Jack." The young boy turned toward the voice confused. "Yes, Lazar is the great fallen angel made demon by Lucifer and placed here for misconduct against his master. No, Lazar is not the 'thing' that screams with his echo following." Jack noticed her voice seemed to be coming from behind a great tree, setting within the forest. He was studying the tree and wondering if he would see her when she suddenly grew anxious. "Please Jack, hurry! Jack, I am behind the great tree, hurry!" Jack couldn't understand her urgency for him to hurry. The forest hadn't changed and all seemed still except for the two of them speaking. "Jack, get over here before it sees you!"

"It?" Jack looked around the quiet forest and darkness was creeping in through the woods instead of the fog he had experienced out on the old road. Jack could see the bright flashes of lighting on the other side of the dense forest line and he could hear the rain was belting down just outside the Forbidden Forest. He gazed back in the direction of the large tree. "Miss, do you mean Lazar when you speak of it? Is he nearby?"

"Jack please, for the love of God, GET OVER HERE NOW, BY ME!" The girl spoke up anxiously "Jack, if you remain where you are, you'll be same as lost forever!" Feeling sudden panic, Jack raced over behind the tree and noticed a big opening in its lower trunk. "Quick Jack, go inside the tree! It won't see you there, my friend, and you shall be safe."

Still standing just outside the big opening, Jack looked all around him for the young lady and jumped when he felt someone give him a push inside the opening where it closed quietly behind him. Blinking back his sudden shock being in the total dark, Jack whispered, "Lady, are you in here with me?" once again he felt nervous about getting trapped in.

"Jack, I am right beside you." The girl spoke just above a whisper. "I have not trapped you inside this tree." Once again Jack noticed how the invisible girl read his thoughts. "I just saved you Jack, from 'it'. Now for your own good, keep still. It's right outside and its sense of hearing, as well as smelling, is powerful. Listen, you can hear the roofs prancing back and forth."

Jack suddenly froze, his eyes wide in terror as he listened to familiar screaming coming just outside the large tree, its echo dancing all through the deep forest. He listened closely, almost afraid to breathe in fear its keen ears could hear him. Hearing the sound of roofs moving restlessly over the mossy ground, Jack imagined some kind of giant beast riding atop a big, black stallion. Jack lifted his head when he heard a different sound coming from the thing, a low, deep, and strong voice.

"Who dares to come inside these woods and hide from the great WarZar? I was resting across the thundering water and felt your strange entrance! You did not walk through the Forbidden gates, yet I sensed you standing! I galloped here with great speed to catch you standing just this side of the old road but you found a way to slip through my fingers, small one. Yes, young one, I knew you were here waiting. Waiting for what boy? Daylight light perhaps? A friend to try and help you through the portal of no return. You poor misguided boy. You will find daylight cannot penetrate the forest of Lazar. Besides, even though you should see your friends searching from the other side, they could never see you through the great invisible veil placed around the perimeter of our boundary.

Young one, you cannot hide from me forever! That is how long you must be among us!" Jack tried to picture what this thing looked like speaking to him. He knew he must be somewhat intelligent to be able to speak so plainly to him and he was capable of powers not known to man. He could sense him at a great distance and even know he did not just walk in. Jack knew he probably never had anyone getting pushed inside the forest before, so this felt strange to this scary thing. This WarZar even has a name close to the evil demon Lazar and somehow this beast knows he is a small boy.

"Boy, thoughts I can sense from you and there are many hidden questions and wonders you have about me, yet you do not speak to me. Nor do you show yourself. You are wise, young one. WarZar does not make friends with humans. The great Waradocks has been known to dine on a few though after the great one is through with them. Fair warning JACK, humans are my enemies and when given a chance, I enjoy slaying them. Many would have preferred a quick death over Lazar's demands! Are you one of the GOOD ONES JACK? Is that the magic from which you hide from me? Are you like the girl? The GOOD girl that cannot be touched? There has never been another like her except the GOOD man that carries book of words!" Jack could hear the sounds of horse-hoofs, as he pictured this thing seated upon a great stallion with red eyes. "It amuses me how you fancy my appearance, Jack. To be frank boy, I dare say there isn't a horse strong or big enough to hold the great WarZar!" A rumble of laughter caused Jack to cover his ears. "Too bad I cannot find your secret hiding place Jack by hearing your thoughts. Enjoy your freedom Jack, while you can. WarZar will not sleep until you are in my control. Do not waste your free time trying to escape this place. It is impossible, young one, or I would have been gone many years before! There is one more thing, JACK! 'Tis sad to be so young a victim, for your long years ahead will be filled with great agony and unfounded pain. Lazar's hate for humans far outweighs mine, fair one. I leave now, Jack, and abide my time, or do I merely trick you into believing me." A loud roar came from the thing's throat and then everything outside the large tree turned deathly quiet.

Still unsure of the things whereabouts, Jack pondered his threating words and just assumed the horrible thing was waiting just outside, standing guard over the tree, hoping the boy's youth would cause him to be careless and slip out. Knowing human habits, the great WarZar could be waiting for Jack to get hungry and come out in search of food in the forest. Jack knew this thing was capable of hanging around as long as necessary to get his prey and like a trapped helpless animal, Jack quivered at the thought of spending weeks cramped up inside his safe shelter.

The young scout wasn't prepared for the girl's soft hand to take his as he watched the floor of the shelter tree open and a dim light shown on the fight of stone steps. Without a word, the girl led Jack down the steep steps inside the giant tree and through a tunnel, lit up by a single torch held in the hand of the mysterious petite young lady, with flowing blonde hair. Jack Spencer got his first glimpse of the girl who knew his name.

CHAPTER 7

Reverend Howard Preston had been feeling a little uneasy ever since the fog drifted in and now with the thunderstorm raging right over them, the anxious scout leader worried about getting all his scouts back to the campground safely. He felt sure the end of the Old Wagon Road was getting close and when he spotted what looked like two headlights up ahead, the worried preacher prayed that it would be the scout bus waiting to take them the rest of the way. To his relief, it was. Howard let out his breath and said a silent "Thank you Lord" before stopping the troop of scared scouts.

"Good news boys, our rescue bus has arrived to take us back to camp. Climb abroad and have a seat in the nearest spot so I can do a head count." Waiting outside in the pouring rain, the scout leader waited until Tom Bruster stepped up, the man who had the rear of the line. "Tom, is that it? Are you certain there weren't any scouts behind you?"

"I can say truthfully Howard, I kept all the scouts in the rear in front of me so I could watch them." Tom Bruster patted the preacher's wet sleeve. "Looks like the Lord gave us all a real-good baptism this afternoon!" Tom laughed at his own remark and noticed the preacher's serious face. "I was watching the boys in the back Howard. With Haskell and Mason standing behind Spencer and James, I felt it necessary, if you catch my meaning."

"I noticed the same thing Tom, so I'm glad to hear you had your eye on them." Howard couldn't shake the bad feeling he was having as words from the past came back to haunt him. "Tom, get on and make a head count. I need to know if all the scouts are on this bus."

"Are you having bad feelings preacher? You know, those flutters in your stomach when you feel something is just not quite right?"

"Something like that, yes. It keeps gnawing at me Tom." Reverend Preston looked up at the other leader waiting on the top bus step. "It's something I just can't put my finger on. Just go and check! Waiting won't change the outcome!"

"Maybe it was the sudden fog and storm that made seeing difficult, then slowed us down so slow dusk started settling in around us to add to the hard visibility." Tom Bruster shook his head and

43

climbed abroad to count. Being left alone, Howard Preston said one last prayer before entering the church bus with all the chattering boys. He called his helper up to the front.

"What's the count Tom?" Howard closed his eyes after noticing the worried expression on Tom's face.

"I counted heads three times and came up with the same number Howard. We are missing one scout." Mr. Bruster tried to keep his voice down. "I was just counting hands Howard, so I didn't see any of their faces so I'm not sure who is missing.

"I haven't looked, Tom, but I can tell you it's Jack Spencer." Howard Preston fought the tears welling up in his blue eyes. "I'll ask to make sure. The scouts need to know Tom. They'll find out sooner or later." The scout leader stepped out in the middle of the bus and looked out over the chatting young boys. "Fellows, could I get your attention. I need everyone to listen to me carefully and if anyone can help me, please speak up. One of your fellow scouts is missing. They never made it back with us, so that means that some boy is either left stranded out on that dark old road alone, or waiting next to it for daylight to come or his search party, and the very worst thing that could have happened to him, he could have got distracted for a second, lost his barrens, and wondered too far out on the right side." The scout leader waited for all the panic words going around throughout the bus to die down so he could continue. "Boys, I know this has come hard on you, but I need to find out for sure who is lost out there in the dark. You all had a buddy, so make sure your friend is on this bus. If you cannot find the scout you choose to be with, please, let me know now."

LeRoy James jumped up, tears racing down his cheeks. "Reverend Preston, I can't find Jack anywhere sir! He was with me sir, calling back every five minutes, making sure I was alright. He was looking out for me and I let him down! But I could see him walking in front of me the whole-time sir, even in the fog! He even took off his scout shirt so I could see his white long sleeve t-shirt. It didn't matter to him that it was getting colder with the fog falling over us and that we might get wet from the storm, Jack is so thoughtful and considerate, he just wanted to make sure I could see him." LeRoy took a big breath, then added. "Now my best friend is lost out there in the cold and dark, dangerous place, I hope he puts his scout shirt back on." The boy looked at the minister pleading. "Please, find Jack sir and bring him back."

"That LeRoy, is my sole mission, if it takes the remainder of this trip." The scout leader looked around the bus and noticed Billy Haskell had his hand raised. "Yes Billy, can you add anything that will aid us in finding Jack?"

"I don't know if it means anything sir, but I could barely see Spencer, being the 3rd boy up in front of me, but I did notice one time when he glanced to the right for almost a minute, as if he heard something from that forest." Billy Haskell got dramatic "You don't suppose he thought he could make a short trip over to catch a glimpse of that little mystery gal after the fog got so sense, then the rain started belting down, then he could just find his way back, being the scout of the year and everything?"

"I cannot see Jack being so careless Billy, and that's because he is the scout of the year. Jack Spencer follows rules and orders better than any scout I have ever known, that includes me when I was a ten-year-old scout. I guarantee, if Jack got loss, it was because he was led astray without his permission." Reverend Preston kept his eyes on the troublemaker. "When we find Jack or he turns up on his own, we shall know exactly what happened to him, Billy Haskell. "Now, you say that you saw Jack glance away for almost a minute. Haskell, sixty-seconds can be a long time when you are supposed to be watching the person walking in front of you, to keep from not only getting yourself lost, but all those behind you as well." Howard watched the older scout shrug his shoulders and give him a cocky smile. The scout leader turned back to LeRoy James. "LeRoy, you stated that you never took your eyes off of Jack, correct?"

"Well sir, there was one brief time, when I felt someone brushed past me or tapped my shoulder, but I turned back quickly, calling up to Jack, who was getting harder to see, with the heavy fog and dark clouds mixing in." Jack's friend thought for a moment, trying to recall what had changed. "After I called up to Jack, I thought for a moment he hadn't heard me, so I spoke up over the wind and incoming thunder. "I said, 'hey Jack, are we near the end?' I'm afraid I asked him that question a lot, sir. I was getting very scared out there."

"Did Jack ever answer you son?" Reverend Preston was trying to place the pieces together.

"Yes sir, I finally heard an answer, but it didn't sound like Jack exactly." LeRoy glanced up at his scout leader expecting to find a confused face but all he saw was one of deep concern. "If it was Jack, he wasn't his usual calm self. I thought, at the time, Jack might have begun getting nervous himself, due to sharp lighting strikes getting nearer to us. He almost sounded gruff or aggravated over my constant talking so he almost yelled 'sure kid, keep walking!'"

"Son, you said, but it didn't sound like Jack. Then later you said, if it was Jack. LeRoy, what makes you believe this person walking in front of you wasn't the same boy as it was before someone drew your attention off Jack briefly?" Reverend Preston knew he was on to someone trying to remove their mark in exchange for a decoy. "LeRoy, you told me that Jack had removed his scout shirt so you could see his white-long-sleeve t-shirt more clearly. A sign of a great scout watching out for his friend and buddy. After you were distracted, let say, 15 to 20 seconds, couldn't someone, waiting and ready, whisk Jack away and replace him with a same-size replacement?" The scout noticed how quiet the boy scouts had become as they were drawn into the mystery. "The scout walking in front of you, assumed to be Jack, was he wearing a white t-shirt or his scout uniform?"

"At first, I just thought the dark clouds and heavier fog made it appear Jack had put back on his shirt, but Reverend Preston, I know my best friend, and I can say, without a worry of getting struck by lightning for fibbing, Jack Spencer would have never put back on his dark shirt, knowing I was relying on his white t-shirt for guidance."

"Alright, then who was walking in front of Jack Spencer when the group went into single line?" Tom Bruster had joined his friend, the need to know more about what happened to their brilliant scout.

"I didn't start out up there, sir but after the fog became so thick and I could tell that storm was headed our way, I panicked and squired up behind Mr. Carver when you called stop, to warn us to step it up because of the storm. I didn't feel safe all the way at the back of the line, in front of my brave buddy, who had called me chicken for fleeing. I'd rather be a scared chicken than a brave dead rooster sir." Joel Mason laughed with the boys seated around him. "Anyway, I'll agree with little LeRoy about him and Jack, speaking back and forth. Spencer, always saying things to help the scared fry, and little four-eyes making sure all was well ahead."

"So, you could hear the friends talking clearly back and forth, Joel?" Howard Preston glanced over at the man next to him. "Tom, I thought you said you had your eyes on all the scouts walking in front of you. How did you miss Joel running up to the middle?"

"If you must know, I seemed to have misplaced my fog light."
Tom Bruster rolled his eyes up in disgust for having to admit his loss.
"I had placed it in my back pocket thinking it safe back there, but it
must have slipped out sometime when we were at Saylor's Landing.
I will replace it with all new, state of the art, fog lights when we get
back home Howard. The only scout I could see clearly was Teddy
Crawford, whose size seemed to block the other four scouts in front
of me and so to keep myself from getting lost, I had to depend on
Teddy's need to get back in time for supper."

"Joel, could you see a difference in Jack's demeaner when his
friend called up to him one last time before we arrived here?" The
scout leader knew this boy was covering up for his friend, but he
needed to catch him in some kind of lie.

"You mean when LeRoy claimed Jack practically yelled. By that
time, the wind and thunder had really picked up and I swear I could
barely make out what Jack was saying to LeRoy. It was hard enough
to concentrate and listen to someone else's conversations when all
you had was wind, but every time Jack turned around to speak to his
friend, it got harder to understand with me looking straight ahead and
Jack's head turned, to speak to LeRoy."

Reverend Preston noticed LeRoy shaking his head negative, as
he kept his attention on Joel Mason, who now was watching him
closely. "LeRoy, is there a problem with Joel's statement. It's alright
to tell me son, I'll let no one hurt you for trying to help your friend."

"Jack never one time turned around to look at me sir while we
were speaking. He knew to keep his eyes on..." The boy stopped,
then swallowed when he heard his scout leader say go on. "To keep
his eyes on Max Carver's back sir."

"That's a bald face lie sir! I was walking up there, the whole
damn time! That proves why he couldn't tell a new Pepsi Cola cap
for an old antique bottle cap! Little four eyes James most likely had
fogged-up glasses and that's why he didn't see me up there in front
of Spencer!" Joel gave a sarcastic laugh. "So, what If I thought old
perfect Spencer turned his head just in case old four eyes could not
hear well either!"

"Tell me, Joel, where you the one that brushed past LeRoy then
and it wasn't done intentionally? You were just in a hurry to move
up the line closer to the front because you were afraid?" again,
Reverend Preston, knowing the real truth, but not ready to point
fingers at the troubled young men, did not need any more dangerous

actions from Haskell and Mason. He would deal with them later, but for now, Howard had to concentrate on finding Jack.

"I guess I could have brushed up against James, sir, in my haste to get up behind Mr. Carver." Joel took a relieved breath, thinking that the scout leader had bought his story. Making sure not to look directly at Billy Haskell, the smart preacher could see a proud look on his face and knew instantly, this bad young man had done something unforgiveable to young Jack Spencer.

"LeRoy, I know you're worried about your friend son. I too am concerned over Jack's safety but we must remember, Jack is no ordinary scout and he knows everything there is to know about staying safe whether in the open outdoors or lost inside a forest. Jack's first reaction may be one of shock and uncertain fear, but his scouting training will kick in and that young man can overcome any problem that may arise. You must also remember our Jack has an ally inside that forest. The girl has already found him by now, LeRoy, and has found a safe place for Jack. Away from the thing Jack has been hearing, then this afternoon, we too have heard. Some wild beast that screams, leaving a loud echo throughout the mountains. Jack is a boy of great faith and he will remember our Lord's words. Yes, Lucifer, has put an invisible barrier around the Forbidden Forest that keeps his demon in as well as all those who enter. It is impossible for humans to escape the devil's barrier, but with God, nothing is impossible!" Reverend Preston got down next to the young boy wearing glasses. "Don't you see LeRoy, if for some reason Satan has made it impossible for us to hear Jack's calls for help, God can hear him! Our God is everywhere son, Satan has no power over our Lord. Jack will know to call up to the Lord for help and He will hear his cry and set him free of Satan's bonds! Jack has a dream for his future and the dream he has is coming from the Lord! Jack Spencer will be a great preacher one day! God has set his course and will help him through!"

CHAPTER 8

Down in the underground tunnel, the beautiful young girl led Jack quietly through the narrow passageway His eyes were glued to her flowing white dress and her incredible long blonde hair, that fell loose in a cascade of curls. Without a word, she moved with graceful steps over the perfectly stone-paved floor. Jack just assumed the thing that had spoken the menacing words directed to him personally, was capable of great hearing and could even sense any noise they made even down below the moss-covered ground above them. So, Jack followed quietly, hoping they would soon reach a safe place out of sound or reach from the wild thing that hated all humanity, nor had no desire to make one single friend with a mere human. A safe place to rest and where he could learn more about this beautiful mysterious young lady, like her name.

When the girl reached what appeared to be a dead end, Jack stared up helplessly at a massive underground rock wall, blocking the narrow tunnel completely. Jack leaned his head as far back as possible, holding his neck to help brace it, as he tried to see just how high the massive wall went. It seemed to just disappear out of sight, so the young scout dropped his head and stared into the girl's alluring blue eyes. She gave Jack a reassuring smile before reaching up to a crevice near the left side of the massive stonewall. Sticking her finger into the crack, Jack noticed an oval-shaped stone door opening and light seemed to flood out into the dark passageway. Jack noted, whatever lay just inside that door was obviously well lit. Was it some kind of living quarters for the mysterious girl who had saved his life from the wild thing? Reading Jack's mind, the young lady merely smiled, took his hand and led him inside the door, which silently closed behind them, same as the giant saving tree had done. Jack stared at the door, and thought, "Both of them closed quietly as if by magic!"

"It's not magic that performs these wonders my friend. It is the power of angels." Once again, Jack noticed her beautiful smile and felt relaxed, knowing they could stop holding their words inside for fear of being heard by the thing."

"You call WarZar, the 'thing', just as you did in the vision I saw

49

concerning you Jack." She gave a soft laugh and stepped from what looked like an entrance hall into a large, round room with stone walls. Jack followed close behind, not wishing to be left alone in this unusual place under the ground.

"Where are we and what is your name?" Jack finally got out the question he had been wondering ever since the girl first called his name, wanting him to help save her. "By the way, how do you know my name? Through this vision you spoke of?"

"My young friend is full of questions, many question still to come as well." Another soft laugh came from her perfect-cherry-red lips and the young scout thought to himself how pretty she was whenever she gave a smile or a sudden laugh. "Thank you, Jack. I find your smile quite charming as well, whenever you share one with me." The girl that had young Jack Spencer admiring her could see another question forming in his brilliant mind. "You are wondering how I can read your mind, young Jack. Always so many questions to ask! But, I dare say, the questions you ask your leaders are far greater, wiser, and brighter than any other scout among you, Jack. Even those who have come before you, except Howard, of course. He asked almost as many questions as you, But, I always knew Howard wasn't the one I waited for to save me. It was always you Jack! I saw things far too clearly to make mistakes. In the end, you will save me from Lazar's dungeon."

"I will save you? Up until now, you have been saving my butt!" Jack rolled his eyes up with self-disgust. "Fat chance my saving you now, fair lady, when I too find myself trapped within this dangerous forest with you!" Jack noticed her beautiful smile again and he knew he really liked this mysterious young lady who still hadn't answered a single question of his.

"Very well Jack, I will answer some questions for you to help ease your mind and help you relax. "My name is Alisia Solomon, the daughter of Reverend Joshua and Sara Solomon. I traveled here with my parents in the winter of 1798, when I was thirteen-years of age, to established a church in the Blue Ridge for the mountain settlers and a place for the wondering travelers, passing through the Old Wagon Road. The Todd's were a gracious family that took us in until we could build a home of our own next to the new church, papa named, Mountain Ridge Fellowship. Papa had a dear friend of the family back in our home state of Virginia to draw out plans for the small wooden church with a towering steeple. Its big windows were made to open on hot summer days and close for the mountain chills that fill the air even in mid-summer." Alisia made her way over to a small picture, hanging on the rock wall. "It was a lovely little church, Jack. Filled with faithful followers of our Lord who wanted to hear God's Holy words spoken, then lift up their voices in song." Thinking back at the many different voices singing, the young beauty girl smiled to herself. "Even if some of the voices were merely 'making a joyful noise' as mama called the dear souls that couldn't carry a tune, the little church still felt alive with all the old hymns being lifted up to the Lord of all creation."

"It sounds like a warm and giving church Alisia, like the one I had hoped to preach at when I got older." Jack had walked over to see what had this beautiful girl's attention. It was a perfect drawing of a wooden church, whose steeple stretched up to heaven. He could see it sat nestled in a grove of Formosa trees and there were mountains in the background. "I don't suppose this beautiful old church has any remains after so many years being neglected."

"All that remains Jack is the massive old flower tree where papa and I buried mama, after she caught the fever, right before the Christmas of 1800."

"That is the same year you got the locket neckless. The one you had buried under that white oval stone!" Jack tried to picture the church in the drawing setting on that plot of ground. He knew it could have fit easily, so where was the log cabin located the Todd's had built?"

"Kenneth and Doris's lovely log cabin sat to the left of Mountain Ridge Fellowship." Alisia laughed when Jack looked up with a surprised expression, then suddenly remembered her mind-reading skills. "Yes Jack, I have received the gift of mind reading from Brianna. She thought it may come in handy if I'm ever confronted by Rakes or Reginal, two of Lazard's Razor Warts."

"Razor Warts?" Jack made a distasteful face. "My dear young miss, I'm not so sure I care to know just what sort of creature this Razor Wart is. It sounds rather sharp and lumpy."

Alisia broke into bright laughter and she walked from the picture holding her stomach as she continued her laughter. "Jack, you are a breath of delight! I knew you would make good company, but I wasn't expecting such a humorous young fellow!"

"So, these two Razor Warts, Rakes and Reginal, aren't dangerously sharp and lumpy?" Jack couldn't help but join in the laughter when the beautiful girl once again broke into hysterical laughter. Finding it hard to speak from laughing so hard, Jack managed his words. "Then tell me Alisia, just what are these warts like?"

"They are extremely mean and dangerous little mold-like creatures that the wicked demon created before he found his first human trapped inside with him." Alisia stopped laughing when she noticed how serious Jack had become after she described the annoying little pest. "It would appear old Lazar got so lonely he had to create his own companions, so he started with the mold people. The wicked old demon took an innocent mole and turned it into a hideous little monster who can speak and think. Let's say, if one spots you before you see it, it plots a plan in its razor-sharp head and due to my gift for mind reading, I am always one step ahead of the aggravating Razor Wart."

"May we get back to how you came to be trapped inside here in the first place." Jack had heard enough about the mole-like thing that could talk. It made him feel sick to try to imagine just what a Razor Wart Mole sounded like so he rather here her life story. "If the Todd's cabin set on the left of the new church, where was your home built?"

"We never got around to building our planned home Jack. Like I was saying, mother got very ill and after we buried her, my half-sister Carmela, showed up, after running away over four years before we came here. It wasn't the first time Carmela took flight and all because she didn't want to share papa's love with anyone but herself. Let me go back to before papa met mama and fell deeply in love with the beautiful Christian young lady." Alisa took Jack over to some strange-looking pillows laying on the stone floor and asked him to have a seat, before she sat down to continue.

Joshua Solomon had just turned seventeen and he had been invited to a party in the west end of Salem. The boys he came with scattered out in the big two-story house where the private party was underway. Not knowing anyone there except the friends that left him downstairs holding a glass of spiked punch, poor papa found a seat in the far dark corner of the big parlor where he could watch as couples chatted briefly before heading up the same steps as his friends. Papa was beginning to think the main party was going on up those steps and had thought it probably wasn't fitting for a preacher's son to even be there drinking for the first time in his adult life. Just as papa was about to make his escape, he said the most incredible woman with long black hair and green eyes, stepped out in front of him and asked him to take her with him if he was leaving. Outside, while walking down the dark, candle-lit street, Loretta Angela told papa she had come with friends and they had left her downstairs alone with a lot of strangers. She explained to my papa how she had always been a virgin because she was saving herself for the man she would wed one day. At the time of their meeting, my dear, trusting papa did not know this woman was going to be trouble or that Loretta Angela would place him in her trance so he would believe he was in love with her. Two-weeks later Papa married that wicked woman and in just one week of the marriage, she announced she was pregnant with his child. Papa was overjoyed to think they were going to have a baby and when the little girl was born, Loretta named her Carmela. Then a few weeks later, Loretta announced she was leaving papa so she could move on with Marcus Carmela, her Gipsy lover and the father of her daughter, Carmela. Then the wicked woman left papa with raising the baby, telling him it was her goodbye gift to remember her by."

"I'm surprised your father would ever trust another woman after that horrible ordeal." Jack felt bad for Alisia's father, even though they had never met. "I guess your sweet Christian mother changed his image of women after Loretta."

"It was love at first sight Jack. The moment my parents looked into each other's eyes, they knew they were in love with that person and wanted to spend the rest of their life with them." Alisia looked thoughtful for a moment. "They were married in 1783, then I was born in 1784, and their beautiful love story lasted only seventeen-years." Jack saw the tears falling down Alisia's soft sweet cheeks and he could feel his own heart breaking as he arose from the floor-pillow to offer her a comforting hug. Her beautiful blue eyes met his and Jack suddenly felt odd, something he had never felt while gazing in another person's eyes. She gently touched his face and pulled out a white lace handkerchief, similar to the one he had found, but this one had a butterfly along its border. She wiped away the tears and gave her new friend a smile. "It's been a long time since I recalled that Jack, but my mother's passing wasn't easy on me or my poor papa, who had lost the love of his life. Mama had been teaching me how to be the song leader when she could no longer do the service. I thought I couldn't possibly sing after losing my songbird. But

53

somehow, the good Lord always gives you that special gift of peace so at her grave, I lifted my voice in mama's favorite hymn, Heaven Bound, I'm going home to glory, to see my Savior and King!"

"I don't recall ever hearing that hymn sang Alisia. Maybe you can sing it one day for me to hear." Jack smiled, then remembered the half-sister Carmela and all the other questions of his she still hadn't answered. "Tell me about Carmela? Did she have something to do with you getting lost inside the Forbidden Forest?"

"Reverend Spencer, it's getting late! You seem to be lost in thought sir! I called your name three times before you responded." Julia Parker had left the fellowship hall after the last classmate took her leftover meatloaf and the remaining brownies she had brought and went out to the parking lot to tell the other Senior Sunday school class members goodnight before heading home. They had invited the young minister to join them at their fellowship supper which met a four, giving the older group plenty of time to get home before dark. Four till six always worked out perfectly for the Good Steward Class and now their class president was over making sure the church doors were locked and the security code was punch in. Before she walked out, the sharp seventy-nine-year-old widow, noticed the preacher's car was still in the church parking lot. "We missed you at the dinner tonight pastor Spencer. Are you feeling alright sir? I know you've got that long trip up those mountains in the morning with a bunch of teenagers." The heavy-set lady chuckled when he gave her a smile and reached for his Bible and keys. "Having second thoughts about leading all those active teenagers for five whole days? We'll, dowdily do, Pastor Jack, I'm glad it's not me, instead it's you!" she chuckled at her own rhyme and was pleased when the handsome minister laughed with her.

"Julia, you are a real comedian! Maybe you should come along to keep us all entertained." Jack walked the active member to the door and opened it for her. "You can go ahead and get in your car, I'll set the alarm and be right out." Jack closed the door to set the church security alarm, then walked out, locked the door, and got into his car. He had to grab a bite before he could finish packing his luggage. Morning would come quickly, but Jack knew he probably wouldn't find no rest for the night ahead. There were too many memories to relive and he needed to go back to his last moments with Alisia. Would she still be there after twenty years waiting for him to save her from Lazar's dungeon? If she were there, how would he know what to do? It was her sweet voice that led him before but, he left her with WarZar, so she would be kept silent, same as her father, Reverend Solomon. Without Alisia's mind-reading, who would warn him of the Razor Warts? There were so many new questions and no one to answer them for Jack. Jack recalled who had helped him escape Satan's trap. Would he appear again to help him?"

CHAPTER 9

Jack had noticed the big bag of food waiting on his car hood when he walked out to the only car left in the church parking lot. He smiled down at his thoughtful gift, left by some member of the Good Steward class making sure the single man had a homemade supper for a change instead of some quick hamburger at the McDonald's on Haven Avenue. Knowing there was probably enough food inside that bag for three hungry men, the young preacher would probably have to freeze most of it for when he returned from the five-day retreat.

When Jack pulled in his driveway, he instantly recognized the automobile waiting for him. Smiling at the senior pastor from Grace Moravian, Jack lifted up the large bag and ask as he shook hands with his old friend and mentor "Reverend Preston, care to join me in, no doubt, leftovers from the Good Steward Class's fellowship supper?"

"Did you daydream right through another church social Jack?" Howard chuckled at the size of the bag. "I would gladly take you up on your offer son, but Rachal is expecting me to take her out for Chinese at seven." The minister gave a joyful laugh. "To be honest, your bag meal will be more to my liking, but I let Rachal pick the place for her birthday, and my dearest wife loves Chinese food." He followed Jack to the back door and stepped inside the cluttered kitchen and looked around smiling. "I about forgot what is was like living the bachelor life."

"It's usually not this messes, but I've been trying to do last minutes things so I'd be ready to leave in the morning." Jack started pulling out containers of potato salad, fried chicken, meatloaf, sandwiches of all kinds, ham biscuits, meatballs, bean salad and five-kinds of dessert, cake, pie, cookies, pudding, and homemade fudge. Jack glanced up shaking his head. "These lovely ladies must think I eat like a growing pig."

"And there I was feeling sorry for you going by the fast-food joint and woofing down another cheeseburger special." Howard Preston sniffed the great aroma drifting up from the ladies' good cooking. "I came here for two reasons this evening my young friend and one was to ask if you wanted to join me and Rachal tonight for

Chinese since you were leaving bright and early in the morning."

"And now that we know what my answer will be, thank you for the grand thought, but no thanks. You may intrigue me with the second reason for your visit and join me in one of those chicken legs you keep eyeing." Jack laughed and placed a pack of large napkins out and poured out two glasses of tea. "Have a seat and join me with your appetizer."

"Don't mind if I do Jack! I was holding out very good until I smelled Ruth Johnson's fried chicken!" the senior preacher sat down chuckling. "That little woman really knows how to cook! He gave his young friend a wink. "By the six-fried chicken legs in that container, I'd say, she saved these just for our junior pastor."

"I do think sweet little Ruth knows both her pastors very well Howard." Jack took a big bite of his chicken and closed his eyes in tasteful delight. "Mum, crisp on the outside and juices on the inside."

"And packed with flavor!" Reverend Preston took a sip of the iced tea, then gazed over at his young friend. "Jack, I also came by because I needed to speak to you before you return to Camp Eagle's Nest in the Black Forest Reserve." Jack's old scout leader watched the young minister lay his fork down, then took a slow sip of tea before looking up, his eyes serious, yet calm.

"Has this anything to do with Alisia speaking to you Howard, when you stayed in cabin 17 at ten-years-old?"

"She told you about speaking to me after twelve, every night and knowing my name like she did yours?" Howard had wanted to tell the young ten-year-old Jack Spencer that he believed his story about the young mysterious girl, but Howard had given her his word that he would not reveal that truth to the young scout. "I could tell you were struggling with everything that was happening to you there and believe me Jack, I wanted to share everything I knew with you, but I had given the girl my promise to remain silent and observe. She had informed me that I would be in charge of you and it would be my job to protect you Jack, and to guard her gift to you with my life. The locket was very powerful, blessed by the hand of the Almighty and delivered down through an angel of light. This miracle locket will be the key that opens Satan's magical spell against all who are trapped inside the Forbidden Forest."

"So, it was the locket she spoke of, when she asked me to trust her the same way she trusted me. Don't you see Howard, she meant for me to find her locket and for you to keep it outside the forest until the time was right for me to save Alisia at last." Jack pushed the food away, too nervous now to eat.

"Yes Jack, the same thing accrued to me and that is why I'm here to make sure you take the locket with you and keep it on you at all times." Reverend Preston set up anxiously. "If you get caught inside that forest this time without the locket, you may never get out and your life could be in grave danger."

"So, you knew I would get lost inside that forest twenty-years ago and somehow get out, the first to do so." Reverend Preston knew most men would have grown angry over a man who should be trusted to protect you as a child but hold on to a deep dark secret that could have ended bad for the young scout, but not the young man seated in front of him. The old scout leader didn't hear a 'why, in the name of God didn't you tell me so I would have made sure I would not go inside that forest'? Instead, Jack reached over and gave his old scout master a friendly pat on the back. "If I hadn't went inside the Forbidden Forest, I would have never met Alisia face to face and finally twenty-years-later, be there to go back inside, this time to save the one I love and set her free."

Both men stood up, eyes locked in a deeper kind of friendship. Two men of faith, both knowing a small part of the mysterious Forbidden Forest and everything they knew concerning it was from one very pretty young lady, who had the face of an angel, blonde hair, flowing in swirling curls down her back, and eyes the color of a clear blue sky. Jack suddenly knew what he had forgotten to pack.

"Reverend Preston, I assume you and Rachal came back early due to my departure tomorrow so you could take over the pastor's duties while I'm away. I can assure you, I planned for both our absences sir. Reverend Tanner has agreed to take any calls from members in need of a minister while theirs are away and I have already prepared my sermon for next Sunday, so I will be ready to preach. If for some unfortunate mishap, Reverend Tanner is prepared to fill in for us on Sunday as well."

"You are on top of it, Jack, but now that I have returned early, you need not worry about the business of the church. Just help save our little friend. She trusted me with getting you there twenty-years ago, and yes, before you ask, Alisia, did ask me to bring you and place you in cabin 17 when I was only ten." Howard looked thoughtful for a second. "Alisia, such a pretty name. Tell me Jack, was she as beauty as you vision her to be?"

"Alisia was exactly the way I vision her looking." Jack's thoughts were on something deeper. "You said you were ten when you stayed at Eagle's Nest in cabin 17. How many years did she ask you to wait to bring me there?"

"The girl chooses exact numbers Jack, quite remarkable the way it always works out." Reverend Preston thought back. "Her words were: 'Howard, I wait for a boy named Jack Spencer, who has yet to be born. You will be a grown man the next time you walk these mountains Howard, exactly twenty-years from now, young Jack Spencer will be under your wing as a brilliant boy scout, like you are now. Then, you will be a minister as well as the scout leader for your church. After Jack escapes the Forbidden Forest, he will returned again after twenty years have passed, to save me at last. The young Jack will ask many questions and your heart will want to answer him, because of what you know, but you must promise me never to tell the young scout any more than you must. He will find something of great value and it must be you who will keep it for him to protect it until he is set free. Jack will know to keep it safe always and after twenty-years have passed, my good friend Howard, please be sure Jack has the locket on him when he returns."

"Wow! Alisia knew me before I was even born! She knew my full name as well." Jack knew his mentor would be leaving soon or have a mad wife, so he sped his plea up. "Howard, you were thirty years old when you took us scouts to the Black Forest Reserve. Now I have turned thirty and you are fifty, still a young man yourself." He enjoyed watching his favorite minister laugh. "Howard, what I'm trying to say is, I need you to come with me to Eagle's Nest Campground. I need to have my reliable scout leader beside me when we walk down the Old Wagon Road with our group of young people." Jack laid a hand on the one person he could trust beside him on this dangerous trip. "I need you to be there to help watch after those active teens when I'm inside that deadly forest. But mostly Howard, I need you to pray for all the good ones locked behind Lazar's thick bars, made silent and unable to speak. I need prayers for my beloved Alisia, who gave up her protected freedom for me so I could escape from the hand of WarZar, the thing that screams with trailing echo's." Tears came into Jack Spencer's eyes. "It wasn't easy to leave Alisia with IT, the thing, but my dear lady finally convinced me that it was the only way I could save her in the end. The very thought that Lazar's son had her at last, and yet he looked down on me with confused eyes, the look I can still see and cannot shake. Knowing WarZar would deliver the beautiful girl who had saved me to his evil father, the girl that took me into her underworld home and filled my heart with total love for a girl of sixteen and me a mere boy of ten. She never laughed at my declarations of love for her but she was always sweet, patient, charming, witty, a perfect little lady, and could sing like my song bird! By now, my songbird has been silent for twenty years, so she won't be there to speak to me. To help me know where to look for her?" He looked at his friend pleadingly. "I need you to pray for my guidance while I'm trapped inside that horrible place."

"Jack, my young friend, Rachael thought it strange when I announced on our three-week getaway, that I had to return home! When she asked me why, all I could say was, Jack needs me and I must be there for him!" Howard Preston placed his hands on Jack's shoulders. "It was the Holy Spirit leading me home for you Jack. You are not alone in this final exit from the demon's trap Jack, the Lord will be there fighting along beside you. As long as you have possession of that locket, you will be safe from anything that stalks you inside the Forbidden Forest! Jack, you can count me in for a reunion in cabin 17! I'm coming with you!"

CHAPTER 10

Jack lay in bed, tossing and turning, so being unable to sleep, the young preacher climbed from his bed to recheck his luggage for the third time. Still hidden safely beneath his clothes, Jack smiled at the locked box containing the locket, still rapped securely in Alisia's white handkerchief. To be doubly sure, Jack unlocked the box to make sure the locket was safely resting inside. He glanced up in the mirror at his reflection and wondered how Alisia would feel about him now that he was a man. She had never kidded him about his confessions of love for her and now looking back over the situation, he felt amazed at her beautiful response to a young boy of ten.

"Jack, that was a beautiful thing you said. Such a young fellow, yet your heart is filled with love for a girl of sixteen. I have never had a beau, Jack. I knew plenty of nice fellows in our old church, but I was only twelve and courting was never on my mind. I became thirteen on the way out here to the Blue Ridge and up here boys became fewer. I never gave marriage any thoughts at the time, for we were far too busy building the beautiful church and helping out the Todd's whenever they needed a helping hand." Jack remembered how Alisia turned and smiled at him, causing his young heart to jump with bliss. "Jack, you are the first boy that has ever told me you were in love with me." She had twirled around, laughing with joy. "Many had told me they loved me, but none said it with such grown up passion as you did Jack, at such a tender age. I could almost believe it was that everlasting kind of love my young friend feels for me and it makes my heart sing!" Then she grew serious, Jack recalled her words that gave him hope. "My dear young friend, the day will come when you are grown and I will remain the same, perhaps that love we feel will blossom and we can become as one. But for now, we shall just be very good loving friends, Jack!"

"Perhaps, that love we feel will blossom and we can become as one." Jack closed up the suitcase and walked over to the bedroom window to look out at the starry night. "It was a night just like this one when I stepped from the Forbidden Forest, sad and heartbroken for having left the girl I love behind. I can still see her relaxing on that strange pillow as we talked and learned more about each other.

"Alisia, I want to hear more about this half-sister, Carmela, but first I need a few more questions answered dear friend." Jack took a bite of the sweet-looking apple she had given him. "First, could you please tell me just where we are right now? Is this where you live in this evil forest?"

"I was prepared for all your questions Jack, for I knew you would have plenty." She laughed and enjoyed a bite of her own apple. "When you face WarZar, and you will, you will have many questions for him as well my friend, and he might not be a gracious as I am at answering them."

"Face WarZar? Why on earth must I face that evil being?" Jack sat up and looked over at his new friend. "Never mind. I'm sure to meet up with him sooner or later since I'm obviously stuck in here with him forever! Let's get back to my first subject and could you please stop changing the topic everything I ask you something?"

"Why certainly Jack, it will be my pleasure to share any information I can with you while there's still time." Alisia laughed when he frowned at her for spiking his curiosity once more.

"I'll not ask you why you sound so urgent about our time together Alisia, so just tell me if this place we're at is your home here or not!" Jack easily tossed the apple core inside what looked like a wastebasket then instantly noticed his companion waging her finger why shaking her head. "Did I toss the apple core in the wrong trashcan? I'm new here, remember?"

"A can for trash? How interesting Jack. Our generation did not have such luxuries. We place anything that cannot be eaten on a pile in the gathering yard. After a while it goes back to the earth and keeps our underground garden alive with fruit trees and lovely vegetables, along with luscious grape vines for making angel's wine. We shall enjoy some for our evening meal. Surely you did not think that apple was all I would provide for a growing boy who enjoys eating this strange looking red meat that is shaped like a fat stick with round ends. At least you still cook your meat the same way we do ours, over a fire."

"Alisia, cannot you ever answer a simple question without rattling off about some other subject, like roasting hot dogs over a campfire?" Jack felt like he was losing this need for answers to his many unanswered questions.

"Yuck! You actually eat dogs? Cut them up and make them into these long pods with round ends?" Alisia made a sickening face. "No wonder you put them in the small loaf of bread and stack piles of different vegetables on it!"

Jack burst out laughing as he fell back on the big, unusual pillow. "That is the funniest thing I have ever heard! Alisia, you make a delicious roasted hot dog sound absolutely grotesque! I can assure you this new generation do not eat anything you didn't eat, dogs included. The moto for today's dog owner is 'a dog is a man's best friend' and I wouldn't mind having my German Shepherd with me right now! He could alert me to those Razer Warts sneaking up on me as well as making fast work in getting them down!"

"I'm relieved to know the thing you and your fellow scouts eat a lot of is really just meat with a strange name." Alisia smiled up into a vacant space and tilted her head as though she was listening to some invisible being speaking to her. The beautiful girl graciously nodded her head and smiled back over at a confused Jack as he watched a shadow disappear through a wide opening near the back of the big room. "Relax Jack, she's good. You were asking about this place. It wasn't always here, my friend, but Brianna and the other angels knew I could not survive above the ground for long periods of time in this forest, so they made this dwelling place for me. With blessing from heaven, they formed the rocks into walls, made vast openings with high ceilings. A few angels are angels of light, so they brought light into the dark rooms as well as the fires for my torch and the fires for cooking and heat, although underground there is a constant temperature, so it is always pleasant down below."

"Yes, I was wondering about the lighted room and the torch that awaited you at the foot of the stairs inside the giant tree." Jack seemed to have far too many questions that needed answering, but knew to choose those that were most important for his and her survival.

"Yes Jack, there are a lot of questions filling your young head, but it makes my heart sing to know how much you care about my survival as well as your own, dear friend." Alisia reached over to touch his young face. "I can see a very handsome man inside you Jack when you get grown."

"I can see a very pretty young lady in front of me right now, Alisia." Jack suddenly thought he spoke without considering this girl belongs to a different culture than this modern world. To speak so boldly to a young lady in her era might be considered offensive. "Forgive my bold manner, dear friend, I never meant to sound so outspoken."

"You are quite the young gentleman, Jack. I found your words a charming complement, rare in someone so young." Alisia stood up and pointed up at the smooth stone ceiling, where several round openings had been beautifully cut out of the thick stone overhead. "Each one of those circles are called circles of light. You will find these heavenly lights throughout my underground home and about the tunnel arched ceiling. The torches were a gift from God to light my way whenever I walk through the valley of death or darkness, He is with me. Each circle of light reaches above the ground and above the trees, to bring in much needed air as well as light." She gave Jack a pretty smile. "What is your next question, Jack. I promise not to wonder."

Jack got up and walked around the room, looking at various pictures on the stone walls and vases of flowers as well as other home items, then he looked down at the strange pillows, then back over at the smiling girl.

"You wonder where all these things came from when I obviously came in with just the clothes on my back, same as you Jack, correct?"

"It had accrued to me how on earth you managed to get all these things from your belongings, except of course, those pillows. I have never seen anything like them before, ever." Jack knew she would have a good answer and he was certain it would have something to do with the angels around her.

"Again, my friend has guessed correctly. I learned from the angels I could only get out briefly in spirit form only, so they again came to my assistance and helped my gather what items I wanted to make my new dwelling place underground feel like home. The pictures reminded me of my happy moments with my loving parents, so I chose them first. Then I gathered a few familiar things that made this place look more like home and many of my best dresses, my nightgown," she looked down blushing. "My lace under clothing, a few personal things my parents gave me, and seed, meant for our spring garden that never got planted outside this place. The pillows came from Zion." Her eyes met Jacks. "I left my very favorite gift behind, buried under the flowering tree, beneath mama's white oval tombstone. The angels had warned me to hide it and not ever bring it inside the Forbidden Forest. They told me as long as I possessed the Locket of Love, no soul who believed in the blessed Trinity could be turned into one of Lazar's slaves, to work, without mercy until they grew old and sick and died, then be thrown into a place called the valley of the bones."

"Where are all these other good people you speak of Alisia? Do they live in their own dwelling places under the ground as well?" Jack couldn't control his shivers thinking about all the lost souls that wandered into these woods to meet such a horrible fate. "Why isn't your father living here with you? Surely you need not be separated below the ground where it's safe."

"All the other good souls had already been caught captive by Torren before father and I got trapped inside. Before the evil Lazar found out about the Locket of Love and all the powers it possessed, he had already made the good ones silent and placed them under his head captain Torren who put them working constantly until they collapsed from exhaustion. Luckily for many of the younger ones, the news of the locket stopped their labor and they were taken to the dungeon of Lazar, as was my father, still unaged like myself, where they will remain until our day of freedom."

"Yet, you are free and they are locked away."

"You will learn the reason soon enough my young friend, but you need to know about Howard. I saw the question in your face when I mentioned the young scout's name, correct?" She smiled when Jack nodded his head, feeling a little embarrassed because she could read him so easily. "The angels showed me a vision of my future and how I would be set free from the Forbidden Forest for all times, as well as my beloved father and all the good ones imprisoned. This is where I saw Howard Preston and learned how he would grow up to become a man of God and a leader for young boys, like you Jack Spencer, the one who would help me get my freedom and go home at last." Jack felt paralyzed at her last four words, "go home at last." He didn't want to lose this fascinating young lady he had grown to love. Was it just his young, inexperienced heart that hadn't given any thought to her real age and what would happen to her earthy body when she stepped through the invisible blocked border. Did this girl he had fallen in love with mean going home to heaven at last?"

Reading the young boy's thoughts, Alisia's heart was lifted with new hope, that this boy really would become the man she was meant to fall in love with, just as Brianna had told her. The young Christian girl knew she had to ease his mind over what lay ahead so she walked over and gathered his hands in hers.

"Jack, we must not worry about what will happen to us when at last we walk through those trees. God has a plan for us and we must put our trust in his will and rejoice in whatever He has waiting for our future. My dear one, let us just enjoy our time together as we build a close friendship that will mature when you return to me in twenty years. If it is His plan that I go to heaven and wait for you there, then rejoice with me and the angels that I am finally home and can see my dear mama again. If his plans are to let me have a life on earth with you, then, my dearest Jack, the joys that will fill my heart will sing a new song for our life together."

"Alisia, I'm know I just ten-years-old, and most boys my age are dreaming of having a new bike with all the latest features or another planned adventure with the scouts." Jack moved his fingers around until he was holding her hands. "Since I heard your voice speak my name, something new and exciting happened within my heart and my dearest Alisia, I too had a vision of what you looked like. I could see a young teenage girl in a long white flowing dress with hair, the color of moonbeams cascading down her beautiful back in curls and her eyes like a clear blue sky. I saw the young lady I wanted to spend the rest of my life with, you Alisia." Jack noticed her beautiful sincere eyes reflecting love of her own for him. "Alisia, I am truly in love with you and when I am older, I want to make you my bride."

"Jack, that is a beautiful dream and one I want as well." Alisia gave the young boy a smile. "But for now, we need to have our supper, then I'll tell you about my half-sister Carmela and how she tricked my papa into following her into the Forbidden Forest."

CHAPTER 11

Jack had been surprised to see a table set for two and two steaming bowls of fresh vegetables stew sending a heavenly aroma throughout the grand room, where a super large bird cage came to life with songbirds of every color of the rainbow. Jack watched as two wooden goblets were suddenly being filled with rich-red angel's wine, while some kind of flat bread appeared on the plates beside the bowls of stew.

"You are in for a special treat Jack, if you have never tasted the food made by angels." Alisia took him over to a water pump and showed him how to wash his hands for supper. "As soon as we say our good blessings to the Lord, we may eat. Juniper doesn't like to see her meal grow cold, so make haste with your cleaning Jack."

After waiting for Alisia to say grace, Jack picked up his wooden spoon and spooned out a big helping in his mouth. As he chewed the tasty stew, his smile grew bigger. "Dang! I thought my granny made the best stew around, but nothing could top this stuff! It's, well, it's."

"Heavenly Jack, this stew is heavenly!" Alisia winked at her young friend enjoying his meal, as she did the same. "In heaven, Juniper is known for her gift of cooking and to have her come down for me is truly a blessing." She lifted her glass and took a sip and noticed Jack had not touched his wine. "Dear friend, be not afraid to drink the wine of angels, for it cannot harm you like the wine made by human hands. The angels make their wine with the blessings of heaven, so it does not intoxicate the drinker, it merely gives you a fabulous tasting drink that is pleasant to the taste buds."

Jack lifted the full goblet of rich red wine and took a small sip and instantly found it to his liking, so drank a bigger gulp. "You are right my friend this wine is super! I shall enjoy it indeed!"

After the couple enjoyed the fine meal, they carried their wine through what Alisia referred to as the back door, to a lovely rose garden, where wooden benches were placed facing each other. Jack looked around at the underground garden and felt as though they were actually in the open outdoors instead of under it. "This place is remarkable Alisia!"

"The angels have made my dwelling place very inviting and

charming. Like the songbirds in the dining hall that serenaded us while we ate." The beautiful girl led Jack to one of the benches and took a seat, as he fell down next to her and smelled the rose-scented air around them. "I come out here to read. I brought all my favorite books here, as well as the holy Bible my parents gave me when I turned twelve. Its pages are a bit worn, but it is still my very favorite book."

"As it is mine." Jack smiled down into her warm eyes. "I guess the angels keep you from getting lonely, being here day after day, week after week, month after month."

"And year and year." Alisia took a deep breath. "I cannot begin to tell you what a blessing it was for me when I heard my guardian angel start talking to me. It wasn't easy being alone after Torren took papa away to lock him in Lazar's dungeon." Alisia leaned back on the back of the bench and took a sip of her wine, then closed her eyes and she remembered how she got trapped in the forest.

"Papa said Carmela was a wild, unrulily child from the moment she could walk and talk. She would never listen to him and her constant sassing and kicking when she didn't get her way, only grew worse with age. The girl refused to behave in grade school and racked havoc on her classmates and teacher. The last resort for papa was to send Carmela to a girl's finishing school to see if they could help her become a lady with good manners. While she was away, papa finally had time for himself, so he started attending the neighborhood church where he met a pretty young Christian woman named Charlotte Russell. They fell madly in love and were married within a month. Word came to papa that Carmela had been dismissed from the girl's school for bad behavior so they sent her home. She instantly took a disliking to her stepfather's new bride and treated her horribly. Carmela was used to getting all of papa's attention, and now he was given his new wife more than his spoiled daughter. After a year of mistreating Charlotte, Joshua had enough and told Carmela to behave or get out. So, she packed her things and left, stealing all the money papa had in his wallet."

"Did she ever return?" Jack could see how this girl could cause trouble for Alisia and her father.

"Carmela returned six-years later, and I had just turned six. Mama was pregnant before my stepsister left and when she saw me, the jealousy started all over again. In front of mama and papa, Carmela pretended to adore me, but when left alone with me, she would jerk me around and break my toys, then threatened to hurt mama if I told on her. After my parents found me hiding with bruises all over my legs and arms, they ran Carmela away again, but this time papa told her she was not welcome in his home again unless she changed and learned how to give love instead of hate.

At the time, we didn't know where Carmela had run off to every time, but we had to learn it the hard away, the day she showed up at Saylor's Landing, dressed like a nun and telling us she had had an awakening while she considered committing a deadly crime with several friends. They were to set fires at four churches while the service was going on, filled with worshipers. Her words still ring in my ears."

"I was standing outside the small white church and could hear the congregation singing a beautiful old hymn, All Hail the Power of Jesus' Name. My hand was upraised, holding a fiery torch and then a bright light fell down over me and I heard a soft voice say my name. He told me how much he loved me and although I have never shown love to anyone, including his dear servant, my father who had raised me with love. Then he said, listen, listen to the voices and the words they sing." I can recall Carmela's tears as she sang those words to us softly, the words she claimed the Lord had her to hear. "Sinners, whose love can ne'er forget the wormwood and the gall, go spread your trophies at his feet, and crown him Lord of all! I fell on my knees and asked the Lord to help me see, to help me love, to forgive all my wrongs. As if his hand had taken away the flaming torch, it had simply disappeared and I was kneeling at the altar in that little white church!" then she looked down at mama's grave and wept before asking me and papa to forgive her."

"She must have sounded truthful and to bring tears after being so hateful made her appear sincere, I'm sure." Jack knew this story was going to take a turn for the worse and this stepdaughter was merely giving them an astounding performance. "What happened next?"

"I recognized the hymn immediately as one of mama's favorite. I had heard her sing it since I was nine. Music was embedded in my mother's heart and she could tell you who wrote the words and who wrote the music, plus the date, each was written. All Hail the Power of Jesus' Name was written by Edward Perronet in 1779 and the music came later in 1792 by Oliver Holden. Mama taught me a great deal about the old hymns when she was preparing me for the church song leader." Tears formed in Alisia's eyes. "I guess when I heard Carmela singing verse three, I felt I could trust the prodigal daughter finally came home.

One night, Carmela slipped away inside the Forbidden Forest, to meet one Lazar, a gift presented to the witch of Salem by her real master, Lucifer. Carmela had asked for a demon to wed, one who had a kingdom over people. Carmela had become so corrupt that she drove herself to hate all humanity because of her personal rejection from her once doting father. Now, it was her goal to place him and his perfect daughter under the spell of Lazar and she would watch them suffer forever with delight. The powerful witch who had run away to Salem, Massachusetts to learn her witchcraft from her mother Loretta had learned of the Forbidden Forest and how close it was to Saylor's Landing. It was a perfect plan and Lucifer had promised his servant who had proved her loyalty by destroying many Christians, instead of her lie about her saving miracle, they led her to become a nun, which she lied again about. The sad truth was, Carmela had killed the nun whose robes she wore in disguise."

"How could one person be so mean and horrible! To be filled with so much hate and envy for you and your precious mother, and to destroy her stepfather's entire life after he had showered her with so much love." Jack felt deep pity over this lost girl, whose bitter hate destroyed her very soul. "Is Carmela still here with Lazar?"

"She is his queen and the evil lustful demon cannot get enough of her, nor she him." Alisia looked out at the red roses. "She delights in papa's silence, but she detested the fact he cannot become a slave of Lazar's. She wants the locket of love, but not for the right reasons. She wants to make life miserable for all the good ones, especially me and papa."

"Then, she shall never get her evil way! As long as I have the locket of love, you and all those good ones are safe from her evil hands!" Jack knew it was up to him to save this beautiful girl and in doing so, he would save all the good ones. "How did she convince your papa to follow her into this evil forest?"

"Carmela returned, telling papa the Lord had led her to find the lost people and had kept her safe from the evil being seeing her. She reported their conditions were horrible and the poor souls were worked without rest. Then the Lord told her what his plans were and he asked her to return for papa. He was to bring his Bible and dress in his vestments, and this would make them both invisible to the demon.

70

Carmela informed me that she would fill papa in on the plan and they should return by morning, with all the righteous people who had been trapped inside the forest. Morning came and no Carmela or papa. Around noon, I was beginning to worry that something had happened to them, so I decided to go wait by the edge of the forest for papa. I never saw Carmela slip up behind me until she gave me a hard push into the tree line and I fell on my face, just like you did. She was surprised that she could not touched me once inside the Forbidden Forest, so she slipped away and that's when I heard Brianna warn me to hide my locket outside the forest that it was what saved me from Carmel's evil powers. She took me to the giant tree and hid me while the angel brought out my spirit to flow through the holding shield and back at mama's gravesite. Brianna lifted up the headstone at mama's grave and had me wrap the locket in my handkerchief, then she placed it under the stone for safe keeping, telling me, as long as the locket of love is out of their reach, they cannot harm you. I have placed a blessing over it so your evil step-sister cannot ever find its hiding place. It will be what saves you and all the good ones one day when your true love finds it and rescues the woman he loves."

"So, we were meant to be together Alisia. I don't understand about the part about having to wait to free you. Will I simply grow up here and after I'm a certain age, then my spirit will find where Reverend Preston took the locket and I'll wonder there and bring it back?" Jack looked confused.

"You are completely wrong over the details Jack, but you will know soon." Alisia picked a rose and lifted it to the boy's nose. He sniffed the beautiful aroma and smiled. "Do you have anymore questions for me tonight, Jack. It's almost bedtime."

"There is one question I have for you Alisia. You stated that when you and your father arrive here sometime in 1800, a creature named Torren was Lazar's captain over the slaves. When did this scary WarZar arrive in the Forbidden Forest?"

"Let me go back to when this new creature arrived in the forest." Alisia settled down to tell the story. "When my half-sister arrived in the Forbidden Forest, she was not alone. As I told you earlier, Lucifer, the once great archangel that was thrown from heaven, helped Carmela after she learned about Lazar, the forgotten angel, had been punished for treason against his master, Satan and was banished inside the forest forever. The very forest that set close to her father and Charlotte's new church. She saw a way to get even with me and mother, as well as papa, for sending her away instead of us. With Lucifer's help, Carmela found the rock palace of Lazar, built over a long time by captured slaves. Using enchantments and potions, Carmela placed a spell on the self-made king Lazar and he became completely smitten with the raven-hair woman with green eyes. Knowing that only the good ones remained youthful, Carmela worried about her lover's loyalty after she started showing her age. Satan felt her distress and gave her the gift of eternal youth.

King Lazar found Carmela different from all the other humans and ask her to be his bride, so they had father marry them and she was crowned queen of Lazar's forest. My evil sister really liked people waiting on her and after a year passed, she grew tired of hearing the king argue with his captain for not following his orders. Carmela gave her husband a solution to his problem.

"Lazar, my very handsome lord, let us have a son, a prince that can take over the role of captain over the slaves." The wicked demon marveled at the ideal of creating a son with his enchanting queen. So, the night Carmela got pregnant with the creature, part man and part beast, the practicing witch, boiled a potion from an enhancing drug and stirred it in two large goblets of strong wine and handed one to her husband while she drank the other drugged wine. Their lust for each other built up and after four straight hours of powerful sex, the baby was conceived. It was a hard delivery for Carmela, due to her son's great size, but after several hours of labor, WarZar was born.

WarZar was everything they had hoped for, he was strong and capable of having supreme authority over all the lost people made into slaves to serve both him and the king and queen. His father Lazar gave the prince absolute power and that made the son equal with the father in strength and evil. WarZar became very handsome, the perfect strong muscular male body standing ten feet tall, with roofs for his feet and great horns protruding through his thick-raven-black hair that hangs in curls down his back."

"So, this creature you have just described is the thing that threatened me while we hid quietly inside that big tree?" Jack swallowed back his fear as he tried to picture the beast Alisia had just drawn in his mind.

"Jack, this forest is not like any place you have ever been to. There are many strange creatures roaming these woods and most of them are nasty little devils out to hurt you, but all of them are petrified of WarZar. The humans that come inside this forest that are nonbelievers or just haven't found the Lord yet, are easily turned into mind-dumb slaves and like I told you before, they are made to work until they die or get too sick to work. Then WarZar makes other slaves carry the sick or the dead to the Valley of Bones and they are thrown on the pile below." Alisia wiped her tears away. "I can only pray that those dear souls that were still alive didn't have to suffer long or get eaten alive by one of the wild animals that roam this forest."

"I have never known such hate and cruelty toward human beings." Jack suddenly felt sick, the thought of facing the evil prince and captain over the slaves, whose minds had been erased. "I will get us out of this place Alisia if it's the last thing I do!"

"Yes Jack, this you will do when you return for me, but for now, we must have our rest for tomorrow we face WarZar."

"Why must we face WarZar Alisia? And why are you saying I will return for you when I will be taking you with me now?" Jack was totally confused.

"Jack, WarZar cannot touch us right now, until we bargain for your release." Alisia touched his lips before he could respond. "Please Jack, let me explain why. You cannot save me until you bring the locket in here with you in twenty years. And before you ask Jack, you must be a man when you return, that is the only way heaven's plan can work for all the good ones. By then, you will be a minister Jack, so bring your Bible, WarZar refers to as book of words. Both the holy book and the locket of love will make you powerful and the prince is hungry for freedom and truth. Jack, all that poor beast has ever known was hate and I believe if you befriend him, he can be moved. Remember the words of our Lord Jesus, Jack! Love your enemy! Pray for them. WarZar is lost Jack, help him find the light of Christ and he will help us in the end!"

"Alisia, you make it sound possible to change the ugly wicked beast into a charming prince." Jack yawned and quickly covered his mouth. "Please excuse my manners, I guess it is getting late."

"It has been a trying day for my young friend and I could see you were exhausted." Alisia led the sleepy scout into a small room where a bed of soft leaves and another angel pillow awaited. "You may rest here the night Jack. It is safe down here with the angels on watch. I'll be right next door in my room, so good night, friend. I'll see you for breakfast."

"Good night, Alisia, and thank you, for everything." Jack stretched out and didn't even remember closing his tired eyes.

CHAPTER 12

"Jack, today you will meet WarZar but we shall not bargain with him until he gets to know you better. Like me, the beast cannot touch you, so you are free to say or do anything you like, except of course, challenge him. You must never put yourself out there for him to claim, even if you feel it's something you can do better than he can. The prince may look like a beast Jack, he may even act like a beast for a while to see if he can rattle your nerves, but in truth, WarZar is very smart and thinks more like a human than he does a demon, thanks to Carmela's portion. She deliberately wanted her son to be smart and full of knowledge so she could have a normal conversation with him, unlike the ones she has with her fallen angel husband, whose constant thoughts are on wickedness." Alisia had waited for the young boy to awaken before she served breakfast, so as they dined on fruit and cheese, she filled him in on their day. "You shall have all day to get to know one another and I will be there to make sure you keep your distance."

"Don't worry Alisia, I don't plan to get anywhere near that thing!" Jack took another slice of cheese from the wooden bowl. "Will we just go back up and wait around for WarZar to gallop up or do we go to him?"

"You never go to him Jack, besides no one has ever been inside his dwelling place before, not even the slaves. I have been told by the angels that WarZar made his own home, under a great waterfall. He likes his privacy and has even forbidden his parents a welcome inside his private world."

"Then I will keep my distance and speak when only spoken to by the beastly prince." Jack got up when Alisia stood and walked over to get her long cape before handing Jack his scout jacket she had found inside his backpack.

"The mornings are damp and cold inside the forest, so we need to dress warm." As she led the way down the long tunnel, Alisia filled the young boy in what he needed to be aware of concerning WarZar. "The prince can sense fear Jack, so you must be brave today and know the Lord God is with us! I know you know your Bible well my friend and there is a lot of scriptures that will come in handy when you face IT. Like I said, the great beast will try to frighten you and when he sees you are not afraid, he will stare at you for a few moments, then laugh out. That's when you and he can get acquainted and learn how each other thinks and feels." She led Jack up the steep steps that came out inside the giant tree. "Once we're outside, we will wait. He will come Jack and you shall know when he is near for the beast will let out one of his terrorizing screams that echoes throughout the mountains." Alisia laughed. "It's his way of announcing his arrival."

"Then I will ask God to grant me the bravery of David, when a shepherd boy." Jack stepped out and could see sunrays sweeping down throughout the overgrown forest. "So, daylight can penetrate this evil forest!" Jack smiled over at the pretty girl who was busy picking blackberries. "Need any help with those blackberries Alisia? You don't seem rattled at all about that giant beast headed for us."

"There's no need for fear Jack when your heart is pure and good. We are as safe in the wicked forest as we would be in church with a lot of sinners, seeking forgiveness." Alisia smiled down at the bucket that appeared for her berry picking. "Thanks Brianna, I thought Juniper could make us a desert out of these ripe berries for supper, since this will be our last night together for a long time."

"I'll gladly enjoy Juniper's desert with you my beautiful Alisia, but to think it will be our last night together before I return in twenty-years breaks my heart." Jack stopped speaking when he heard the wild screams coming from the distant forest. "It's WarZar! He sounds about a mile away, according to the scream and spreading echoes. "My guess is that he moves swiftly."

"Very swiftly Jack. This forest contains fifty miles of land, rolling hills, valleys, mountains, waterfalls, creeks, streams, a large river and lots of forest. The six-mile stretch alone Old Wagon Road is like a panhandle to the rest of the great estate of Lazar." Alisia grew silent, then pointed to the sound of gallops. "He runs quickly toward us, so stay brave my dearest Jack and all will go well."

Catching his first glimpse of WarZar, caused the young scout to catch his breath from the wild man's magnificence. Jack was expecting a hideous monster, instead he witnessed a grand Titan, like those in Greek mythology. One of the races of giants, children of Uranus (heaven) and Gaea (earth), banished to the underworld for rebelling against the gods. WarZar was one such being, a person of great strength.

"Small one! Now you show yourself to me! Do you think not I can take you prisoner and wipe all thoughts from thy head and turn you into my slave?" The beast bared his sharp canine teeth. "Yet, your young flesh has not grown old, nor your bones weak and brittle." WarZar held out his hands as though he were measuring Jack's height. "Mum, I'd say, 3ft. 9" a little short for my roasting spindle."

"Would it help if I were exactly 4ft. sir?" Jack showed no fear, and the beast narrowed his green eyes. "Is that the length you're looking for?"

"Are you offering yourself for my tasty meal, young Jack?"

"No sir, never would I lay down my life so you may have a roast dinner, but the fresh pork from the wild boar that just wondered inside that thicket, would be mighty tasty, if you ask me."

"Roast boar? Young one, does the skin not taste horrible?" WarZar had never encountered young boys as clever as this one before. The beast thought how much like the girl he was. "Do you make a jest or have you eaten boar before Jack Spencer?"

"I have eaten my share of pork, WarZar. Bacon, sausage, bar-b-q, and yes, roasted pork, same as the wild boar, only raised by farmers." Jack could see total confusion on the tall gallant man's face. "I keep forgetting I'm years ahead of those inside the Forbidden Forest. The farmer raises the hogs, kills them, removes the hide, cuts the pork up in choice pieces. Hams, shoulders, tenderloins, etc. He cooks the large amounts of fat to make lard for frying and baking with. Bacon is made by smoking shoulders. Sausage is made by grinding up the meat and adding various spices to the meat. For you WarZar, remove the hog's skin and hide, then removed all the icky stuff inside, place on your spindle, then turn it to roast for several hours."

"Several hours? I'm not sure how to keep that time, Jack. Does it take a hog the same time to cook as it does a human?" He watched Jack carefully, hoping to get a nervous or sick reaction, but all he saw was a smile.

"I'm sorry sir, but I cannot help you there. I would never take another person's life much less roast one." The boy kept his cool. "If I ever did anything so demonic as that, I'd be a heathen, a worthless lost child." Jack glanced down at his new watch, never needing batteries due to the solar panel on it and it kept perfect time. "You know WarZar, if you and I were friends, I would give you my brand-new watch so you could tell time and know exactly when your supper is done and know the time of day." Jack shook his head. "Too bad you don't want any friends, WarZar."

"May I see that fine time piece you are wearing Jack?" Alisia waited until the young boy removed the watch and fastened it on her slim wrist. "I have never seen anything like this before Jack. It is unusually exquisite. How does it work?"

Jack ignored the beastly prince lifting his hands to his hips in dismay over their casual conversation and easily ignored his impatience. "It is simply called a solar watch Alisia because it runs non-stop as long as you are in the sunbeams for several hours of the day. This is a diagonal watch, so you can see it shows 11:00 a.m. (morning). When it is p.m. (afternoon) a light shows up in the far-right corner." Jack moved in close while WarZar stared down at the cute pair. Jack pointed up through the tree opening toward the sun. "You can tell by the sun it is about one hour away from straight up, noontime. With the watch, you won't need to check the sun and if its raining, the time will still show up for you. It stays charged a long time."

"You've got a fine time piece Jack." Alisia started to take it off and Jack stopped her. "Oh, Jack I couldn't possibly take your beautiful wrist clock, and it's far too small for WarZar's big wrist if he ever decided you'd make a great friend."

"Who needs a ridiculous piece of jewelry! Real men do not wear a woman's trinkets!" WarZar flipped his leather strap with bones tied to the bottom. "WarZar wears man of war ropes, bragging on the many wild cats I have caught with my bare hands." He laughed at the watch for a moment then smiled down at the boy. "You did well by giving it to the good girl, Jack. It looks far better on her delicate arm. You need to hunt the big cats and make yourself a rope like mine, if you wish to impress me."

"Killing something for bragging rights and to have more bones than the other man is not for me WarZar. I only shoot animals with my camera." Jack knew he had stumped the beast again with an unheard item. "It's in my backpack and I'm afraid its not with me now or I would take your picture and have you a copy made."

"Take my picture?" The beast narrowed his eyes on the small boy. "Would you dare come inside my dwelling place and steal something I suppose to have?"

Jack bent over double laughing at the ideal that this prince thought he meant he would take something belonging to him. "I have no intention to come to your home uninvited WarZar and if I did, at your invitation as my friend, I would never steal anything from you!"

"But, you said you would take my picture!" WarZar frowned over at the girl now, laughing along with Jack. "Alright, what is so funny small ones?"

"WarZar, a picture is an image you put on canvas, like those drawings in my papa's book of words you saw." Alisia winked at Jack, not sure herself about taking a picture with a small camera, when the only one she had ever seen was a massive wooden block covered with a cloth. "I guess me and WarZar don't know much about your modern generation my friend."

"Then the first cameras were around when you were on the outside?" Jack had hoped Alisia's picture was in the locket.

"It was a very modern thing back then Jack and had not gotten out for the average citizens when I read about it in the gazette. They were still trying to perfect it so I never got to see it work." Alisia could read Jack's disappointment. "But Jack, we did have great artist, who could paint portraits close to real life."

"Excuse me, but do you mind, kids! I haven't got all day to stand around listening to a lot of human chit-chat!" WarZar found a large tree stump and sat down. "Come closer Jack! I don't bite."

"Then you fibbed about eating me?" Jack stayed put. "I'm fine right here your highness! I wouldn't wish to get in arm's length of you."

"You are a smart young fellow, Jack Spencer." The beast scratched his head, as he thought. "I give most good ones a chance to fight me before I make them silent and throw them inside the king's dungeon. Would you challenge me to a fight to avoid the dark cold dungeon, Jack?"

"If I were David, I might." He smiled at the beast's dismay.

"David? Who is this stupid boy who would dare take me up on a fight?"

"He is long dead on the earth WarZar, but lives again in heaven with our holy God, three-in-one! You can read about this young shepherd boy, about my age, who was faced with his own giant bragger. No one in the land would fight the giant Goliath. They were all scared of him, like many are of you."

"But, not you Young Jack?"

"Like David, I have no fear WarZar, because my God is always with me! David walked out unafraid with only a slingshot to slay the evil giant warrior. Goliath made fun of the small child, and brag about feeding him to the birds but in the end, David killed the giant with just one smooth river rock from his slingshot and the Almighty God beside him." Jack gave the serious giant seated in front of him a big smile. "So, you see your highness, it's far better we be good friends than enemies. Besides, my Lord as told me to LOVE my enemies and pray for them."

"LOVE me?" WarZar jumped up laughing. "I do believe our young Jack is a little crazy in the head."

"Not one lick, WarZar, old buddy! I've just got a lot of love in my heart." Jack smiled.

"I know where your head is boy, I've witnessed my father taking off a few, but this heart, where is it on your body?" the beast remained serious, the need to know.

"Your heart is not on the body my friend, it is inside the body, inside the chest." Jack knew the beast had become quieter as though he fought his own feelings. "Dear friend, you can feel it beating when you are lying down and all is quiet around you. It goes, thump-thump-thump. This is what keeps you living and this heart can be filled with either hate or love and the simple truth is, it's your choice to make. Do you want to have hate in your heart for everyone and be miserable for the rest of your life, or do you want love in your heart and learn happiness and joy?"

"And freedom? What about freedom Jack Spencer?" The beast started pacing back and forth, and Jack could hear the same sound he had heard outside the large tree. "I have been trapped inside this damned forest for all my life! I have longed to get out and see more, be more, do more!" He gave a great roar. "How could I, being a beast? Humans would run from the sight of me! I would be hunt down and trapped again!" his eyes fell on the young scout. "What hope is there for me Jack Spencer, whether I choose hate or good! If I chose good, my demon father would have my head and my bitch mother would boil me alive and dine on her own son's flesh!"

"Hate is all you have ever known WarZar and if you would let me be your friend, me and Alisia, we could help you."

"Help me! How can a mere boy help the magnificent prince?"

"When I am older and return to your forest, I will have the answer you need my friend, but like you stated, I am yet just a boy, but when I return, I will be a man of God, and the powers of the

Almighty will be with me. Humans only see a beast when they look at you my friend, but our God looks on the inside, at your heart. It will be our Lord who will save you dear friend, if you choose this love I told you about." Jack could see a change come over WarZar, as his eyes softened. "Soon I will be leaving, but I promise I will be back to get my bride, Alisia. For now, I am too young, but when I'm a man, I will be free to marry my beloved and if you are truly my friend, and I will know the truth, then I will set you free as well. Free from this hate that lives inside your heart and free from your bondage of unhappiness."

"Young one, you sound far older than your years and you make me believe this can really happen for me, if I so choose you for a friend." Jack felt Alisia take his hand, was it a warning for him not to trust this beast just yet.

"Time will tell, my friend. Until then, you must earn my trust as well as Alisia, whom I incredibly leave behind until I'm more mature." Jack smiled. "If I see an hourglass at the camp store before we leave for home WarZar, I will get you an hourglass so Alisia can help you tell time by."

"When do you dream you are leaving this place, young Jack?" WarZar gave a small laugh at the boy's wishful thinking. "And should you manage the impossible, do I wait for your return for my gift?"

"Never would I make you wait friend. If I find an hourglass, I will bring it outside my cabin tomorrow night and toss it gently into your forest when I tell you goodbye." Jack smiled when WarZar narrowed his eyes.

"Will I see you before you leave, young Jack?"

"We shall meet you here tomorrow morning WarZar, same time as this morning." Alisia smiled down at her new watch. "I shall be right on time with this beautiful gift from my dearest Jack."

"Then I'm off!" The prince paused before giving Jack one last glance. "And Jack, should you managed to escape Satan's trap, I'll let you know I'm near your cabin tomorrow night when you here, thump-thump-thump, my tapping sound to mock my heart! It will be our signal Jack, yours and mind."

"Then I shall listen for your tap-tap-tap WarZar. Will it be the tapping of a loving heart, my friend, or one still filled with hate?" Jack Spencer was serious now, knowing he had to know the difference when he returned. Would this beasty prince only pretend to be his friend just to get him, or was he sincere about wanting his freedom?

"I shall see you both in the morning!" he gave Jack a cunning smile. "Do rest well tonight in your hideaway." In a flash, the beast galloped away.

CHAPTER 13

"Jack! Are you ready to go!" Reverend Preston knocked once again on the young minister's door. He stepped back when the door flung open and Jack came out juggling his luggage and a cup of coffee. "Need some help there, son?"

"Just open your trunk for me so I can drop these bags in. Sorry I'm running late Howard, but I was up pretty late last night. I couldn't sleep so I got up for a while." Jack Spencer got in the minister's car and let out his breath. "I cannot believe twenty years have passed since I was in that forest and now I'm heading back."

"So, are you still planning on going back inside the Forbidden Forest, my friend?" The faithful friend and minister had watched the young scout grow up into a terrific preacher and he didn't exactly trust him getting out a second time. He drove his car up behind the church bus, which was loading up with the ten youth and the other guides, servers and cooks. "I'm glad we decided to drive up behind the bus Jack. It will be loaded from hood to rear with luggage and riders. Tom Bruster has rented a U-Haul trailer that has been stacked with food, bedlinens, towels, wash rags and anything else we might need. Clayton Weatherspoon has volunteered to drive it up in front of the bus with Tom riding along to give directions."

"This arrangement is a lot better Howard and ten times quieter than ten-active teenagers chatting all the way up the mountain." Jack laid his head back and closed his eyes. "I have to go back in, Howard. Alisia has been waiting for me for twenty-years and I just pray WarZar is ready to make friends."

"WarZar, the thing that screams with echoes." Reverend Preston watched the bus pull away, so he started his car and followed behind. "You know you cannot just leave the group and walk into that forest Jack, not after telling the young people how dangerous it is and that you will be trapped inside forever. They will think you have gone over the bend my friend."

"Howard, I'm not certain how it will happen, but somehow it will. According to my beloved, everything has been planned in heaven so sometime along that six-mile hike or at midnight in my cabin, I will be made to go inside the Forbidden Forest. I must keep my Bible and the locket on me at all times."

"So, that is why you brought that big backpack." Howard Spencer glanced over at his rider.

"Yes Howard, for the Bible and a few more needed things while I'm inside the forest. The locket is safe around my neck."

"Did you ever figure out how to open the locket cover Jack?" Reverend Preston had often wondered what was behind the cover. If it was a portrait it was most likely painted.

"It's the most exhaustible thing I have ever seen my friend. I swear it cannot be opened. I even took it to a fine old antique dealer who after several failed tries, swore it had a fake cover, securely welded into place." Jack gave a soft laugh. "I finally asked Alisia the secret to opening the cap before WarZar showed up the last day I was there. It was a sad time for both us."

Down inside the underground home, Jack and Alisia knew this would be goodbye for a long time, so with tears filling the young girl's eyes, Alisia gave the young ten-year-old Jack Spencer a kiss on his cheek. "Dearest friend, I shall miss you dreadfully and knowing I will be locked away for twenty-years, I can dream of your return and our joyful reunion. For then, my dearest Jack, I can kiss you as a man, the man I love."

"I will have you back in my arms soon, my darling, and gladly kiss you with passion and deepest love." Jack had grown up inside and knew he was in love with Alisia Solomon, but he didn't know what future they could have together once she stepped out from the magical forest that kept her eternally youthful.

"My beloved Jack, we mustn't dwell on tomorrow but live for just today and the day you return to save me and those loved ones waiting with hope." Alisia looked down at her new watch. "It's time Jack. We must do this thing now, so you can return to your leader. Your time will go by like the flight of a hawk making its way across the vast sky to places unknown. Your life will be caught up in studies and schooling. I will dream away the hours, the days, the months."

"The years, until I return to claim what is mine, you, fair Alisia. I want to make you my bride, if just for one night." Jack knew if he took her outside the forest she could quickly return to dust and like Romeo and Juliet, at least they would know one another one special night.

"This is my greatest hope, Jack, to become your wife when you return and Papa is more than ready to perform our ceremony. The poor man was locked away before Carmela pushed me." Alisia grabbed her cloak and waited for Jack to put on his scout jacket and backpack. She watched him look around the familiar room. "You will be back Jack, but for now, we must go out and wait for the prince."

Outside the underground refuge, Jack and Alisia stood waiting for the strong giant. Jack slipped his hand around the beautiful girl's trembling fingers. "You're scared, Alisia. Please dearest, let me stay with the beast and you can go free in my place."

"Jack, dearest friend, your love for me shines from you like a beacon of our Lord, but it cannot be me that leaves now Jack. It must be you for you are our only hope out of this place." Alisia squeezed his hand. "You must not worry about me Jack. Brianna will always be at my side and, even though my voice may be silenced, she and I can speak in sweet spirit. Even sing in happy harmony. Juniper will follow to serve me delicious meals the whole time I'm imprisoned and Abby can supply me with angel's wine and fresh flowers every day. Crystal and Starlite will supply me with all the light I need so Jack darling, you need not worry about your lady being lonely, but she will be missing you every single day you are away."

"I'll be missing you as well, fair Alisia." Jack heard the scream of WarZar and knew he would soon arrive and their time alone would be gone for twenty years. "The locket, how does it open Alisia?"

"You cannot open the locket until it is ready to be opened dear Jack." Her soft fingers caressed his face. "Remember dearest Jack, there is a reason why it's called the locket of love. When the time is right, it will easily open for you and all will be revealed." As they looked into each other's eyes, WarZar came galloping up and stopped short of where they stood and gazed down at the odd-looking pair, sharing warm words.

"Excuse me! Am I interrupting something private going on here between a young lady and a mere child?"

"What you are witnessing yon prince are two future lovers, yet to become such, until the day I return a man. We are sad because our years apart will seem like an eternity for two people in love, even though I am still a child, as you so bluntly put it, my friend." Jack held tight to Alisia hand and noticed the trembling had ease up with his touch and words to the beast.

"So, young Jack, just what is the deal here? By now, even you must know one cannot just prance out the forest the same way he

84

came in." The beastly prince watched the couple closely, to see just what they were up too.

"WarZar, I have been told you are very smart, full of knowledge, so you can communicate with that devilish woman who gave you birth, Alisia's own half-sister, Carmela Solomon." Jack needed to check this beast out and see what he might be capable of concerning Alisia. "In human terms, this would make my girl your aunt, WarZar. So, if Alisia is your kinsmen, wouldn't that count for some loyalty from such a gallant prince?"

"An ant? I just don't see it, Jack! Alisia is far too pretty to be a stinky black ant that crawls around pulling dead pray ten-times its size into a red mound of dirt." The beast made a distasteful face.

Jack bent over laughing and was joined by Alisia. "WarZar, you are a hoot! And before you say it, I am not calling you an owl!" he continued laughing. "I said aunt: A-u-n-t, not an insect ant: A-N-T!"

"Oh, I get it, aunt is same as half-sister. So, which half belongs to Carmela?" The beast looked from Jack to Alisa as he watched them shaking their head. "That's not right either?"

"Nowhere close pal." Jack suddenly felt like a teacher to a retarded child. "Listen close and try real hard to understand what I am saying here. Carmela's father is Reverend Joshua Solomon, the man with the book of words, Alisia's father is also Reverend Joshua Solomon. Both girls have the same father but different mothers and I'm not even going to try and explain Carmela's birth father."

"I'm glad because I understand same father but different mothers. Got it! So, what's this stupid loyalty about kinsmen got to do with anything?" Feeling a little aggravated over all the formalities, the beast was growing impatient. "I hate my mother, so why should I care what happens to her half-sister?"

"Because your mother hates her half-sister, that's why? The overbearing witch is jealous over my charming and beautiful lady who has God's blessings for her eternal youth, while poor evil Carmela committed some gruesome crime for her devilish wish to stay young." Jack felt the words flying from his young lips and he could not control them.

"I see what you're saying Jack Spencer. Carmela wishes to make life miserable for fair Alisia and you want me to protect her for you until you return. Does that about sum it up for you?"

"I would find that a show of friendship WarZar and your pathway to finding the right choice for when I return." Jack knew

Alisia was looking at him with amazement, for she too felt his words were driven by a godly source. "WarZar, I know it feels hard to learn to trust a human being and to except them as a friend, but I believe with all my heart fair prince, that we can be the best of friends, if you just listen to your heart and learn to feel the love that's inside it, just wanting to come out and remove all the hate that has kept it captured inside."

"If I protect her for you Jack Spencer, it will be my choice to make, but she must be hidden someplace my parents cannot come." His eyes burned down on the small boy. "I have NEVER allowed a soul to tread my domain and I'm not sure I wish to start now!"

"Please WarZar, Alisia is helpless without your protection. How, can I leave the lady I love if my friend refuses to keep her safe for my return. Surely there's someplace within your fine mansion under the waterfall she can stay, out of your way. She need not worry you with anything my friend for her angels keep her well supplied with food, wine, flowers and companionship." Jack looked up at the serious creature looking down, his eyes softened and somewhat sad. "Dear friend, make her silent only if you must, but if you can give her the gift of song you will never feel lonely, this I promise."

"It will be for me to decide young Jack although all your words are locked away inside my great mind." WarZar continued staring at the amazing young boy who indeed seemed older in years. "I am a bit older than you are Jack, so it's only natural I know a good deal more than you, young sprout!" He laughed at the thought of their age difference. "Do the math boy and you shall see I am telling you the truth this time. I managed to crawl myself out of that wicked woman in 1802, two years after the enchanted witch charmed Lazar and became his queen. "He gazed down at the beautiful girl. "Alisia would not be your girl Jack had she been much bigger, like me! I fancy her beauty, her gentleness, her perfect body and her magical locket of love."

"199, WarZar!" Jack looked up seriously and ready to fight for his young lady.

"Huh?" the beast made a confused expression. "199 what?"

"Your age sir! You were born in 1802 and it is now 2001! Do the math, if you know how, genus!" Jack placed his arm around the beautiful Alisia and looked up with defiance. "Find yourself another girl your highness! This one is spoken for, remember that and treat her like a lady, who is engaged to your only friend, if you don't lose him before you except him!"

"Calm down Jack. I have no intention of stealing what belongs to you and I will protect her from the evil ones and all I require for your agreed departure, without interference from me, and her safety, hidden from everyone, is, the gift of her golden locket of love and an occasional glass of that angel's wine you spoke about." The beast looked from Jack to Alisia. "Just hand over the locket Alisia, and Jack goes free and your stepsister will never find you, this I promise."

"Dear beast, I cannot give you the locket. I have already given it to my dearest Jack, and he hasn't got it on him." Alisia spoke softly knowing that anger was building up inside the prince. "Please WarZar, do as Jack says and he will return in twenty years with the locket and his book of words. Right Jack?"

"I will have both on me when I come back, my friend and I promise your reward will be far greater than the locket, meant only for me and Alisia's love." Jack felt better about the beast wanting Alisia for his princess, so now he had to convince him to permit his departure and to protect his beloved from the evil forces inside this wicked forest. "You seek your freedom from this life of hate and torture to those innocent humans who simply made a mistake by stepping over Satan's barrier into your world. You feel trapped inside this never changing wickedness with no hope for happiness and joy." Jack grew excited with the possible prospect of changing WarZar's heart to the good side. "By helping you find love fair prince, your life will start turning in a new direction. One without hate, one without torture to those lost souls who can also learn by seeing the change in you. So, as that love grows inside your big, beautiful heart, it will start bearing fruit and your treasures will start to accumulate in heaven."

"This heaven, what's it like? Is it another type of forest to get trapped in?"

"The Forbidden Forest has been your home forever WarZar, so you cannot imagine another place without large amounts of wooded areas, fed by natural water ways, such as you have here. You've known only the worse kind of creature, roaming these woods and caves. Humans become mind-dead zombies, obeying every order or facing severe punishment, even death. Hate and evil fills the very air you breathe."

"That pretty much sums up my lovely homeland Jack." WarZar

made a face. "Does that describe this new place call heaven?"

"For starters friend, heaven was here long before this old earth was created so it's far from new." Jack chuckled at the thought of heaven being anything like the Forbidden Forest. "I'd say the only place close to your homeplace is the dwelling place of Lucifer, the devil. Heaven is the most beautiful place anyone can imagine and its borders are endless, so if you're blessed by going there to live among angels and the holy creator, the Almighty God, your stay will be eternal! Forever! You would never feel trapped inside the majesty and glory of God's Kingdom. One might wonder to and fro, from place to place, but never run out of land, mountains, rivers, and lakes! Colorful forest with singing birds, laughing flowers, all giving praise to their God! Mansions lining streets of gold, where one can walk, run, float or even fly and never grow weary! There is always light, radiating from the Son of light, our Savior, who you will hear of when I return." Jack felt Alisia tap his arm. He glanced down into her blue eyes, treading for this moment to come.

"It's time Jack. Deacon has made himself known. He stands by your right side, waiting to take you through the invisible shield." Once again, Alisia's slim fingers trace his face, as tears fell from her incredible loving eyes. "I will wait for you Jack. Never forget how much I love you."

"I could never forget such a beautiful declaration of love, dearest one." Jack felt his lips tremble, the anguish of leaving her behind and the urgency of returning to find her safe and unharmed. He knew he had to put his trust in this wild beast waiting to take her from him and prayed that God would in the end protect the girl he had given his young heart to. "Alisa, I promise to return for you, not as a child any longer, but as the man who is very much in love with you."

"Why shucks, what good is that locket of love for two people who hold that much love for each other already?" WarZar had witnessed what real love looked like and it please him, far better than the bickering back and forth from his wicked parents when one or the other didn't get their way. "You go, Jack! Go and grow up, then come back in twenty years. You will find nothing has really changed around this prison except for new slaves added to my growing list." The beast roared out a laugh. "My numbers have increased since I took over head captain. Old wicked Torren either worked the wretched slaves to death or delivered final judgement on them if they disobeyed his commands or stopped to take a break." The young boy couldn't read his cunning smile as he added. "I found permitting them to have a few scraps to eat, a bowl of water to drink and a more hours to rest, helped their work, so I got high praise from Lazar who asked what I desired for my great job. Care to guess what I asked for Jack?"

"My guess would be a place all your own, my dear friend, since you had rather spend your off time completely alone instead of with nagging parents, or silent murmuring from the slaves and empty stares." Jack knew it was time to go and he welcomed any time left with the one he loved as well as the big brut who had crept slowly into his unsuspecting heart.

"Again, my bright boy is correct, so if I choose to hide Alisia away, it will be, without her gift of song nor her physical appearance for me to gaze upon within my closed mansion. I will tuck her away from my sight and wait for her gift of promised wine, whenever she has a goblet."

"Be a lonely old beast then, if that's your choice, but this 'IF I CHOOSE TO HIDE HER AWAY' remains part of our bargain, I might just decide to take her with me now, leaving you no chance to find God's gift of love inside your heart. When I have no reason to return." Jack hid the fact that he was bluffing, but he needed reassurance where Alisia was concerned. "What's it going to be WarZar? My girl treated fairly and safely hidden in your oversized mansion, or you remaining here until our Lord and Savior returns to judge you along with the rest of the heathen population, then sentence you to the lake of fire for all Eternity! Even this horrible place will seem better than your end, if that's your choice."

"Promise me Jack, you will return if I hide this girl and protect her from everything wicked inside this forest?" WarZar held out his arms for the girl, his eyes focused on young Jack Spencer. "You will give me my freedom and teach me about this 'love' and help me escape that fiery lake, that is never quenched?"

"My friend, when I return to find Alisia well and safe, then I promise to do what it takes to save you and set you free from your bondage." Jack felt Alisia squeeze his hand one last time as she gave him a reassuring smile.

"I will be fine Jack. I trust WarZar to keep his word, so I'll wait for you." She let her fingers slip away and started over toward the big-strong beast, who scooped her up into his waiting arms. "I'm not afraid my love for I am never alone, same as you dearest Jack. I won't be able to greet you when you arrive in the Black Forest twenty years from now, but I know your heart will find me Jack. Just listen for heaven's call."

"Get going boy and try not to worry. Just remember we are waiting for your return! If you fail to come back Jack Spencer, my promise is no longer valid!" the sincere look was back in the prince's eyes as he added. "I'll be seeing you at midnight for one last remainder of our deal."

"I'm sure I won't have any trouble hearing your call friend. If I find you an hourglass at the camp store to help you time your pork roast, I'll toss it out to you and Alisia can help you learn how to use it." Jack felt his heart breaking just looking at them standing just a few feet away, both watching him. "I guess I better get moving. This is not goodbye, I'll simply say, I'll be seeing you both!"

Jack felt the hand take a firm hold of his arm and the warm soft male voice close to his ear. "We must leave Jack, while the window is open. Brianna will keep watch over your loved one." The patient angel let the young boy glance back to see them both still looking back sadly, then Deacon turned Jack's head away to face the forest edge and walked him through. "There's no need to turnaround Jack, they're gone."

Jack Spencer dropped to the ground and wept.

CHAPTER 14

Halfway up the mountain, Howard Preston had driven silently as his young friend recalled his last moments inside the Forbidden Forest. "Never had I felt so much sadness than I did when I stepped out, leaving part of my heart behind. I couldn't get her sad face out of my mind and I fought running back inside, but I knew it would be the wrong thing for me to do. I didn't care what time it was, nor what day. I just wanted to grow up quickly and rush back in after Alisia." Jack looked over at his dear friend. "I never knew you were outside, waiting for me to come out until I heard you say my name."

"We had left the other scouts with Max and a few volunteers from the kitchen staff and drove out to search for you when the storm passed by. After having no luck and a difficult time seeing due to the growing darkness, Tom and I decided to wait for morning, knowing if any scout could survive the elements it was you, Jack. Tom and I were back out on Old Wagon Road at first light and remained searching until Bruster declared you lost inside the evil forest. The next morning, I packed up a few camping supplies and headed out on my own and around eleven a.m. I watched you come out of those woods, clean and unharmed, the sadness youngster I had ever seen." Reverend Preston noticed the tears welling in the young minister's eyes, so he reached over to give him a friendly pat before grabbing the stirring wheel back.

"My heart was breaking just observing your incredible sorrow Jack, just as it is now." Howard Preston gave his signal to turn into the Black Forest Reserve and quickly wiped away his cold chill bumps. "I guess I'll never get use to coming in here."

Jack looked around at the familiar surroundings and smiled. "The beastly prince said things would look the same when I returned in twenty-years. By the looks of this road, he is right." Jack knew the Eagle Nest Campground was only three miles up the road, so he turned to watch the Black Oaks passing by. "I recall you slept right through my visit from WarZar at midnight the night before we left for home."

"I'm afraid I did Jack. I was so exhausted when we finally turned in, I didn't recall ever shutting my eyes when you switched the lamp off next to you." Howard and Jack had arrived back at camp with happy jeers and excited young boys, needing to know everything that had happened to their hero and how he had managed to escape when no one else ever had. Jack had only told them bits and pieces about his adventure, saving his private feelings to himself. After a farewell supper with pizza and ice cream and cake, the happy scout leader awarded Jack Spencer the Eagle Scout Award for his bravery and survival for being in the Forbidden Forest and the first to walk out. "I guess it was your youth that helped you wake up at midnight, Jack. You never did tell me what happened."

"I awoke to the beast screaming and his echoes seem to sweep inside the cabin that night and surround me as I slipped from bed and out into the darkness, my gift in my hand." Jack smiled over at the confused driver. "I had promised WarZar I would get him an hourglass if the camp store sold them. I never expected to find one, but there it set, on sale for five bucks. A pretty big one at that, so I just thought the old timers used to use them so it was a keepsake to remember your trip by."

"An hourglass? In the camp store?" Reverend Preston raised his shoulders with uncertainty. "I just don't recall ever seeing one before when I tried to find my beautiful wife a souvenir before we left for home. That would have made her happier than some of those childish gifts I was stuck with."

"Maybe they had it tucked away and decided to put it on sale." Jack noticed the cabins coming into view. "Who knows where it came from Howard. All I know is it made my appearing as a friend who had kept his word satisfy the handsome beast because after I tossed it into him, like I promised, I could hear the tap-tap-tap. Our code for one another."

"How did you come up with the three tapping sounds?" Reverend Preston pulled his car up behind the church bus and looked out at the familiar campground, before switching off the motor and turning to face his young friend. "Was this code your ideal Jack or that things?"

"WarZar was asking about the heart and I had mentioned that it made a thump-thump-thump sound so after our conversation about it, he said it would be our code for getting in contact with one another." Jack recalled the tall Titian scooping up a stick and striking a nearby rock three times, making the same sound, tap-tap-tap.

"Did you ever see this WarZar when you went out and delivered your gift to him?" Both men had gotten out of the car and were unloading their things, while those chosen to be over the youth's cabins showed them where to go. The first cabin #1, went to Clayton Weatherspoon. Cabin #2 and #3 went to Joe Keaton and Carter Davis, the men over the young men who were in Cabins 4, 5, 6, 7, and 8. Cabin 9 belonged to Tom Bruster, then the teenage girls were in 10-14. Cabin 15 and 16 belonged to the girl's chaperons, Taylor Nance and Mattie Wagner. As planned, Jack Spencer and Howard Preston were bunking in cabin #17, the end cabin that sat next to the tense forest. Those helping in the kitchen had new cabins located directly behind the large kitchen and chow hall, so no one felt cramped.

Jack had heard his old scout leader ask him about seeing the magnificent beast before he left, so inside their cabin while they divided the drawers and closet space before unloading their clothes, the young minister felt he could answer his friend's question now, without a lot of listening teens. "I didn't see WarZar at first, so I thought he might be waiting for me to say goodbye first. When I left them inside the forest, I had refused to tell them goodbye and told them that I would be seeing them soon. Goodbye just seemed so final. I knew he was out there, somewhere watching me, waiting and listening, so I said:

"My friend, the gift I threw in to you is the hourglass I promised to get. When the sand is all in the bottom, turn it upside down and you will see it sifting back down. Once it all gets back down in the bottom, you count it one hour, so, every time you turn it over it starts another hour. I've never roasted a whole pig over a fire before, but my guess would be four hours, to get it well done, so that's four flips of the hourglass." The young boys laughed, trying to picture this big giant roasting a skinned boar on a spit, over at fire. "You might want to ask Alisia if I'm right about the time." Jack stared out into the quiet darkness. "WarZar, are you there or am I talking to myself?" Jack smiled to himself when he heard a chuckle near bye.

"Young Jack Spencer, I shall miss you." WarZar stepped from behind a big tree and stared down at the young boy wearing pajamas. "Did the man waiting outside the forest this morning decide to keep his eye on you tonight, Jack?"

"Reverend Preston? No, my friend, he understands more than you think. My scout leader is the only one I can share my story with and he won't think me mad." Jack smiled up at the serious face. "I'm going to miss you too WarZar. It's hard to leave your friends."

"But, you will be back, right young Jack?"

"I promise to return in twenty-years, your highness." Jack suddenly became concerned over this beast not knowing just how long twenty years were and he had threatened Jack he would withdraw his promise about keeping Alisia safe if he failed to return. Forgetting the beast' ability to read thoughts, Jack jumped when the handsome Titian laughed out.

"Relax Jack, I know how years work. My mother gifted me with knowledge, remember? There are 12 months in 1 year and each year consists of 365 days. You informed me that this is 2001, so in twenty years from now it will be 2021, so if you do not return in that year, my promise to you is valid!"

"Thank you for easing my mind, WarZar. That was the act of a good friend." Jack gave him a big smile. "I'm sorry I didn't have my camera with me to take your picture, but I'll be sure to have one with me when I return. Is there anything else I can bring you when I come back?"

"Just my freedom, like you promised."

"If I can see a changed heart in you my friend, that freedom which you want so desperately will be granted, I promise." Jack knew in his heart this beast was sensing something he had never felt before. Once again WarZar read his thoughts.

"You are different from all the others Jack, except the girl and her father, of course. Lazar got to Reverend Solomon before I was born, so I never got to share any words with him before he was made silent to please my wicked mother." The beast raised his head proudly. "Alisia is very wise, for a female, but neither Lazar nor WarZar take council from a female."

"My friend WarZar might not regard the female gender as someone to teach you the things you desire to know, but your demon father does not hold all females as lower beings. I am certain Carmela has her say on most matters. Would you not agree, my friend?" Jack wouldn't argue with this giant over their traditions on human status, even though Jack regarded women as equals when it came to knowledge on certain subjects."

"I gather your ideals on a woman's capabilities outweigh mine, young Jack, but as for my demon father's weakness when it comes to his lustful wife, I must agree with you." WarZar sneered. "I was referring to the average normal female, Jack. Not my wicked witch mother who can conjure up a potion to get any knowledge she requires."

"I am sure it was both your parents that made you believe a female was created to serve man and obey their will, never to offer any opinions of their own." Jack was only ten years old, but he had found there were some ladies who possessed a bountiful supply of knowledge and his Alisia was one such girl.

"I will not dispute your claims about the fair Alisia endless knowledge Jack, and your young years is also one of the reasons I hold you different from the others. To see in the weaker sex's more than just a mate is remarkable at only ten-years of age. Your views differ from those of my wicked father and mother and from their teaching I have been taught that the male is above the female in all things. What do you believe Jack? Are we men the ruler of our domain and the women under us?"

"In the Old Testament of the book of words it does state men will be the head of the house, over the woman in making decisions for the family. It also states, the male and female will be made one and the man is to love his wife with the same kind of love as he does the Lord. It will be my beautiful job to love and protect Alisia all my life, for as long as the loving God gives us together. Jesus, God's Son, welcomed women who wished to serve him and he treated them with the same love and respect as the men who followed him. To show any child of God the love and respect they deserve by letting them speak what is on their heart, is following Jesus' commandment, to do unto others as you would have others do unto you."

"Can you make that a little clearer, Jack?" WarZar was thirsty for the truth and knew he would never get it from his parents and Jack would soon be gone for twenty years. "I promise, this will be the last question for now. Just show me how to give this love and respect, you speak of."

"By following that commandment from Jesus my friend. Just start treating all those around you the same way you want to be treated. It's just that simple my friend." Tears came to the boy's eyes. "Please keep my girl safe and treat her with kindness. When I return to your forest WarZar, I will be older and far wiser in my knowledge of the book of words so you can feel free to ask me any questions you have. I'm sure Alisia can write them all down for you or better still, she can teach you how to write words and know their spelling." Jack gave his big friend a sad smile. "Don't feel too proud to ask her friend. My Alisia is filled with the love of God and will gladly teach you."

"This sounds like goodbye Jack, so I shall remember your promise to help me learn more about this truth. Reading and writing were never taught me by either parent, saying we had no need in our captive world for such nonsense. I might take you up on her service to keep all my questions down for me though." Sadness clouded the beasty prince as he gazed down for the last time on the young boy who had stolen into his life unexpectedly. "I will wait this time to come to you Jack at your return. Just make the tap-tap-tap and I shall hear it and come with haste."

"I shall remember our secret code dear friend and announce my arrival." The tears could not be retained as they fell from the young scout's eyes. "I love you WarZar and I shall truly miss you "

"Jack, I am sure you recall my words on making friends with humans, that this is something I will never do! I have of yet to call you my friend, nor do I plan to, at least not just yet. I must see if you keep your word, to both me and the sweet girl, I keep safe for you." Tears were new to this Titian and so was a breaking heart. The thought of not seeing or speaking to this young boy had touched him deeply, like nothing he had experienced. "Please Jack, don't let us down. Alisia and I both need you. My young one, you are our only hope for saving freedom."

"Only death could keep me from coming, dear friend. I promised to return, WarZar, and a friend never breaks his promise. In the summer of 2021, you will hear my tap-tap-tap and I will wait for our happy reunion! See you!"

"See you, Jack! Stay healthy and alive!" With that, the beast was gone and the sad boy wandered back inside and to bed.

CHAPTER 15

Two days had passed and the youth group had been kept busy with activities which included swimming, hiking down short trails throughout the campground, boating on the Swan Lake and several other fun games chosen for their age before and after supper was served. Wednesday had come in a few degrees cooler and it would make the long hike down the Old Wagon Road a lot better for a group of teenagers used to shorter walks and longer swimming and tennis time. Today's hike would take up their entire day, so Jack Spencer and his helpers had their work cut out for them. Teenagers didn't get as excited over things like treasure hunts for old trinkets or a history lesson on the old timers. So, Jack was discussing the situation over with his good friend Reverend Preston.

"If Saylor's Landing doesn't interest this group, I hope the Forbidden Forest excites their visit to the area. Up until now, they have been kept busy with things they enjoy with each other and their camp dance on the last night seems to be all they talk about."

"Well, maybe Tom's dramatic telling of the old timers at Saylor's Landing will hold their attention for a while, then we can stop for lunch and the group will brag about not being afraid over any dumb forest." Howard rolled his eyes in disgust. "If teenagers could have the same respect for their leaders as all my scouts did." He noticed Jack's eyebrow go up. "That is, all but two of my scouts, right Jack?"

"I wonder what ever happened to Billy Haskell and Joel Mason." Jack strapped his backpack on and checked under his shirt and smiled at the locket hanging secure. "They both sure were out to get me in that foggy storm. I guess I was the last thing they suspected on our last day at camp. I noticed when they spotted us coming in the campground, the smirk on the faces vanished. They watched me with wide-terrified eyes, as though they saw a ghost."

"I knew they were guilty of your disappearance Jack, but I had no proof and you never pointed a finger a them. The sign of a loyal scout brother and another reason I awarded you with the Eagle Scout award." Jack's scout leader had watched the young ten-year-old scout react to what had happened to him with true honor and no finger pointing. "Jack, you set an example that day for all those boys who looked up to you and they all admired you for your scout pledge of scout loyalty. It might help you to know your troop that always admired you wasn't the only ones that had a change of heart that day. Joel Mason broke away from his old friend Billy after we returned home and he set his course to follow your example. As for Billy Haskell, he is still serving a forty-year sentence for bank robbery and attempted murder."

"I knew it was Billy who grabbed me and pulled me over at the edge of the forest." Jack didn't make light over his old enemy's troubles; he just knew it was time to tell his friend what had happened on that stormy evening. "I had been keeping my attention on Max Carter's back and informing my scared friend behind me our locations. LeRoy got nervous when his glasses got fogged up so I kept speaking to him to reassure my buddy I had his back and we were almost at the end of Wagon Road. When it got dark from the storm clouds, I knew LeRoy wouldn't be able to see my scout shirt as well so I took it off so the white t-shirt could be made out clearer. The thunder was sounding closer and I reassured my friend to keep watching my shirt and before I could make ten more steps, some big hand grabbed around me while the other hand clapped over my mouth. I kicked and squirmed all the way. The big brut dragged me toward the right where he switched on a fog light behind me and lowered his voice in disguise. The next thing I knew, he let go and gave me a shove through the tree line where I fell on my face, trapped inside."

"So, that's what happened to Tom Bruster's fog light." Howard shook his head. "Haskell's stealing started long before he grew up. Tom thought it had slipped out of his pocket. It slipped out alright with the slick fingers of one Billy Haskell."

Jack checked his new watch and noticed it was time to go. "He might have thought he was sending me to a hellish place, and I admit at first I was a case of bad nerves, but when I heard her voice, my whole world changed and now, I cannot wait to go back inside that Forbidden Forest." He walked over to the door. "And I feel this is the day!"

"Then let us depart for the Old Wagon Road." Reverend Preston stepped out and notice their group getting on the bus. "I know you have grown anxious my young friend having no contact from the woods next to the cabin, but you did say the beast would wait for you to send him the secret code when you come inside."

"You're right of course Howard. I'm not yet sure how it will happen but something will take me inside that forest today, I just feel it." Jack led the way to the bus and climbed on with the still quiet group, who had been treading the long hike and had already assumed it would be boring.

"Cheer up youth! We promise your day will be exciting! It was super exciting for me when I was a boy scout and found the best treasury ever found at Saylor's Landing." Jack looked around at all the sour faces and gave a chuckle. "What do you think I found? An old rusty nail? A broken piece of china? A rusty horseshoe?" He smiled over at Tom and Howard, knowing all three of those items had indeed been found that day when Jack surprised the group with his find.

"So, what did you find, Reverend Spencer? The bones from a dead horse?" Jason Berry laughed out with the other teens.

"I bet our handsome young minister found an old Bible, with yellow pages and words in Hebrew!" Emily Faircloth slapped her friend's arm as they laughed.

"Are there any ghost floating around the old grounds?" Gil Steele pretended to shiver. "Ohhh! I hope not! It's not even near Halloween yet!"

"It's easy to make fun of something when you have already decided it's not worth your time or interest." Reverend Preston stared out at the ungrateful group sporting their faux smiles. "I can tell you, without a doubt, that the majority of my young scouts had more respect for their leaders than any one of you! You are a disgrace due to your obvious bad manners and unless you change your attitude and try to enjoy this hike, we will think twice before bringing you on another youth retreat again!"

"Reverend Preston, maybe if these rude kids hear what Jack found, it might make them show a little respect for the time all the leaders have devoted to them along with Mr. Bruster's lovely gift so they could have this retreat in the first place." Mattie Wagner had sat listening to the mean words by the unruly teens and she, for one, was almost ready to pack up and take them home.

"Thank you, Mattie, I think that might make this group stop their cute remarks about the treasure hunt when they find out what Jack found and how he found it." Tom Bruster glanced back at his quiet granddaughter who had glanced down when her grandfather started speaking. "Amy, wouldn't you like to hear about Jack's find?"

The cute blonde smiled up at the handsome young minister. "I would love to know what Jack found twenty-years-ago grandfather." She had wanted to speak up for the charming young preacher she had a crush on. "And, just how did you find the very best treasure ever found there, Jack?"

"I heard a voice from a young lady and she led me to her secret hiding place under what she called a flowering tree." Jack had everyone's attention as they rode down the long road to the far entrance of the Old Wagon Road. "She told me to look under the white rock. Of course, all the other rocks I had seen were dark colors so I questioned her and she told me to look behind me. I twirled around to see a giant Formosa tree and underneath was an oval shaped white stone. I heard the scout leader, Reverend Preston say five minutes and I knew he would soon be counting down the last sixty seconds and I had to be back in front of him before he said sixty, stop!" Jack could see every ear was keen on his story, so he continued. "The girl said with urgency in her sweet voice, hurry Jack, look under the rock, get it! I lifted the stone away and saw a beautiful white silk handkerchief and stood up and opened it to find a golden locket on a gold chain. Then I heard Reverend Preston start the count down and I raced up the hill with my treasure."

"Needless to say, Preston and I were flabbergasted over such a great discovery. It was dated December 25, 1800 and the handkerchief was still white and in excellent condition." Tom Bruster was relieved to see the teens interested in Jack's story, but he could also tell several of the girls had a crush on their young minister, including his granddaughter, Amy. "So, I'm sure you can understand why Jack won the top prize."

"I hope that dumb badge wasn't the only thing Jack got!" Shawn Harper gave his young minister a smile. "You got to keep one of those treasuries didn't you preacher?"

"Jack got to keep both of them Shawn and the smart fellow decided to keep them instead of becoming a millionaire." Howard Preston stood up when the bus stopped at the end of the Old Wagon Road. "Well kids, this is it! I hope you wore some good shoes today although the dirt road will be easier on your feet than a paved one. Get out and we will line you up with a leader in between the small groups."

The group was divided up with Howard and Jack in the lead, the two cut ups Lori Robinson and Shawn Harper, directly behind their ministers, then Joe Keaton, the head coach from Graceland High and one of the men over the boys behind them. Walking next to Coach Keaton was one of the girl's counselors, Mattie Wagner and behind them walked Amy Bruster, Tammie Wexford, William Brown, the only African American in the group, and Gil Steele, walking in twos. Following them was Tom Bruster, who insisted on walking near his granddaughter, then the last four teenagers were behind Tom, walking in twos. They were, Juanita Martinez, the only Mexican, Emily Faircloth, Ron Bailey, and Jason Berry. Behind them walked Carter Davis, the boys' counselor, and Taylor Weatherspoon, another girl's counselor.

The group had walked down the tree-divided road for almost five miles as Tom Bruster pointed out various trees and asked if any youth knew what kind it was. Emily Faircloth seemed to know almost every tree as well as its history. After listening to the girl continuing to answer Tom correctly, Reverend Preston stopped the group and smiled back at the knowledgeable young lady.

"Emily, your knowledge of trees is remarkable for one so young. How do you come by all these perfect facts on all the trees and some that grow only in Black Forest Reserve?"

"It's really quite simple Reverend Preston when you bring a book on trees on the hike with you!" The book worm held up her book for him to see and he laughed.

"What a clever girl you are Miss Faircloth." Howard looked around at all those facing forward. "Your very wise president is referring to her book titled: The Trees in the Black Forest Reserve!" His eyes fell on an irritated Tom Bruster. "Brother Tom, with you asking the perfect questions and Miss Faircloth giving the perfect answers, you both make a great team. Wouldn't you agree Jack?"

"If we didn't know better, your head leaders would declare you planned the entire thing!" Jack laughed and everyone joined in, except Lori Robinson, whose hand was up for a question. "You have something on your mind Miss Robinson?"

"Where you are concerned, sir, lots of good things, but the reason I lifted my hand was to ask, wouldn't what Emily did be cheating. You know, like, having the answers to a test right in front of you?"

"Only if this had been a contest, Miss Robinson." Jack overlooked her personal comment regarding him. "There were no set rules for asking the question Mr. Bruster has asked about the trees, so Emily has done absolutely nothing wrong. Now, let's keep moving. One more mile we will be at Saylor's Landing and if anything can impress a group of teenagers these days, then this place and its history will 'blow your mind!'"

As the group stepped out into the large clearing, it was obvious to the leaders most of them were impressed with what they saw after seeing nothing but thick forest on both sides of the road for a far as you could see.

"Wow! What happened to all the trees on this large track of land?" Jason Berry turned a full circle, taking in the barren land around them. "Man! I was trying to picture how a bunch of wagons could fit in anyplace, but now I know!"

"This place appears to be almost a desert! Reverend Spencer, did you really see a large Formosa tree around this place or did you just imagine it?" Amy Bruster looked down at the black and brown stones, then shook her head. "And I do recall you telling us you looked under an oval shape 'white' stone! Right?"

"That's right Miss Bruster, way over by the drop off, the only place on Saylor's Landing where the wagons didn't park for the night." Jack had pointed in the direction he found the locket. "Mr. Saylor was the first keeper of the wagon rest, that's what they called the spot the wagons stayed on. Besides having the land named after him, it was thought he had a one room log cabin down on the land where I found the locket. Kenneth and Doris Todd were the second keepers and they built a larger log cabin, big enough to accommodate anyone needing a place to stay, and this was where the young lady I heard, stayed with her father and mother while the church they were building was completed along with a home for them, which they never got to complete."

"Why Jack? Did something happen to prevent them from finishing their dreams?" Taylor Nance looked over at the drop off and figured it had to be deep to hide the tops of a large tree.

"The girl's father, Reverend Joshua Solomon, was tricked into going inside the Forbidden Forest and was captured and never came back out, like he had promised his daughter. The sweet and beautiful young lady had just buried her dear mother only days before her father went missing."

"So, what happened to this beautiful chick, Reverend Spencer?" Shawn Harper wandered how this man could possibly know what a girl who lived in the 1800's could look like. "Did her ghost become visible for you, man?"

102

"I couldn't tell you how I know Shawn, and you wouldn't believe me anyway if I did." Jack wasn't going to share any of his personal feelings with a bunch of teenagers who would only make fun about his story.

"Say, Handsome, I just remembered you telling us the mysterious girl knew your name. She did call you Jack, right?" Lori's eyes lit up with mischief when his eyes met hers. "I can see how this lovely ghost chose you to speak to, Jack Spencer."

"For starters, Alisia is 'not' a ghost! She is trapped inside that evil forest and has remained young ever since she entered!" Jack was getting aggravated over the two agitators, constantly implying things they didn't know anything about. "One word of advice to anyone who has any thoughts about slipping inside that trap, thinking its all a hoax and you can just walk right back out! If you are thinking in those terms, then I am telling you now, as you leader, do not try or God forbid, Lazar finds you and turns you into a mindless zombie, never to know anything but torture and work for the remainder of your life!"

"You seemed to know a lot about the Forbidden Forest Jack, as though you saw things inside for yourself." Joe Keaton had never taken the fable serious until now, and the high school coach didn't wish to lose a single student.

"I would never have disobeyed my scout leader and deliberately went inside that scary forest, Joe." Jack looked back at him with a serious expression. "I wasn't expecting to get pushed inside that forest, brother Keaton, but for everything I experience I would not have changed my fate if I had the chance to do it over." Jack looked around at the listening group of young people. "I am not giving you a green light to have your own experience inside that forest, my young friends. I can assure you things wouldn't work out the same for you. I was the first to ever step out from that invisible shield that surrounded the large track of land and I owe my released to the young lady."

"Then, are things as bad inside that forest as we have been told Reverend Spencer?" Amy had been warned over twenty times by her over protecting grandparent, who had insisted on coming along just to keep his eyes on her. "Is there really a demon trapped within those woods by Satan himself?"

"I know for a fact Lazar, the demon of Lucifer, is inside those woods and has been for a very long time and I am certain the evil being would not choose to be there if he could get out." Jack had never seen the wicked demon for himself, but WarZar was living proof and his beloved Alisia would have never lied to him about his existence if he were not real.

"Jack's story only proves the tale that has been passed down through the generations about the devil standing on this very ground below us and placing a curse on Lazar for his disobedience, to bound his fallen comrade inside a substantial amount of woodlands forever. The legend goes, the devil was so angry, fire rose around him and covered the surrounding countryside, destroying every living thing on it. Knowing his fate, the screams from the demon could be heard by tribes throughout the mountains." Tom Bruster could not remain quiet another second, recalling how excited the young scouts had been over this revelation. "After soil samples had been taken and analyzed by experts, they could only find traces of ashes and old brunt embers, deep down inside the worthless earth." He gazed over at Jack and smiled. "I guess the only way to find out how that Formosa tree grew below the ridge and not much else, our young preacher will have to ask his beautiful 'young' friend where it came from."

"Tom, you might recall I wasn't shy about asking questions when I was ten, so I do recall asking Alisia about that Formosa tree standing tall and alone on that barren land." Jack could tell by the silence and every face watching him closely, they too wanted to hear this answer. "When the Solomon family came over the mountain from the state of Virginia, Charlotte Solomon, Alisia's mother and Joshua's true love, had grown very ill with scarlet fever. Young Alisia nursed her loving mother inside the wagon while her father drove the team of horses down the narrow mountain road toward Saylor's Landing. Nestled tucked away between their few belongings, sat a four-foot Formosa tree, potted safely inside a big barrel, they would eventually wash out to collect rainwater in. Charlotte had wept over her flowering tree left behind in Virginia, a wedding gift from her devoted husband Joshua, who knew it was her very favorite. But a ten-foot tree firmly rooted in the ground could not be dug up and moved. So, Joshua did the next best thing to help make his love happy. He thanked God for the small seedling growing under the wedding tree and dug it up to plant at their new home. Charlotte had a glad heart knowing she would be taking a part of her love-tree with them and that was where they buried her, several months after they moved to the Black Forest." Jack could still see Alisia's tears as she told him about her beautiful mother's passing and the tremendous sadness her father had felt. "In Reverend Solomon's sorrow, he took the white oval stone he had brought to place at the church entrance for a step and used it for his wife's head stone. So that is how the tree and the rock came to be sitting on this barren land."

"I hate to stop all the questions you are hitting my young friend with, but due to time restrictions, we must move on with the agenda" Reverend Preston could tell his friend was getting weary over all the personal questions, so he decided it was time for the treasure hunt. After going over all the park rules, he asked anyone interested in searching to begin and the others to have a seat and watch, speaking quietly if they wanted to talk. Three teens sat it out while the other seven spread out looking.

Slowly and one-by-one, the teenagers began to find small items, sticking up from the rain the night before or in one case, wedged between two big rocks and took some strategy and a slow process to figure out just how to get the article out without disturbing the big rocks. Unsure of how to retrieve his great find, William made eye contact with Jack Spencer.

"I think Will has found something that looks interesting and he is not sure how to get it without breaking the park rules." Jack had bent over to whisper to his friend Howard. "Maybe if we offer advice to any teen who needs help, it would make it fair to see what he needs."

"I see your point Jack and watching the other flustered-looking kids, I can't see that it will hurt. We are not handing out badges this go-round. Just a chance to find a treasure they can keep as a souvenir." Howard stood up and blew his whistle. "Look kids, you have ten more minutes and it appears some of you look puzzled over what you found, so, we have decided to offer any help for those who request it. I think Jack has spotted one needing assistance so you may ask any other leader if you need too."

"What do you have Will?" Jack followed the young man's dark hand to the object wedged between two big rocks. Jack got down for a closer look, followed by the tall young man.

"What do you think it is Pastor Jack? My guess would be some type of sword, but all I can make out is the handle and just part of some kind of blade." William Brown glance over at the interesting young minister, that he had always admired.

"Son, if we can find a way to get this great antique out from these rocks without disturbing them, I believe you have found one great treasure." Jack examined both rocks to check for looseness and found one of them moved slightly. "I've got an ideal Will that might work. While I wiggle the lose rock, you pull gently on the handle, keeping it straight. If you should move it up or over it might snap and the blade will be lost forever under the rock." Jack looked up and gave the nervous boy a reassuring smile. "I know you can do it Will. I've watched you painting with confidence, on that church mural. Fine straight lines that take a steady hand. Just pretend that handle is your paint brush handle and the blade is the brush resting just before falling in the wrong paint."

"Yes sir, Reverend sir!" The young man smiled with confidence and slowly wrapped his long fingers around the handle as Jack jiggled the rock, then with a steady calm movement, Will began pulling the stuck blade loose from its burial place. When the point tip came out clean and unbroken, both Jack and Will laughed out. "We did it sir! We got ourselves an old soldier's sword!"

"Correction son, you have found yourself one terrific treasure, to keep or to sale!" Making sure the boy held the sword safely down, Reverend Spencer gave the young teen a big hug. "Congratulations!"

The sixty-second countdown was completed, and other than Tammie Wexford's old coin find, William Brown had found the very best treasure of the day.

"Alright youth, we will have our lunch break before we head down the most dangerous part of the Old Wagon Road and let's pray we don't run into the same type of bad weather we did back in 2001, when a young Jack Spencer was pushed inside that wicked forest by another scout who was jealous of the bright young scout." Reverend Preston looked over at Jack to continue.

"I am asking that all of you respect each other and do not try to frighten those who are already nervous about walking past that forest. If I hear or see anyone of you misbehaving while walking passed the Forbidden Forest, you will be placed between me and Reverend Preston for the remainder of this hike." Jack looked over the group and noticed a few smiles. "Believe me, getting trapped inside that forest is no picnic. It was the most terrorizing experience I have ever had. The loud screams from the beast called WarZar can be heard miles away and its echoes linger long after its screams die down. The great Titian stands nine to ten feet tall. His feet are roofs and great horns protrude from his huge head, covered with thick black hair that falls down his strong back. If you don't look where you step, you might end up with a Razor Wart clamped on your leg. Lazar and his evil witch mate, will wait for their son, WarZar to catch you and turn you into their mindless slave forever! You will be thrown on a pile of the dead at the Valley of the Bones when you die or grow too sick or old to work. Other wild creatures roam the land, captured inside with Lazar if they were unfortunate enough to be there when Satan set his trap." Jack looked out now at every face, serious and somewhat nervous about walking by such an evil place as the Forbidden Forest. "I tell you these truths so you won't be tempted to prove yourself to some girl, fellows, or girls, to any fellow you're trying to impress with your bravery. This is not a time to show bravery, young people. This is the time to show your leaders and all your classmates and friends, just how caring and smart you are and what kind of Christian you are."

"You all heard Jack's warning, so be smart and stay safe, then you can be around to enjoy the big dance on Friday night." Howard noticed the teens remained quiet and smiled at Jack. "Enjoy your lunch kids."

CHAPTER 16

"Alright young people, we are about to walk down the six-mile stretch where once again we will be flanked on both sides by thick forest. The big difference now is neither forest running along beside Old Wagon Road are the same. The forest on your left is very similar to the forest we just walked between for the first six miles with many of the same trees as Emily described. The forest that runs the full length of the six miles on our right and comes out close to the campground, is the Forbidden Forest. Believe me the old timers that named that forest knew its history and danger." Jack had watched as the leaders lined the youth up in the same groups as before. "I think we covered most of the reasons not to go near the right." He noticed Shawn Harper's hand raised. "Shawn, you have a question?"

"If all the 'old farts' knew that forest was so darn dangerous, how did so many idiots get trapped inside?"

"Yeh, Shawn is right Jack!" Lori shook her head in agreement. "If there really is a Valley of Bones somewhere on that property and those dead or dying, perish the thought, was throw down on a 'stack' of bones, there had to be hundreds of "idiots' going inside those woods."

"I take it both you and Shawn think I made up all this and it's a bunch of nonsense. This is the exact attitude all those people that did go inside think. They must have considered the story ridiculous, same as you two and ended up captured by either Torren or WarZar and made into mute mindless slaves!" Jack knew every group had the troublemakers and doubters. These two were theirs "Are you going to be like the disciple, doubting Thomas and have to see it to believe it! Well, if that's the case, be prepared for hell on earth young people, because that will be your fate!"

Howard knew by Jack's demeaner he had had enough with both teens and sent them behind the first group. "Shawn, you and Lori can stay smack in the middle and for you own sake, keep on this road, eyes straight ahead!" Reverend Preston looked out over the group. "That will go for anyone else who doubts our word! Jack and I are both men of God and we would never bare false witness! Leaders, keep your eyes on the two teens in the center and get prepared to walk!"

The group remained quiet for the first three miles, letting their eyes wander to the right from time to time and noticing the complete stillness within the tense forest, while the forest to their left was alive with all kinds of nature. An occasional whisper could be heard among the young people as they discussed the complete opposite woods. After three miles, Jack held up his hand to stop the group. From past experience, Jack glanced up and noticed dark clouds in the Western sky and shivered recalling the exact same weather change when he was the young scout waiting in the line. Jack and Howard exchanged glances before Jack spoke.

"We have just completed the first three miles down this dangerous stretch of road, but this is where things get even hairier. This old wagon road has been reserved the way it was when the first travelers came through the mountains, so over the years, the vines and vegetation has crept closer in to the old road making it narrow. As long as the sun is shining things don't look so ominous and forebodingly evil with the Forbidden Forest just nine-feet away but that faithful day in 2001, things took a turn for the worse when a thick fog fell over the road and dark thundering clouds blocked out the sunlight." Jack could see all the teens were listening to his every word and even Shawn and Lori didn't act as brave as before. "For your safety my young friends, we must walk the rest of the way in a single line, making sure that you stay in the middle of the road at all times. Tom, would you tell the youth about how Mr. Saylor made this road."

"My pleasure Jack. It might ease some of the worried youth, considering the road was made between both forests." Tom cleared his throat. "When Mr. Saylor decided to run a 10-foot road through the Black Forest to help weary travelers find a place to camp for the night, he knew to keep away from the deadly Forbidden Forest. Since the forest was flatter along this path, he realized he would be near the evil forest so he chose to take all the land from the safe forest, so he dug it out sixteen-feet away from the Forbidden Forest. Unfortunately, the land wasn't as flat over the last three miles, so he has to narrow it to 8ft. Then the vines and vegetation came out later on both sides of the road, so now both forests are only nine-feet away from an 8-foot dirt road." Tom Bruster waved his hand dramatically. "So, I'm sure you can understand why we must walk in the center of the road and not stray over to our right or we might find ourselves mindlessly digging our own graves!"

"Would someone please tell me why we are even putting ourselves in this scary situation in the first place?" Juanita Martinez asked, her voice shaking with fear.

"I can answer Nita's question Jack!" Amy Bruster narrowed her eyes at her grandfather. "My very adventurous grandfather thought this road of horrors would be lots of fun to a group of teenagers who are into horror movies and things that go bump in the night! I guess paw-paw wanted all of us to have a story to tell when our teacher asked us, 'What did you do over the summer kids? Anything exciting?'"

"I, for one, think this day has been very adventurous and educational!" Ron Bailey gave a-two-thumbs-up. "Listen gang, I was sure we were in for one dull-boring day and what we got has been anything but! After today, there's not a Halloween haunted house anywhere scary enough for me!"

"I'm with Ron!" Gil Steele spoke up. "I haven't been this excited since dad let me drive his old Corvette! I say we play it smart, stay cool and listen to Reverend Spencer and Reverend Preston. For ministers, these guys are awesome!"

"The guys are right! We are having a new adventure, unlike anything any of us have ever done! Just buckle up all the jitters, throw your worries to the wind, stay in line and act mature and when we're sitting around the campfire tonight or back home reliving our story again, you will be proud you were a part of this not-so-brave group today!" Emily smiled up at the young minister who had been listening with his own grateful smile. "As your president, I say it's time to follow our leader and listen to his wise council and take his words seriously."

"I could not have said it better! Let's walk!"

Near the last mile, the dark clouds began to drift overhead as the wind picked up, making it hard to keep loose things from blowing. Thunder could be heard in the distance as traces of fog began floating around them. Jack turned to see Howard searching the dark sky. Was it his imagination or was this the same spot the storm grew bad before? Jack stopped and took out his fog light and gave his old scout master a discouraged look.

"Howard, I swear this is the same spot you stopped 20 years ago to warn us scouts about the dangers of the changing weather."

"I wouldn't disagree with you Jack! It always seems to get hazardous near this spot!" The minister's spoke softly so they wouldn't frighten any teens. "The road starts to make a turn here, a slight curve toward the left. I recall seeing the curve when I was a scout and the same sort of storm came up."

"So, the road seems to start turning away from the Forbidden Forest at this spot." Jack looked thoughtful and he could hear the youth whispering to one another.

"What are you thinking Jack? I can tell you are on to a possible reason for storms to strike in this area around the same time."

"Lucifer knew about the wondering lost souls traveling this road and let's say, just suppose he relished in the ideal that people were either accidentally or on purpose, walking into the Forbidden Forest and getting captured by his trapped demon. Satan knew once caught in his trap, they could not escape and eventually die, never having a chance to find salvation. Since these people had only six miles to get tempted and he saw the last mile quickly coming to an end, he devised a plan. An evil plan that could assure at least one or two careless people, unable to see clearly due to his trick of sudden fog and a devilish storm made worse with the howling wind, would make their way into the forbidden tree line and lose their eternal soul to him!"

"I know it's just a theory Jack, but what other explanation do we have." Howard glanced back at the frightened teenagers and leaders. "We best get moving and if this is where you are meant to leave me my friend, I promise to wait for your return for as long as it takes."

"You're a good friend Howard and I trust you with my life! We will walk out of there. I'm just not sure if I will be the only one left when we do." Jack took a deep breath and lifted his fog light. "Leaders, light those fog lights now and keep them down on the road! We do not want to stray toward the right! If you have anything on you that might blow away in this wind, let it go! You can always replace a cap or scarf, but not your life! I will personally buy you another one. Keep your eyes on the person walking in front of you and keep moving! Let's go. There's only one more mile!"

The wind grew blustery and Amy Bruster had to take her cap off, for fear of losing her favorite autograph cap she had worn to Justin Beaver's concert and was overjoyed when he had signed it. All the other girls had been envious over her wealthy grandfather buying her a front row seat, directly in front of the star she adored.

Lori Robinson had spotted the cap held tightly in the rich girl's hand, so she punched her friend Shawn Harper and pointed at the girl waking in front of him. "Look how the little rich snob grips that prized cap like she was just one of the lucky girls to get her idol's autograph. Every girl in school knows her paw-paw paid that singer big bucks for that personal signature. To beautiful Amy! Love, Justin!"

"Too bad that gusty old wind didn't lift it off her royal head." Shawn laughed along with his jealous friend. "You want me to act like a big buff and ripped that prized cap right out of her hand?"

"Ha! What a neat ideal! Poor little rich girl will think that mean old wind just whipped her favorite cap right out of her ring-covered fingers!" Lori glanced back and noticed Tom Bruster was looking at the road with his fog light. "The coast is clear! The rich grandfather has his eyes on the road!"

With quick movements, Shawn grabbed the pink cap from Amy's fingers and let it go, sailing up toward the Forbidden Forest. In her panic, Amy yelled out. "STOP!"

Hearing his granddaughter's frantic cry, Tom Bruster made his way up by her side. "Amy precious, what happened?"

Up in the lead, Jack called back with concern, "Everyone stand where you are and do not move!" He tried to see down the long row to where the scream came from. "Who asked us to stop? Did anything happen to you?"

"My cap, my very special favorite cap in the entire world was ripped from my hand and blew up over toward the right! Please, let me go get it Jack! I promise I won't get near those woods but if I see my cap lying on the open ground in front of that evil forest, it will be safe for me to just get it and get back in line."

"Amy, remember what I said about the possibility of something blowing away in this wind? It is far too dangerous for you to wander over by those woods just to get a cap." Jack knew she was proud over her special pink cap, but the risk was too great. "I'm afraid I must say no, for your own good. Maybe the young entertainer can send you another signature cap, right Tom?"

"Of course, he can sweetie. I'll have my secretary on it first thing Monday morning." Tom Bruster patted her drooping shoulders. "Now be a good girl and turn back around." The rich banker called up to Jack. "It's settled Jack, you may start the walk before the rain starts."

Just as everyone started to move, Amy Bruster grabbed her grandfather's fog light and took off to where she last saw her favorite cap, leaving her startled grandfather's yelling "STOP!", this time.

CHAPTER 17

Amy Bruster had found her cap, lying on the ground halfway between the clearing and the Forbidden Forest. She smiled when she noticed the cap's bill was facing out, so she thought, all I have to do is get down and slowly reach for the tip, then pull it free. The spoiled girl jumped when she heard Jack Spencer call out to her.

"Amy, move away from those trees now! Just forget that cap and get over here at once!"

Amy turned around to see Jack standing just a few feet away with her grandfather and Reverend Preston. "The cap's bill is facing out and all I have to do is take hold of the end and pull it out! I can do it!"

"Amy Bruster, just get your butt over here with your paw-paw this instant!" Tom Bruster had never felt so much anxiety as he did at that very moment. "I promised your parents I would look after you!"

"And you have paw-paw, practically every second I've been here!" The irritated girl spit back. "I am old enough to take care of myself! I'm not going to do something stupid!"

"Then get up slowly and back over toward us right now Amy." Jack Spencer kept his voice calm. "Be a smart girl sweetheart and move out of harm's way. Those trees might look harmless, but they are misleading. There are evil things lurking just inside there and if you so much as touch that cap, they can and will jerk you in, when they're ready."

"Reverend Spencer, you were pushed inside that forest and I do not recall you ever telling us of anyone who had gotten yanked in while standing innocently on the outside." Amy smiled when the handsome minister dropped his eyes. "Do you know for a fact that anyone has been jerked inside, as you stated, or is that just a guess?"

"Amy, there was no records stating how all those people ended up trapped inside that forest, but are you willing to take that chance and regret it?" Jack had witnessed the powers of those inside the forest and in his heart, he knew the evil that lived inside the Forbidden Forest could have the means to suck anyone standing too close or taking their bait. "Amy, I personally believe this will happen to you so please, dear girl, do not prove me right. Those evil forces could have pulled your cap just within their reach knowing your mindset and the temptation too great to resist. We all love you, Amy! Jesus loves you and he wants you to make the right choice. So, just get up and step away from the demon's trap."

"Amy, listen to Jack. He has been inside that evil place and has seen just a small part of the horrors those captured endured." Reverend Preston knew this girl had always got everything she wanted from her parents and her grandparents, and she could be overbearing to those less fortunate. To get this spoiled girl to take her leader's orders was very doubtful. "Amy, couldn't you for one time in your life listen to those who care for your welfare? This is one time you do not have to get your way!"

"Blah-blah-blah! Grownups always think they know what's best for the youth! "

"Amy Marie! Stop that sassing right now young lady!" Tom Bruster had just about all he could take with this spoiled grandchild. "Your daddy should have turned you over his knee a long time ago!"

"Give it a rest, old man! I'm sick and tired of being told what I can and cannot do!" Amy stuck up her chin. "I am going to get my cap so we can go back to that boring old cabin with no television!"

"No! Please baby-girl, paw-paw will get that singer to send you ten caps, one of every color!" Tom Bruster watched in horror as his granddaughter reached for the cap's bill and gave it a pull. "The darn thing is stuck!" She fell back tugging on the cap. "Get loose, you" before she could say another word, Amy Bruster was sucked inside the tree line, along with her prized cap.

"Oh my God!" Tom Bruster started to run forward, when Jack and Howard stopped him. "Let me go after her! The poor kid, she'll be frightened out of her wits!"

"Listen Tom, it won't do either of you any good if you get caught too." Jack glanced over at his friend. "I know what you're thinking Howard, the foolish girl asked for everything she got after we both tried to warn her what would happen."

"I guess this is your time to go back inside now Jack, right?" Howard Preston had tears in his warm eyes. "Stay safe my young friend until you get with WarZar and Alisia. I'll get the young people back to the campground safely."

"I know you will Howard. You are the best leader around." Jack handed him his fog light and picked Tom's up where Amy had

114

dropped it. "Don't worry about your granddaughter Tom." He handed him the flashlight. "I'll make sure she gets out safely but I cannot tell you how long or when so you might want to hang around with Howard who will be waiting for my exit."

"Thank you, Jack and may God go with you and keep you safe." Tom Bruster threw his arms around the young minister.

"I know I go in with the Lord's protection Tom." Jack looked into the worried man's eyes. "And Brother Tom, if you should learn that Amy's cap didn't get ripped away from the wind but a harmless prank that went poorly, try not to judge those young people too strongly. My guess is Shawn and Lori were behind the getaway cap, but never intended for anything bad to happen to Amy. They are probably feeling pretty bad right now and blaming themselves for Amy's foolish actions. I'd say there a lot of blame to go around, wouldn't you?"

"Starting with Amy's parents and grandparents Jack." Tom Bruster tried to smile. "I'll not judge those young people. For what you're doing for our family by going in that forest to help our spoiled granddaughter, I will even try to help them not blame themselves."

"Then I'm off, first to find Amy, who shouldn't be too far away, then see to her safety before seeking out my big friend." Jack disappeared inside the Forbidden Forest.

He stopped to listen and could see no sign of the young girl who had been too stubborn to listen for her own good. Absentmindedly, Jack touched his chest and felt the locket and immediately he could hear a nearby chattering noise. He slowly moved toward the noise and froze when he saw a large razor wart had Amy backed up against a tree. Jack thought to himself. "That little devil is what pulled Amy in the forest and now he is holding her hostage until his master comes to collect his next slave."

Jack slipped up behind the unsuspecting oversized rodent after picking up a heavy tree limb. He placed his finger over his lips when Amy spotted him, so she wouldn't give her hero away. Lifting up the heavy limb, Jack came down hard on the razor wart's head, causing it to scream out in loud squeaks. Seeing Jack standing over it, the scared little varmint dashed away as Amy ran into her hero's arms.

"Jack! Thank God, you found me!" The young girl could not control her tears. "I'm so sorry Jack! I should have taken you seriously! I'm just a stupid spoil brat and I don't deserve you having to be trapped too!"

"Amy, your life is worth saving sweet girl. I know you're sorry for what you insisted on doing, but its done, so you must promise me that you will start doing everything I tell you, especially inside this forest." Jack knew she had learned her lesson even though it had to be the hard way. "I know a place where you can be safe until I locate my friend, but you must promise me that once I take you there you will stay put and wait for my return, no matter how long. You won't go hungry or thirsty, this I know, for it was where I stayed when I was trapped inside this place twenty-years ago."

"I promise you Jack, I will stay where you take me." Her eyes wandered around the scary woods. "Anyplace is better than these woods with those fuzzy-little creatures with razors on their head."

"That was a razor wart, an evil little rodent that rounds up people for the demon, it's master, then keeps them hostage until Lazar appears to take his victim." Jack drew quiet and whispered for Amy to keep still. He could hear something galloping toward them and he knew he had not given his big friend their secret signal yet, so Jack suspected either Torren or Lazar, himself, was heading their way. He looked around frantically and saw the giant tree just a few feet away. He grabbed Amy's hand and raced over to the tree and prayed that he could find how it opened. Releasing her hand, Jack ran both hands over the spot where he had entered as a boy and nothing happened.

"Hurry Jack! Those horses are getting closer!" Amy whispered, her fear rekindled.

"I know Alisia opened it right here!" Jack suddenly remembered the locket's power and touched it, then like magic the hidden door opened and he pushed Amy inside and jumped in behind her to watched the secret door close. "Amy, do not say a word nor think any thoughts when you hear them right outside. If WarZar could hear my heart beating and the things I was thinking when I hid inside here from him, this evil being can do the same." Jack looked down and noticed her eyes were on him. "They're here, quiet." He spoke just above a whisper and they could hear two horses moving around in front of the massive tree and snorting out from their big nostrils.

"Starky, you little razor wart, just where did you leave that girl?" It was an angry male voice, which was obviously seated on one of the horses. He sniffed the air. "I can spell her flesh! She couldn't just disappear!"

"Over by the rutty scrubs, O Great One!" came the croaky voice from the razor wart as Amy made a distasteful face realizing the

116

fuzzy rodent could actually speak. "I was keeping guard over your slave when the giant slipped up and clobbered me on the noggin."

"A giant Starky? Surely you do not refer to WarZar, my strong handsome son?' the other rider was indeed a female, so Jack knew who this 'great one' had to be and who had ridden out with him.

"Never would I mistake the great and powerful Waradock, whose strength and height outshines any other!' the nervous creature shivered at his mistress' stare. "Your son, WarZar, has not been near this place in some time, your majesty. I dare say ever since the small one departed."

"The small one? You speak of the ten-year-old boy who was pushed through the veil by some wicked boy." The woman sneered. "It is a shame Weed was too slow to sweep out and capture that Billy Haskell while he was standing close enough! My guess is Weed was taking a nap at the time he was on watch and only awoke when he felt young Jack Spencer fall through the trees and on the moss-covered ground. Even though that was twenty-years ago, I can still hear Weed's frantic call, alarming every creature and his royal masters that an invader had just arrived inside the forest and he had been unable to capture him."

"That was then my tempting wife! It is the present I am concern about!" Lazar looked in every direction. "Dearest, are you sure this is the spot where you sensed the humans?"

"Unlike you and Lucifer, my tongue is NOT forked and laced with lies! There is no mistaking their presence being around this area for I feel the power of the locket of love! My slippery sister's magical locket and once I possess it, I will have total control of her and my father!"

"So, it wasn't the human's you sense being in our mist, it is the very locket I have wanted ever since I learned of its heavenly powers!" Lazar had dreamed of owning such an object, so powerful it could aid his escape from this place of confinement.

"Sorry my king, but this locket will be of no use to you and will not aid your longing freedom, that you so desire." Carmela gave her demon mate a curt smile. "I made a deal with your powerful master darling to be able to come and go from this very forest at any given time and to become a forever beautiful queen, the wife to a powerful and handsome demon, who could always satisfy my every need." The enchanting witch reached over to stroke her handsome husband's face. "Cheer up darling, I'll not grow tired of you and leave your side for another, as long as you treat me right and" her smile instantly dropped into a serious face. "Never look upon my pure sister with lust in your heart when I have her in my domain!"

"Orders to your king, Carmela!" Lazar gathered her long braid in his hand and pulled her head close to him. "I could strangle you with your own glorious hair or lift your bossy beautiful head right off its shoulders!" his eyes wandered down her shapely body and he could feel himself growing aroused. "My queen pretends to be better than her intelligent husband and her evil master, who now possesses her wicked soul, same as he does mine! If we find this human that has the locket on their being, we will share the power it gives! I have spoken!"

"And this is why I am so crazy about you Lazar. You take total possession of me and turn me on with your painful actions and evil words!" Carmela reached over and laid a fiery kiss on his full lips. "I'll expect to feel you completely my sexy demon, when we return to our private chamber, but for now, we must concentrate on finding the foolish, spoiled girl and my sister's boyfriend. They cannot be far and there is nowhere to hide forever!"

"Alisia has a boyfriend, from the outside? How on earth could this man stay alive outside this magic forest for over 200 years?" Lazar just assumed the young lady had left her boyfriend on the outside of the Forbidden Forest when his cunning wife pushed her sister through the tree line. His mind didn't wrap around the beautiful Alisia falling in love with someone from the modern-day world.

"My saintly sister had means to learn about one Jack Spencer, who at ten-years of age, was pushed inside at this very spot and at the time of his first entrance, our son WarZar came out to find the intruder for himself. As it is with us now, WarZar could not locate the boy. He had simply vanished, even though our powerful smart son could hear his heart beating nearby and even read his thoughts, to the boy's dismay."

"Tell me you are kidding dearest one. You are trying to convince me that your, very charming and brilliant younger sister Alisia is in 'love' with a mere child?" Lazard laughed at the absurdity of his queen's statement.

"My dear husband, are you so dense you cannot see the reason for the boy leaving her behind twenty-years ago?" This time it was the irresistible Carmela laughing. "My poor darling, Jack Spencer left so he could grow up and become the man my sister plans to wed, then with the aid from the magic locket of love, be free to leave this place along with 'our' father and all those other 'good souls' rotting in your drafty dark dungeon."

"Over my dead body!" the demon yelled out with anger. "No one leaves this forest! Once inside, there they must remain forever!"

"Lazar, have you forgotten, you cannot die!" Carmela took a deep breath, aggravated over knowing Jack Spencer was hiding someplace near and obviously listening to their every word. "This man knows the power he holds and he will not give it up lightly. Already he has fooled the dull brain razor wart into believing he was larger than he really is. I'm not sure Mr. Spencer knows just how powerful that locket really is. When he finds out how to use it, he will use the locket to his advantaged."

Amy had been listening with Jack and hearing about the power Jack had from the girl's locket, she felt more confident in their position and was unaware of the trap being set for either hidden person who felt it safe to speak. Even though Amy's words came out very soft, "The locket will save us." Jack instantly knew their hidden place could easily be found. He quickly folded his hand tightly over Amy's lips and silently moved his head in a negative.

"It came from over near that big tree!" Lazar rode his horse around the tree and could see nothing. "If they were hiding behind this giant black oak, where the hell did they go?"

"Don't be stupid Lazar!" Carmela had ridden over by his side and looked up the tree. "They hide somewhere on this tree! Its limbs stretch far above our sight, so it is impossible for us to view the top branches. You are a demon husband! Fly to the top and find them!"

"Me? The royal master and king?" Lazar bellowed out. "Starky, you little squirt, find Scabs and Bumps immediately and without delay! I need the little climbers to go in search of the intruders!"

Inside the giant tree, Jack knew what he must do to keep Lazar and Carmela from eventually cutting the tree open and finding them. With haste, Jack opened the trap door and pulled a frightened Amy down the steps. He pulled her deep within the thick tunnel and saw what he had been searching for, a thick, hard stick. Going next to the tunnel wall, Jack struck three times, the secret code meant for his big friend to hear. Jack only prayed WarZar would hear his tapping and come to their rescue.

He quickly led Amy to the end of the tunnel and she gazed up the high wall, shivering at the sudden thought that this was where Jack was going to leave her. To her relief, Jack reached up into a small crack and mashed it. An arched stone door magically opened into a massive living quarters. Inside with the door shut, Jack could finally speak.

"This is where Alisia lived until she was taken by WarZar in exchange for my freedom." Jack's eyes were serious when he looked down at the young teenager. "Amy, you must promise me that you will remain here until I come after you. Now, I have to go back up and wait for my friend to come. WarZar is the only one that can save us now."

"Those evil being's son? Jack, you heard that razor wart, describe that beast!" Amy grabbed his arm. "Please Jack, you cannot put our lives in that evil thing's hands! Let the Locket lead us to Alisia! She will know how to help us!"

"Alisia is with WarZar, Amy! I know you are scared and you have every right to be but you must trust my judgement for once! Had you trust it the first time you would not be in the predicament." Jack took her hand away from his arm. "Promise me you'll stay put!"

"This place is pleasant compared to that forest! So, I will gladly stay right here Jack, I promise." She looked around at the quiet surroundings. "I recall you said I'd have food and water to drink here, right?"

"They will serve you Amy, don't worry. The locket let them know of your presents." Jack knew he must be going up so he wouldn't miss WarZar's arrival or if the 'climbers' had arrived to go up and search.

A scared expression fell on the girl's face as she whispered. "They? Who are they or should I say, what are they?"

Amy turned around as soon as the sweet voice spoke behind her. "We are angels, my dear, sent from God to take care of you while you dwell within this underground dwelling. We shall keep you company and Jack needs to get back up to hear what is happening just outside the magic tree. Help is on the way and, he needs to be sure it is WarZar that waits just outside the tree alone and not the trick of the evil ones."

"Oh! By all means Jack! Go with speed!" Amy watched the handsome minister dash out the door and up through the tunnel.

Jack slipped up inside the massive tree and listened. He could hear the sound of critters scurrying up the tall trunk to the top branches. The next sound he heard brought out his big, relieved smile, the loud screams of the beast, galloping swiftly toward the search party. WarZar had arrived.

CHAPTER 18

The loud voice of WarZar filled the air. "What goes on here? Does my king and queen dare take over that which is rightfully mine?"

"Forgive me my son, but just what are you referring to darling?" Carmela could not resist her wicked flirting, even to her own incredible handsome son. "Your father and I were out on a hunt and discovered a couple intruders had slipped inside our forest so we decided to hunt them instead of the wild boar we were after."

"Congratulations mother, you now lie almost as good as the evil king!" The clever beast saw through her words. "Your thoughts are on the locket of love and you are in hopes this one intruder has it on him, correct my queen?"

"You are aware I have been seeking the locket for many years and have even gone out in search of it!" Carmela lifted her eyebrow in defiance. "I want it! When the locket is in my control, I will have power over everyone!"

"Everyone my wife?" Lazar had kept silent to hear what would be said and his anger was kindled. "Your power will never be as great as your husband's woman! Should you try to take over my throne, I will not hesitate to turn you into a mindless slave to give me what I desire and you shall be unable to enjoy it for yourself!"

"You do not scare me Lazar. The fact is, even if you turned me into this mindless lover, the passion would never be the same. A one-sided affair is not delightful and there would be no spiked wine for your sexual taste buds!" Carmela laughed out. "You forget my dearest, Lucifer is on my side, and he will never permit you to touch me in a harmful way!" She patted his red cheeks. "Cheer up husband, you will still be my king, now and always! You know your queen will share the power with her king."

A big smile fell on the demon's face. "That is more like it!" Lazar turned to his beasty son. "I see your point son! This is not a job for your master. The intruders are your responsibility, so we shall leave them to you. Should you sense the locket present, get it from Alisia's lover and bring it to the palace at once."

"You think that this pure girl who has the ability to hide from us is capable of having a 'lover'?" WarZar smiled at the thought. "Only a wicked mind could have such thoughts concerning this angelic creature. Being gone from the love you knew in heaven has made it hard for you to recall how pure a virgin can be."

"My son, how do you know about me ever living in heaven?" Lazar had not thought about the place he was thrown from ever since Carmela came into his life and to hear his strong son speak of it was disturbing "Who have you been talking too, to know these facts about me."

"Your master, he is the one that shared the information with me Lazar." Jack was listening and knew WarZar had been in the presence of Lucifer at some time.

"When did Lucifer come inside this forest without my knowledge of his evil presence?" Lazar knew his old master was deliberately avoiding the demon that had betrayed his command and only wanted to see for himself the beastly child they had created.

"Satan was amused over my appearance." WarZar got his mother's attention. "He expected to see a half human- half demon son and seemed pleasantly surprised to learn I was some type of Titan, half man-half beast." The handsome giant grunted. "That devil laughed in my face as he spouted out, "To be born of such a beautiful-shapely woman and a handsome, well-built demon, you turned out to be a hideous beast with great horns and roofs for feet!"

"I waited for his laughter to cease before I spoke and told the thoughtless serpent what I thought!"

"Son, you did not say anything to make the great one angry at you, did you?" Carmela suddenly felt nervous for her handsome son as well as herself for bearing one who would speak disturbing words to Lucifer.

"Actually, Lucifer admired my bravery for speaking my mind regarding his hateful and disrespectful words about my appearance." WarZar noticed the instant relief fall over his mother's face. "That is when he sat down to have a long chat with me, telling me about the war with God and how he had been thrown out of heaven along with all his followers, which included my very own father, you Lazar."

"Better coming from the devil, himself than one of those good ones who have been made silent!" Lazar stared up the tall tree. "This one named Solomon read from the big book of words many an hour before I made him silent, tired of hearing the constant 'Thou shalt nots' and praises to the one and only God in heaven! The same loving

122

Creator that tossed us down into the deep along with our self-admiring leader!" The fallen angel watched one of the ugly small creatures scrambling down the large trunk. "Scab? Have you found the intruders yet?"

"You sent climbers up that massive tree?" WarZar couldn't resist his laughter. "Humans could not have made such a high climb Lazar in the short time it took your horses to gallop here once the razor warts sent out their warning of intruders." Still laughing, he looked from father to mother. "What made you both think the intruders climbed this giant tree?"

"We both heard a girl speak and her voice came from this tree!" Carmela watched as the other climbers slid down the tall tree making a chatting noise as they slid. "We did not send you up there to have fun coming down Spits! What have you found?"

"No sign of humans up there, your greatness!" came the squeaky voice. "Not a one!"

"One can see a lot of the big forest from such a high tree!" came another high voice. "All the surrounding ground was bare of any life, except for you royals below the tree. They must be invisible, great one."

"Invisible? Don't be ridiculous! They are here someplace very close, hiding from us!" Carmela stared at the massive tree trunk and noticed it was plenty large enough to hold humans inside its belly. "With help from that magic locket, the intruders may even be hiding inside that tree right now, laughing at us and making us look foolish chasing up the tree after them!"

"It is I who is laughing mother at that ridiculous notion!" WarZar continued to laugh, only to cover up the truth he knew but would never share with his evil parents. "I know for a fact Jack Spencer has tricked you both the same way he tricked me twenty-years ago!"

"And just how can this Jack Spencer trick us, a powerful demon and a cunning witch?" Lazar roared with anger. "We heard the girl speaking plainly at this tree! How could that be a trick?"

"That is what I thought myself before I learned the truth about the young scout's talents. I stood outside this very tree and could hear his young heart beating with fear. Then I could read his thoughts and when he finally got brave enough to talk, the sound came somewhere around this tree." WarZar lied, knowing the ten-year-old never spoke a word while he threatened him outside, so the beast had left to wait for another time to meet up with the boy. "I found out later that the young boy wasn't anywhere near the big tree, but was watching from a safe distance where he threw his voice, to make it sound like he was there. Other times he would mock a girl's voice and the young fellow got great at throwing his voice, so he could make his escape while I searched where the voice could be heard." WarZar shook his head. "I can tell you for a fact you are wasting your time searching around this big tree. Jack Spencer made you believe he was at this large tree and while you have been here searching for the clever young man it gave him time to escape from under your nose. Now Spencer is long gone and well hidden, maybe even with the young lady you seek and cannot find." WarZar stepped away from the big tree and out to an opening wide enough for him to stretch his great height.

"Can this human ever be found if he possesses such magic?" Lazar sat up in his saddle. "Where do you suggest we look WarZar?"

"Just go back to your palace and wait sir. This is not a job for the royal king or his queen to worry about. I'll gladly search for Jack Spencer personally. He might have escaped me before, but I know all his tricks now and he cannot hide from me forever. Now that the human is a grown man instead of a slippery kid, staying just one step ahead of me, he will be more easily spotted and at 30 instead of 10, the age difference will show. As a child, the boy ran full out, never worrying about what obstacles lie ahead. The more mature Jack will run the chase with caution for what lay ahead that might trip him up or slow him down." The tall handsome beast had to sound convincing to have his way. He got down on one knee and bowed to show his father respect. "Father, trust me to find this man that made a fool out of you and your queen, my beautiful mother. The intruder who showed you no respect, O mighty king and ruler of the Forbidden Forest, in the kingdom of Lazar! Your son will make him pay a deadly price for this disrespect toward the great Lazar! This I promise! It shall be my soul purpose until I hunt him down and destroy the little weasel!"

"WarZar my son, you make me proud! Such loyalty will not go unrewarded!" The handsome demon could now have eye-to-eye contact with the tall beast, still down on one knee in royal honor. "I shall give you all the time and space you need to search out and find this man named Spencer. What more do you request my son, to aid you in your mission. Just ask of me and you shall have it, no questions asked."

"You may start by removing all your spies from the forest! This is one time I and I alone desire to make the hunt. To avenge my mother and father, I will search him out from every corner in our homeland! Eventually there will be no place left for the human to hide from me, since I know this land of my birth far greater than any other." WarZar stood up proudly, staring seriously ahead. "Promise me complete authority over these woodlands, hills and valleys and I will catch this intruder for you!"

"It is as you wish my son. Complete authority over all that is mine, from corner to corner and all in between, for as long as it takes to find and take prisoner one Jack Spencer! I will place the order on all my guards, the climbers, the spies, and the snitches, to keep out of your way and from under your foot. They shall remain in the barrows, caves, or underground lairs until you give me the word to release them back out on duty!" Lazar turned his stallion toward the slave's quarry. "I leave at once to inform Torren, your second in command over the mute ones, to stay put and watch the workers so that they do not grow slack with their labor. I require many stones for my building projects and the palace upgrades made by your exciting mother keep growing!" Lazar blew Carmela a kiss. "It's a good thing we have a house full of mute and mindless workers who don't mind cleaning the ever-growing palace." Hearing the many little sounds coming from the chatting guards, Lazar whipped his horse around, stirring up a dustbowl around the furry little varmints, causing them to cough and sneeze. "Enough useless chatter! You all failed me so this is no time for celebration or great mirth! This time off will not be a vacation for any of you! I order you to make out your year's report on every single intruder you personally captured! The first to be summon back on duty will be my loyal snitches, the only creatures who have not let me down on any of my orders."

"My son, when you find this slippery young man, search him for the locket, then bring it to your mother." Carmela smiled over at her husband. "It will do your father no good to possess it." her cold eyes fell on her son. "Nor you, my delightful-handsome boy. I'm afraid it's charms only work for the human race. Not for angels, never fallen angels nor beast with great horns and roofs for feet, my poor misfortunate son."

"Spare me your pity mother. I have learned to except who and what I am!" WarZar's eyes burned into hers. "I had no other choice after your bad choice to create a powerful brew just to make your lustful night together irresistible. It was so powerful, it created me, the hideous beast with great horns and roofs instead of feet!" WarZar turned to his father. "Torren has the habit of leaving his post whenever he grows weary of his job or becomes filled with jealousy and uncalled for suspicion on what I am doing so long. Make sure he stays put and does not sneak away to find me or you may be finding yourself another second in command after I destroy the sneaking shadow!" This time, the handsome beast wasn't far from the truth. "Just make sure all those creatures stay inside until I have completed my mission, including your devoted snitches!"

"WarZar, you have my word son! I will inform Torren if he leaves his post this time, he will face execution! As for the creatures, including the dependable snitches, I will make them remain inside their dwellings until further notice." Lazar swept his arms out over the woodland. "Son, you have complete command of this forest until you catch Jack Spencer." The demon glanced down at all the furry creatures swirling around and making a mad dash to their living quarters and the howling sounds coming from the hills proved the snitches were inside their caves. "If any creature disobeys my command and tries to interfere or override my order, you have my permission to destroy them!"

With that, the mighty demon motioned for his wife to follow him and they galloped away, leaving their son standing alone in the massive forest. His smile fell on the great tree and his heart leaped with joy, just from knowing the young boy he had missed and longed to see for twenty-years was waiting inside the large trunk.

CHAPTER 19

WarZar moved over by the giant tree and lend back on the one beside it, then called out. "I heard your signal Jack and came at once, knowing you were in danger! I'm sure you heard our conversation regarding you and now are aware my parents are out to get you and the locket they both assume you have with you."

Jack had also heard his big friend promise his evil father that he would get Jack Spencer for him and his wicked mother and after twenty-years being away, the young minister couldn't help but wonder if WarZar's real loyalties belonged to them and he had been merely playing around with the young Jack's mind."

"Jack, my clever boy, you can trust me! The coast is clear. I alone stand outside your hiding place. And a very clever one at that."

Jack wanted to put his trust in his big friend but knew in reality he didn't really know this beast at all. He had declared his hate for humans when he first heard the giant raving outside his hiding place and Jack recalled just how scared he was at that moment. Jack knew a friend helped another friend, but again, WarZar declared he wanted no friends! Maybe this was a trick to get him to come out only to find Lazar and Carmela waiting with their powerful son.

"This friend thing really bothers you, doesn't it Jack?" WarZar had read all Jack's doubts concerning him. "I need time before I can decide if a friend is right for someone like me, but the truth is if I ever decided to take a friend it would be you, Jack Spencer! How do you think I know you are hiding inside this tree? I could have never figured it out on my own although my evil mother came very close to learning the truth. Had she found you inside there before I got here to throw them off your sent, that young girl that got yanked inside would have been found as well, hiding below."

The side of the tree opened up and the young minister stepped out to see only his big friend, resting up against the opposite tree trunk. "The only way you could know these things my friend is from Alisia." Jack stepped over and gazed into WarZar's warm dark eyes. "She had to trust you to tell you her secret dwelling place."

"Jack Spencer, you have a very wise and loving young lady." WarZar remembered back to the day she shared her secret with him.

"The trust did not happen overnight, young Jack, it took almost fifteen years before she felt safe to open her heart to me. It was right after I decided to tell her my dreams and how I wished more than anything they could come true."

"You had been having a recurring dream?" Jack noticed the questioned look come over the handsome face. "A dream that returns night after night!"

"Yes Jack, every night, I have the same dream." WarZar got up and looked around at the quiet forest. "We'll speak of this at another time. To remain here for long might not be wise." He looked down at Jack and could still see the young boy inside him. "You have grown into a fine young man Jack, but your features are still the same ones I've also seen in those dreams. We must be very careful not to be seen making our way back to my dwelling, the only safe place to hide you at."

"I heard your mother speak about her sister, Alisia and her determination to get hold of the locket of love so she can control its power." Jack knew this wicked witch had hurt his friend's feelings over her claims that she alone could possess the locket and control its power. "Carmela will never get near this locket WarZar! Your mother could never touch the one that has it and even if she managed to destroy me, she would find it impossible for her to remove the locket of love from around my neck!"

"Then you do wear this prized possession my wicked parents are seeking! Jack, this puts you in greater risk while in this forest!" WarZar showed real concern. "Could you not place it inside the carry pouch you wear on your back?"

"I wear it proudly my friend, for it is this locket's power that will save my beloved and set her free at long last." Now it was Jack who was looking serious. "Is Alisia safe with you WarZar? It's obvious from your evil mother's words, she does not know her whereabouts."

"Did I not tell you I would keep my word, Jack Spencer. Your Alisia is safe and as beautiful as the day you left her with me." The beast finally smiled. "I took her the long way around the day you left and it will take us sometime to get to her since I will be taking you around the homeland to get there, same as I did her twenty-years ago."

"Do you mind telling me why we will be making the longer scenic route when you obviously came from your dwelling place to get here a much shorter route, since you got here in less than twenty-

128

minutes?" Jack gave a sarcastic laugh. "Even though, listening to your evil parents just outside my hiding place, it seemed more like a two-hour wait for your arrival!"

"I have a very good reason for taking the longer, safer route Jack! The short route goes right past my parent's large estate, where guards are posted to keep watch for any intruders getting too close to the royal palace." WarZar smiled at Jack's big eyes. "The same guards acknowledge my passing every time I galloped past, so you would be instantly spotted! So, we shall move around and far away from the palace grounds. My father promised me complete domain of the forest and surrounding homeland until I caught you, Jack Spencer. Lazar cannot be trusted to keep his word. If he grows weary of waiting and hearing no report from me, he will not hesitate to call out his snitches and have them hunt us down. Lazar is a chronic lair just like his old master, Satan, and he cannot be trusted to keep his word." WarZar knew they must start moving to get to his place before his father sent out his snitches to spy on his progress and to keep him informed.

"Well, at least I can see more of the Forbidden Forest this time. I never got past the entry woods on my first visit." Jack silently hoped he wouldn't have to run to keep up with WarZar's giant steps. "Just how many miles are we going before I can be with Alisia?"

"There are several miles the way we must go Jack, but I did notice you have on the right kind of shoe for this trail. We'll be hiking over hills and one small mountain, so there will be rocks under your feet. My hoofs are used to all the rough places." The friendly beast smiled down at his companion's frown. "Don't worry Jack, I'll slow down my usual fast gallop and if you get too tired of walking, I'll give you a lift! It will be a better view up here! Let us go before the moss starts to grow under our feet!" WarZar led the way, far beyond the tree line that had been familiar to the young minister, to places unknown. As they walked further away from the Old Wagon Road, Jack began to notice the woods getting less dense and an open meadow started to come into view. Looking around at the green grass and rolling hills in the distance, the young minister sensed the feeling of tranquil peace within the Forbidden Forest and he realized this place wasn't the reason for the people's fear, it was the one that called it home. WarZar had noticed the sudden change in his young friend, where before he had been tensed with his surroundings, now he seemed relaxed and his anxious pace had slowed down.

"Jack, I see you have noticed my homeland is not as gloomy as it appears inside the forest, where all the humans that wonder passed our border fear getting sucked in if they get too close." WarZar had deliberately slowed down so his companion could feel at ease walking next to such a tall being. "There are many such places as this on our property Jack. Our highest hill in Lazar is not much taller than Echo Ridge, the small mountain near Eagle Nest Campground, where your scout leader led you and the other scouts up to the crest, where the Bawl Eagle builds its nest, raises its young and dwells permanently year-round." The beastly prince enjoyed speaking to Jack Spencer, the only human he had ever liked, besides Alisia Solomon.

"I will not ask my friend how he knew about our hike up to Echo Ridge to witness for ourselves how the American Eagle made their nest and fed their young. My only guess would be you just happened to be up on your mountain that sits adjacent to the one we climbed and saw us." Jack smiled up at his big friend. "Reverend Preston pointed out the nest and the great Swan Lake below it in the wide meadow where he said the eagles could catch as many fish as they needed to survive on the mountain year-round."

"I did not witness your climb for myself Jack. Alisia has told me many things that were outside the Forbidden Forest, the prison I was born into." WarZar could almost hear the young woman's laughter as she recalled many happy moments watching the ten-year-old scout without his knowledge and he gave a soft chuckle. "You were right about her volume of knowledge Jack. For a girl, Alisia is highly educated, much like mother. The big difference between them is, mother is wicked, evil, and thinks only about herself while Alisia is sweet, charming, filled with love and genuinely cares about everyone trapped inside their own bodies and being treated worse than animals. Her words, spoken straight to my face and without fear." He glanced down at Jack and noticed he had his companion's complete attention. "I see what I tell you about your beloved woman has intrigued you. So, I might as well confess that I have heard the little songbird sing and she sounds beautiful. Her sweet melodies lift my spirits and make me glad that I am alive."

Jack stopped walking and gave a happy laugh. "So, you never made my girl silent after all! Did you tuck her in a room far away from you like you said, or did you give Alisia a beautiful room to live in while she's been with you, my friend?"

"I didn't see any reason to place her away in some far room when I found I delighted to be in her company, same as I do you, Jack!" Pausing to form his words correctly, the beast sat down to have closer eye contact with his young friend. "I cannot explain my feelings toward you Jack, but I have never sought out a human to be close to before, but you are different. I sincerely care about what happens to you and this might sound funny coming from a monster, but Jack Spencer if it meant losing my own life to save you, I would gladly do it." WarZar looked down with confusion written on his handsome features. "Tell me, Jack, what makes me feel this way? Why do I hold you in such high regards and loyalty?"

"What you feel my friend is love, a gift given only by the Almighty God! WarZar, you and I are more than just good friends, who care deeply for one another, we are actually brothers of the heart." Jack reached over and touched WarZar's hand, an act that had never been given this incredible being. Tears filled the dark eyes of the beast as Jack said, "My friend, my brother, you are not a monster nor are you a hideous beast. You are a very special creation, made by evil parents, true, but of no fought of your own, and with our Lord working through me, we will make you a more loving, giving and caring man."

"Jack, you are the first human to touch me and I could feel this incredible love you spoke of radiating inside me." The voice came soft and tender. "Never have I needed a friend, nor have I wanted one, not until now Jack Spencer. I am happy to call you friend! I am even happier to call you my brother!"

They began walking again and this time there were smiles on each face as WarZar picked up where he had left off speaking about Alisia's living arrangements. "I could not bring myself to silence such a remarkable guest, with tales to tell and songs to sing. I felt it would be a total waste, especially when I had so many questions needing answers and having to wait for your return 20 long years help my decision." WarZar chuckled and gave his small companion a wink. "Your lady informed me that some of my questions were too deep for her to answer and I'd have to wait for you."

"My girl is wise, my friend." Jack suddenly remembered the hourglass and roast boar. "Tell me friend, how did the hourglass work for timing your roast pig?"

"If you are talking about food Jack, you must be getting as hungry as I am." WarZar laughed and pointed to a fig tree, hanging ripe with figs. "Figs will have to make do for now, my friend, but I will roast one of those, fine boar for us to celebrate your homecoming and being with fair Alisia again. As for the timer, it did the trick, with your girl's help. I must admit her angelic cook has made my life a lot better and the angel's wine is super good!"

"I remember! I cannot wait to enjoy a glass with two of my favorite people, you and Alisia." Jack stopped at the fig tree and popped one inside his mouth. He found it soft, chewy and perfectly sweet. "Mum, this is very tasty, friend. Stop me if you see me eating too many."

"Eat all you like Jack! This will be our little secret!" WarZar placed three inside his mouth and made pleasant sounds as he chewed. "We will walk a little further before night falls over the woods. I know the perfect spot we can stay the night then be up at first light to head home, the faster way."

"What way is that my friend?" Jack knew this tall beast was not referring to them running, since Jack would automatically be left behind.

"I would not expect my friend to keep up with me running, so stop fretting." WarZar pointed down into a valley where a clear brook flowed. "We go down to have a drink, then clean off the sticky hands before heading up Raven Knob, to my secret cave. Tomorrow morning, I shall carry you on my shoulders down the other side of the mountain then through the path that runs by Wolf Creek all the way to Rockford Falls, my dwelling estate."

Both friends headed down to the clearwater brook, chatting about the difference in this place and the modern world lying just outside the hidden veil that kept them prisoners, where no waterway was safe anymore to just enjoy a drink.

CHAPTER 20

The cave on Raven Knob had proved to be bigger and safer than Jack had vision. The clever prince had stacked plenty of dry firewood near a back wall to assure dryness and with skills obviously learned over the many years of outdoor camping, WarZar had a nice warm fire going in no time. Always prepared, the gentle giant had one wall lined with plenty of warm cover and bedding, in the form of black bear pelts. After shaking out two large ones, WarZar draped the fur around his companion's shoulders.

"That should keep you nice and warm during the cold night, my friend, with aid from the fire, I'll see keeps lit."

"Tell me brother, did you have to stay one night inside this cave or elsewhere, when you took Alisia to Rockford Falls?" Jack was trying to picture his perfect lady sleeping outside with this person before she knew if he could be trusted. "It was still early in the day when I left so I just wondered how far you traveled then."

"By, carrying your girl the entire distance, I managed to make it to Rockford Falls just before sunset, running all the way like a cheetah." The big beast rubbed his hands together before studying his fingers. "Your girl always knew the right words to make me feel better about being myself. Once I was carrying on about my ugly hoofs and bull-like horns and her sweet little voice reminded me that with such perfect hands and handsome fingers I should be grateful and filled with Thanksgiving."

"Now that you mention it, you do have a set of perfect hands and they are not much bigger than my own hands." Jack studied his friend for a moment. "I think we guessed you to be ten-foot tall WarZar. I am exactly 6'-5", so that would make you 3' 5" taller than me."

WarZar held out his hoof and shook his head, then lifted Jack's foot up to measure. "So, you're saying I'd be as tall as ten of your feet?"

Jack could not resist his chuckle over his comparison's remark. "I guess there are some tall gentlemen who have size 12 feet, my friend. My actual shoe size is an 8-1/2. I was referring to a 12inch ruler." Jack had taken off his backpack, so he unzipped it and pulled out a ruler. "Walla! This is a 12" ruler or I foot. Placed this end on end ten times and it would be at the tip of your head."

WarZar reached for the wooden ruler and studied it, then stretched out his hand over it, then both before he smiled over at his young friend. "I guess if a person has hoofs instead of big feet or a ruler, he could measure with his hands. So, if two hands take the place of a one-foot ruler, that would make me 20 hands high, right?"

"You are absolutely correct my mathematical friend!" Jack laughed happily, seeing his friend's fingers stretched exactly end to end on his ruler. Glancing back down inside his backpack, Jack saw the polaroid camera he had purchased from the antique shop in Graceland. He reached in and lifted it out and noticed WarZar's attention was fixed on the strange looking object.

"Is this another measuring device Jack? It doesn't appear as easy to use as the wooden ruler does?"

"This object I hold in my hands is the camera I promised you I would bring to take your picture, remember?" Jack smiled as he set it up for his shot and lifted it to his eye and focused in on the handsome face, who was looking back into the leans watching with uncertainty. Jack tilted his head away from the camera and looked at his unsure companion. "WarZar, I can assure you this thing is not a weapon. It will only take your picture. Make an image so you can see what you look like."

"Take your picture first Jack Spencer, then I might let you take my picture!" The great serious beast folded his arms stubbornly.

"Very well, I shall try to hold the camera far enough away from my face." Jack got it ready to snap, stretched it out in front of him, smiled and snapped the shot. He set the timer. "Now we wait a few minutes until the picture shoots out finished. This is an old camera so the photo will be in black and white. Color prints came later. With today's technology, now the sky's the limit for taking pictures, both still, like mine, or moving pictures."

WarZar had been watching with excitement and when the photo popped out, he set up like a child, waiting for Christmas morning. "Let me see Jack! Let me see how a hand device can draw a portrait and in such a short time."

"Sorry to disappoint you my friend, but there is no talented painter inside this little camera, the print you will be looking at is actually my face on paper!" Jack smiled at the great shot and handed it to his wide-eyed friend, whose stare stayed on the very face he had grown to love. Then WarZar looked from the print to Jack's smiling face and back down to the print. "You may keep it if you like my friend. I know I want one of you, so I'll make two so you can have a print of your face as well."

The teary-eyed beast held the picture of Jack to his chest. "This will be one of my cherished possessions, dear friend and brother." Holding the prized gift in his lap, WarZar set up and gave Jack a smile and holding the camera steady Jack took this beastly prince's picture for the very first time. As soon as it popped out, Jack snapped another shot of his friend, then handed the first one to WarZar, so he could see himself for the very first time.

WarZar slowly traced his facial features with his finger and smiled when he saw Jack had taken it only from the waist up, same as he had made his picture. Jack held his photo of WarZar up for him to see, they were very similar in looks. "Thank you, friend, for leaving off my hoofs! Those I can look down and see anytime."

"So, what do you think my friend? About your handsome face and great head of hair?"

"I say, we could pass as brothers, Jack!" he held the photos side-by-side and smiled. "Two great-looking brothers, out to take on the whole world!"

"One tall and one shorter, but whose watching our height when they can check out our good qualities and matching features!" Jack laughed at the unusual comparison then noticed WarZar's sudden change. His laughter had died away and his eyes held serious thoughts. "What's on your mind friend? I can see there is something bothering you."

"I was thinking about those dreams I have Jack. When night falls and all is finally at rest in the forest, I know when my head touches my pillow I will dream the same dream once more and I just don't know what it means." His dark eyes met Jack's loving blue ones. "I was hoping you could tell me what the dream means, my brother."

"The Bible, the big book of words, tells of a man who could interpret dreams through God. Even the dreams a very wealthy king kept having. King Pharaoh had two very disturbing dreams, both very similar and through the power of the most-high God, Joseph, a slave and prisoner, wrongly charged for a crime he did not commit, was brought out of the king's prison to interpret the dreams and he did and was made second in command under Pharaoh for knowing its meaning." Jack pulled two Hershey candy bars out of his backpack and pulled the wrappers off and handed one to WarZar as he enjoyed a bite from his. "You will love candy, my friend, so while you are enjoying it, tell me about your dream and I will pray for the right answer."

The big beast lifted the candy bar up to his nose and gave it a sniff, then gave Jack a happy smile before he tasted candy for the very first time. "Mum! This dark block taste extra good Jack!" He settled back to enjoy the rich chocolate treat as he told about his recurring dream. "I dreamed I was taking a nap beside the crystal pond behind my dwelling place and when I awoke, I felt different inside. I rubbed my fingers through my hair to straighten it up, being careful not to poke the end of one of my great horns. It was my tradition to swipe my hands up and down my smooth horns to give them a quick shine and" his gaze met Jack's face, serious and listening carefully. "The great horns were not there, they had simply vanished. The only place I could see myself halfway clearly was the crystal pond, but it was always wavy and blurry. I got up to go over to the pond and that's when I noticed my hoofs were gone and I had two perfect feet. The other thing I noticed was how much closer my feet seemed to be when I gazed down in total disbelief. I rushed over to the pond, hoping to be able to make out my appearance and again I was shocked to find myself staring back up at me, clear as the noonday sky." WarZar reached for Jack's hand. "Jack, I had become a normal man, just like you. That's when you appeared beside me and I noticed I wasn't as tall as before and it made me feel overjoyed, then I awoke" his eyes fell "and nothing had changed. I was still the giant with great horns and hoofs instead of feet. Please tell me what my dream means Jack, weather good or bad, I just need to know."

"WarZar, this dream could mean one of two things will actually happen to you in your very near future. The most likely scenario would be that you will become a believer in the Lord Jesus and due to becoming His you would go to heaven when we stepped outside this forest, whose magic has kept you young and alive for 219 years. Your old body will stay behind, most likely turned into dust, but your living soul will be taking up to heaven where you will receive a perfect new body and live in love and happiness forever." Jack noticed his big friend's sad face. "There is no need for sadness dear friend, heaven is filled with loving people and Jesus, our Lord, Himself."

"But, what about you Jack, you're still a young man and yet I saw you standing next to me. Surely this loving Jesus would not take you up too early, just for me." WarZar didn't want to be made new if his brother and friend were not around to be with him. "What about fair Alisia, my friend? She too is of a great age! Must she be taking up away from the one she has loved and waited for all those years? Not just the twenty you know Jack, but that girl has been waiting for you ever since she was pushed inside the Forbidden Forest. I know this because she told me how the angels comforted her when she arrived by telling her about the one great love who would come into her life two centuries later and his name would be Jack Spencer." The giant reached for Jack's hand again. "Jack, if not for me, I hope your second scenario means Alisia and I can somehow survive and dwell with you here on earth before we all travel to that loving heavenly kingdom where my demon father used to call home."

"Then I think my friend will like what my second theory is, although the chances for it are slim. To be honest WarZar, I too would like to see both you and my beloved Alisia somehow remain here with me, but it would take a true miracle of the great Jehovah, the Lord our God to see my dear friend, given a second chance to live a normal life in my hometown of Graceland, with me and Alisia. To find the perfect mate for you my friend, to share your life with. A bright girl who is beautiful, adventurous, fun to be with, smart, a great cook, great with children, very available and waiting for her perfect mate." Jack smiled up at his friend who was listening to his every word. "These things are not out of the question WarZar for someone who has faith in what he wants. Jesus said, ask, and you shall receive, by faith, your prayer will be answered."

"Jack, I long to hear more about this faith you speak of. This one called Jesus, who has the power to give miracles, even for someone like me if I learn to believe like you." WarZar curled up on the cave floor and covered up with the bear fur, then watched his young friend do the same. He gave Jack a big smile. "You can fill my head full of this faith as we make our way to my estate in the morning. For now, we need to close our eyes in rest as dreams invade our sleep. There is just one more thing you can tell me before we rest, this mate you described for me, it was as if you know such a perfect girl. I'm sure you are not speaking about your Alisia so who do you speak of Jack? Maybe it will be her I dream of this night, now that my dream has been interpreted."

"I was describing my baby sister, Veronica, who just turned twenty-five and is all those things I said and much more." Jack couldn't contain his yawn. "I couldn't think of a better match for my adventurous handsome friend!"

WarZar closed his eyes, thoughts still on Veronica. "Does your beautiful sister look anything like you Jack? You know, black hair and blue eyes?"

"My glamorous sister has long chestnut hair and enchanting blue eyes. She has a fashion-model figure and stands almost as tall as her 6' 5" brother." Another yawn as Jack drowsily closed his tired eyes. "With your new height being a little taller than me, it will be a perfect fit."

"I'd say in my dream I was about 7' 5", not bad for just an average normal tall man." The beast smiled when he heard his friend's steady breathing and knew Jack had finally fallen off to sleep. So, checking the new logs on the fire, WarZar closed his eyes in sleep. Morning would come early.

The friends had gotten up at the first rays of sunlight that drifted through the arched opening to the cave. The thoughtful beast had picked a small bucket of figs the evening before so they would have something to eat before heading down the mountain and then the long trail back to WarZar's dwelling place. The beast stomped out the remainder of the fire as Jack hung back the warm furs on their wooden pegs. Stepping out into the fresh morning air, Jack almost forgot he was in a dangerous place, with strange little monsters and a demon with a witch for his bride. Jack gazed down into the silent forest resting some distance away and he turned to see the eagles arising in their great nest on the opposite mountain.

"It appears the great eagles are the only ones up besides us around here." He could see the spot he had been standing twenty-years-ago and noticed nothing had changed except his looks. "Is it always this quiet this early in the morning?"

"Don't let the quietness fool you, my friend. When the snitches are out on their prowl, they can remain extremely still." WarZar strapped on his gear as Jack followed his lead. "They are very cunning, quick and deadly."

"Tell me WarZar, what does a snitch look like, just in case I spot one first." Jack heard his friend laugh. "What? Listen, I have you know, my eyesight is excellent and when something gets lost, I'm always the first one to find it, no matter how tiny!"

"Snitches started out as mountain wolves, coming into the forest to hunt prey and they got trapped inside, like anything else that made the mistake of crossing the forbidden line. Father would not tolerate their wiping out our meat sources, so he trapped them and turned them into his loyal group of spies and the runaway slave's worse nightmare."

"Why? Just what do these snitches do to those poor unfortunate people?" Jack knew the answer would probably be gruesome, but he had to know everything that went on concerning these poor lost souls he was also sent to try and save.

"Lazar sends them out on a hunt Jack." WarZar paused when Jack made a distasteful face. "The pack is anxious to find and catch their prey. It is the only meat their master permits them to eat."

"O my God! What horror those poor people must suffer." Jack felt nauseated over the thought. His eyes met his friend's. "Please tell me the snitches kill their prey before they eat them?"

"I'm sorry Jack, but I cannot lie to my good friend. The poor unfortunate souls that grow too desperate to run are tracked down by these cunning hunters, who with decades of practice, have become experts in killing for their human food. The snitchers move in slowly, unseen and unheard by the scared runaway until they find themselves trapped by the surrounding demon wolves. Their fear intensifies when they notice the slow stalkers gums are pulled back reviling all their sharp-pointed teeth, one unique sign of a wolf from hell. The other is their red eyes that glow in the dark, a sickening horror in itself if it's dark when they find you." WarZar knew this part would come painful to this good man he had grown to care about. "Hard as it will be for you to here, my friend, it is no easier on me to have to tell you, since these evil deaths bring a cheerful delight to my demon father and my wicked mother, but have never brought me anything but sorrow. When the snitches reached their victim, they go into a feeding frenzy and ripped the scared slave apart alive and eat them, leaving nothing but the bones. The many bones I have collected and carried to the valley of bones have been endless." Tears ran from the beast's dark eyes. "Not just men, Jack, there have been families trying to escape the forest before they met the same fate like all those they had witnessed working in the stone quarry. Husbands, wives and children."

"Such innocent small ones having to face the demons of hell instead of enjoying being a child. I do not know how or why parents would think to bring their children inside this forbidden place, but I do know we must put a stop to this savage attacks and killings on the children of God. I knew demons were evil beings, but I know now just how evil they really are!"

"Jack, I too have grown tired of the cruelty and hardships these humans endure, just to serve my evil father and his wicked wife. In a way, I am a slave to my parents as well. The only difference is, I work at a higher position, but we all hold the same long hours. While they work endlessly chipping out stones, then stacking them up to be hauled away in wagons to building locations directed by the queen mother, who is over all things built by stone. Dwellings, stone walls and bridges over the many different water ways. But it is I that sees to labor moving, dwellings, walls, and bridges being made, collecting trespassers and making them into mute-mindless slaves." The beast gave a sarcastic laugh. "I ask for the position when I witness Torren mistreating the humans, both in the rock field and where they slept and what they ate.

Since Lazar demoded him to second in command, he has looked at me with jealous eyes and standing back, planning, seeking, and hoping I will slip up and he can turn me in then resume his hateful leadership.

Torren did a lot of whipping when he was the one in charge. If a person grew weak from hunger and collapsed, the evil man would practically drown him with water to wake him then beat him to a pulp before sending him back to work swearing, if it happened again, he would feed the worthless bag of bones to the king's snitches." WarZar started walking around to the other side of Raven Knob, Jack following right behind him. "He made the people sleep outside, year around, no matter the weather. In the cold winter, I'd see mothers or fathers covering the small children to keep the warm during the night and many a parent froze to death, protecting their babies. Torren never cared what happened to his fellow humans. He had been chosen by Lazar because he was a big strong mean brut, who hated everyone and he made sure he stayed warm and fed his oversize belly. Torren had the slaves he punished build him a stone cottage with a big fireplace and a root cellar to hold lots of produce and smoked boar and trout."

"Are those poor people still having to sleep out in the cold and elements, rain or snow?" Jack tried to visualize the lost souls living conditions now that his friend was in command.

"I saw that they had a warm place to live with a fireplace and root cellar that I keep stocked along with bear furs for each family member. I sought out the women that knew how to sew clothes, so I had descent clothes for them to wear instead of the ones they came in with, now mostly rags." WarZar led Jack down the mountain trail toward the bottom. "You were wondering why parents would cross our evil line, risking their children's lives. Many of the families that came in were the first Indians, who knew nothing about Satan's trap, then after the first settlers came to these mountains, they too did not know of a place called the Forbidden Forest, so they had no one to warn them like your scout leader warned you. Those with kids after all the warnings came out to stay away from the right side of Old Wagon Road, didn't stop a few adventurous kids from escaping their parents only to find themselves unable to get out, so?" the beast turned around and waved his hand for Jack to finish the obvious statement.

"So, the frightened parents dashed through the tree line to rescue their poor helpless runaway child." Jack smiled. "Say, I just remembered! What did you dream about last night WarZar? The recurring dream or did you dream about a pretty young lady with chestnut hair and blue eyes?"

"A very beautiful girl Jack, with flowing chestnut hair, that shined in the sunrise and the most hypnotizing blue eyes I have ever witness." WarZar laughed as he kept walking. "I had to be a normal man Jack because she kept running ahead of me, glancing back as if to tease me saying, 'catch me if you can Zar baby!'"

Jack burst out laughing. "That's my little sis alright friend! She has been working out in California for seven years as a movie director's assistant, where everyone is baby this or baby that! The last trip home to Graceland she called me Ack baby!"

"I've always dreamed of having a mate, but I know with my great size this is impossible. Turning one of the bigger female black bears into a mate was suggested by Lazar, who had gone through the trouble of drawing a sketch of how he would make her more human but couldn't guarantee our offspring wouldn't be odd looking cubs." WarZar glanced around making a face. "I told father to scrap those plans if that's the only mate suitable for his beast of a son. Then my overheated mother came up with what she called the perfect solution. Her plan was to have another baby with Lazar by drinking the same wicked potion she had stirred up when I was conceived but this time instead of placing male a mite in her brew she would add female, a mite and create the perfect mate for her handsome, lonely son."

"My friend must never take such a woman for your mate for she would be your blood sister! This act would never be right in the sight of the Almighty God." Jack had stopped walking over that revelation and he drew the princely beast aside. "After you learn about believing in your Savior and what He did for everyone born, you will understand why I must rebuke the ideal of you taking your own sister to be your wife. It would be far better if you had no one than to commit this carnal sin by having sex with your sister."

"Jack, I do not want to do anything that would keep me from becoming what you are and believing in this God and Savior you speak of." WarZar looked around and saw what he was looking for, the right size rock. "Jack, this is where you start riding on my back friend. Climb on top this rock and I'll bend over so you can climb up, then we can continue our conversation the rest of our journey to Rockford Falls."

"Wow! It's really high up here my friend." Jack settled on and the tall giant picked up his pace, moving steady and making it look easy. "Since we have some distance to go WarZar, I'll tell you all about salvation and what you will gain if you choose good and what your future looks like if you remain with evil."

"Believe you me, I want to know everything my brother. I have always felt it wrong to treat the humans like animals, with no regards to their health or happiness. Whenever I had new intruders to change, it came harder to go through the ritual of placing them in my trance, then delivering their judgement to be a mindless-mute, to obey my every command, as well as Lazar's and Carmela's. Before I became the Captain over the slaves, Torren had to rely on Lazar to do the ritual. A human could never do this act granted demons and witches, so I had double power to perform the ritual." Speaking at such a fast-walking pace did not make the beast out of breath, for he was used to long runs to get from one point to another with great haste, another trait giving to Satan's demons.

"To show your loyalty to the Almighty God and to prove you truly have a change of heart concerning these mistreated humans, is it not possible for you to reverse this ritual and restore what you have taken away from those lost souls." Jack knew to save these lost children of God, he had to have their minds restore.

"I would gladly do this thing you ask of me Jack, but only after great planning." WarZar stopped briefly, deep in thought. "If I chose to perform the reversed ritual before our plan has been set into

142

motion, this large group could rebel against us before you could even calm them down enough to preach the words they need to hear."

"I see your reasoning my friend, and I agree, a plan is in order." Jack was amazed at how smart WarZar was. "When we reach Rockford Falls and I can finally be with my beloved Alisia again, the three of us can start making plans as to which way would be the safest to go. Lazar and Carmela are both very powerful and to help protect you from their wrath, it must appear you captured me. This will throw them off guard for our final escape."

"Then, the three of us shall work out a perfect failproof plan together to make sure everyone, the slaves, the good ones, waiting in prison, that girl Amy Bruster, hidden below in Alisia's old dwelling, and us, will make it to the entrance next to the Old Wagon Road, then passed through Satan's invisible shield to better places."

"Now, to tell you about Jesus, the son of the Almighty God, the maker of heaven and earth and everything in and around it. Our most Holy God is a Triune God, three in one and He is the one and only God, the Creator of everything. He was and He will always be the only God! The three in one consist of the Father, the Son, and the Holy Spirit." Jack could tell his big friend was drinking in every word of the living water the Lord Jesus had promised all who would believe. "Before God created the earth, where we live, He created His angels, who lived in Heaven with the Triune God, where only love and beauty flourished. Lucifer, one of two powerful archangels decided he was better suited to be God, so he hatched a plan to take over God's throne. His punishment had him along with around 10,000 beautiful angels who unfortunately followed Lucifer and was thrown out of heaven down into the deep, a round globe of water which would one day become earth and the home for God's future children he would create, in His image."

"So, Lazar chose to follow that evil angel and now he is doomed forever?" WarZar wanted to know if his parents could be forgiven like him.

"I'm afraid your father had his chance to ask for forgiveness before he was thrown out of heaven, by Jesus Himself, who had offered every angel committing treason full pardon if they would repent of their acts toward their God." Jack knew Carmela had once known of Jesus' love when she lived with David Solomon before she moved up to Salem to live with her wicked mother, Loretta. "As for your mother, she has committed some evil acts during her lifetime,

143

but if she truly repented and fell down on her knees in front of the Lord, he would forgive her."

"Forgive someone that wicked? Jack, then should we try and save Carmela with the others or let her stay with this evil demon, who can never be forgiven now?" WarZar never cared before what happened to his evil parents because he just assumed they would always be there and in control of their land.

"We cannot risk everyone's life by taking that chance that she can be saved." Jack knew he had to help his new friend understand the difference in lost souls. "Many of these slaves who are lost have never known the Lord Jesus, either through unsaved parents who never prayed or took them to church, others might have been told but got caught up with worldly matters and things and pushed religion to one side, thinking they had time to sew their seeds first, then settled down to matters of the faith. Carmela had been raised by a very religious man who taught her at a very young age, right and wrong, the salvation that comes from believing in Jesus, our Lord, who came to earth as a baby, born of a virgin, that is a young girl who had never been with a man. The third part of the Holy Three in One, the Holy Spirit, came to the virgin Mary and gave her the baby, God's son. When he reached the age of thirty, he left his mother Mary and his earthly father Joseph, to start His three-year ministry, teaching everyone the love of the Father, what he expected of each child of His. Jesus performed miracles, He turned water into wine, he made the blind see, the cripple walk, the deaf, hear, the numb, speak, drove out demons, healed the sick and raised the dead. He fed over 10,000 with a few small fish and a couple loaves of bread, he calmed the sea and walked on water and so many other things his twelve followers could not write it all down. Then the time came for Jesus to complete His reason for coming down from heaven to earth. Jesus, our Lord and King, would ride into Jerusalem on a donkey with shouts of hallelujah and by the end of the week he would be beaten, crowned with a braid of thorns, and crucified on a Roman cross." Jack removed the crucifix he wore and dangled it in front of WarZar eyes.

"But why would His Father send Him down here to be killed in such a horrible way? If Jesus is the third part of the Triune God, why did this have to happen to someone so perfect and without sin?" WarZar needed to know as his tear-stain eyes stared at the man hanging on what his friend called a cross. "What held up the sacred body and kept him from falling?"

144

"First, Jesus was nailed to that cross, a very painful way to die over 2000 years ago when our Lord walked on the earth He created. Remember all three trinity were here before Creation of the earth. The first sin was committed in the garden of Eden, right after creation, caused by Lucifer. Due to this sin, sin fell on every child born on earth and since no one was without sin, they could not be saved for heaven. God sent His Son Jesus to die for all our sins, since he would be the only child born of woman who had never sinned. WarZar, if you believe in Jesus and that He died for your sins, same as he did for me and Alisia, you will be saved and when you die from this world, your soul, that beautiful thing that lives inside your heart, that makes you breathe and think and act, will continue to live and return to heaven, where it began when God created it."

The deformed creature stopped and lifted his smaller friend off his shoulders and lowed him gently. Suddenly this special being felt there could actually be some hope for him, but there was one more important question the beast needed to know. "Jack, there is nothing more I want any more than to be free! Free from the prison I have been trapped inside of since my birth. Not just this place, but this body, part human, part animal. I have been taught to hate all humans, except my mother and Torren, and never to trust them. I was also taught to respect my parents' control of me and my great powers, I think for their self-fear of what they had created taking over their kingdom through my great mind and power. When you spoke about the Lord Jesus, and how much He has done for us, to die on that cross for all our sins, has only proved just how much he cares and loves us. My heart leaped with happiness, knowing I too could be saved, my friend, by confessing my belief in the Son of God who died for my sins and ask him to forgive me. I do Jack! I truly do believe in our Savior, Jesus Christ, because I can see his light shining through you and Alisia. Your faces, your acts of kindness and you both excepting me for what I am." WarZar looked down with pleading in his eyes. "Jack, my one great fear is never having received this soul you speak of. With a demon for a father and a witch for a mother, how would this loving creator have created my soul in his heavenly home? How did I receive it when I was born a hideous monster?"

"WarZar, every living creature on this earth has the breath of life. Even the smalless of God's creation has a heart. Every human born of woman, including you, my beloved brother, has been given a soul by God, Himself. The moment Carmela conceived you, God placed his child's soul inside you and when you tell Jesus you believe in him with all your heart and soul, then ask for forgiveness for all your bad doings, our Loving Savior will send the Holy Spirit down inside that soul and it will be lit with everlasting life, through Jesus Christ." Jack took his big friend's hand. "The story does not end with Jesus dying on that cross WarZar! Jesus was buried inside a tomb and on the third day, which is our Easter Sabbath, He arose from the dead, just as he had told his people. Because He lives, we too will live WarZar, for all eternity in His heavenly kingdom when we leave this world."

The tall prince fell on his knees, his face lifted to the heaven above, and feeling the hand of his young friend laying on his head, WarZar gave his life to Jesus Christ.

CHAPTER 21

WarZar stopped when the roar of the great falls could be heard. He reached up to lift his friend off his shoulders. "Hear it, dear friend, the Rockford Falls, our gateway to my dwelling place."

"So. It's the waterfall that keeps all unwanted guest out?" Jack followed beside his tall friend as they made their way toward the roaring water. "Do we have to walk under the falls to get inside your grounds? You did call it your gateway to your home."

"To most people, it would appear one must risk going under the great falls if they tried to enter my estate, but for you Jack, I will take you through my secret passage, known only by me." WarZar smiled over his genus discovery for going under the falls without getting wet. "This is the only safe place in the Forbidden Forest, my friend. That's why I have no worries of someone snooping around my personal belongings while I am away. Demons, witches, humans, and all their evil creatures would never risk coming through the falls to get to my place in fear of drowning."

They stopped when the great falls came into view and Jack could see why everyone and every creature was terrified of walking under such powerful falls. "So, this loud roar does not keep you awake at night my friend?"

"Not unless you intend to camp down near the falls instead of inside my large stone villa which sets far enough away to keep from hearing the powerful water at play." WarZar smiled and pulled Jack through a thick hedge and down a narrow path lined in a high wall of rocks that led to the side of the waterfall where they simply walked though, never getting wet. "Jack, if you have ever doubted that I am your friend, then, now is the moment to know! You and Alisia are the only people I have ever permitted to come inside my private world."

"Then who built your villa WarZar?" Jack felt good inside that the beast he had once feared was now a best friend. Reading Jack's thoughts, WarZar chuckled.

"It was my job to put fear into you Jack and being just ten-years of age made my job very easy." He stopped when his big-magnificent rock mansion came into view. "I suppose a normal man might think a place this size took a whole fleet of workers, but the truth is, it only took one, very ambitious, big, strong beast who wanted his own private place, away from everyone and everything." He laughed when a bird flew over his head. "But, there are some things you just cannot keep out. So, my companions have always been singing birds. That is, until I brought Alisia here to hide. She has been a joy to have around and I must admit, the angel's food and wine are much better than what I made."

"You are amazing WarZar! This stone mansion is breathtaking! You have done a remarkable job." Jack knew the girl he had dreamed about for twenty-years was somewhere inside that large stone dwelling and he was suddenly anxious to see the young women he loved. "Is Alisia inside, waiting?"

"My friend grows anxious to see his woman!" WarZar lightly patted Jack's back. "Come, my friend, the two of you have waited long enough." The prince walked inside the massive door that stood 12 feet high and called out. "Alisia, I have brought Jack home!"

Footsteps could be heard running through an upstairs hallway then she appeared at the top of the tall staircase, she paused to looked at the young man she had been longing to see. After saying his name softly, Alisia ran down the twenty steps and into Jack's waiting arms.

"Jack, my heart is beating with such happiness and joy, I can hardly breathe."

"My beautiful Alisia, has it really been twenty-years since we last saw each other when you look just as you did when we said our tearful goodbyes." Jack had held her back to take in her incredible beauty. "Nothing has changed, except, the dress. You are wearing a very beautiful blue dress that seems to match the very color of your enchanting eyes."

"I am wearing a new dress Jack, just for your arrival. A gift from my charming host when he noticed me checking over my white dress that I have been wearing ever since Carmela pushed me inside the forest." Alisia took a step back to take in Jack's grown-up change. "My, the young boy that left with my heart has turned into quite a handsome young fellow." She heard WarZar chuckle and gave him a wink. "Wouldn't you agree dear friend, that our Jack is a very handsome man?"

"As a matter of fact, fair Alisia, your Jack and I did discuss last evening before we shut our eyes in rest, how much we resembled one another and could almost pass as brothers."

148

"That is an honest statement WarZar, since both of you are extremely good looking, although your height might give you away." Both Jack and WarZar noticed the loving girl never mentioned his hooves or horns. "But then, plenty of families have short brothers and tall brothers."

Jack grabbed her and gave her a long-awaited kiss. "My daring, I have longed to kiss you for so long and now that I finally have you, I know I need you my love, to be my bride. I have longed for my wedding night to come so I could finally make love to the woman I love with all my heart."

"I too have longed for our wedding night to arrive my darling Jack, so if these are the only days we have together before I must leave you, at least let us know one another first." She held him tight, not wanting to ever let him go again, but knowing her chances to remain with him once free from the Forbidden Forest, would take a miracle.

"We must not give up on hope, dearest Alisia. We serve a loving God who knows the hearts of all his children." Jack felt her quiver in his strong embrace. "I have put in many hours of prayers for that miracle that would restore both you and WarZar to be able to live again! To love and serve His Holy name."

"For now, we must have our evening meal. For Jack and I came straight way from Raven Knob where we last ate a few figs and even though I can see my friend has thoughts only for his reunion with you, dearest one, we need to stay strong so in the morning we can put our heads together and make those perfect plans for getting everyone out of the Forbidden Forest for good and let Lazar and his bride reign over those who have given them their loyalty and do their work to please their masters." WarZar laughed. "We will not leave them without someone to boss around. Torren can take charge over the volunteer palace workers, the gate guards, the field workers who praise and admire their evil masters. The queen mother has stacks of building stones waiting in the quarry and the evil creatures will learn new commands, for the locket of love will block the entrance into the Forbidden Forest, so no one else can ever be trapped inside."

"WarZar is right Alisia, we must plan this exit well so no one will get hurt. For now, I wear the locket, but we must show our faith and trust in our big friend here when the time comes for him to fool his evil parents." Jack knew in his heart the locket would only permit a saved person to wear it, so Lazar or Carmela could not order their

149

son to hand it over. "Come my dearest, let us eat, then we can snuggle some more before saying goodnight. To make a perfect-failproof plan, we must get our rest."

"And once we have father free, he can perform the ceremony my darling, and I will be your bride." She reached for his hand as they followed behind their big friend and host. Jack smiled down before kissing her sweet lips.

"And I will be your happy groom, at long last."

The evening had gone by quickly and after a much needed rest, the new day dawned in bright, with the aid of the heavenly helpers permitting the sun a space to shine down on Rockford Villa. The three friends had gathered around the big table WarZar had built for eating his large amount of food. Plans had to be made and each stage of their plan must be done carefully. There were a lot of souls at risk if something went wrong, so the three great minds joined forces to create the perfect escape from the Forbidden Forest.

"First, I must let Lazar and Carmela know of my success in hunting down the invader who had gotten away when he first arrived." WarZar knew that his presence must be made known before they could move forward. "They will see my loyalty was to them and that I had kept my word, to Torren's dismay, I'm certain." He chuckled. "Then I will be placed back in charge of the slaves and dismiss Torren, sending him on a long errand."

"They will want to see me for I feel these two cannot even trust their own son's word. So, I suggest I go down among the slaves and pretend to be made mindless and mute like the rest, where you will show them, to satisfy their doubt. By making me dumb, you could remove my locket and have it around your neck when you first arrive."

"Jack, I cannot take the chance that one of them might have a way to get it from me." The prince was deeply concerned, knowing the locket was the way out. "Maybe I could tell them you never had it on and maybe they sensed Alisia nearby."

"WarZar, Jack is right about wearing the locket." Alisia had been listening to her favorite fellows discussing what they must do to get everyone out safely. "My wicked sister knows I do not have the locket with me and she was aware I had hidden it somewhere outside the Forbidden Forest. Even you told me she had been outside the forest in search of the locket but could never find it. The angel standing guard over it kept her from knowing its location so when

Jack came to the campground with his scout troop, he would be the one to find it, with my help." The beautiful blonde smiled over at the young man she loved so dearly. "Carmela knew about Jack and me falling in love, so it was only a matter of time she realized who had the locket and why he had escaped the invisible shield the first time. That's why my sister insisted to her husband that they should be the ones to bring in the intruders when Jack arrived this time. They only pretended to go in search of a boar. Anyone should have seen through that little scheme since Carmela is terrified of the wild boar. To be honest, that pampered little spoiled brat would never go out to hunt for her own food. No, my sister wanted to find Jack and take the locket of love away from him so she would have all the control and her search for me would not stop until she had me locked away like poor papa."

"Alisia is right WarZar, if the queen sees you have the locket, her hopes will grow in knowing her beautiful half-sister can never have it and use its power to take their father out of the forest." Jack gave his girl a wink of approval. "After announcing you found me and turned me into one of the slaves, you can show them the locket is around your neck."

"Jack, then please tell me how I am supposed to explain to my parents just how I managed to make a 'good one' a slave, when up until now this was impossible, so we had to lock them in the dungeon. The only thing we could managed was to mute them, to keep the silent so they wouldn't disturb the royal couple with their prayers, Bible reading, and singing their praises to their God, our God."

"It's really quite simple my friend. You can proudly brag on how you changed a good one into a mindless, silent, slave. You had promised your parents that you and you alone would go in search of this man who insulted and made fools out of the royal king and his queen. You can say, your anger toward me had built up so strong that when you finally found the little coward, your temper was boiling over and in the high rage, you easily performed the ritual and through your loud screams that echoed through his mind, you won! You would say, the slave would be mine, the locket would be mine, since I ordered my mindless slave to place it over my head!" Jack could tell by the listening beast that he was liking the ideal.

"Then, what if the queen orders me to remove the locket and place it over her head?" The beast knew his mother well.

"Tell my sister this! Tell her you can never remove the locket from where the good one placed it on. Should you try, the great power will instantly destroy you as it sends electric shock waves throughout your body and through your heart. Only those who know and live good is safe from the locket's power." Alisia reached over and patted the smooth hand of the beast. "You may warn your mother not to get near it, but Carmela does not take rejection well so trust me, she will try, only to fail. And I truly doubt the jealous witch will ever get over the shock."

"If that's the case, I hope Queen Carmela does try to take it!" WarZar chuckled at the thought of his mean mother getting a painful shock from a helpless-looking piece of jewelry. "Don't dismiss my demon father from trying. He knows nothing can kill him but he most likely will think he can and will get it for himself."

"Nothing evil can get within four feet of this locket so there is no way either of your parents will be able to take it from you." Jack felt good about their plan so far, but wanted to assure his friend that he would be safe wearing the powerful locket. "The part about the locket killing you would not be true, my brother, but these evil beings do not need to know you are one of the good ones now."

"Alright, the plan so far has WarZar back and giving a good report to his trusting parents, so just give an award-winning performance and we shall have phase one down." Alisia noticed Jack's uncertain look and she gave him her perfect smile. "What is it darling, did I say something wrong?"

"No, my love, you are quite right about act one of our performance starting us out on the right foot." Jack returned her smile. "I was just wondering how you knew about rewards being handed out for some actor's great performance, that's all."

"Oh, I keep forgetting we live in two different centuries Jack. I was referring to the traveling play-actors who put on what they called their award-winning performance spectacular, each summer, when they traveled from town to town putting on the same play for the year. Our town was on their list and if the show was descent enough for a young Christian girl, then papa would happily take me to see them perform." Her eyes met his seriously. "Do actors still travel from town-to-town Jack or did that go out with the stagecoach?"

"Entertainment is much different now, Alisia, sweetheart. Actors still perform on stage, a few may take their show on the road but most of them perform in big cities or in small town theaters. Many people had rather take in a motion picture show, we call movies, or just stay at home and watch their favorite shows on the television." Jack noticed both his companions had confused expressions, so he simply laughed. "Somethings are better seen than explained, so if we are blessed with your remaining on earth with me, I promise to take you both to a movie and let you watch my big screen television." Seeing them smile at one another, Jack continued. "But for now, our time is running out before Lazar grows suspicious of his son's absence. I say our next move would be to get Reverend Solomon and all the good ones set free and smuggled to Rockford Falls. WarZar, you know the palace's layout and your parent's routine. What do you think is the best way to get them out? To where there are no workers around and with the assurance that no one will grow suspicious where your parents are concerned. No spies to watch the escape and make haste to report it."

"My wicked mother does not have many fears and her senses are strong, but there is one thing she cannot tolerate. Rats! The queen hates the sight of a rat! Even a small little mouse causing her to dive on top her bed screaming for her servant girl to come kill it." WarZar stood up and walked around the room, hatching the perfect plan. "I will go to the palace, with one of my slaves carrying a cloth bag, tied up. Inside the moving bag are four big rats, to show my mother, who will back away petrified, just witnessing the moving bag in my slave's hand. My unafraid father will stand his ground, waiting for me to announce why I'm there and what is in my bag." WarZar turned to give his companions a smile. "I shall inform the royal couple that it had been brought to my attention that the palace dungeons were infested with hundreds of rats and that if I did not go down to remove them immediately, they would soon find their way up into the palace and overtake every room, stinking up the place with the horrible stench of the rodents."

Jack joined his big friend. "I can see where this is going and I like the sound of it, my clever friend. Your mother will go into a panic. The very thought of stinking rats overtaking HER domain was out of the questions. So, frightened and ready to have her way, Carmela orders her son to get them out!"

"Exactly! But Lazar is still not so easy to convince and this is the reason to present them the evidence, which will be all mother needs to see to demand her husband to stay out of her son's way until every Rat is dead and gone." The tall handsome beast smiled down at Jack.

"Then my slave, whose head is covered out of respect, and lowered, as not to be seen, you Jack, will open the bag and lift out by their tails all four rats and hold them up." He laughed out when his young friend made a distasteful face as Alisia jumped up and ran over.

"WarZar, you are kidding, right? What if Lazar and Carmela recognize Jack? He could be in mortal danger."

"Yeh, by holding up four stinking rats that could bite me and give me some sort of disease!" Jack had the creeps just thinking about carrying the wiggling bag and now learning he was to pick the ugly rodents up by their tail. "Wouldn't it look better if the big-strong son lifted the rats up and dangled them in front of his parents for a closer look?"

"Don't sweat the job my friend, I was going to lift the rats out anyway, but I do need you there with me, to help with the break-out. We cannot trust anyone else, so it has to be the two of us. Besides, the good ones will feel better when they see you with me and don't start to worry about why I'm removing them and taking them away." WarZar went back to the table and took his seat, followed by Jack and Alisia, after they kissed one another.

"Fellows, wouldn't three working to free all those prisoners go a lot faster?" Alisia asked excitedly, feeling the need to do her part. "If they saw me, they would instantly relax and wait to be set free, then follow us without any trouble."

"She does have a good point WarZar, but how can we hide her appearance so her sister would not recognize her or smell her scent?" Jack draped his arm around her and pulled her close to him as she snuggled inside his arms. "Three getting rid of hundreds of rats might look more convincing as well."

"You both have good points. We can disguise beautiful Alisia by dressing her in man's attire and covering her head like all the slaves do. It is expected of all slaves to show respect to King Lazar and his queen, by keeping their head lowered at all times and bowling when I order it done. They will know you both are my personal workers, so they won't suspect anything." He gave a soft sneaky laugh. "And you must forgive the scent you will be given, fair Alisia, for it is the only smell that can cover up such a perfect flower."

"Dear friend, I dread hearing what smell you are referring about, that is strong enough to keep my sister's witch-senses from sniffing my scent." Alisia sat up straight. "But, nevertheless, whatever this horrible stench is, I will endure it for the sake of freeing my dear

154

father and all those lovely people, wasting away in that dark-dank-dungeon, with only scraps of bread to eat and a little water given to keep them alive."

"There are those who have been known to enjoy the scent of a skunk, dear one. So maybe, it won't be so bad." WarZar could not control his chuckle over her twisted face.

"A skunk?" She ran her hand through her hair. "Then I shall smell like a charming, furry, black and white little stinker, your highness. Then on my return, I shall have a nice-long soak in your very large washtub!" Hearing Jack join his big friend in laughter, Alisia turned around and playfully slapped her true love arm. "It might not be so funny for the one who has to catch the little stinker for me." She laughed when they grew serious, and Jack's attention went to his big friend.

"I hadn't considered the one who had to round up the skunk, friend, but since it was your bright ideal, I'll let you have the honors!"

"No problem. Little friends! I have rounded up many a skunk in my back garden without so much as a squirt!" He smiled over at the pretty girl. "You may count on me fair Alisia to round up a large skunk without getting any of its perfume on me, so it will have plenty to spray on you. I grant you, no one will be bothering you or asking you to step forward." The giant could see the scene unfolding in front of him. "I'll march in after my presence has been announced and my workers will respectfully stop behind me. Jack, holding the proof in a wiggling bag and Alisia holding a basket, filled with lots of empty white bags, ready to fill up when we reach the dungeon."

"Knowing hundreds of rats will take a long time for three workers to bag up, it should give us plenty of time to get everyone safely out and moved to Rockford Falls where you can deprogram them, so they speak again." Jack felt the need to have help with so many confused people being let out of their trance at the same time and he knew it had to be done where no one could witness their work. "WarZar, I know having to share your very private place with so many strangers will not be easy my friend, but I just cannot think of a better alternative. Have everyone brought here. It is the one place no one working for Lazar and Carmela can come to, even you parents themselves have been forbid entry inside your private world."

"You are right, Jack, this is the one place safe enough and with the space to accompany such a large group." The handsome prince glanced around the room at his familiar things he knew he would be leaving behind, but he had no regrets in going. WarZar had wanted his freedom for a very long time and now the time had come for him to depart the only home he knew.

"My friend is thinking about leaving all of this behind when we stepped through the invisible veil, aren't you?" Jack reached for his hand, their eyes locking. "It's only natural to grow sentimental over the things you have always known and find yourself ready to leave them all behind to start over. My dear brother, I can promise you the life you knew here will soon be just a faraway memory and as your new life begins to grow in the riches of pure love even those bad memories will start to fade away and be replaced with true happiness! Unlike anything you have ever known." Jack gathered Alisia in his arms, his attention still on his big friend. "And should that new life began with me and my beautiful bride, we will become a family and with love just around the corner waiting for you, you too will know the sweet bliss of romance and then marriage to the one you love."

"I feel much better Jack! Thanks!" WarZar sat up smiling at the prospects for his new happy life. "After I release the mute-mindless state from the people, then it will be up to all the good people to convince each and everyone of those lost souls to ask for forgiveness and give their lives to the Lord. If we fail converting only a few, what will happen to the others Jack? Will Torren be put back in charge and make them suffer again or for running away, will Lazar send the snitches after them to have a banquet feast? If they are not changed to good ones, they cannot get out! They could remain here, but sooner or later they would be found when I failed to show up."

"Surely they would all choose to trust in the Lord after seeing evil face to face!" Alisia's heart was breaking for the poor lost children of God. "WarZar, when a heathen hears the word of God spoken by true men of God, like my father and my future husband, their tortured souls and hearts will be so uplifted with new hope in the saving grace of the Lord, Jesus, they will gladly repent of their sins and give their lives to him."

"And if Reverend Solomon and I cannot convince them, telling them about their future to remain here, about the demon wolves hunting them down and eating them alive, then their soul will go to an even worse place after they are dead. They will go to hell, to be tortured until Jesus Christ returns to judge all people, and never being

156

saved, they will join the devil and his demons in a lake of burning fire for all eternity." Jack knew he had not told these facts to WarZar when he was deciding his faith. He had seen the goodness already shining through this beast and he felt there was no reason to mention his other alternative, if he had decided to remain the same.

"So, you are saying, if I had not chosen good, and ask the Lord to forgive me, I would have been thrown into this lake of fire that never went out?" WarZar noticed Jack removing the cross around his neck and was moved when he placed it around his own neck.

"Dear friend, you must keep your beautiful faith hidden for now." Jack dropped it under his top. "When you are around the evil ones, you must not let them know you too are a good one now, but should they be there to watch us leave, guarded by the locket of love, you can proudly show them that you're a Christian!"

"Thank you, my brother! This I will do proudly for I will never be a shame to show that I am a Christian!" The tall prince gathered his friends into his arms. "After we have saved the all the slaves, Reverend Solomon can marry you two and I will personally whisk you back to Alisa's dwelling place under the ground, take the young lady back with me, and leave you lovebirds to enjoy one another."

"Then sadly, with our beautiful night behind us, we will meet all of you up near the entrance facing the Old Wagon Road, where Alisia will release the power of the locket and the shield of the Almighty God will divide the good ones from the bad ones, and they can do nothing but watch us leave their evil forest forever, leaving them double blocked in." Jack felt good about their plans.

"And with God's shield in place, my half-sister will be trapped inside with her demon husband and her protector, Lucifer, will be unable to get back inside the Forbidden Forest to help her with Lazar. She will have to become second then, under her king, and this will drive the wicked witch mad with green jealousy."

"At least mother will still have her workers to order around. Those foolish people who chose to give them their total loyalty, like Torren, just to spare being turned into mindless mutes!" WarZar rubbed his hands together and walked to the door. "Alright kids, the act is on! Let's round up our costumes and one big skunk for later. First thing is to visit my parents with the good news, then tell them to meet me at the stone quarry so they can see my latest slave, the first good one!" he laughed. "I'll get rid of Torren first by sending him out on a boar hunt, agreeing to give him half for smoking. He will gladly take up my generous offer and the chance to get away from working, then you can go down and mix in with the workers and pretend to be one when they arrive to look down into the pit."

"Give me a pic and an ax, and I'll start whacking or if you prefer, O great master, help with the stacking!" Jack laughed at his own rhyme.

"Stop it, Jack!" Alisia was laughing so hard she was bent over. "I am marrying a real poet!"

"Is that what you call it?" WarZar laughed. "Slave, you may be better at stacking instead of hacking!" he laughed. "You see my brother, we even rhyme alike. Just watched that those real mindless slaves don't mistake you for a rock and stack you up!"

Jack removed the locket and placed it over his big friend's head. "Remember what we told you about the locket dear friend. Even though you can actually touch it with no harm, Lazar and Carmela must never know."

"Then I'm off to get our plan rolling. Stay hidden behind the falls until I come fetch you after I send Torren away." He opened the door. "Just get into you disguise Jack and don't worry about my performance where my parents are concerned. I know them better than they know themselves. They are too busy admiring their own self to see what they're really like. I'll be back for phase two with my mission accomplished!"

CHAPTER 22

At the palace, the royal announcer stepped forward to let the king and queen know of their son's arrival. "Your great royal majesties, your son has just arrived, to bring news of his great success!"

Remaining on their thrones, the royal king waved his hand, palm up, the sign for excepting the visitor's request to address his monarch. Head held high and proud, the magnificent beast stepped in and bowled.

"My Lord, my Lady! I have come with great news! One of triumphant victory! I tracked down and captured the invader, Jack Spencer. You may rest in knowing, this good one is now my slave, mindless and mute!"

"This is great news son. Your mother had no doubt in your success in finding this human. Unlike your dear father who was beginning to grow restless, from no word of your whereabouts." Carmela had always tried to make a division between her and Lazar's loyalty to this powerful son, so to give a bad report of Lazar's mistrust pleased her greatly. "I told your father to be patient, that our devoted son would not let us down."

"My dear wife, are you quite finished putting me to shame in front of our magnificent son?" Lazar narrowed his eyes at the outspoken women he couldn't get enough of. "WarZar, I was merely concerned for your wellbeing, my son. I never doubted for one moment that you would not accomplish this task you set out to do! To avenge our good names, you kept your promise, despite your mother's constant bickering over wanting that damn locket and wished you'd return with it so she could at last have it for herself!" Lazar gave his angry wife a nod, as if to say, ha! Got you back!

"Speaking of the prized locket, did you by any chance take it off this good one once you blocked out all his earthy thoughts and" the evil sister could not resist a chuckle. "The desire he felt for my saintly half-sister. Poor wretched Alisia. Wasting her entire existence waiting for this Jack Spencer to gallop in and save her and her precious papa!" her laughter turned to anger. "Well, he was my father first! She shall never have him again, the little thief!" Carmela's smile quickly replaced her frown. "Now that the locket will be mine,

I will see that the little beauty is locked away in her own dark dungeon, alone."

"What makes you think that I have the much sought-after locket, madam? And even if I now possess the powerful golden trinket, what makes you think I would hand it over to you mother?" WarZar stood unafraid, knowing he could easily take down both his parents, wounding his father and killing his evil mother, but his new-found faith taught him to never kill. "Aren't you in the least bit curious about how I managed the impossible, when even the mighty demon could not?"

"It did strike me as quite a surprise when you declared performing the ritual on the good one son." Lazar spoke up, glad the locket subject had been dropped for now. He knew his beloved would never let the topic grow cold. "It's just after your mother made me look like I had betrayed my word to you and sent out a possible spy or two to check on you that I didn't wish to question how you managed this feat." The king looked up sheepishly. "So, just how did you manage turning this good one into your slave son?"

"Through my incredible anger toward the little weasel and how he had treated my parents! To fool them into believing he was actually near that big tree and how he had escaped two of the worlds finest trackers on earth!" The tall giant laughed loudly, its echo bouncing off the high ceiling. "Catching his frightened eyes in a stare, I commenced to roaring my great scream, letting the traveling echo to penetrate through his skull and deep down into his mind! I knew the moment his eyes rolled back into his head I had completed the ritual and this one would be mine forever!" he smiled down cunningly. "I then ask my slave to place the golden locket around my neck and there it will stay! I will have all the power mother, not you, not father!"

"You are to show total respect to your queen WarZar! Do you think because you are my son it gives you any rights? Nay! In truth WarZar, you are just a step above all the slaves and workers in the forest and you WILL OBEY US!" Anger dripped from her wicked tongue. "Satan himself promised me the golden locket would be mine and I would be the ruler of my kingdom." She gave Lazar a flash of a smile. "Even over you dearest!"

"Over my dead body bitch!" Lazar yelled. "I, and I alone will rule this forest! It has been mine from the moment my damn master cursed me and sent me flying through those wretched trees!" He got

160

in her sneering face. "If anyone has that locket, dearer, it will be me! Get it witch?"

"Do not flatter me with those words, you loser! You idiot!" She placed her hands on her hips, anger dripping from her lips. "Did you really think you could override the great dragon? Lucifer was on to your treason the moment you had the thought to commit it! Who do you think created everything evil and sinful!"

"CARMELA! LAZAR!" WarZar yelled out. "Could you both just try and get along. At least while I'm here, bringing such good news. As for the locket mother, the reason it must remain with me is to keep me from dying! Only the good ones can touch the locket of love! It is around my neck only because a good one placed it there! But, if I try to remove it, the lightning that comes from the locket will penetrate my body and fry me!" Now for his best performance, the handsome prince forced real tears to fall down his face. "I only wish to spare my beautiful mother's life by telling you I alone can possess it. It would go far worse for you or Father if you even came near it. I only speak what is true."

"Darling son, you have warmed your mother's heart with you sweet words of concern, but even if your evil demon father cannot grow near the beautiful locket, you sweet mother can." Carmela gave him a faux smile. "Can you just show me where it lies around that handsome strong neck, my son?"

"I can show you mother, but it will do you no good to see it, then want it all the more and be unable to get it." WarZar pretended to have pity for the anxious woman as he bent over and the locket dangled form his neck, perfect and sparkling. "Please mother, it will hurt you if you try to take it."

"Let me be the judge of that darling." With her wide eyes locked on the treasure she had been searching for, Carmela moved toward the locket. As she started to stretch out her hand, a flash of a lightning bolt went streaking toward the frighten woman and slammed her up against the wall, her long black hair standing straight up. Stun and tingling from the electric shock, Carmela was made speechless.

"Poor stupid darling!" Lazar couldn't resist his chuckle. "I do hope the effects stay with her a while. I had forgotten how nice things were before her loud mouth came here!" Lazar turned toward the swinging locket. "Do not try to stop me son, for I know I, the powerful demon, can and will get that locket off your body!" he glanced back at his shaking wife. "Take over my throne, will you!

161

I'll show you who will have the power!" Without hesitation, Lazar took a step toward his son only to get the lightning bolt to strike him in the head, sending him spending in circles. WarZar tried hard to hide his laughter as he watched his father whirling around for what seemed like fifty times before it slammed him up against his wife.

"I did try to warn you about the locket's power and its distaste for evil beings!" With his parents completely dazed, WarZar walked over and picked them up to place on their thrones. "This should wear off in about one-hour folks and when it does, ride down to my station at the slave's quarry and I will point out Spencer for you." He reached down to pat his mother's dizzy head. "Cheer up mother! I now have the locket ,so Alisia has no more powers from it. You may still be able to get your revenge on the pretty little lady, if you can ever find her." He walked to the door smiling to himself knowing phase one had been a success. He called back over his shoulder. "I shall be waiting to show off my latest slave, hard at work, stacking up lots of building stones, just for you!"

After successfully sending Torren away on a hunt, giving him two days off with promised awards, WarZar had slipped Jack in among the workers. Seeing his young friend stacking the stones, the big beast laughed, remembering their silly poems. Hearing the sound of horses galloping his way, WarZar knew his parents had come to check on their son's greatest recruit for the stone quarry.

Carmela slid from her saddle and made her way quickly by her son's side, then stared down into the deep pit. "The pit is grown so deep since we were last here. Darling, you are really making great progress with that mountain of new stones, just waiting to be laid on one of my many achievements! Why, before I set foot in this place, Lazar was living in a sweltering slab with a thatch roof! I brought civilization to this remote, wooded kingdom and changed it into a real kingdom, fit for me, the queen." She smiled back at her husband. "And, of course, my very handsome king, who deserved to have the very best." She pinched his cheek. "That's why the darling demon chose me to wed! Right dearest Lazar?"

"Why certainly my enchanting beauty!" Lazar stared down, trying to find the new man-made slave. "From up here, they all look alike son. Which one is Spencer?"

WarZar pointed down by the stone pile, near the middle. "There, the tall man dressed in dark brown with a tan head cover."

Carmela had pushed her way up to see for herself what her

sister's lover looked like. "He does have a great body!" She knew Lazar had stopped watching Jack Spencer, instead his eyes burned down on his flirty wife. Still peering down, she knew her husband's jealousy was building. "But, he still could never compete with my beloved Lazar. There not a man born who could satisfied me now that I've had a taste of my sexy demon." From her side, she could see the demon smiling, and she knew she had once again fooled him. "Congratulations WarZar, my big handsome son." Carmela blew him a kiss. "Do come around more often my darling. I do so love your company!"

"I shall come if I have the chance mother, but my job keeps me busy and I have been away from this one far too long. I wouldn't want Torren to undo what I have got going!" WarZar kept his distance as they walked back to their mounts. "I gave Torren a couple days off to go hunting for us, so maybe you will have some good roast pig very soon."

"Such a clever son, WarZar, to give the man who challenges you at every turn, time to go hunting! I'm surprised you didn't give him some hard labor to do instead, especially since he begged me to let him go out in search of you when you were gone so long." Lazar smiled from the saddle.

"That does not surprise me father. Torren has never forgiven me for taking over his position and he is one to harbor a grudge for as long as he breathes!" the tall giant laughed. "The jealous human knows there's nothing he can do to hurt me and how easily I could crush his skull in! No, Torren is no real threat, but should he have tried to track me down while I was on my important mission to avenge my parents, I would not have hesitated to smash his fool head in and feed him to the snitches!" He simply gave them a wave and walked back to his watch stand as they rode away, feeling proud to have had a son like WarZar.

Phase two had been aced! Now for the dramatic performance! Their bold plan for releasing all the prisoners in the palace dungeons.

CHAPTER 23

WarZar came back inside his big mansion laughing as Jack helped Alisia with her head wrap. The tall beast continued to laugh as he walked into a big closet and came out carrying a large basket filled with white cloth bags and ties.

"This is going to work better than I had hoped!" The handsome prince set the basket down on the big table and checked out the beautiful woman's transformation. "Young lady, if I didn't know a very shapely, attractive lady was under all that disguise, I would swear you were a boy!" WarZar laughed out. "At least your foul scent will make better sense! A pretty young lady would never reek like a skunk."

"Is my attire what you were referring too when you arrived laughing, dear friend?" Alisia checked herself out while Jack held up her small looking glass. "I'm just glad I don't have to speak my part."

"Then you will be safe, being my mute slave, Harvey!" WarZar smiled when she playfully slapped his arm. "To answer your question about why I declared this next phase would work out better than I had hoped, it is because two of the palace workers came out to me at the job site, all excited and scared. They said it was their duty to clean out the dungeons, so as usual they made their way to the back entrance with all their cleaning buckets and as soon as they opened the thick wooden door, six huge rats came charging out. So, in a panic, they slammed the doors shut and to save their necks, they rushed around gathering as many rats as they could. The number of rats they captured were exactly four! Both frighten workers handed me one of the buckets, covered and I took it from the trembling hands and told them I would take care of the rest inside the dungeon." WarZar laughed remembering their shocked faces.

Previously at the stone quarry:

"The rest? Your greatness, are you saying there can be more inside that big-dark-scary-underground prison?" the female worker shivered at the thought of hundreds of stinking rodents running around her feet.

"At least in the hundreds, maybe more! They multiply very rapidly." WarZar kept his face straight, the need to laugh making it difficult. "What about you Mr. Blanking? Surely a few hundred rats wouldn't bother you, would they?"

"It's my old heart, young master. I just do not think I could help with such a large amount of the icky-ugly-biting- scurrying around-dirty rats!" he shook at the very thought. "We thought, maybe you could take a couple of your mindless slaves to help you clean out the infestation!"

"Consider it done! But I need to keep these four handsome specimens to show his royal highness my reason for going into his dungeon." The giant noticed their relieved faces. "I will need for you to come before the king with me when I arrive, rats in hand, to inform them of the rat invasion and why it must be dwelt with immediately."

"Excuse me, your excellence, but won't the royal king want to know why you are cleaning out the rats instead of us?" Mr. Blanking wrinkled his brow. "They may insist we help out and if we do not off with our heads!"

"It will never happen to you, I promise!" WarZar checked the sun for time and knew he had to get back to Rockford Falls to load up his big wagon with everything they needed for the prison escape. "Just be there when I arrive. I'll inform my parents your help is not needed." With that he dismissed them and left for his home.

AT ROCKFORD FALLS

"I see the Lord's hand in this WarZar! Four rats caught! The exact number we had planned to get." Jack stopped, looking puzzled. "Where exactly where you going to find four giant rats anyway, friend?"

"And how are we going to rustle up a hundred or more once we are inside that dungeon along with papa and every good soul down there?" Alisia had been thinking about the possible real number of the stinking rodents they would be facing.

"First to answer fair Alisia's distressful question about all those rats! You can relax sweetheart, there are no more rats inside that dungeon. And before either of you ask me how I know, it's because I planted the six rats they saw scurrying out just at the entrance, where I blocked the little varmints from going any further in the dungeon. So, Jack, I found those four early this morning at the quarry and now they are waiting for us in the wagon!" He laughed at their relieved smiles. "Now for Alisia to meet her fairy little stinker who is waiting in the garden under a wire cage! Once the skunk sprays his fragrant perfume on our Alisia, we can be on our prison break!"

At the palace:

"Your majesty, your son has just arrived with some disturbing news sir." The head usher backed away when Lazar's eyes blazed on him.

"DISTURBING NEWS?" the king bellowed.

"Well, it could be worse, your grace. WarZar has something to say concerning your living conditions sir, should a certain subject be ignored by the royal couple."

"O Franklin, for the love of God, please cut out the dramatics and show our son in!" Carmela stormed out, discussed with her afternoon ritual of drinking spiked wine ruined. "Do not keep him waiting!"

"Yes, your highness! I shall show your son in." the nervous usher rushed out and WarZar stepped in, two slaves behind him.

"WarZar, just what is so important that you once again come unannounced?" Lazar lifted his eyebrow.

"It is good to know you really wanted my visit and I can assure you I had no other choice unless you enjoy lots of nasty invaders racing around inside your fine castle!" WarZar smiled when his mother sat up, now interested in what her son came to say.

"Do go on son. Forgive your father's rude welcome darling, but he was about to feel the effects of his sexual drink." She gave her husband a knowing smile.

"Yes, I was, as was your sex starved mother." Lazar returned her wicked smile then turned to his giant son. "You wear that dangerous locket still, I see. Please keep your distance, my son, and tell me what is about to invade our privacy, uninvited!"

"It was brought to my attention my two of your loyal workers in the dungeon that there has been some unwanted visitors down there! When they started inside the big outside door to clean, six of your guests came running out under their feet."

"Under their feet?" Carmela made a face and set her wineglass aside when she noticed the moving white bag in one of the slave's hands. "You wouldn't happen to have one in that bag, would you darling?"

"Not one, Mother, four, very large-stinky rats!" WarZar tried not to laugh when his father squeaked out and his mother gave a little scream. "I have come to clean out your dungeon and get rid of all those unwanted rats, with your permission."

166

Lazar, never trusting anyone, raised his eyebrow as he checked out the two quiet slaves, then turned back to his son. "Show me what's in that bag, Son! I need to know if you are being honest with your king."

"You doubt my word father" WarZar stood proudly and stared down coldly as he held out his hand for the slave to step forward. "Open the bag slave, so I can show the king what will be shortly up inside their living quarters if I do not get rid of the multiplying varmints in the dungeon."

"Inside my palace?" Carmela jumped up and stared as her son lifted out four huge rats by the tails. She backed up against the wall shaking her head back and forth. "Put them away WarZar! I cannot stand to watch their squirming around! Lazar, I will not have those horrible rodents invade my space! Send our son down at once!"

"How do you know those rats came from our prison WarZar? You have no way of knowing what goes on down in my dungeons! A multitude of rats invading the palace, nonsense!" Lazar stopped speaking when his son waved in the two workers.

"They will tell you how I know about all your invaders father! If you do not believe them, I shall turn around and go out that door and let the rats take over your entire living space! And that includes your bedchambers!"

"LAZAR! LET HIM GO AND CLEAN OUT THOSE RATS THIS INSTANT OR I WILL NEVER LET YOU TOUCH ME AGAIN!" Carmela was shaking all over at the thoughts of those rats running around all over her bedroom and in her bed. "Listen to the workers if you must, fool!" She grabbed out her lace handkerchief and covered her nose. "And that horrible stench that followed you in here from those rodents! I would be a constant wreck! Sick to my stomach every second!" she waved her hand in front of her face, trying to whisk away the skunky smell. "My God, I knew rats smelled bad, but—"

"But they are stinkier than a skunk!" Lazar covered his nose as the breeze behind Alisia blew through the castle. "Let the workers speak and see what they say! Then, I shall decide what I will do!"

WarZar motioned to the usher to bring the man and woman in. They both stepped into the royal couple's presence, heads lowered and the gave a respectful bow. The man spoke, with quiet respect. "Yes, your excellency, you ask for our account regarding the horrible rat infestation?"

167

"Infestation!" Carmela took a deep breath, inhaling the repulsive fumes coming from the strong smell. She suddenly felt regret for her unfortunate reaction to this worker's words. "Just how many rats did you see down in the royal dungeons?"

"When we opened the door madam, six of the ugly varmints attacked us!" the female worker had the bad habit of stretching the truth, and this poor habit was well known by WarZar, since he was the one in charge of all the workers in the forest. "That's when Mr. Blanking thought quickly to slam the door shut before anymore escaped, giving us time to capture the ones that came out and take them to Master WarZar for further orders."

"Miss Startle is spot on, sir." Mr. Blanking, being a pest exterminator before getting trapped inside the forest, knew that if you saw more than one rat in a basement, the odds for having more were great, so, he spoke what he believed was true, not knowing that WarZar had planted the rats at the entrance just for them. "Before I came to serve such a powerful king and queen, my other life was to know all about the habits of insects and rodents. The cold hard fact is if a person sees a mouse or a rat, there are likely many more in the house. If they are not taken care of sir, I can assure you they will find their way up to your living quarters and make your pampered lives miserable."

"And you feel my son is the best person for this job, Mr. Blanking?" The queen felt the need to rush this meeting so the rats could be dwelt with.

"Yes Blanking, my wife has a good point there." The king rose up from his throne and ordered a window opened. "Will you and Startle be assisting my son with this rat clean-up?"

"Due to the dungeons being so dark and with so many places for the rats to hide into, Miss Startle and I only thought it best to let your brilliant son seek out and destroy the hundreds of the ugly-smelly rodents." Mr. Blanking swallowed, afraid he would end up down below cleaning out the varmints and glanced for the woman who helped him.

"Sir, my assistant has spoken only that which is true and there is yet another reason why your son could clean them out faster and completely." She felt the king's eyes on her, and her knees began to knock. "The truth is, I am petrified of any sort of rodent!" Miss Startle looked hopeful at the queen. "Surely your majesty the queen can sympathize with my feelings where mice or rats are concerned!

If I have a heart attack, I'll do you no good."

"My dear Miss Startle, I am well aware of your feeling concerning those creepy-pest and we need your work below to continue, so your help with the rats will be excused." Carmela had gathered her fan and was waving it in front of her face quickly. "But what reason could Mr. Blanking have for not helping. As long as my son is there to use his special senses to track those horrible rodents down?"

"It's his eyesight madam. The poor man took a spill and tripped over his eyeglasses and broke them. Now the poor soul cannot see an inch in front of his nose without help." The woman of tales looked over at her flushed companion with pity. "The poor man would be more of a burden to your son, unable to see where he's at in the dark dungeon. When we work together, we work as a team. I help him find his way and he helps keep me from getting nervous over every little bump in the dark halls."

"There, folks! This is why I brought two of my younger workers with me to help out." WarZar had listened to the woman's made-up excuses and was glad he didn't have to come up with another reason for him and his slaves to do the job. "Robby and Randy have been my personal slaves for many years and I can depend on these boys to get the job done without jumping over every rat that runs up their pants!" The giant laughed. "They couldn't scream if they wanted to and they are brain dead to things around them, which makes rounding up disease carrying rodents a breeze."

"Then it is settled! WarZar will clean out the dungeons!" Carmela spoke up, her eyes on her demon husband. "Any objections my king? The faster this problem is settled, the sooner my dearest Lazar can have a fresh glass of spiked wine for our planned festivities tonight."

The overheated demon knew his wife was determined to have her way and if he was going to enjoy her body for the night, he would have to give in to her will. Lazar felt the swell in his pants and knew she had the upper hand, so he gave her a loving smile then turned to give his big son a positive nod. "The job is yours and your slaves WarZar! See that it is done quickly!"

"Quickly? That shall be determined on the number of rodents down below, but a fair warning to all, the dungeons must be off limits for at least two days due to the terrible stench the rats have made." Still holding the squirming rats by the tail and listening to their high-

169

pitch squeals, the beasty prince noticed his father waved the rats away and WarZar turned to the slave holding the bag open to receive them, then he quickly tied it shut. "My king, we will do this job as quickly as possible and haul the rodents away for the snitches to enjoy. The guard at the gate is aware of our job here and he will inform you when the task has been completed." The prince gave the word for his personal slaves to give their respect to the king and queen, and instantly both silent boys bowed down on one knee, then arose slowly. "Remember my warning about staying clear of the dungeons until the open vents to the outside have time to freshen up the air." He laughed. "Let the prisoners enjoy the wonderful fragrance for a couple days, dear parents. It's only befitting that they should have something pleasant to enjoy in such a dreary place."

"How wonderfully charming WarZar!" Carmela had moved to the open window, where she had stuck her head out for some fresh air. "Poor papa, it will take him some time to thank his worthless God for that smell!" she broke into laughter and Alisia narrowed her eyes under her hood, suddenly wishing her hateful half-sister would tumble from the window.

"It is quite a lark!" Lazar joined his wife and took a big breath of the fresh air. "And I thought the smell of sulfur was rancid! Those good ones cannot hold their breath that long and if they try to eat their leftover stale bread, it too will stink just like those nasty rats!" He joined in the laughter and unseen by either of them, WarZar was now even happier he was a part of releasing all those trapped souls below in his parent's prison.

"Then, with your permission your highness, I will take my leave and get busy below."

"Of course, my son, the faster the better!" Lazar was not only anxious about getting back to his romantic evening with his sexy wife, but he wanted those stinky rodents removed from his presence. "Do take those nasty rats out of the palace and be about your job!"

WarZar gave his parents a bow and walked out, mission half-way accomplished. Now to remove all the silent prisoners without being seen. The three friends walked back out and got on the wagon and WarZar drove the team of horses around to the back of the palace and noticed only one man at work in the royal garden. Recognizing the man, the tall prince knew how to get rid of him in a hurry. He stopped the horses and got down, then motioned the interested party over. Unsure and nervous, the gardener walked over to where the king's son was.

"You wish to speak to me your highness?"

"I did notice how you were watching me and my slaves, so I was wondering if you might like to join us in removing all those unwanted rats waiting down in the dungeons?" WarZar knew this man was a big coward and afraid of his shadow, so he felt safe in asking him, knowing what his reply would be.

"Me? Help remove rats?" the man stuttered with his words and began backing away. "Golly, your majesty, I would like nothing more, but I have had my orders from her majesty, Queen Carmela to trim the hedges at the front of the palace, so I'm afraid I cannot be of any help down here."

"Then, of course you must obey the queen's request." WarZar laughed softly as he watched the frightened gardener dash up the hill and around the palace. The tall prince noticed his two companions had joined him watching the man. "Poor old Lester, he wasn't afraid that he could not help us, he was just plain afraid!"

"Then you knew what his answer would be WarZar." Alisia caught her breath. "For a moment there, I was concern he might except your offer."

"Never dear lady." WarZar headed down the stone steps to the huge wooden door. "That poor man is scared of his shadow and he wouldn't be caught dead down here." He continued laughing when he stepped inside and lit a lantern by the door. He commenced to take down the wire cage he had put there to keep the rats from escaping into the long hallway. "Follow close behind me. This underground prison doesn't have many outside opening to permit light to come in."

"Everything is so quiet down here." Jack moved slowly behind his big friend, holding tight to Alisia's hand. "Are the cells divided?"

"Divided and spaced apart, to keep the good ones from seeing each other." WarZar had once thought these dear people deserved their punishment and that his parents' policies were the only way to rule, but now, the handsome prince saw things more clearly, thanks to Alisia and Jack. The big giant had never known happiness, not until he met his dear friends. "Soon, they will all be free, but we must hurry and get them under the tarp in the wagon."

"You are right friend. The faster the better." Jack had noticed Alisia had stopped and moved over toward the first cell. Both men moved up behind her and when the prisoner saw the beast standing behind two obvious slaves, he began to worry about his daughter's safety. WarZar held up his hand to the frighten man.

"Reverend Solomon, there is no need for you to be afraid of my being here." The friends noticed the uncertain look on the good man's face. "Please sir, I am not here to hurt you. We have come to set you free from this dark dungeon." They noticed his lips move trying to speak

"To save me? To save all of us?"

Alisia moved up next to the cell and put out her hand, and instantly he saw she was a young girl in disguise and not a boy. "Papa, we have come to get all of you out of here! Carmela and Lazar believe we are down here removing hundreds of rats. Instead, the rats are still up in the palace drinking their wine while we remove God's children to safety, then out of this forest at first light!" Both daughter and father had tears falling after the beautiful girl removed her hood for him to see her after so many years apart. She turned to her big friend. "WarZar, do you have the keys to the cell doors?"

"I do not need keys dear friend, when I have these strong hands!" He laughed and yanked the door off the hinges. "See Alisia, no need for stupid little keys!"

Alisia walked over to hug her big friend before running into her father's arms. "Papa, WarZar is one of us now. He is a saved Christian, same as us and the best friend Jack and I could possibly want. Without the kind man, none of this would be possible."

"True sir, but these two saved my life by showing me their great love." WarZar motioned the group to follow as he commenced to break down each cell door to release each good one down there. "For now, we must go to our safe place. When we get outside, make a run to the long wagon and get in the bed, then lay down. Jack and I will place a large tarp over you so the guards cannot see what is under it. They will think it's a lot of bags with rats, so move around like a bunch of trapped rodents for the royal guards to see."

Alisia smiled at each thankful face. "When we return to Rockford Falls, the home of our friend WarZar, he will undo Lazar's ritual to make you silent."

"Once that is done, WarZar and I will round up all the mute slave workers down in the stone quarry pit and take them to WarZar's estate." Jack had noticed how frail and sickly all the prisoners looked so he knew a good hot meal made by the angel cook and a much-needed rest would make the journey out a lot easier. He looked over at his future father-in-law and smiled. "I love your daughter with all my heart, sir, and it would make me very happy to have your blessing for our marriage, once you can speak. Then sir, you and I must convince these lost souls what their two choices will be, to continue to not believe means the devil will win their soul, or to learn of salvation, trust in the Lord and believe on the name of Jesus and ask for total forgiveness and they will enter into everlasting joy and love."

Reverend Solomon looked at the religious young man and knew he had to be a minister as well. He gave him a big smile and walked out the huge wooden door, glanced back to give Jack a thumbs' up, then ran to the wagon where WarZar was waiting to lift each weak person up.

Once the wagon was loaded, WarZar drove up to the gate, stopping at the guard stand. "You may report to the king all rats are secure and ready for departure." The freed prisoners moved around under the tarp making it appear to be hundreds of unhappy rodents trying hard to free themselves.

The guard smelled the skunk spray and held his nose. "Smelly varmints, aren't they?" He looked from WarZar back to the moving tarp, and nervously moved around in his stand. "You do have them tied securely, I trust?"

"As of now Rolland, but if I don't get this wagon to the snitches den pretty soon, those angry rodents will chew their way out of those bags." WarZar fought to keep a straight face watching both guards moved away.

"Then, don't let us hold up your delivery young prince." The nervous guard bowed his head. "I will inform the head usher immediately to take word to his royal majesty about the successful capture and your rush to get them away from the palace grounds before they escape."

"Have a good day fellow's and stay alert." WarZar drove away laughing as he made his way quickly to the large waterfall.

CHAPTER 24

After taking all the prisoners safely to Rockford Falls over the Rockford River bridge a half mile below the falls, WarZar drove his horses around the other side of the falls to his other secret entrance. The one he used whenever he needed to use the big wagon. The intelligent beast had an even bigger wagon that he intended to use the following morning to deliver all those trapped inside the forest, both the good ones plus the slaves, that he would bring in just after nightfall, to avoid any spies from witnessing the move.

The three friends had planned all the details for the final escape down to the last possible objective. Now, inside the big mansion, the clever beast reversed his father's strong mind control on the ten good ones and their tongues were loose so they could speak again. The first words that came from the mouths were praises to the most-high God, for hearing their inward prayers and sending his servants to set them free from their silent bondage. David Solomon lifted up his arms to sing praises to his Lord and Savior, for bringing Jack Spencer among their mist and into his loving daughter's heart, an instrument in which to save His people. Both those made prisoners and those lost souls made mute slaves, with no mind of their own.

"Jack, my boy, you ask for my daughter's hand in marriage, and this I will gladly give. But son, surely you must be aware your married days are numbered, due to my daughter's age." The minister watched the young pastor seriously. "The way I see it Jack, when we walk through Satan's trapped veil and back into the land of the modern-day world, our destiny will surely be heaven and these bodies, made young through demonic powers, will turn instantly to dust while we take on our new heavenly bodies."

"Reverend Solomon, sir, I am aware of the possibility that once I marry my beloved Alisia and we come together as one, that we may only be blessed by the Almighty God to know each other for only one night. If this should be my one and only night with my beautiful bride, I cannot deny my heart will be completely broken. As it will be if the Lord takes my dear friend away and our last moments will be in this forest saying farewell." Unseen by Jack or anyone else, the big beast fought to hide his tears, for his love for Jack was the best thing that had ever happened to him. "I love WarZar, sir. He has one of the most loving, giving hearts I have ever witnessed. There's only one other man in my life that has touched my heart the same and that's my good friend Howard Preston, my life-long pastor and the most devoted scout master any ten-year-old boy could ever have." Jack felt the locket back around his neck after his big friend gave it back to him and he remembered Alisia's words about the locket of love:

"As long as you have the locket of love Jack, something wonderful will happen. You just have to believe darling."

"Reverend Solomon, I am smart enough to know storybook ending do not always happen for two people who are deeply in love. But sir, I am a believer in prayer and the hope we have being believers in Jesus who said, ask, and it shall be given unto you, seek, and ye shall find, knock, and it shall be opened unto you. I am a believer in miracles, big and small and God's holy angels, many of which was sent to protect, feed, and give comfort to your daughter, while she was alone in this hell of a place. The same angels that assisted her spirit to leave the forest to hide the locket and return to lead me to it, when I was that ten-year-old scout. The same scout that was shoved inside the Forbidden Forest to be saved by your sweet girl. I grew up that summer sir because I had falling in love and I knew, as hard as it was, I had to leave in order to grow up and become the man you see today. After twenty years had passed, I returned. This time to save Alisia as well as any souls that would choose good over evil." Now it was Jack who watched Alisia's father with serious eyes. "Sir, deep down inside me, I truly believe somehow, someway, I will see Alisia and WarZar again before I leave this earth for my heavenly home, and somehow the miracle lies in this golden locket. Alisia told me she received the locket for Christmas, 1800, which is engraved onto the locket's back. Something this beautiful and made by fine gold could not have come cheap for you to buy so my guess is you never purchase this powerful neckless at all and that it just miraculously appeared, most likely around my darling neck on Christmas morning on December 25, 1800, the Lord Jesus recorded birthday."

"Jack does have a point daddy. I do recall waking up early that snowy Christmas day and discovering the beautiful locket around my neck." Alisia had excused herself the moment she arrived at Rockford Mansion to have a warm-relaxing bath in WarZar's giant tub, the angels had prepared for her arrival. Now she was clean and feeling refreshed, knowing her wedding night would be this very night and she was not getting married smelling like a skunk. The preacher's daughter had overheard Jack and her father's discussion as she descended the high steps. "I also recall overhearing you and mother worrying about having me nothing for Christmas on Christmas Eve as you both stared down at the bare floor under the small cedar sparsely decorated with red berries and pinecones. I was aware we were having finance problems due to sinking most of our savings into building the church, so I had prepared a Christmas Letter to my loving parents, explaining why I did not want anything for Christmas that year because having them with me to celebrate the birthday of our King inside the Lord's house, was the best present ever!"

"Alisia, you were always so much like your saintly mother. Showing strangers, you never met more love than they probably ever had. Helping build the church, day in and day out, serving workers food and drink so they could take a much-needed break from their labor." David Solomon gathered his daughter in his arms. "My beautiful girl, your mother said you would understand not having a present and except it with grace and charm, and of course my Charlotte was always right sweetheart, but I recall telling her it just didn't seem fair, that someone as loving, as caring and one of God's beautiful earthly angels, would not receive a special gift on the Lord's big birthday like she has every Christmas before."

"Daddy, I never expected a present for Christmas in 1800, and when I awoke and knew the first rays of daybreak was waking up in the eastern sky, I knew I wasn't alone in my small room." As Alisia recalled that Christmas morning, a glow radiated her face. "I remember setting up and looking around at all my familiar things, but something was different. There was a silence around me that made me relax and the wind I had heard blowing through the cracks in the walls, had died down, so that the stillness of the morning stretched even to the outside. I climbed quietly from the warm covers, expecting to feel the normal chill that came with the morning fire going out during the long night, but my room felt cozy and warm, as if I had my own personal fireplace, blazed with a nice warm fire." Knowing she had everyone spellbound with her story, she continued. "I walked over and looked from my window, but I was not prepared for what I was about to witness. "A fresh snow was falling and the white ground indicated it had been falling all night. But this was not what took my breath away that Christmas morning, for it snowed often in the mountains of North Carolina. It was what I could not take my eyes off, that had been watching in wonder. I knew in my heart at that instant I had been given a Christmas gift. Not given from my loving parents nor any earthly friend or family member, but a Christmas gift from the Lord God Himself. All around the snow was falling down except in one spot. High in the eastern sky, there shone the bright and morning star! The star of Bethlehem shined down bright, it's lower point lighting it way to the earth onto a lowly stable." Her eyes met Jack's "I never told a soul about my Christmas miracle. I suppose I was afraid they would say it had to be a dream, but I knew I was as awake as I am now. It wasn't until after I got trapped inside the Forbidden Forest that I realized just who and why I had been blessed with this vision of the birth of Jesus so many years later. It was when the angels appeared to help me when I was lost and afraid I'd get captured by Lazar and my wicked half-sister. I learned that angels can do things humans could never do. One such then is lifting my soul and carrying me outside the forest. This is when I learned what had happened that Christmas. I was warm that morning because it was my soul that Brianna, my guardian angel had woken up on Christmas morning while I lay sleeping in my warm bed. She led me to the window to see the snow and the Christmas miracle which happened so long ago, and before she left me, she placed the heavenly golden locket around my neck and said it held a powerful secret that would one day make the impossible be made possible by the blessing of Jesus Christ." Her story was finally out and both her and Jack could not control their tears. "My darling, this is why I said, as long as you have the locket of love with you, nothing can be impossible."

"Yes, my beloved! We must hold on to that hope until the Lord reveals His plan for us." Jack checked his watch. "The hour grows late WarZar. By the time we drive the big wagon to the slave quarters, it will be getting dark and they will be coming in to rest the night. Wouldn't it be better to gather them on the wagon as they arrive?"

"It will be faster that way Jack." WarZar made his way to the back door, a look of worry on his brow.

"My friend is worried over managing the thirty slaves and their children?"

177

"Nothing like that Jack. Ordering the slaves will come easy, for they obey my every command. This group of mindless mutes will not acknowledge I am loading them up for travel." WarZar chuckled. "Most of them will probably fall asleep from exhaustion on the trip back." The big beast changed the wagon to the larger one and both men rode away. "If you're wondering what I was fretting about, its where I am going to put up all these guests for the night. It doesn't sound fair to bring them out of their blocked condition then have them sleep on a hard-cold floor."

"Is that all you're worry about!" Jack glanced over when he heard his big friend grunt. "You can relax my friend and stop fretting over being an unthoughtful host. Alisia and I had already counted your rooms and the amount of people who would be spending the night in your big house. Just to be made whole and know they could be on their way out of this forest safely would make every single person staying here proud enough to curl up anywhere in your warm home, but after counting the rooms, including the two Alisia and I used, now that we will be in her dwelling tonight, you have amble room."

"Oh, I have the rooms alright my clever friend, it the furnishings I do not have!" WarZar narrowed his eyes when he heard Jack chuckle. "What? You think it's funny to place people in rooms that have no beds? No wash pans with soap and rags? No chair to take off your shoes from?"

"Does my friend recall all those angels who have been assisting Alisia and now you, since you took her in?" Jack wiped his eyes. "WarZar, Alisia and I made our rounds the day you left to report to your parents that you had returned with me. We found the rooms empty just as you described and the angels heard us discussing how we were to find enough beds for the influx of people coming for a stayover. That's when the beautiful heavenly being said they would fill all the rooms for us and they knew the number of souls and there would be plenty of rooms available for that one night." Jack gave his friend a smile. "So, you see, there is nothing for you to worry about! The big meal will be prepared as well as the rooms furnished, perhaps even more rooms than you normally have! Angels are sent by God to serve us We are sent by God to serve Him by saving the lost souls and bring them out whole, fully restored through salvation by Jesus Christ!"

At the Slaves quarters, WarZar parked the wagon at the far end of the shack row and tied the horses secure. "I will see if Flax is releasing the workers like I ordered him. You can stay with the wagon Jack, but keep your head covered in case some spy wonders by. Just act numb and mute if one should stop and speak to you. Remember, Slaves do not speak. The few children can, but are too afraid, so they remain still."

"I'll be on alert WarZar." Jack pulled up his hood. "Try to hurry this along."

WarZar gave him a big smile, sensing his friend's anxious feelings over it growing dark and this group of workers would be wondering in soon. "I shouldn't be long. Just keep watch."

Jack remained quiet and barely moved in his high seat, afraid someone besides the slaves might see him and wonder about the wagon setting there with only a slave aboard. He noticed the shadows growing tenser down the gravel drive and he perked up at the sound of gravel moving under someone's feet. Jack could tell it wasn't the sound of hooves coming behind him so he began to sweat when he noticed a strong stout man stop below him and stare up, as if he were trying to figure out the reason for a wagon to be down at the slave huts. Keeping his head down and remaining quiet, Jack could easily make out the sneering lips from the broad man wearing a black long coat and a wide brim black hat. He shivered when he realized he was being watched by Torren, himself.

"Well now, what have we here? This wouldn't be a getaway wagon now, would it boy?" The voice became gritty and deep as Jack knew to remain mute, as if he didn't understand this voice. "Speak up, you no good scamp! You be playing dumb with me boy?" Jack noticed the big man tilted his head and felt his heart drop when the hefty bully climbed up for a closer look. "What 'sha hiding under that hood slave? How did you get out of the pit and up here in this fancy wagon? Did you go and steal it boy, to free the other slaves maybe?" He gave a chuckle close to Jack's ear. "You know you won't get fer before the big king Lazar sends out his snitches to hunt you all down. They be real hungry for meat too, since I went and ate the pieces of boar I was supposed to feed them!" He looked around to make sure he was alone before pulling back Jack's hood. "Well look here, if it isn't that Jack Spencer! Old WarZar's prize find! I might just let you take all those slaves off so I can send out the snitches and watched them eat all the big giant's slaves alive, then the king will be so angry at the great lost and WarZar's failure to stop

179

you, he will be removed and I will be made head captain again!" He laughed out, never knowing the WarZar was watching in the shadows.

Jack, not knowing that his friend was close by, suddenly remembered he was wearing the golden locket and its power would knock this big-mouth bragger into a spin and maybe even down into the pit, after the latter had been taken up. Knowing this man was standing in their way instead of obeying WarZar's order to go hunting for two days, Jack realized the deep stone quarry would keep him imprisoned long after they had gone out of the forest so without warning, Jack jumped up and took out the locket, pointing it directly at the evil man.

"What's this? You little—" The powerful blast that came from the locket sent Torren into a spinning whirlwind as he whirled across the road toward the deep drop off. Jack heard his big friend laugh out loud and joined him in laughter. They watched with delight as the big blow fish blew over the cliff out of sight, while at the same time, saw the slaves coming across the yard with the big ladder on their shoulders. Torren was trapped and he could not get out without the ladder.

"Great work Jack!" WarZar smiled up. "You saved me from knocking the lazy traitor over the quarry myself! Now, to order the workers on the wagon before we send another spy friend down to keep my enemy company."

WarZar made quick work of loading the slaves, for they obeyed him without question and the children were glad to go with the young man who had sent the mean Torren spinning into the stone pit. The loaded wagon rolled away from the slave's quarters for the last time. Their next trip in the wagon would be on the road to freedom.

CHAPTER 25

Once WarZar and Jack got the helpless people inside the beast's big mansion, he ordered them to sit on the floor in a big circle so all the good ones could stand around behind them and help them calm down if they grew confused over the sudden reversal. Knowing everyone was in place, WarZar spoke the words so all those trapped inside their own mind could be deprogramed and return to normal.

As the reversal deprograming took place, their eyes began to flicker open and shut, as their bodies were readjusting to who they were before the strong prince hypnotized them and took their sense of thinking and speaking away. Looking around confused as to where they were, the group of ex-slaves could see the men and women standing behind them and many of them remembered their faces well, but with their groggy minds they could not remember who they were or how they knew them. The great beast felt the need to speak first as he looked down at their shaking bodies.

"You are wondering why you are here in this strange place and with people surrounding you. These loving people mean you no harm." WarZar saw all their fear emerge when they recognized the great one speaking, and it caused their fears to mount. Sensing all feelings, the loving man gazed down with compassion as he held his hands out in a loving jester. "You need not be afraid of me any longer, please believe me. I only wish to help set you free! Both from your bondage, then from this forest forever, but you must listen to the two fine gentlemen standing beside me. Reverend Jack Spencer and Reverend David Solomon, whom many of you recognize from your past life. You all were made slaves because of your unbelief in the Holy Trinity while those standing could not be. Each good soul is prepared to leave this place in the morning and you could go with them if you just open up your heart to Jesus. Please my friends, do not try to deceive your Creator by pretending to become a true believer, God, who hears all, knows all, and you cannot fool him. If that is your choice, your disguise will be seem through and the miracle locket the Lord gave Alisia will feel that evil and you will still be trapped inside with my evil demon father and cruel wicked mother."

Jack smiled up at his good friend with admiration. "WarZar, I can see if there is a future in this life for you my friend, you will make an excellent preacher. Wouldn't you agree Reverend Solomon?"

"Absolutely Jack! Why, the dear fellow has practically did our job for us." With eyes reflecting great love, Alisia's father reached high to pat WarZar's strong back. "Dear friends, our big friend has become a blessing for each and every one of us humans! First, he saved my precious daughter Alisia by hiding her here in his own private home, hidden behind a powerful waterfall to keep everyone out. I suppose they believe WarZar has found a secret power to escape death when he goes though the thunderous waterfall to get to his land, so don't worry about being found here by anyone living in the Forbidden Forest. Not even his evil demon father or mother, also a human and my stepdaughter, whose mother and real father are a witch and a warlock from Salem, Massachusetts." He looked over the faces watching him and listening closely to his every word. "Everything said by this big man wearing horns, grown there by no fought of his own, was absolutely true. I know for a fact that each person sitting here have been told about Jesus at one time in your life. Perhaps as a child, growing up with one or more faithful Christian. There have been some here who even went to church, mostly for special celebrations such as Easter and Christmas. You told yourself you'd put in an appearance for the sake of a mother, a father or maybe just to show of your outstanding Easter attire or new Christmas coat and matching hat with gloves. It was never for the right reasons, so after a while even those days grew less important when you could be spending that time doing the things you like. Instead of investing your talents, time and finances for God's work, you bought yourself flashy buggies, later years, flashy cars, big houses with the finest furniture money could buy. You dressed in the rich clothes, wore priceless jewelry and furs! Sent your spoiled children to prestigious colleges instead of sending them to church every Sunday while they were young and growing with wisdom. Your life choices had become me, myself and I and you left the only thing important for a perfect life completely out, so your precious children never got to know about their Savior."

"Choosing the wrong path can mean only one thing, you have become attached to Lucifer, God's enemy, and he has been joyfully leading you down his wide path filled with all sorts of temptations and false promises. The number one thing you must beware of concerning Satan is, he is a liar! The very creator or lies and deceit! He saw all of you getting deeper into his worldly trap and the devil knows all your weaknesses. You cannot defeat the powerful foe by yourself or even with thousands of human fighters. The powerful archangel can overtake any human forces thrown at him but" Jack walked out into the middle of the circle. "Satan cannot and will never defeat the Almighty God! Lucifer is seeking your souls, my brothers and sisters, not because you bring him pleasure. No! He is trying to win all your souls because you are children of the Almighty God, who loves you dearly. Lucifer has not the power to give men souls! Nor does he have the power to give men the gift of choice or free will, but your Holy Creator did both. Because he loves us so much, God created his children as well as his angels, in His holy image. If it was God who gave you the gift to choose and the gift of a living soul, a soul that never dies but will live on for eternity, wouldn't you want you and your children to make this eternal life with your loving three-in-one, God the Father, the Son, and the Holy Spirit, that is now speaking though me these words of salvation. It is your choice to make. Do you continue to choose bad, the road to Satan and his hell, or do you choose good, the road to the Savior, to the one who died on the cross to save you from this sinful heart your soul lives in. The Lord made it easy for His children. Just put your trust in the Lord, believe in Jesus as your Savior and ask Him to forgive you, then you will be set free."

"Please listen to Jack and David, people! I turned you all into mindless mutes to labor for me until death took you to hell and more punishment. Yes, I was evil and hated all humans, just as I had been taught since birth by my wicked parents. I knew nothing else! I had never heard anything good about this God in heaven, only bad reports by my demon father and his powerful master Lucifer. I never knew what it felt like to be happy, caring, devoted, sad, joyful, tearful, loyal, or loving, until I met Alisia and Jack. I saw something in these young people I had never witnessed before. They showed me all those traits I mentioned and for the first time in my horrible assistance I felt special and even normal. They never saw me as a beast, they saw me as a good friend and brother. I had never desired to have a friend but there was something different about Jack, even when he was just ten years old, first appearing in our forest. Like all children, at first, he was frightened of me, mostly by my screaming

183

arrival that echoed across the woodlands, then by my threating angry warnings just for him, but he was ready for me when I arrived the second calling and that's when my life started to change for the better." WarZar came in the middle and sat down next to Jack. "Jack became my friend and brother when he returned to the forest to free his true love Alisia, who had stayed behind with me so he could escape as a boy. I had never felt sorrow before, but I could feel myself hurting inside watching him go and I missed Jack every day he was away. Alisia had help me grow in my new feelings so when my friend returned, I wanted to learn everything about this Jesus and how I could be set free from my prison. I chose salvation and the love of Jesus Christ lives inside me now. Jack and I risk our lives to rescue you because we want you to have that same chance to make the right choice. Like Jack said, it's now up to you. I pray you all make the right choice to turn your life around but if you choose to remain in this life, you may stay here inside the safety of my home until Lazar and Carmela misses my presence or sees our departure from the forest." His eyes watched them closely. "They cannot be fooled friends. They will know you are hiding somewhere in this forest and eventually they will find you. My best advice for you who choose staying is to turn yourself over freely to Lazar and give them your total loyalty or they will turn you back into mindless slaves or feed you to the snitches. These are your final choices. Now, pick bad or good!"

WarZar stood up and pulled Jack with him as they walked from the center and joined Alisia and her father. Reverend Solomon lowered his voice to Jack and his daughter.

"My bet is on 100% choosing good, especially after WarZar's finals choices were given."

As predicted, it was a unanimous choice for good, as everyone sitting on the floor lined up for confession and gave their heart and soul to their Lord and Savior, Jesus Christ. Alisia lifted her voice in song as they moved forward with tears dancing in their happy eyes. They would enjoy the first good meal they had since getting trapped inside the Forbidden Forest and celebrated the beautiful wedding between Jack and Alisia. Not having time to celebrate with their adoring crowd, the young couple gave their thanks and gratitude for their guest's warm congratulations and Alisia's father's moving words during their ceremony. Knowing this could be their last night together and their first as husband and wife, Jack and Alisia wanted

184

to get to her hideaway a quickly as possible, so the big friend came to their aid and galloped them with haste to Alisia underground dwelling.

When the three friends entered the massive welcome room, Amy Bruster jumped off of her big pillow, dropped her book and raced to the only familiar face in the group. "Jack! You came back!" Her attention traveled to the ones who stood behind her preacher and froze on the animal-like man, standing heads above Jack. "Who are your friends, Jack?"

Jack had not let go of Alisia's hand ever since he helped her off their big friend's back and he pulled her up next to him. "This is my new bride, Alisia, the reason I agreed to come with the youth group to the Black Forest. We met inside the forest twenty-years ago, the same time I met my big friend here." Jack had noticed her trembling at the sight of WarZar and to make her feel at ease for going back with him, he would have to convince her this tall man was on their side and now a Christian, same as they were. After Jack told her those very words, Jack noticed a new change in the spoiled girl that began changing after she got trapped inside the Forbidden Forest. "WarZar has helped us prepare for tomorrow morning, the day we finally all get out from this evil place."

"Jack, I know all about you and Alisia and the sad fact that this might be your only night to spend together as man and wife." Amy looked sincere as she spoke and it was beautiful for Jack to witness the change. To stop always thinking about self but to think about others and what they were facing. "Alisia, I hope and pray that our loving Lord will grant you both a miracle and that you will be blessed with a life on earth with Jack before you leave for heaven." Amy threw her arms around the beautiful girl and gave her a loving hug. "I'm so glad Jack found you!"

"Bless you Amy, you are very thoughtful to hope for our future together." Alisia gave her a thankful smile. "Jack and I know our possibilities, but we also know as being human, we cannot fandom how we can be together, but as being Christians who believe the words spoken by Jesus, our Lord, 'with God all things are possible!'."

"My beloved is right! Jesus also said if we had faith the size of a mustard seed, we could move mountains, meaning, there is nothing too big or impossible for us to do." Jack pulled over his big friend. "I also want my dear friend here to be a part of my life on earth, and

I have the hope to believe this also will come to be."

Amy smiled up at the tall handsome prince. "I have learned a lot of things since I was jerked inside your forest WarZar. Watching and listening to Reverend Spencer after I came inside made me start seeing myself for the first time for what I really was. A selfish, self-loving, brat and rich snob. I was never grateful for anything I received and I never ran out of my wants or demands." Amy shook her head. "Believe me, I did not like what I saw and I knew it was my fault for my being here and dragging poor Jack inside with me." The young girl gave a bright laugh. "Then I met Alisia's angels and they told me my coming inside the forest was God's plan and he had done this for two reasons. First reason was to make me see myself for the selfish-ungrateful person I had always been and second, He needed for Jack to have his reason for coming back inside to save all his children. Suddenly everything made sense and I wasn't afraid anymore to wait for you to do the will of God for I knew in my heart, you would come back and we could leave this place. Me, a better person when I run into my paw-paws arms and you Jack, for being God's chosen servant to free his people."

"These angels can work wonders, sweet girl!" WarZar finally spoke, knowing she would go back with him without arguing. "They can cook and clean a house far better than I can and whip up something to wear in a flash." WarZar noticed Jack and Alisia had started kissing, so he reached for Amy's hand and nodded toward the loving newlyweds. "Let's give them the privacy they long for Amy. We will return in the morning with all the other good ones and say goodbye to my homeland for good."

As they made their way up the tunnel, Amy felt safe with this half man-half beast. "Won't you miss your home after you leave, WarZar?" She had someone else to be concerned about. Amy Bruster had grown up.

CHAPTER 26

Everything had been made ready for the newlyweds by the thoughtful angels. In Alisia's old bedroom, a large round bed was waiting with real soft sheets and pillows. Roses filled the candlelit room as somewhere soft beautiful music was playing. A decanter of angel wine and two crystal glasses waited beside the huge bed and the couple finally stop kissing long enough to gather it all in. Alisia gave a soft laugh.

"How so much like the angels do make this night special for us my darling husband."

"Before the hours move faster away, my dearest, let us feel one another with complete oneness!" Jack lifted his bride and carried her to the bed, then laid her down. Jack slipped from his clothes and slowly undressed his beautiful wife before joining her on their love bed. While the rest of the good ones slept, two lovers in love knew the complete joys of becoming one, as they made love at last until the morning came.

Howard Preston and Tom Bruster had watched the youth bus and rental truck drive away with the teenagers and with their things packed as well as Jack's, they drove out to the Old Wagon Road and parked Howard's car at Saylor's Landing after renting a space. Both men pulled out the camping gear and headed for the last place they had seen Jack and Amy. They set up their tents and placed their chairs facing the Forbidden Forest. They had been waiting there every day since Jack and Amy disappeared then walked back to the campground to sleep until their time ran out and the youth had to leave and the new campers would be arriving. Both men had gotten permission to camp along the road across from the Forbidden Forest and to stay out of any visitor's way.

Tom poured himself another cup of coffee, feeling anxious and unable to sleep. "Howard, do you really believe we will ever see Jack or Amy again?" He glanced over at his silent companion who sat reading his Bible. "I mean, they could have been captured and we might never see them again!"

The solemn preacher looked up toward the dark forest, darker since night had fallen. They had lit their lanterns to be able to read after eating their roasted hot dogs and the preacher had not given up hope that his young friend would be stepping out soon. "Tom, I cannot explain how I know we will see our loved ones again, but in my heart, I just believe we will. Maybe in the morning, on the holy sabbath."

"I too had great hopes at first, Howard, but it has been so long." Tom Bruster felt so helpless and some how he felt responsible. "If I had not insisted that we come back to this God forsaken place, this would have never happened!"

"I'm not so sure Tom." Howard sat up and patted the big man's drooping shoulders. "I believe God led you to come up with this trip, since you could afford it and He wanted you to bring your spoiled granddaughter." Howard held up his hand to stop the banker from objecting. "You know its true Tom. That young lady has hurt many a feeling by bragging about herself and what she gets while putting less fortunate girls down." His attention went back on the Forbidden Forest. "I believe the Lord wanted to teach your daughter an important lesson Howard and when she returns to you, it will be of a new and loving child."

"Then why did Jack have to go back inside after he successfully got away at ten?" Howard slumped down in his chair, knowing Reverend Preston knew Amy well.

"Jack had a mission from God and it was His plan for Jack to return to the Forbidden Forest as well, to save his people and set them free." Howard heard the banker laugh and glance his way. "Something funny about that Tom?"

"Not the fact that God wanted Jack to be a servant and do His will." Howard smiled sheepishly. "I was just trying to compare our Jack to Moses, chosen to set God's people free."

"Alright, but on a much smaller scale." Howard returned Tom's smile. "Jack is in love with the girl who led him to the locket and he had hopes they could be wed before they walked out the forest."

"The young lady who lived in the 1800's? She is still alive inside that forest?" Tom stood up and stared across the narrow road. "How old would that make her?"

"Jack told me when he came out Alisia was born in 1784, so that would make her 237 years old. Inside the forest she has remained seventeen and that is who Jack saw and fell in love with." Howard knew trying to explain these facts to his companion was near to impossible, but he would give it his best shot. "Tom, the locket Jack found is no ordinary locket. It holds a powerful secret, so powerful it will be the source of setting all the good souls trapped inside free. Most of them will step out the way they step inside, but as soon as they leave the magic of the forest, their earthly body will turn immediately to dust and their living souls will go to heaven."

"You said most. Are you referring to the ones remaining as Amy and Jack?" Tom felt totally overwhelmed by this revelation but from everything that had happened at that place, he could never discount it as not being real.

"Most definitely Jack and Amy, but I'm sure there will be others, perhaps children inside, but soon, much older." Howard joined him standing near the road's edge. "I just pray for Jack's sake, that his Alisia and WarZar can step out themselves, to remain with Jack in this life."

"Do you actually think that can be possible Howard?" Tom stared down at the minister. "I mean, the girl is very old and I'm certain this WarZar, whoever he is, is also old."

"Tom, you ask if this was possible. With faith in God, all things are possible! It was God that led Jack to Alisia. Our loving God would not bring them together in such deep love just to take it away." His attention remained on the forest. "As for WarZar, he is the thing Jack heard that screamed out sending his echo throughout the mountain. Jack saw hope and love in that beast's eyes and that young man truly loves him and hopes to save his soul, to set him free to be a normal person." Howard looked up into the dark starry sky. "Somehow, maybe not right away, but somehow I truly believe our loving Lord has a plan for these three to be together and I will not let my young friend give up on the hope that comes from believing in our Lord's special miracles."

"I cannot say I understand fully everything you have told me Howard, but I will pray for Jack to get that miracle. If not when he steps out of that forest, but in the very near future." Tom felt better over their situation. "Hope blooms in the morning!" He glanced over at the minister, his eyes unsure where those words had come from. "Howard, Where?"

"My old friend, do not you recognize the Holy Spirit when he sings from your heart?" Reverend Preston looped his arm around the man's shoulders and they walked back to their tents and said goodnight.

CHAPTER 27

The first rays of sunlight filtered through the open portals deep under the ground in the warm bed, shared by two lovers. "The morning has come far to swiftly my beloved wife." Jack felt his raw emotions building, knowing all the uncertainty that lay ahead for them once they stepped outside the Forbidden Forest. "I have been dreading this day, yet rejoice in the freedom of every living soul who waits above for our presence."

"Dearest Jack, no matter what happens when we walk out together, I truly believe that even though we find ourselves separated, it will be only temporary." Alisia had kissed him one last time before getting dressed. "I know our loving Lord brought us together and He will not keep us separated for long. Please my darling, even if things are looking helpless and bleak, you must never give up, no matter the loss. That which is lost can be found again in time. When you start to think it's hopeless, you will find hope."

"Then, I shall hold on to those words of trust and faith, my beloved Alisia." He took her hand and walked out the stone door for the last time. They moved slowly down the long tunnel before coming to the steps that led up inside the massive tree. "This is where I first saw you. I knew I was in love with you Alisia, the moment you spoke my name." Jack drew her into his arms and held her tight. "I want to take in your sweet smell and feel you close to me, until our loving Lord brings us back together. I too believe this, as long as I have the locket of love with me, you will come back."

"Never forget the locket of love is powerful Jack. Sometimes it cannot be seen, but you must not let this take away your hope." She pulled away to look into his loving eyes. "Promise me Jack, you will never forget that?"

"I promise, even if I cannot see the locket and perhaps even think it's gone for good, I will remember your words, given to you by the Holy Spirit. To lift me up out of despair and renew my hope in that miracle that will reunite us as one, as well as my dear friend WarZar." Jack gave her a kiss before stepping up inside the tree. "Once we open the secret door, the decent will begin."

"Then, we must not keep all those beautiful souls waiting."

Alisia gave him one last kiss. "It's time darling. There's no turning back. We leave on the holy sabbath to meet our destiny."

"Let us depart, Mrs. Spencer." Jack opened the door as the locket around Alisia's neck gave him the power. They saw the quiet group had arrived and was patiently waiting for their leader to take them out to freedom.

"Thank you for waiting. I know each one of you are anxious about leaving this forest, especially being out here at the same spot where many of you were captured many years ago." Jack had noticed all the nervous people waiting to step out into a place unknown. "Dear friends, this place you leave is almost as bad as living in hell but the new home that awaits most of you soon, will be so beautiful and filled with the incredible love of our Heavenly Trinity. Once there, you will forget all the things you left behind, for the beauty of what you will receive will replace earthly things into glorious things.

Now, you will witness the power of the almighty God working through this very special locket my beautiful bride is wearing. Do not be afraid of the mighty wind that will blow across the land in front of us to create an invisible-solid shield that can never be penetrated by all those evil souls living inside the Forbidden Forest." Jack waved his hand toward the trees behind them that lined the Old Wagon Road. "Once God's shield has been put into place, he will open up the shield of His once beautiful archangel, Lucifer, and destroy it all together and replace it with another blocking shield, to keep his children out of the Forbidden Forest." Jack turned back to his wife and smiled. "Alright darling, speak the words the Holy Spirit waits to speak as you hold up the locket of love."

"Gladly Jack darling." Alisia lifted the golden locket in her hand and held it toward the inward forest. "Thy power Holy Creator is great! There is nothing that thou cannot do! Your children ask to be set free from their bondage, both in their labor and in their past unbelief and to wall in these evil beings that do that which is evil in the sight of their one true God and worship their master, Satan. They delight in the great pain of your children, by torture in their dungeons, by beating their slaves after they make them mindless mutes and treat them worse than animals, they feed the runaway or the dying to their demon wolves and find joy in their suffering when they are eaten alive. Send thy mighty wind Lord and shield inside this forest that drips with thy children's blood, these evil souls that have shown no mercy!"

191

From high above them, dark clouds formed as a whirlwind began to drop down and stretch around the entire perimeter of the Forbidden Forest. A wide streak of lightning swirled around the border, just inside the forest as thunder peeled across the sky, so loud the ground shook and rumbled. Then, there was silence and the morning sun appeared and its rays glistened down the long-high shield created by God.

Cheers and praises went up to God from the happy crowd, for any doubts they might have had had been vanished by the hand of God.

"See, my friends, the heavenly Jehovah still works wonders for his people. Same as He did for the Israelites when Moses brought them out of bondage!" Jack was feeling all kinds of mixed emotions. To witness firsthand God's power to help his people, and the sick feeling not knowing what would happen when he stepped out with Alisia and WarZar. He snapped out of his thoughts when his big friend touched his arm.

"They come Jack!" WarZar was looking toward the inside. "Lazar and Carmela have gathered all their loyal workers and are headed this way!"

"They cannot touch us my friend! The Lord God has made us safe and they will forever be trapped inside this forest with no more human to invade their precious kingdom." Jack took his big friend's hand. "It's alright if you're having sad thoughts about leaving your homeland my friend or even your parents, no matter how bad they treated you."

"They made their choice a long time ago Jack and tried to teach me to feel like they did. Up until I met you, I did act like them and hated the sight of human beings." The handsome prince saw their horses come into view. "I guess I'm just feeling pity for my mother and father. Father for making such a bad choice in heaven and losing his soul to Lucifer, then refusing to ask for forgiveness when he was given the chance by Jesus. Mother, for growing up with David, who loved her as his own child and taught her all about Jesus. Her cold, jealous heart sent her down the wrong path and I find there was no hope for her. Even if we would have tried to save her, she would have betrayed us to Lazar and watched him destroy us."

Lazar pulled his black stallion to a halt and stared out at the humans that had once worn work clothes and slaved in the stone pit. Sheer hate and anger shown from his evil face. "What goes here?

Where do you think you are taking my slaves? Why do they wear these fancy clothes?" his voice grew loud. "Did I not hear them cheering and shouting praises to God?" Lazar's red eyes fell on his son. "WarZar, why do you stand with these people? Was it your power that reversed my spell on them?"

Carmela noticed her father and half-sister waiting next to her son. "Why are my prisoners standing free, WarZar? Did you remove them along with the stinking rats?"

"No mother, I set them free from your cruel bondage. As for the rats, the only rats living in your palace mother are you and father!" Her giant son laughed out. "There were never any rats infesting the dungeons, only innocent people, praying to our God for freedom!"

"OUR GOD, SON?" Lazar stepped forward. "You have become a traitor to your parents! We shall deal with you, Son, and it will not be pretty!"

"Master, let me punish WarZar!" Torren stepped up beside the demon. "I knew he was up to something, but no one would take me serious!" the big brut saw Jack smiling at him and the mean man narrowed his bitty eyes. "You! Shock me with that small weapon you hang around your neck, will you? Why, I will fry your body alive!" he made a charge for Jack and hit the invisible shield of God, that could only be seen by the Christians waiting to leave, and his entire body lit up with electricity that sent him flying back unconscious.

"What the devil was that?" Lazar asked wide-eyed. "It cannot be Satan's trap! It's too far inside! Who did this?" his red eyes blared at Alisia wearing the locket. "Was it you girl? And that damn locket, filled with painful power?"

"The shield placed there to hold all of you inside the Forbidden Forest forever, was created by the one and only God!" Alisia smiled. "It will also keep out any other poor soul for wondering into your trap as well as your old master, Lucifer."

"Lucifer?" Carmela called out loudly. "Surely no shield is strong enough to keep the powerful Lucifer out! Did he not create one just like it to keep all of you inside." She suddenly laughed, thinking those stupid people were trapped between both shields. "At least we have a lot of land on our side, you idiots! I see you only have about ten feet between each shield. Your life is going to get pretty boring stuck inside of such a narrow strip and my big son takes up a big part of it!" She continued to laugh, as her husband finally had something to laugh about.

"Laugh while you can mother. I hate to burst your bubble but, we are not trapped inside here and pretty soon, we shall be making our exit from the Forbidden Forest forever!"

"No, Son! Please, darling, if you go from the magic forest you will turn to dust! You soul will go to hell and my beautiful boy will be tortured forever." Carmela brought on fake tears. "Your home is here, Son, with your parents. Even if you should survive outside in the real world, you would be treated as a horrible beast! The public would have you locked up like a circus animal! Oh WarZar, please darling, don't leave your mother!"

"You never loved me mother, not like my friends have." WarZar knew she was only putting on a motherly act. "You don't need me Carmela. You've got Lazar, the demon you ask Lucifer to let you marry so you could be a queen of a kingdom. You got your wish mother, but now you must hold on to your wicked husband by your own charms and wicked wine, you both lust for. You won't have Satan's help anymore to keep Lazar in line. From now on, you must give him the title King of the kingdom and just be happy you still have subjects to order around."

"If you will excuse me from listening to your empty threats that do you no good, my wife and I are going to start the exit moving." Jack turned toward the road with Alisia by his side. "My brothers and sisters, line yourself up along the last row of trees and at my word, walk out, free people!" Jack could hear Lazar and Carmela yelling hateful things to the people lining up but all they could hear was the beautiful sound of music coming from the open veil of heaven. "May you trip upward being a happy one! You may walk!"

Just outside the forest waiting across the road, Howard Preston stood up slowly as he had watched a group of people line up just on the other side of the tree line. Without taking his attention off the people, Howard called out to his companion, who sat lost in his book.

Tom Bruster jumped up and moved next to his old friend and saw the people waiting on the other side of the trees. "Howard, where did they come from?"

"They just appeared on the other side Tom. I believe these are the first group to be sent out by Jack. My guess is that they've been there a very long time and as soon as they step out, they will simply go to heaven." Howard closed his eyes and sniffed the air. "Can you spell it Tom? The veil has opened to heaven. They are waiting for them to come out."

"If they go to heaven Howard, what will become of their bodies?" Tom Bruster could only stare at the unusual sight and the banker just didn't have the gift to smell heaven's scent when it fell down. "Will they leave a stack of bones for us to bury?"

"My guess is, they will simply turn to dust and blow away in the wind." The men watched the group moving forward and when they stepped out they quickly turned to dust, that swirled around where each person had stopped as their soul moved upward into the glory of heaven in beautiful new bodies.

"You were right, Howard." Tom gazed over at his companion with amazement. "How on earth do you know so much about all these strange happenings?"

"I have done a lot of research on many different subjects on the unnatural and miracles of God." Howard did not budge, for he knew his young friend would be the last soul out. "Tom, remember when the sky grew dark overhead earlier and you were worried we were in for a bad storm?"

"How could I forget! That was the biggest dark cloud I have ever witness and when I saw that tornado coming straight down just inside the Forbidden Forest, I was scared something bad was going to happen to Jack and Amy!"

"Tom, I didn't understand what that storm meant at first, but now I realize that it had to be the power of the Almighty Jehovah, creating some type of protection inside that forest for Jack and those people he was sent to save." Howard reached over to pat his worried friend on the back. "Ever since Jack found that locket and got lost inside that forest, I knew God had a plan for him, so I chose to do all my research to help my young friend. He and I have been moving forward with this assignment for twenty years Tom and when Jack steps out of those woods, he won't be alone. Jack will be clinging to his new bride, not knowing her fate and fearing the fact it might be their last few minutes together, as well as the friend he befriended and loves deeply. Both Alisia and WarZar are of a great age and they could very well turn into dust like those other saved souls. This is why I wait and watch. Maybe I'll see something that Jack misses and help him keep having hope for that miracle." Howard stopped when he saw the five children step up inside the tree line. "Look Tom, five small children are to step out next."

"Please don't tell me they will turn to dust as well?"

"I think not friend, but they will become adults, the instant they emerge." Howard waited and watched, ready to help them once they step out in children's shoes and into adult ones.

"My brave little friends, you watched your parents being lifted up to heaven and now each of you will find yourself grown up and adults when you make your step outside this forest." Jack patted each of the small heads and their big eyes smiled up at their hero.

"We will be big and brave like you Jack!" one of the boys gave him a grateful hug and was followed by the other four, giving Jack their own thankful hug. "Will you be coming out soon Jack?"

"I will, my brave children. I'll send Amy out with you so you won't have to go alone. Once outside, my good friend will be waiting to help you and Amy's grandfather can see his granddaughter safe again." Jack smiled down at the young teenager. "Thank you for volunteering to go out with these children, who will be older than you once you are outside."

Amy smiled, but could not control her tears as she first hugged Jack, then Alisia and WarZar. "Dear friends, I hope and pray I shall see you both again! If not when you step out, in the very near future. I have seen the love between all three of you and I just know God will bless you with a miracle." Amy turned, tears racing down her pretty young face, gathered two of the smallest children's hands and stepped out of the forest with five adults as a more giving and loving young lady.

CHAPTER 28

Reverend David Solomon stepped up in front of his daughter and smiled into her beautiful sad eyes. "My precious girl, you have always been the joy of your mother and my life. We have always been so proud of you. The way you always thought about others first, before yourself. Like you dear mother you could sing like an angel and I could tell many of the congregation listened to your beautiful voice, feeling uplifted with the presence of our Lord." He gathered her hands in his. "Alisia, my place is with my beloved Charlotte, whom I have missed ever since the Lord took her home to sing with His angels. I look forward to going! To be with my Savior and give Him grateful praises filled with thanksgiving." David closed his eyes and smiled. "To run into Charlotte's waiting arms and walk hand-n-hand throughout our Lord's heavenly kingdom." Alisia's father turned to Jack, then back to his daughter. "Charlotte and I had many loving years together sweetheart and I want this for you and Jack. I have seen the incredible love you share and I know our loving God did not just place you both together for such a brief time. Jehovah has plans for you both, as well as WarZar, so I know this is goodbye for now, my beautiful child. Your mother and I just want you to be happy Alisia and I can see how happy Jack has made you ever since you met him twenty years ago. Never forget, your mother and I will be watching you to share all your happy moments, like all the births of our grandchildren." Reverend Solomon looped his arms around Jack and gave him a warm fatherly hug. "Take good care of my little princess Jack."

"Yes sir, I will love your beautiful daughter forever, just as you love your beautiful Charlotte." Jack tried to hold back his tears but they came nevertheless. "You may share this with mother, Charlotte, for me, tell her, our first son will be named David, after his loving grandfather and our first daughter will be named Charlotte, after her loving grandmother."

"God bless you, my son." Try all he could, the preacher could not control his tears as he gave WarZar a hug, then his daughter. "I cry down here darling, for leaving you behind will be the only thing I shall miss seeing every single day, like it was before getting trapped. I love you with all my heart Alisia. Just be happy! I know you will, as long as Jack is in your life and—" He smiled at the sad beast. "—and WarZar."

"This is not goodbye, Daddy!" Alisia smiled through her tears. "Like Jack told me and WarZar twenty-years ago, goodbye sounds too permanent, so I shall simply say. I'll be seeing you daddy! Tell mama I said Sing a song for her daughter's happiness, then send it down on the wings of a dove! Please tell her I love her."

"I will give her your messages darling." He stepped away. "It's time to go. The other good ones who were in the dungeons with me, are waiting. "I'll be seeing all of you in heaven!" Reverend Solomon turned and walked over at the edge of the forest and smiled back, waving. "I can hear the song of the angels, Alisia, coming down from glory to welcome us, and your mother, my Charlotte, has joined in their singing for I would know her beautiful voice anywhere. May the Lord bless and keep each one of you, and may He shine His face upon you and give you peace!" Alisia's father was gone and the three friends waiting and watching, could see each soul's light rising up through the clouds to heaven.

"Daddy is gone and now he can be young and happy again with his Charlotte." Alisia wiped the tears from her eyes and took around the man she loved. "My heart wants these moments to linger, my dearest, for I do not want to leave your side." Alisia buried her head in his chest and took in his manly scent. "We have only found love Jack and I believe our God has made us one for more than just to help set his people free from this place. I realize WarZar and I cannot just walk out and remain like we are, me 237 years old and WarZar 219 years old."

"I had another dream last night." WarZar felt sure the dream meant something like the other dream did. "See what you think Jack. I dreamed we all walked out of the Forbidden Forest together and the instant we stepped out to freedom, Alisia and I found ourselves in the most beautiful garden I have even seen. There were colorful flowers everywhere and sparkling clear water. Never have I seen so many different kinds of fruit trees and the sounds of singing birds filled the clear blue sky. Alisia looked exactly like she did when we left the forest, but I had changed into the man I had seen in my first dream." The handsome prince looked down hopeful. "Jack, there was only one person there beside us and he had the most incredible eyes I have ever witnessed. His hair was dark and fell in waves around his face, then touched his shoulders. He had a well-groomed beard and mustache and the white robe he wore shone like the morning sun. Was we in heaven Jack or did we go someplace else?"

"Did you feel yourself leaving your old body when you drifted up, my brother?" Jack knew WarZar had been in the presence of Jesus but he needed to know if he drifted up like the others.

"That's just it, Jack, we didn't drift up like everyone else. No dust floated around us! We simply vanished and were standing in the garden with this angelic person." WarZar knew his young friend was onto the truth.

"You did not go to heaven if you saw no dust, nor drifted upward." Jack had remembered reading of such a place in the lost Bible, old scrolls that had been found in a cave. "The place you just described to me was the Garden of Eden, the only place on earth made in the image of heaven. Jesus brought you both there to renew your lives so you could return to me." Jack laughed, feeling the hand of God in WarZar's dream. The reassurance of his holy word and the loving gift that only the Savior could provide.

"God has given us a message through our dear friend's dream!" Alisia joined Jack laughing, for new hope had replaced her dread of leaving the man she had given her heart to.

"Then, my dream was good?" WarZar noticed Jack shaking his head proudly before grabbing his big friend in a strong hug. "God gave ME the dream to lighten all our burdens!" the giant roared with laughter, as his mother and father looked on sadly.

"Lazar, never have I seen our beautiful son happy." For the first time in her life, Carmela was feeling something new. The hate and bitter anger she had felt earlier had melted away and now she only felt joy for her son. "WarZar has never known happiness Lazar and to see him like this warms my heart." Carmela moved close to the shield and spoke his name softly. "WarZar, my son." She waited for him to look her way. "To see you so happy, fills my heart with hope for you. I'm sorry I was never there to give you the joy you have inside you now, but, even if you don't believe me. I'm happy for you, Son. Go with your friends, Jack and Alisia. They gave you the one thing I couldn't, love. I gave that beautiful act away when I sold my soul to Lucifer. Enjoy your new life WarZar! You deserve to be happy. Life never treated you fairly in our world and you deserve so much more." Tears raced down her face. "I may be punished for saying this, Son but, I love you WarZar. I have always loved my little boy."

"I believe you mother." WarZar had his own tears for the one he wished he could help. "I am happy now mother. Jack and Alisia are my family now and I am proud to be a Christian like they are. It's never too late mother to ask for forgiveness if that is what is in your heart. Jesus died for all our sins and he will lift you up out of this place if you ask for forgiveness and believe in Him again."

"Thank you for caring WarZar and for those words of hope." Carmela knew her son would be gone soon. "I'll miss you every day."

"I will remember you too mother and" he looked deep into her sad eyes, knowing this time she was not acting. "I love you. This is goodbye unless you turn your life over to your loving Lord, then this is: I'll be seeing you Mother, in heaven!" The beast turned and took Jack's hand, then Jack gathered Alisia's and they moved to the forest edge. "I love you both very much."

"We love you too my brother." Jack squeezed his hand. "This is it." His eyes fell on Alisia, tears reflecting back in hers. "I love you with all my heart, my dearest Alisia. You will be in my heart forever."

"As will you dearest Jack. Never give up hope darling, remember all I have told you."

"With my heart filled with love and hope and the promise of our Lord and Savior, lets walk out together now." They stepped out together and Jack found himself standing alone on the grasses knoll, looking desperately around for the two who had vanished.

Reverend Howard Preston had made his way over beside his young friends, who now was down on his knees searching frantically for the locket that had been around Alisia's neck. "Jack, the locket is not there, son." Jack glanced up at his devoted friend with tears in his eyes and seeing Howard's extended hand, Jack took it and stood up, shaking his head.

"This is harder than I had imagined, Howard." Jack could hardly speak. "I took both their hands and we walked slowly out together. One moment I felt their fingers in mine, the next, they were gone and my hands were still warm where they had clutched them tightly." Jack's sad eyes met his old friend's and he could not control his emotions any longer as he broke down in his scout leader's strong arms.

"It's alright to have these feelings, Jack. I know things seem so helpless right now, but son, I have been watching as every soul stepped out from the Forbidden Forest." Howard knew he had his young friend's attention because he had stop crying and gently pulled away to listen to what his dear friend had seen. "Jack, I saw the first group of people lining up down the tree line and when they stepped out, they immediately turned to dust. As it swirled around where each person had been standing, I saw their soul, like a light, floating up to heaven's open veil." He noticed Jack's questioning eyes about heaven's open veil. "You're wondering if I could see the open veil, perhaps a little, but I knew without a doubt the veil to heaven had divided to receive all the souls below because I could smell its distinct smell that is like no other."

"The children and Amy followed the men and women who had been made slaves before finding salvation." Jack knew this was leading up to the last three to step out, but he knew to remain patient and listen to his wise mentor. "Were they very old when they came out? Going from a child to an aged adult could be tragic for someone unprepared."

"I thanked God when the young children stepped out to find themselves no older than teenagers. They seemed please as well, most likely fearing they would be very elderly when they emerged." Reverend Preston smiled over at the youth chatting with Amy as she filled them in on what it was like to be a teenager in the modern society. "I don't know what happened to Amy Bruster inside that forest, but it certainly changed the girl for the good." He watched the new teenagers laughing and picking with one another. "Looks like they are typical teenagers now, all child-like behavior is gone now."

"Howard, I just assumed by the year their parents said they were born, they would be a whole lot older. All of them in their eighties." Jack couldn't wrap is mind around how they didn't come out their birth age. "How could this have happened?"

"Have you forgotten the words of Jesus my young friend? Yes, with us humans, this should be impossible. But, with God"

"All things are possible, Howard! Even getting our miracle is possible! Just because I cannot see the locket of love, doesn't mean it is lost!" Jack lifted his drooping shoulder and stood up straight. "My beautiful wife told me that and that the locket can be invisible! You saw Reverend Solomon and his friends turn to dust, that swirled around where they had stood as their souls lifted to heaven, correct?"

"I did Jack and that is why what I tell you next will make you joyful." Howard laughed when Jack grabbed his arm.

201

"Tell me, Howard! What did you see when the three of us stepped out?"

"I was watching as the three of you stepped up to the tree line. I could see all the emotions on each of your faces as you clasped hands tightly as if you were hoping if we hold on tight to each other, we will remain together on the outside." Howard thought back. "I could tell each of you dreaded to take that final step outside and all of you could have even wondered if you shouldn't just remain on that thin amount of land inside the Forbidden Forest and considered if you did not step out the three of you could be together forever."

"It did occur to me for a brief moment, but I knew that wasn't what the Almighty God wanted so in the end, we all took that hard step out together and I found myself alone on the outside." Jack needed to hear what his old friend had seen. "What did you see, Howard?"

"I saw all three of you stepping out together, but just as soon as you cleared the forest, Alisia and WarZar simply vanished into thin air." Howard reached for Jack's hand, knowing this was the good news he had waited for. "They never turned to dust Jack! The veil to heaven had already closed after Alisia's father and friends went up. Can't you see Jack! The Lord never took your wife or great friend to heaven! He took them somewhere where no human can go and plans to renew their life."

"Somewhere humans cannot go! Jesus plans to renew their life!" Jack now could not control his happiness as they began laughing, recalling his big friend's dream. "Howard, I know where the Lord has taken my beloved and my friend and brother! I know how he will give them new life there!" Jack could not stop laughing. "My giant friend had dreamed some dreams that he couldn't understand, so after praying for guidance to help translate WarZar's dreams for him, each interpretation made sense. The last dream he had was on this very topic. WarZar had dreamed he and Alisia came out with me holding my hands and simply disappeared to a beautiful garden. There were all kinds of flowers and fruit trees, crystal clear water and beautiful songbirds. I recognized the place immediately! The Lord had taken my loved ones to the garden of Eden! The closes place on earth to heaven and at the tree of life, Jesus renewed each of their life. My beloved Alisia as she was and my giant friend into a normal human man, no more with great horns protruding from his head or hoofs, instead of feet and standing ten feet tall."

"Of course, Eden was designed to be like heaven on earth so the first man and woman could feel close to their loving Father Creator. Jesus walked beside them in the garden and His light remained in that one special place just as it does in heaven!" Howard looped his arm around Jack's shoulders. "The tree of life was off limits to all people after Adam and Eve were put out of the garden for disobeying God's command not to eat from the tree of life but from ever other tree in the garden, where there were many to choose from. But again, the same thing holds true where Alisia and WarZar are concerned. They could never touch the tree, but Jesus could and it was his hand that pulled off the fruit of life, blessed it with his special miracle, and gave to them to share."

"So now, I must be patient and wait." Jack looked back at the last spot he had seen his bride and dear friend, just inside the Forbidden Forest. "Somehow I will know where to find them. Without the locket I feel lost and uncertain what to look for. Will it be some sort of a sign?"

"Whatever it will be Jack, I know it will not be here." Howard smiled when his young friend glanced up at him. "It's a fact Jack, the Lord will not send your loved ones back to this place. My guess is somewhere in Graceland, near your home." He patted the young minister on the back. "Your things have been packed and are waiting in my trunk with mine, Tom's and Amy's luggage. It's a good thing my car can seat lots of people, now that we have five extra teenagers to take back. Nine riders will be a tight fit, but we will manage. Let's go home, Jack. Home is where you will find your answer."

CHAPTER 29

Howard Preston had dropped Tom and Amy Bruster off at his big mansion, along with the five teenagers, whom Amy had asked to help teach the things they needed to know as well as giving them a place to stay, until they could find proper homes for each one of them. Tom Bruster was happy to pay for anything the young people needed, for having his granddaughter back from the Forbidden Forest in one piece and a more giving young lady. For the first time in her life, Tom could see Amy was now caring about the needs of others and not thinking solely of herself. The grateful grandfather had noticed his granddaughter walking out holding on to the two smallest children's hands and she wasn't wearing her prized cap that caused her capture in the first place. When the thoughtful grandfather asked her about it, she just gave him a soft laugh and said, earthly things were not as important to her anymore. She told him it was time to start laying up her treasures in heaven and give more to the less fortunate.

Amy's parents were amazed at the change in their young daughter, as was her grandmother Helen, who had noticed the change in both her husband and her granddaughter. The only thing the girl insisted on was that the two teenage girls with her would be staying in her old bedroom and the three boys would have the nicest guest room. Amy declared she would be happy staying in the upper attic room until all the young people found families of their own.

Howard Preston had helped Jack carry his things up to his back door. As he set them down, he watched his young friend tumbling with his house keys until he hit the key hold and turned the key to open his door. "Jack, I can see you are still upset son. Just let me stay this first night back, in case you need someone to talk to. My beautiful sweetheart will understand."

"She might understand Howard, because your wife is one of the most caring, unselfish and understanding ladies I have ever known, but friend, I know now how true love works and by now the two of you deed to be together." Jack managed a smile. "Howard, I really appreciate your kind offer, as well everything you have done for me, but what I really need is some rest. This had been a long trying day, which started out with just me and Alisia, lying hugged up in bed, where we had spent the entire night knowing each other. Neither of us closed our eyes in sleep for we both knew this might be our only time for consummating our marriage." He reached a weary hand up to pat his dear friend's arm. "I'm not even going to unpack my things until morning. If I can manage brushing my teeth, taking a quick shower and putting on some fresh Pajamas, then I can get some much-needed sleep so I can be alert to any sign shown me regarding Alisia and WarZar."

"Alright Jack, if you're sure you are going to be alright." Howard took his car keys out of his pocket as he watched Jack set his luggage and backpack inside the door before stopping just inside the open door.

"I'll be fine friend, once I get some sleep. You go on home to that pretty little wife of yours and go to bed." Jack gave Howard a knowing smile. "And if you're not too tired from that long drive back to Graceland with a carload of chattering teens, then show your beloved just how much you missed her."

"I will, you rascal!" Howard walked down the sidewalk and opened the car door. "If you need me for anything Jack, please don't hesitate to give me a call. I'm probably the only one around that understands just what you are going through."

"Yes Howard, I am well aware of that and should I have any news to share with you concerning my beautiful bride and good friend, I'll be sure to give you a call, day or night." Jack tried to cover his yawn.

"Please do Jack, no matter how big or small the clue, we can figure it out. Do call me, son, anytime. I am always there for you." Howard climbed inside his car and drove away as Jack entered his back door and switched on the kitchen light, then laughed softly at the mess he had left behind.

"I'll clean up this mess in the morning along with all my dirt clothes waiting inside my suitcase." Jack made his way to his bedroom and switched on the bedside lamp before going back to cut out the kitchen light. After setting his luggage on the floor near his closet, Jack's gaze fell on his backpack when he remembered the photos that had been taken with his Polaroid camera. He quickly unzipped it and pulled out the items he had placed over them to protect the photos from damage. Jack carefully turned the first picture over and grew emotional as he looked at his big friend's face and could see the love from WarZar looking back. Suddenly the memory of that day filled his mind. WarZar had taken Jack to his secret cave to stay the night. Both men could feel their friendship growing as they made their way to Alisia and Jack had learned so much about his big friend and just how intelligent he really was. Jack propped the photo up and stared at it as he recalled the last moments he had seen his strong friend and how Jack had asked him why he had packed such a small bag to carry out with him.

THAT MORNING, AFTER JACK AND ALISIA HAD COME OUT OF THE HUGE TREE.

"You cannot have much in such a small bag, my friend." Jack looked at the small bag in his big friend's hand. "There cannot be too many favorite things from your home inside such a tiny carrier."

"I have nothing here I wish to take with me Jack, so I gladly leave them all behind for someone else to enjoy, should they learn the secret way around the waterfall." WarZar had a serious expression as he lifted up his light load. "I only carry out my most cherished possessions Jack. The first pictures you made of me and then yourself. My words were true when I said we looked like brothers, my friend, because in my heart, we are."

BACK IN GRACELAND: JACK'S BEDROOM.

"I feel the same way my brother and I long to see you and my dearest Alisia very soon." Jack flipped over the next photo and tears filled his eyes just seeing his enchanting and beautiful wife smiling back. "Oh, my darling, what I would do to have you in my arms tonight. To kiss your sweet lips and make passionate love to my incredible loving bride." He carried the photo to the window and looked out at the starry night, the exact starry night sky he and Alisia had sit under while staying at Rockford falls and had gotten lost in each other's arms. "Alisia, my darling, are you gazing up at the same stars, in that magic place the Lord has taken you? And, if you are my love, are your thoughts about me and the night we shared, not so long ago?" Jack stared up at one bright star that seemed to shine down directly on him. "My love, you are there, I can feel you in the star's beam. I love you Alisia. I will see you soon sweetheart."

THE GARDEN OF EDEN.

The Lord had kept His promise and on the morrow Jesus would

be taking Alisia and WarZar to their new home. After Jesus had guided the beautiful girl to a quiet spot he had her to looked up in the clear blue sky. Alisia watched her Savior with happy love as he waved his hand toward the clear sky and it suddenly fell into a starlit night.

"Sweet sister, even though there is no night in Eden, I made an exception this special day. For night has fallen in Graceland, North Carolina, and the sky there is filled with the same stars we are witnessing.

There is one sad young man looking up as these very stars right now thinking only about the bride he watched disappear from his side. Listen my child and hear what he says." Jack's words flowed lovingly into Alisia's ears. Jesus pointed out her star, the one that fell down on her beloved husband and she gazed up and saw another one that shined down on her.

"It is Jack's love for me, Lord?"

"The love you both share goes beyond this world Alisia, as my angels can testify. Speak your words to Jack and his heart will hear,"

"Jack, my love, I am always close in your heart, as you are with me. I know you are thinking about our night together under these very stars while staying with our dear friend. I miss you too my dearest and I love you. I'll be seeing you soon."

GRACELAND, NORTH CAROLINA

Jack smiled up at the beautiful sky shining with promise and new hope. He knew he would be with his loved ones very soon, but for now, his weary body needed rest. Hope always comes in the morning!"

CHAPTER 30

Jack Spencer slowly opened his rested eyes as he listened to the distant church bells tolling out six o'clock, then the distinct sound of the daily newspaper being tossed on his front porch. He sat up and stretched, feeling well rested and revived after sleeping eight-straight hours. After his usual morning bathroom routine, Jack went to the kitchen to put on a pot of coffee, then gathered all the unwashed dishes in the sink and placed them in the dishwasher, before washing off the countertops and putting things left out, away.

He poured himself a large mug of coffee and after stirring in just the right amount of creamer, he carried it back to his bedroom to start unpacking his suitcase. He opened it and gave a chuckle when he noticed the quick packing by his good friend.

"I can see Howard didn't spend much time sorting these things." He began pulling his soiled hiking clothes out and tossing them in the laundry basket. When he was lifting out his pajamas his hand touched something hard, so he quickly gave them a toss to see what had been laid in the bottom, Jack knew his toiletry case would feel softer and had seen it sticking out through his socks. Brushing his underwear aside, the young minister's eyes fell on the box he had kept the locket in. Being caught up with the normal household chores, he had blocked out his anxious feelings and worries about finding Alisia and WarZar without the locket of love. The last place he had seen it was around his beloved neck and Jack had just assumed it would drop to the ground when she vanished and he would simply place it back around his neck to help guide him to his loved one's whereabouts. Now, everything needing done did not seem important to the young man for once again his heart was aching and all his unanswered questioning returned with the sight of the empty box he looked down on.

"Oh Lord, if only the loving locket was still waiting inside this box and not gone! My beloved did tell me to keep the locket with me! That it would help lead me to her!"

"Jack, did not Alisia also tell you about the locket's great power and that sometimes it would seem invisible to you." Jack had turned at the sound of his friend's familiar voice. Reverend Howard Preston stood holding up the morning newspaper. "I rang the doorbell, but couldn't get you, so I started to knock on the back door and noticed you had left it unlocked last night after you went inside."

"Unlocked?" Jack looked over forlorn and dropped on the bed next to the open suitcase. "I was sorting my dirty clothes and spotted the box I kept the locket in. I guess it just brought reality back to me and the fact that the locket is missing. If only it would just reappear inside this box, but that would require a miracle of its own." Jack picked it up and, believing it to be empty, tossed it behind him and heard a clinking sound inside. Both Jack and Howard exchanged glances as their attention fell on the box. "It can't be Howard! I saw Alisia wearing the locket around her neck so it's impossible for it to just show up inside the same box I brought it in!" Jack picked it back up and gave it a slight shake and he could hear something sliding back and forth inside. "Maybe someone placed something inside as a prank or Tom was helping you and saw the empty box and threw a few of my things inside it."

"Jack, there is only one way to find out son. You must open that box right now so your mind can relax." Howard watched his young friend staring down at the closed lid. "Jack, maybe you're just afraid if you do open the box, you won't see the locket and as long as it remains closed, you feel some hope."

"You're right Howard and I know the odds are almost zero that I will find the heavenly locket waiting inside that box." Jack felt his fingers tremble as he slowly lifted up the lid and let out a gasp when he looked down at the shining gold locket, safely secured inside his box, just as he had packed it from home. "I—I do not understand how this special locket got back inside this box, but praise God, here it is waiting for me to find."

"Jack, maybe the sign you're looking for is inside the locket!" Howard watched his young friend lift the locket out and turned it around in his hand. "Try the cover, son, and see if it will open for you now."

Jack let his finger roll around the top of the cover and suddenly he heard a click, as the lid snapped open to reveal a photo. Howard watched in amazement as the young minister's eyes grew wide with surprise. "I cannot believe it Howard! This is truly a blessing sent from the Lord!"

"What do you see Jack? Is it your Alisia?" Howard had grown excited for his young friend and the need to know just what Jack was staring at was eating away at the older minister.

"Here my friend, see for yourself and you will understand why I am completely overwhelmed." Jack laid the open locket in his long-time friend's hand and Howard merely shook his head, overcome by what he saw. "Howard, this is a picture of my wife and good friend standing on either side of me in front of WarZar's stone mansion."

"WarZar's stone mansion?" Howard lifted the photo up toward the light, to see the magnificent mansion behind the three friends. "Jack, did your beast friend's mansion have a name?"

"Yes Howard, it was named after the enormous waterfall on his private property. He called his self-made mansion, Rockford Falls." Jack titled his head as he watched his old friend studying the photo closely. "Howard, is there a purpose for your asking me this question concerning WarZar's estate?"

"Jack, I have no doubt this is you in the middle, so I know the beautiful young lady is Alisia, because she is exactly the way you described her looking, and the ten-foot man with horns on his head and hoofs for his feet, has to be WarZar, but son, this mansion may look a lot like your friends old home, but I recognize the stone mansion looming up behind all of you and it's not in the Forbidden Forest Jack, it just twenty-miles away from Graceland, in the country side."

Jack grabbed the locket back, jumped up and walked into the kitchen to get a magnifying glass. He went over to the bright window and looked down to see if he could notice a difference in both the mansions. The moment Jack saw the large double front doors, he knew this was not the home WarZar had built with his own bare hands. First, WarZar's big door had been made straight across and the ones in the picture were fancy oval doors and the footing was done in massive handmade bricks. Where his friend had one row of stone steps in front of the door, this mansion had a cut-stone porch floor with three wide steps rising up to the grand portico.

"Howard, are you telling me this magnificent mansion is just out from our town twenty miles? Why haven't I ever known about such a magnificent old place. I have lived here practically all my life."

"Its understandable young people would know nothing about the old Rockford estate, since the last owners didn't wish to share their time or money with the town." Howard saw Jack sit up at the announcement of the family's name. "William and Katherine Rockford moved here in the late 1700's and built the lovely old home on two-hundred acres of good farmland. It had everything a farmer needed to make a great living with his trade. It had lots of green meadows for pastures, streams, a creek and a rushing river, which he named the Rockford River and it was perfect for the grinding wheel in the mill he built, for grinding his own corn for cornmeal and making grain to feed his many chickens and livestock. There was also a bountiful supply of river stone to build his large mansion with, and there was always a never-ending amount of the rocks being smoothed down for everything he wanted, including the long-high wall that surrounded the estates three-hundred acres, to keep his cattle and horses in as well as keeping any noisy neighbor's out. The one great thing that came with his property had always been the main attraction for the citizens of Graceland so with the wall keeping them from seeing it, they could only stand near it by the great wall and listen to its loud roar."

"Howard, I know you cannot be speaking about a mountain lion, these people long to see but can only hear." Jack's heart was beating with anxious anxiety knowing where this was leading. "They were all missing the great waterfall they had always enjoyed watching before this rich man came into their lives and blocked it off for good."

"Yes Jack, and not just an average waterfall, but a very high, free falling, roaring waterfall, also named Rockford Falls." Howard grabbed his weaving friend to steady him, knowing all this description had sounded too familiar to his young friend. "Jack, did WarZar's estate mirror the Rockford Falls Estate, here, near our small town?"

"Howard, not only does it mirror my good friend's place, but it is named the exact thing! You just described Rockford Falls Howard! A very high, free falling, roaring waterfall! It was that scary waterfall that kept everyone in the Forbidden Forest away from us! It helped keep us safe! This has got to be the sign I have been looking for Howard! I am supposed to meet Alisia and WarZar out at the estate!"

"But Jack, the Rockford Falls Estate is still owned by the ancestors of William and Katherine Rockford! Every single one of those Rockford's have kept people out. They only permit workers to come in if they need repairs done on the house or if something breaks down. They still grow most of their food, raise livestock and chickens and as far as I know, still grind at the mill." Howard felt bad over the latest situation and for the first time was unsure of how he could help his friend."

"Howard, I believe with all my heart, our Savior himself, has His hand in this miracle and somehow Jesus has opened the gates for me and my loved ones at this home." Jack self-consciously picked up the morning newspaper and opened it up, letting out a gasp.

"Jack! What have you found in the morning paper?" Howard joined his young friend and stared down at the large print and the bold letters above it. Howard began reading what it announced out loud. "NEW OWNERS! THE ROCKFORD FALLS ESTATE HAS BEEN WILLED TO ELIZABETH AND WARREN ROCKFORD'S ONLY REMAINING KNOWN KIN, WARZAR ROCKFORD, SON OF THE LATE CARMELA ROCKFORD. THE PREVIOUS OWNERS HAD SEARCHED FOR THE LAST REMAINING FAMILY MEMBER FOR SOME TIME. FINALLY FINDING HIM, THEY WILLED THE ENTIRE ESTATE IN HIS NAME BEFORE PASSING AWAY AT THE RIPE OLD AGES OF 100 AND 101. THE NEW OWNERS SHOULD ARRIVE SOMETIME THIS MORNING AND PLANS TO RE-OPEN THE WALL NEAR THE GREAT FALLS FOR THE TOWN'S CITIZENS TO ENJOY AGAIN! GIVE PRAISES TO THE LORD, FOR HE IS GOOD! NEVER FORGET JOY COMES IN THE MORNING!"

"The locket led me to the place I will find my beloved wife and dear friend, WarZar!" Jack grabbed his old friend in a bear hug, at last feeling new life inside him. "Howard, I must not wait another moment! Can you tell me how to get to Rockford Falls from here?" Jack laughed. "Better still, how would my dear friend like to go with me and meet my beautiful bride and great friend and brother?"

"Son, I would like nothing more!" Howard walked quickly to keep up with his excited young friend. "This has been a long time coming, Jack! Did you ever dream when you left on that scout trip with me twenty years ago, it would come to this?"

"Never in a million years, Howard! I was just a happy young boy going to another adventure with my favorite scout leader and preacher." Jack opened his car door and started the motor. "I never imagined I would end up inside the Forbidden Forest with the most incredible young woman I have ever seen, much less fall in love at ten years old. Then hear the screams and loud threats from WarZar, only to wind up being best friends and brothers." Jack smiled over at his mentor. "Life certainly has a way of turning things around sometimes, doesn't it?"

"When its God's plan Jack, yes it does! This was supposed to be your destination all alone, to meet Alisia, fall in love and have deep

212

feeling for the man you once feared. All, so you would return when you were older to save his lost people and help his righteous ones to freedom, along with the young man trapped inside a horrible beastly body."

"I wonder if I will be the first to arrive at Rockford Falls mansion. This modern world might take some getting used to for both Alisia and WarZar." Jack drove down the tranquil country road. "Isn't it funny Howard? I have driven down this country road many times but never realized there was such a place as Rockford Falls Estate just off this road.

"I'm sure you probably saw their gate well hidden by the overgrown trees and scrubs and thought it was just an old, abandoned place, forgotten over the years of neglect." Howard smiled over at his young friend. "It is exactly twenty miles from town so it should be coming into view so you best slow down so we don't pass it."

Jack slowed down, but the old gate was no longer overtaken by overgrowth, but had been trimmed down neatly, probably for the new owners and the old gate now shined like brand-new and stood wide open, to welcome the new owners.

"I cannot hardly recognize the place, Jack!" Howard looked up at the shiny gate and down the long-tree line driveway, that seemed to go out of sight. "Someone has really done a lot of work in here since I've been down this road."

"It certainly looks like they have made it welcoming for WarZar. Let's drive in and see if they are here yet." Jack drove through the gate and down the long-winding tree line drive until he came to a large stone courtyard and pulled his car around to the front of the exquisite mansion standing four floors high and stretched out from end to end. "Dang! This thing is huge!" He climbed out along with his friend, who looked up and around with total amazement.

"It seems to be pretty quiet around here Jack. Maybe you did get here first." Howard thought he saw motion to his right and glanced over to see a tall handsome young man walking around the side of the large mansion. "Jack, we have company."

Jack turned to see who his old friend had spotted and he saw him for the first time as he described himself in the recurring dream he had kept having and asked Jack to tell it's meaning. Jack took two steps toward him, tears filling his loving eyes as he called out. "WarZar! My friend! My brother! You're home!"

"Jack!" The tall handsome prince ran across the manicured lawn

213

into his friend's arms. "Jack, when the Lord told us He would be taking us home, I never dreamed it would be to my new Rockford Falls!" WarZar still had the same loud laugh, but now the handsome man stood 7' 8" with no horns or hooves, just a thick head of long hair and average feet for man his height. "Look at me brother, just like my dream!"

"Yes, I can see! We really could pass for brothers now my friend!" Jack grabbed the tall man again in a brotherly hug. "Wait until my sister gets a load of you friend. All those movie stars she's being eyeing out in Hollywood will seem to lose their glow after she sees you, my friend!"

"Then, I look forward to meeting my new dream girl real soon Jack. We will be keeping the romance in our family, right Jack?" WarZar laughed out and noticed the man who had arrived with his friend. "Let me guess! You are Reverend Preston, right?"

"Why, yes, I am. Did Jack tell you about me and that I would be waiting for him to come out of your forest?" Howard already liked Jack's friend and understood the close connection they felt for each other. "I'm glad to finally meet you WarZar. I heard a great many of your scary screams before though, several times when I was the young scout who was in the end cabin and then when I brought Jack back as one of my young scouts."

"That's right! Little Howard Preston, the small boy shaking under his sheets inside the cabin next to the woods. And I thank you for bringing ten-year-old Jack to Eagle Nest Howard. That was the best thing that has ever happened to me." The handsome prince could not resist hugging Jack's old scout leader and pastor. "Thank you for your loyalty to my very best friend. Well, besides Alisia, my only friend. Defiantly my first friend ever!"

"I can see the loving friendship you both share WarZar and I am certain God brought you two together." Howard could see his young friend looking around. "WarZar, I believe our Jack is looking for his young bride." He noticed the tall man smile and nod his head in agreement. "Do you know where she is?"

"Yes, I do." WarZar looped his arm around Jack shoulders and spoke close to his ear. "There is a songbird waiting in the rose garden for her mate. Just go in the direction I came from, Jack, and you will find your beloved waiting for her husband."

"Thank you, friend. I do love you!" Jack smiled up at him and almost ran toward the back of the big mansion to find Alisia.

CHAPTER 31

Once Jack found his way around the big house, he noticed the massive walled-in garden that stretched far behind the large stone mansion. Going through the open gate, he looked around for any sign of his young bride among the paths that ran down rows of colorful rose bushes. Jack noticed marble benches, tucked away inside of archways and niche's, along the garden path. Hearing the sound of running water, Jack knew a fountain had to be near, so he continued down the long span until he saw the spectacular fountain, consisting of angels with great water pitchers, pouring out the gift of the Lord's promise in supplying His living water. The crystal-clear water that poured gracefully from the six angel's water pitchers fell into a large pond of living fish, with Lilly-pads floating around in an array of colors Still, Jack could see no sign of Alisia and thought she might have gone inside the large mansion before he came around.

Jack stopped suddenly when he heard the voice of an angel singing nearby and knew right away it was his little songbird lifting her praise up to the heavens. Picking up his pace, Jack found himself in a grove of full-grown Formosa trees and standing directly in the middle of the bright blossoms stood his beautiful Alisia, dressed in a long white dress, her long blonde tresses blowing in the morning breeze. Seeing her at last and looking as she had in the forest, Jack stood taking in her incredible beauty and listening to her enchanting voice, afraid if he moved or spoke out loud, he would wake up from a beautiful realistic dream.

Suddenly feeling she was not alone, Alisia Solomon grew silent and turned slowly around, her eyes falling on the man she had been waiting for. A big, happy smile fell on her luscious lips as she picked up her skirt-tails and race over into Jack's awaiting arms. "Jack! My dearly beloved! Have you been here long, dearest? Why did you not greet your wife the moment you saw me? Was it my song that froze the words in your handsome mouth or did the sight of me bring confusion to your sight, as I look just as you remembered?"

"I was but afraid I might still be dreaming and this place with such a storybook garden was just my imagination." Jack held his bride close to his chest, feeling relieved to know everything he had witnessed that incredible day was a real God moment. "Your song did enchant me, my beloved, and all the while standing inside these flowering trees you and your mother loved so well. As for your perfect appearance, never have I seen a more beautiful woman as you Alisia and the sight of you took my breath away, so another reason for my mute voice."

"As for you, my wonderful husband, you grow ever more handsome each time we are together." Alisia smiled up at his incredibly good-looking face. "Speaking of handsome, what do you think of our dear friend WarZar's looks? With the horns and hoofs gone along with his great height, he will have no trouble finding a mate now."

"And I have told WarZar of the perfect woman for him and he cannot wait to meet my younger sister Veronica." Jack gazed down at their empty ring fingers and knew their hurried wedding didn't afford wedding bands and without a legal marriage license, they would not be considered married by law.

"My darling has grown quiet and his mind seems far away." Alisia had noticed her husband checking out their left hands and considered what his reasons could mean. "What are you thinking Jack? I know it has something to do with our rushed wedding. I can assure you sweetheart, daddy did not leave anything out and you and I are very much married."

Jack gave his young wife a reassuring smile. "Alisia, my beautiful wife, I am having no doubts about our wedding vows being complete, but our government might have a hard time believing how and where we got married and by whom. And, with no marriage license to prove our perfect wedding day, we need to have another ceremony just to make it legal with today's laws." Jack pulled her into his warm embrace. "It won't change the real fact that we are husband and wife, sweetheart, but to legally take my last name and start a family, claiming property as a married couple, we need a marriage license." He glanced down into her luminous eyes. "It would not be all that bad to get married a second time to the woman I love and have another wedding night together again. Only this time, we need not worry about being separated anymore. So, what does my bride think about another beautiful wedding and this time in the house of God."

"A church wedding sounds wonderful Jack! Your good friend Reverend Howard Spencer can perform the ceremony. The same young scout I saw before you came to Black Forest years later. "I wish mother was here to sing for us. Maybe my message to her about singing a song for me and sending it down on the wings of a dove will be our wedding gift from heaven. Father did say he and mama would be looking down at all our happy moments and share in our blissful celebration."

"That would certainly be a heavenly blessing for our special day and I am sure Howard would be honored to perform the wedding for us." Jack was happy his different century bride understood about the modern laws regarding marriage. "Howard and I both preach at Grace Moravian Church, so the congregation would wish for us to be wed there so they could all attend." Jack glanced down humbly. "I don't wish to brag dear, but everyone at Grace Moravian adores their ministers and would bend over backwards to please them. So, this means the Moravian women would want to give us a big wedding reception after the ceremony and I'm certain there will be plenty of wedding gifts to open, unless we choose the loving people to donate a small gift to a worthy charity, such as Graceland Home for the orphan children or Forever Young at Heart, a retirement community for the less fortunate senior citizen."

"Since I'm not used to receiving a lot of gifts darling, maybe we could help both places you named. Small-helpless children need kindness and loving care as does our older family of friends." Alisia's family had always been known for helping out the less fortunate, even if it meant giving some poor-hungry soul their last loaf of homemade bread.

"I have married not only a beautiful songbird with the voice of an angel, but a kind and giving young lady with a big heart for anyone in need." Jack took her hand and began walking to the garden gate. "Alisia, I did not come here alone, so there is someone I want you to meet."

"You brought Howard with you, did you not?" She smiled up as they made their way from the large garden and around the big mansion. "Is he waiting next to your carriage darling?"

"He is waiting around the front Alisia but I didn't exactly arrive here driving a carriage." He chuckled at her confused face. "I came here in my car, one of today's transportations for getting around."

"A car?" Alisia wrinkled her brow. "Is that some kind of a cart, with seats?"

"My car is absolutely nothing like anything you knew in the

217

1800's." Jack stopped when the car came in sight and he pointed at the white BMW parked out in the front." There it is honey, my 2019 automobile."

"Jack, has someone already unhooked your horses from your car?" She walked up and stared at the front. "Just how do you hook your horses to this strange carriage?"

Howard and WarZar had stopped speaking when Jack brought Alisia around to show her his car. Howard placed his hand over his mouth to hold in his laughter.

"Alisia darling, you cannot see this car's horses. They are all under the hood." Jack slapped the car hood and winked at his old friend smiling over.

"Jack, do not make jokes like that! You expect me to believe there is actually horses under this thing you call a hood?" Hearing Howard laugh out, she glanced over, noticing him and WarZar watching with interest. "WarZar, did you know this strange looking carriage puts it horses on the inside?"

"Alisia, I do believe dear Jack is pulling our leg!" The handsome prince shook his head at his best friend. "Jack, Alisia and I know not even one horse can fit under that piece of metal!"

"Not just one horse my friend, but 425 horses!" Jack bit his lip to keep from laughing at their expressions as his glamorous wife gave him a playful slap on the arm.

"Jack! Tell us how this strange carriage runs without the aid of at least four-strong horses!" she took a deep breath. "WarZar and I know you cannot be serious about 425 horses hidden under that top!"

"And there aren't 425 real horses underneath this car hood, there is just one very large motor, another invention, first called the horseless carriage, the later the automobile or car, maybe a truck, which is built to haul things around in place of the horse drawn wagon, like WarZar had."

"Still has, Jack! I have been searching inside my many new barns and have found not only different length wagons but three handsome carriages with which I can attach a few of the many horses that graze the pastures just beyond the big red barn!" WarZar laughed now at Jack's expression. "So, who needs this horseless carriage when I can use the real thing! Right Alisia?"

"I do enjoy riding in a carriage. It will bring a little familiarity in my new world life." Alisia gathered her husband's hand and walked over by Howard Preston. "It is finally good to meet you Howard.

You have grown into a handsome man since your shy scout days in the Black Forest. You were a part of God's plan my friend, to become a minister and help rear a young Jack Spencer into the man he has become. Jack has told me how you have been his mentor and good friend, helping him at every turn to get to where we have come." Alisia walked into his arms and gave him a warm hug. "We could not have done all of this without you Howard, so thank you dear friend and God bless you with great health and a long life."

"Jack was right about you Alisia. You and he will make the perfect life together." His attention went to the tall friend, waiting with his head down, "And I know the two of you will always have room in your heart for your dear friend and brother WarZar." Howard smile at the handsome man when he looked over smiling.

"Howard, Jack and Alisia are my family now and I want them to move in with me so we can be together all the time." WarZar felt Jack place his arm around his shoulders and the tall friend pulled the young minister in close. "I will give them the rooms of their choice and plenty of private moments." He laughed.

"Besides, I too will have a mate one day and our rooms will be at the other end of this grand mansion, where we can enjoy our own private moments."

"All of that sounds wonderful for each one of you so whenever you meet that right lucky girl young man, I would be honored to perform your wedding." He glanced at his young friend and the beautiful girl standing next to himself. "I guess we need to have a redo of your wedding vows as well Jack, just to make it legal in today's society."

"You practically read our minds Howard." Alisia gave him her beautiful smile, then kept it for Jack. "Jack and I decided to get married again inside Grace Moravian Church and let you do our ceremony this time. It would make us very happy Howard."

"Alisia is right Howard and" Jack smiled up at his tall friend. "Once my brother here meets my sister Veronica, there may just be a double wedding. That is, if they hit it off as well as I believe they will." An ideal was building in Jack's mind. "And to move things along, I will send for my active-adventurous sister and have her fly out immediately to meet my new best friend. I will inform her if she does not act swiftly, another pretty single gal will be giving my friend the make."

"The make?" WarZar wrinkled his brow, unsure of this new

word. "Just what would this young lady be doing, Jack?"

"Flirting with my very strong and handsome friend. Trying all her feminine tricks to make you fall in love with her." Jack laughed when the tall prince grunted.

"Female tricks? Sort of like Carmela did to Lazar, to get him all crazy about her?"

"Well, she won't use enchantments or stir up witch's brew." Jack laughed along with Howard and Alisia.

"Dear friend, what my funny husband is trying to say is, when certain women see a man they want, they will dress with fewer clothes and rub their hands up and down your back." Alisia noticed both ministers had stopped laughing and were eyeing her seriously, causing her to laugh. "I saw one such women on the stage once doing that very thing to make the male actor notice her and fall for her. I personally would never stoop to such bad behavior."

"Alisia, my love. You think that is bad behavior? I can tell you women today do far worse things to gain a man's attention, but I know my sister and she is nothing like I described." Jack gave his old friend a knowing smile, since Howard had known Veronica for as long as he had known Jack. "Wouldn't you agree Howard?"

"WarZar, Jack's beautiful sister is a very special young lady and she will come here thinking she will be the one being wanted and desired by you instead of her falling head over hills and have the need to chase after you instead." Howard laughed at the notion of this outgoing young woman finally seeing someone she really wants instead of being the one wanted. "I cannot wait to see how Veronica reacts when she lays her eyes on WarZar."

"Well, I know she already has my heart, Howard." The tall prince noticed both Howard and Alisia staring at him after his bold statement about being in love with a woman he had never met. "Listen, I know it sounds ridicules, but after Jack describe his sister to me, I had a dream about her and I was trying hard to catch the runaway beauty as she kept shouting, 'catch me if you can, Zar baby'."

"Zar baby?" Howard glanced over at Jack. "Did you by any chance mention how your sister puts baby at the end of everyone's name? "

"Not until WarZar told me about his dream about Veronica and her calling him that." Jack looked up at the big house. "Have you both been inside yet to see what it looks like?"

"No Jack, Alisia and I have been waiting for the rest of our family to arrive so we could all tour it together for the first time." WarZar held up the big brass key. "The key to the door! Shall we go and check out our new dwelling place?"

"Howard, do you have time to take the tour? I know it's large, but I feel sure my old friend has always wandered just how it looked inside as well as outside." Jack patted his old friend's back. "What do you say friend? Are you needed back home yet?"

"I told my beautiful flower that I might be late, so I would love to check out the inside of your new home, dear friends."

"Great!" WarZar stepped up to the arched door with the lock and placed the big key inside. "My family, welcome home!"

CHAPTER 32

The four touring the large mansion could not believe its size as they went from room to room, floor to floor and after about two hours of looking over massive rooms with high ceilings, filled with the best furniture money could buy, mostly antiques, they came down to the entrance hall.

Jack noticed Howard looking at this watch and knew he was probably getting anxious to go home. Taking Alisia's hand, Jack made his way over to his old friend. "I know you must be wanting to get back to my place for your car Howard. I need to take Alisia and WarZar out shopping anyway for a few things to wear and personal items they may need. It will give me time to pack a few of my things, before I return later to clear out my things for the next renter."

Before Howard could object, Alisia gave her husband a happy smile, knowing she had some happy news to share with the man she loved. "You will not need to take me and WarZar shopping for anything Jack, the rooms we chose had closets loaded with beautiful dresses and sleeping gowns. The drawers in the vanity I picked is filled with pretty silk unties and petticoats."

Jack laughed out. "My big friend will look pretty ridiculous wearing beautiful dresses and dainty lady's underwear!"

"Jack Spencer, I was describing my large wardrobe, yours and WarZar are very masculine! Everything a fine gentleman requires!" she narrowed her eyes as he continued to laugh. "Now what is so hysterical?"

"Those clothes where left here by the old owners darling and unless you want the three of us to be wearing outdated fashions, we need to go shopping."

"Jack Spencer, you have not even looked at your wardrobe yet, but I have and I do believe they are your own clothes!"

"My clothes? Here, in one of the large closets in our room?" Jack studied her face to see if she was making everything up. "I'd say, those things belong to one William Rockford and since he up and died, he does not need them anymore, so there they hang, waiting for a costume party."

"Jack, are you or are you not wearing the locket of love?" Alisia

222

finally got his serious attention. "That is right my darling husband, you witness for yourself the power of the locket and my guess is that is how your clothes have ended up here." Alisia reached up and patted his serious face. "You did find the locket Jack, did you not? How else could you have known to come here to find us?"

"After you disappeared when we stepped out of the Forbidden Forest, I searched the ground frantically, thinking it would slip off your beautiful neck if you suddenly vanished but quickly learned you must have kept it on you. I was beside myself with worry, thinking it would be impossible to find you if the locket was missing. I knew it was a big part of my finding out where the Lord had taken you and WarZar, especially after Howard said he had watched everyone come out and how those who went to heaven would turn into dust that swirled around where they had stood as their souls entered into the new heavenly bodies and floated up toward heaven's open veil."

"Jack's right Alisia. I also saw the veil close behind your father, Reverend Solomon and the others, while you and WarZar simply disappeared, leaving nothing behind." Howard heard a horn blow and smiled at his young friend who had faced him quickly. "Jack, I called my wife to come here and pick me up so you could spend your time with your wife and good friend." The loving minister knew his young friend would reject, feeling the need to return his friend back where he brought him from. "And Jack, before you get upset for my going behind your back to get a ride back to your house, I did it also so I could show my kitten, my nickname for my sweetheart, your rental house since we promised our son to help find a small starter house for him and his new bride Betsey." Howard gave Alisia a quick hug and patted Jack's back. "Whenever you're ready to move your things, we can give you a hand."

"Listen Howard, most of my furnishings are practically new and as you have seen, I won't need them here." Jack walked his old friend to the front door. "If Jason and Betsey like my things, I want them to have them, as a wedding present. Alisia says my clothes are already here, angels I supposed, sparked on by the power in the locket." Jack laughed and opened the door, then waved at the beauty woman waiting for Howard. "I'll take my family for a ride over to the house and check out what has been left behind, then I'll call Fred Womble and tell him he has a new renter."

"Jack, you let me speak to Mr. Womble for you, son. You have enough to do planning that perfect wedding and playing matchmaker." Howard Preston gave him one last smile before heading for his wife's car, got in and they drove away.

"I really like your friend Howard darling." Alisia waved as they drove out of sight. "So, that's how a horseless carriage works!"

"And, it's a whole lot smoother on your backside as well. I'll take you and WarZar for a drive in the morning, but for now, we have some catching up to do in the bedroom."

Later that evening, the three friends had finished eating a very good meal prepared by the household cooks, that had been waiting inside along with the maids and butler. Due to the oversize-drafty house, a warm fire had been started in the large living quarters where the friends had settled down to talk and were interrupted by someone banging the door knocker loudly. Jack started to get up when the butler waved him back down.

"Permit me sir. I shall see who is at the door." He walked out, his back straight, face serious as he opened the door. "Oh, Mr. Baker, it is you." He took the man's hat and hung it on the gold hat tree, then led him to the new owner. "Mr. Rockford, sir, there is a Mr. Stanly Baker here sir, the Rockford's attorney from Graceland."

"WarZar, Mr. Rollins, is speaking to you." Jack could tell by his friend's looking around for the person named Rockford, he was confused over the butler's announcement.

"Oh! You are speaking to me Rollins!" WarZar noticed Jack rise up from his seat, so he did the same and waved the stranger in. "Please, Mr. Baker, come in and join us. We were just discussing this huge house with just three, well hopefully four people soon, living here."

"There are all of us here as well, Lord Rockford." The butler took a step back when the tall man whipped his head around at him. "Did I say something to disturb you sir?"

"Rollins, there is just one Lord, and I promise you I am not good enough to share his title. Just call me WarZar, like everyone else!"

"Yes sir, whatever pleases you, WarZar," he said cautiously. "I will leave so you gentlemen can talk." The serious man slipped quickly from the room, while the lawyer removed some papers and something resembling an old scroll. The entire time he did this, he kept looking at the only familiar face in the large room.

"Reverend Spencer, I was not aware you knew any of the Rockford's. Yet, here you are, sitting in their grand living room." The lawyer smiled over at his friendly minister. "To be honest pastor,

I am really happy you are here to witness these strange documents for yourself." The hefty lawyer's attention went on the new owner of the Rockford Falls Estate and gave a nervous laugh. "What I am about to say young man, means no disrespect or comparison to you sir. Ever since the Rockford family moved here, decades ago, they have all been a strange lot. Walling in their big estate to keep all the friendly citizens out and only allowing workers living outside our fair town to come in to repair what got broken or needed replacing. They sold their beef, pork and chickens to neighboring towns as well as produce from their gardens and orchards, grain and cornmeal from their mill, but not one thing in Graceland. It was as if they had a vendetta against the entire town." Mr. Baker fumbled with his stack of papers. "Needless to say, I was flabbergasted when I received a call from the last Mr. Rockford, asking me to handle their estate will to their only living heir. A young man they never met but had heard a great deal about from his mother Carmela."

"Do you know when Carmela spoke to her relatives concerning her son, Stanly?" Jack sit up on the edge of his chair, wondering if she had actually came here or just called them.

"As a matter of fact, Jack WarZar's mother was here at the estate two years ago, telling her cousins about her big powerful son." Once again, the lawyer checked the tall handsome man out. "Her description of you, was somewhat over exaggerated WarZar. Carmela Rockford swore that her son, a prince, was a giant, stood 10 ft tall, with great horns protruding from his head and walked on hoofs instead of feet." He gave WarZar a smile. "Your ancestors would have approved a beast living in the grand mansion, since the ceiling were extra tall. I, for one, like the man I see much better."

"So, you're saying the Rockford's knew about my friend's old appearance and would have preferred him as half-man and half-animal?" Jack and WarZar exchanged glances before the tall prince spoke up to calm the big-eyed lawyer, now shocked by the reality that WarZar had been this incredible giant his mother had described.

"They may have preferred the old me better Mr. Baker, but the Lord and I preferred me more human." Ready to change the subject, WarZar pointed at the stack of papers the lawyer was gripping tightly. "Are those papers for me Mr. Baker?"

Stanly Baker snapped out of his trance and looked down at the papers shaking in his fingers. "Oh, these papers! Yes, yes, they are things that might interest you and your friends." The lawyer laid all but one letter aside and gave a nervous laugh. "And maybe one of you could in light me as to what some of these things mean."

"Sure Stanly. Would the one you're holding be from the previous owners?" Jack got up and moved over next to one of his church members and pulled up a chair to have a closer look. "This looks like the will WarZar. It certainly is short and to the point. "All our belongings, land, mansion and all there in, livestock consisting of horses, beef cattle, pigs, and chickens, all out buildings along with the mill, every item inside all barns and outbuildings, fields, gardens, pastures, streams, creek and the Rockford River with its great waterfall, everything seen on the Rockford estate goes to WarZar Rockford for as long as he lives, then he must pass it over to his first-born son." Jack gave his tall friend a wink. "It's now legally yours my friend."

"Now Jack, this letter is from WarZar's mother Carmela for her son, should he be found." Stanly handed the letter to Jack as he shook his head. "This is one of those strange things I was referring to earlier. I cannot read the private contents, but the outside is clearly marked by these words: Please give this to my precious son should he leave the home where he belongs."

"Stanly, I do not see anything wrong with her words. Carmela sounds like she fears her son might find a reason to leave his homeland, the place where she too dwells but as long as she gets help from her dark friend, she can leave the forest while others are trapped inside, she assumes forever, including her son WarZar." Jack glanced back at her words. "She has merely asked her cousins to hand her son the letter for her should he leave and come there."

"Jack, although I cannot understand what the devil you are talking about where Carmela can get out from some forest when everyone else is trapped inside and can never leave." His nervous finger pointed at the date. "It's the date Jack! That is what gives me the willies!"

Jack stared down at the date, written in Carmela's hand, then over at Alisia and WarZar. "This was the very last time Carmela could have gotten out! The date is for this past Saturday morning! Somehow, she managed to sneak out, come all the way here in fast spirit form, and leave the letter with one of the staff members, due to both Rockford's being buried weeks before."

"You said the very last time she could have gotten out! Did the woman die after she came here?" The lawyer was even more confused.

"Stanly, have you ever heard about a place called the Forbidden Forest?" Alisia had stayed quiet long enough. "Legends have been passed down through many centuries, telling how people go inside the evil forest but have never returned. Satan trapped one of his demons inside that forest many years ago and he has captured everyone who stepped over the forbidden line. Once inside, they are trapped just like the demon, due to Satan's invisible blocking shield. Carmela is my half-sister, earlier adopted as a baby by my loving father, who thought the baby was his, then found out her mother was a practicing witch, like she became. Her dark friend my husband told you about is Lucifer, who she befriended and he offered to help her get Lazar, the demon, to fall for her and making her his queen. The demon and the wicked witch drank a strong brew, stirred up by Carmela and nine months later, our friend WarZar was born. My evil sister has become trapped inside herself this time by the power of the Almighty God that help all of us trapped inside to freedom."

"Wow, that is quite a story!" Stanly Baker had sat quietly listening to the beautiful young woman explain why it had been the last time they had seen Carmela Rockford. "Then if Carmela was a witch and her husband was a demon when they had you, WarZar, how did you escape the devils trap?"

"By finding a friend who sincerely loved me and taught me about the Savior, Jesus Christ." WarZar glanced over at Jack, brotherly love radiating from the handsome man's face. "Jack and Alisia taught me how to be a Christian and how to love others."

"Without my big friend's help Stanly, I would have never been able to carry out the will of God and get all those good souls out." Jack looked at his church member seriously. "WarZar did appear just as his mother had told the Rockford's, 10-foot-tall, horns and hoofs, but as his lawyer Stanly, you do not need to tell this to anyone else. The only thing the citizens of Graceland need to know is WarZar Rockford is a prince and heir to the vast fortunes of the late Rockfords and he has shown his love for the children of God by making the Rockford Falls open for everyone to enjoy."

"Your story is safe with me, young WarZar." The lawyer lifted up the scroll, his eyebrow arched in question. "The Rockford's hired me some time ago to find their lost heir and we were having no luck until Carmela showed up. She never said how she had found out about the long search, but one day she just appeared at the front door, complete with family records. After she left, we realized she failed to tell us how to reach her son, then this scroll showed up and the only address it had on the outside was, Zion! There are just a few places in the states named Zion and after searching the smaller ones I contacted Zion, Utah and no one seem to know how a scroll got mailed off or just who would be sending such an outdated thing."

"Then it must have come straight from the real Zion Stanly, since the Lord was the only one who knew our plans." Jack tried not to laugh at Stanly Baker's shocked expression. "What did the heavenly message say?"

"It simply said, written in old script, 'We know the whereabouts of thy heir and will gladly inform him, and bring with haste the new owner of the land.'" Stanly glanced at Jack's two friends. "I got a call from Rollins this morning informing me that Mr. Rockford had just arrived and was waiting outside with a Mrs. Spencer for her husband to get there." The church member just stared at his younger minister. "Jack, when did you get married? No one even knew you had been dating."

"That is because I hadn't been dating Stanly. I met my bride twenty-years-ago when I got trapped inside the Forbidden Forest." Jack did not wish to discuss how his beautiful wife could be so young unless she was just a child when they met. "Forget trying to figure up the math Stanly, just know Alisia and I fell in love and planned to get married when I returned to save her." To change the subject, Jack added. "As for how Carmela found out you were looking for her son to become heir, the one who informed her was Lucifer, who must have been pretty proud of the Rockford's family behavior until the last heir came along with the aid of our Lord."

"Well then, this news will be both appreciated and sad. Appreciated for a friendly owner, but sad for all the single ladies in our church who have been trying to get your eye ever since you became Reverend Preston's second in the pulpit." He turned his attention on the tall new owner. "But there is still hope for one lucky young lady WarZar. You will be the talk of the town and all the available ladies will be seeking you out! You have what it takes to make women flock! Great looks, muscular and well-built as well as the richest man in town." The lawyer passed the handsome prince the legal papers to sign after Jack had read over them. "I'd even go to say, women from every state will be sending you their personal information along with photos. Just get yourself a computer and log on to Facebook!"

"Stanly, that won't be necessary brother. My sister is coming in tomorrow morning and those two will be a match made in heaven." Jack gave his tall friend a playful wink. "If anyone can tame my kid sister down, it's that guy."

"Veronica is a good match for you WarZar! That will leave many heart-broken women in town, but you cannot fight love." The lawyer put away all his papers and zipped up his briefcase. "I never considered your showbiz sister Jack. I guess I assumed she was planted in Hollywood, always the beautiful face behind the movie camera."

"All it takes my friend, is the right man to come along and finally turn her head away from that camera." Jack put his arm around his bride, wanting this meeting to end so they could finally go up to bed. "If that's all Stanly, I'll show you out. I know this has been a long day for all of us."

"Yes, I must admit this has been a most interesting day and I can see you all must be tired, so I can see myself out Jack, as I have done many times in the past." Mr. Baker walked to the door. "Enjoy your new home WarZar." His attention went to his young minister holding tight to his pretty wife. "And you two as well. I'm sure WarZar welcomes your company in such a huge mansion. See you at Church on Sunday, Jack?"

"We will be there Stanly." Jack stood up and walked toward the door. "Goodnight then."

"I'm off! Goodnight to you all!" The lawyer left the house and the three friends moved up the wide staircase to their rooms. WarZar to dream about his new mate coming in the morning in something Jack had called an airplane and the loving couple to finally be in each other's arms again after their time apart.

CHAPTER 33

The three friends were seated around a large round table in a bright airy room the butler had called, the breakfast room, waiting on the servants to bring out their morning meal. WarZar watched in wonder as the young servant girl brought out a tray filled with three large plates, loaded with country ham, scrambled eggs, fancy hash browns, fresh fruit, croissants with butter and honey. Not used to gratitude, the pretty girl paused after each person seated told her thank you, and had sincere smiles on their faces. After she had set down her last plate, she returned a smile to them, suddenly feeling happy with her job in the big house.

"You are all welcome. My name is Greta, so if you need anything, just ring the bell at your place and I will see to you. Please, enjoy your breakfast."

"I am sure we will Greta." WarZar watched Alisia pick up the white cloth and lay it across her lap, so he did the same. "You seem to be very young Greta. Have you already finished your schooling?"

"My schooling." The petite young girl smiled down shyly. "I have graduated high school sir, but couldn't afford college, although I could never have gone anyway. My mother worked here as a servant until she slipped and fell, and the doctor told her she'd have to stop working, so I replaced her. My father died when I was five so I needed to work to pay our bills."

"Miss Greta, please stop bothering Mr. WarZar and his friends while they are trying to have their breakfast!" Mr. Rollins had walked past the breakfast room and caught the young server chatting about her family troubles. "You need not worry the new owner with your pitiful family crisis!"

"Mr. Rollins, will you lighten up on Greta." WarZar could see his parents in this man and he knew if he remained his head butler, Rollins would have to change his attitude. "I asked the girl a question and she was polite enough to give me an answer. You will find I prefer all my helpers to be friends and find me easy to work for and speak to. That includes you Rollins! So, if I see you acting like my hateful parents again, I must let you go! Do you understand?"

"Yes sir, you like a friendly person, well behaved and not bossy."

The Butler relaxed, suddenly glad for the change. "Greta, please except my apology and if you are finished with your story, you may return to the kitchen." He gave a bow and walked out.

"Greta, go on back to your job for now, but please stop worrying where your money will come from to pay those bills." WarZar stood up, walked over and patted her head, like he used to do Jack. "When you finish your day's work, find the college you wish to attend and let you precious mother know all her bills will get paid as well as someone to attend to her needs while you're away getting your education."

So, overcome with joyful emotion, young Greta threw her arms around WarZar's waist. "God bless you WarZar! I promise when I become a doctor, I will repay you for everything!"

"Just become the best physician you can young lady and help make God's sick children get well!" The tall handsome man turned her toward the kitchen, "Now fetch us some more of that great stuff called coffee!" he smiled when she took off laughing.

"Dear friend, that was the most generous thing I have ever witness from a rich man." Jack smiled over at his good friend after he sat back down and started eating. "How do you like our country breakfast WarZar? Did you realize the meat on your plate is pork?"

"Dang It is!" WarZar suddenly remembered what he wanted to ask Jack. "Jack, you never did tell me and Alisia how you knew where to find us."

"You are right brother!" Jack picked up his coffee cup when Greta came out with a fresh pot and refilled their coffee before going back to the kitchen. "I guess it was all the excitement of seeing you both again, then taking the tour of our grand mansion. I had thought Alisia disappeared with the locket around her neck."

"And I did Jack." Alisia gave him her beautiful smile. "Then after we arrived at Eden, Jesus asked me to give it to Him, so I did without question. I supposed somehow the Lord would make sure you got it back darling. So, did you?"

"After I got home, I was both sad and worn out over the long day and not getting any sleep the previous night, for obvious reasons." Jack heard his big friend laugh and gave him a knowing smile. "I did not unpack my large suitcase that had been left at the cabin until yesterday morning and that's when I saw the box I had kept the locket in. Just looking at the empty box sitting closed the way I had left it when I took the locket out and hung it around my neck, made be depressed again. Howard showed up with the morning paper and finally talked me into opening the box, because when I picked it up and tossed it on the bed behind me I heard something inside it sliding around. I did open the box and was shocked to see the locket had been placed back inside. When I took it out, the cover finally snapped open and once again I looked down with wonder at the three of us standing in front of a rock mansion." Jack knew he had both their attention because they had stopped eating and were waiting for his next statement. "I thought it was taken at WarZar's rock mansion in the Forbidden Forest until Howard pointed out the arched doors and three steps instead of just one step."

"Did Howard know about this Rockford Falls mansion, Jack?" Alisia was trying to come to terms with how the Lord made a photo of the three friends standing in front of a house they had never been to until yesterday.

"Howard knew all about this old stone mansion but had only seen pictures of it. After finding the locket with the photo of me standing in the middle of you two on either side, I absentmindedly opened the morning newspaper and the Rockford Falls Mansion and write-up about the new owner was on the front page. Howard knew the way here so we got in my car and drove straight out!" Jack removed the locket and handed it to his bride.

Alisia passed it over to WarZar, who looked down shaking his head. "This is defiantly the work of the Lord! You did say once, with God, nothing is impossible, so here we are standing on the stone steps outside this big mansion, and neither of us knew anything about it! Amazing."

All three friends jumped when the door knocker announced an arrival. Jack jumped up, checking his watch at the same time. "If that is my kid sister, she got here faster than I thought. I'll go and check."

"Jack, may I be the first to greet Veronica into my life." WarZar was up and standing next to his friend. "You and Alisia can come wait behind the door. Jack, I have never had any female desire me before so this is new to me, but I feel the need to welcome her."

"Of course, you may welcome the young lady you have been waiting to see." Jack touched his friend's arm. "Go and enchant my sister with your handsome face and haunting charms, my friend. I may have to sneak a peek at her face when she gets a load of my friend. I wanted her to drop her busy shoot and come here to meet."

"That will be fine brother, just do not let my soon to be mate see you spying on us." WarZar laughed and made it to the front door before the stiff butler. When he opened the door, the handsome man noticed the tall-shapely woman had her back turned away from the door as she looked around the vast courtyard. "Veronica?" came the deep voice behind her and she turned quickly and let her eyes wonder up the tall well-built man standing in the open doorway. The usually talkative movie director could only stare up into the luminous dark eyes looking back at her. "You have to be Veronica Spencer. Jack described you down to the stern facial expression when you are studying a scene you are filming. I can assure you madam, I do not act anymore to frighten people, but I am looking for a leading lady in my lonely life."

"You are lonely?" Veronica studied his expression to see if he was joking with her. "Forgive my confusion but I'm having a hard time believing a man as incredibly handsome as you are with all the perfect features, are having any trouble finding this leading lady in your life."

"I have only seen her in my dreams and there she tries to run from me." WarZar liked what he saw and he was already smitten with Jack's beautiful, raven-haired sister.

"I think you must be seeing your dreams in reversal." She noticed his confused face at the word 'reversal'. "It's like when I am making a film and me and my team want to view the scene, we just shot so we reverse the film, or run it backward. This is how you really see the girl. Instead of running away from you she is actually chasing after you, trying to catch you for herself."

"Is that a fact woman! Then why on earth are you always running away from me looking back, laughing while saying, 'catch me if you can Zar baby?"

"Me?" Now it was Veronica looking confused. "Well, it does sound like me, but how could you possibly dream about me when you have never met me? Unless my big brother showed you my picture. That's it, Jack showed you a photo of me. Rats! I hope it was one of my better ones."

"Veronica, Jack never showed me any photos of his amazing sister, he just merely described you after I told him you called me Zar baby." WarZar noticed the three pieces of large luggage beside her. "Looks like you knew I was going to ask you to stay here with me."

"Huh? Stay here? With you?" Jack's sister swallowed and

noticed he was looking at the three large bags. "Oh!" she laughed, assuming the very handsome man standing over her had just noticed all her bags. "You are referring to my three large suitcases. That's a relief WarZar! You had me going for a minute there."

"Going? No! I do not wish for you to leave and I certainly would not wish to give you the impression that I wanted you to go a minute from now after you just arrived." The strong man reached for all three bags and easily carried them inside the big mansion while she watched his power with fascination and amazement. After WarZar had set down the luggage he took her by the arm and pulled her over the threshold and closed the door, revealing Jack and Alisia standing there trying hard not to laugh over their big friend's misunderstanding and his wild behavior showing through the gentleman he had become.

"Surprise Veronica! I bet you have never met another man like my best friend here!" Jack grabbed his baby sister and gave her a big hug. "For starters kid sister, my big friend here does not understand modern slang words due to living inside the Forbidden Forest all his life where the lifestyles were more 1800's. Another warning, although I believe you will enjoy it sweetheart, my friend WarZar may at times resort back to his beastly role if you don't let him have his way. This guy is incredibly good at everything and a terrific friend Veronica. You might have to teach him the basic acts in romance, hugging, kissing, etc., but the handsome fellow is more than ready to learn, when the right girl comes along." He got close to her ear. "And if you play your cards right and don't do anything foolish, you just might be that perfect mate for WarZar."

"Mate? What am I dealing with, dear brother? Another Tarzan perhaps?" The glamorous girl turned to checked out WarZar's big muscles. "Well brother, your friend could certainly play the handsome jungle man if he ever considered acting."

"I can tell you right now Miss Hollywood, my incredible friend has no intention to become an actor or even go to California for that matter." Jack knew persuading his sister to settle down right here in Graceland was the only way things would work out for her and WarZar. "Listen Veronica, there was a reason the Lord brought WarZar here to Rockford Falls. The Almighty knew he would have a hard time fitting in with today's world and this place is almost a duplicate to his estate in the Forbidden Forest where he lived all his life after growing old enough to leave his evil parent's palace."

234

"Palace? His estate?" Always suspicious of her big brother's matchmaking for her, she narrowed her eyes at him. "What exactly is this handsome man's title darling brother?"

"He is a prince, the son of King Lazar and Queen Carmela, who will reign in the Forbidden Forest for many years to come." Jack felt like this was something WarZar should tell her and get everything out in the open. A good relationship should never have secrets and his sweet sister had her own secret past she would have to share with him as well. "I'm sure when you get to know WarZar, he will tell you all about his previous life and I expect you to do the same for him. If anything is to become between you two, then first you must be friends and share your failures as well as your successes with one another."

"Jack is absolutely right, Veronica, and I would like nothing more than to go for a walk with you in the rose garden. It is quite pleasant outside today and the garden is a perfect place to get acquainted with one another." WarZar waved the butler and footman forward. "Rollins, will you please take the lady's things up to her guest chamber." He smiled down at the beautiful face smiling back. "If you need to follow Mr. Rollins up to your chamber before we go for that stroll, I will be happy to wait for such an intriguing young lady?"

"That is very thoughtful WarZar, I think I would like to freshen up a bit and visit the lady's room." She glanced down hoping the sheltered man wouldn't require about the 'lady's room', but was relieved that he did not. "I came here straight way from the airport when I noticed a cab part out in front of the terminal waiting for a ride."

"Airplane? Airport?" the tall handsome man asked confused. "So, you came here from California on an Airport. Jack said you would be taking an airplane." Veronica glanced over at her laughing brother and finding it hard to hold back, she broke into her own brilliant laughter. WarZar, flabbergasted, looked over at Alisia who just shook her head and raised her shoulders, completely dumbfounded herself. "Did I say something stupid, Spencer's?"

"No WarZar, it is no fault of your own that you do not know the difference between an Airplane and an Airport." Veronica frowned at her brother who couldn't stop laughing at the funny statement, as he tried to picture his sister flying up in the air inside an airport with huge wings "Jack, will you stop seeing me flying in the L.A.

235

Airport." After she said it, she couldn't help but laugh as she too, vision herself flying across the sky looking out of L.A.'s large terminal windows.

"WarZar, sis and I aren't laughing at you my friend, we both were just picturing her flying here in Los Angeles' large airport, a very large building where people wait for their ride on the big airplane that flies up into the sky and straight across the country." Jack pulled his bride in his arms. "I just bet both you and my girl here has heard those big planes flying over the Forbidden Forest many times and did not know what they were."

"So, the big thundering birds where really just airplanes?" WarZar couldn't resist his own laugh. "I'll wait for you, my lady. Rollins and Willard have already gone up, but I'll get Glenda to see you get there. She will be your personal maid while you stay with us or if things work out, I shall be your personal helper." The handsome prince had a twinkle in his dark eyes as she gave him a quick wave and dashed up the steps behind the smiling maid.

CHAPTER 34

Coming from the back entrance of the large mansion, WarZar escorted Jack's beautiful sister down the wide and gracious steps that led into the enchanting rose garden. Veronica looked around in wonder at the massive size of such a spectacular place.

"Oh WarZar, this is one of the loveliest gardens I have ever seen!" she glanced up at the handsome man who watched her closely. "Tell me friend, was your garden in the Forbidden Forest as lovely as your new one?"

"When we left Rockford Falls, pretty lady, it was every bit this magnificent, thanks to Alisia's angels." WarZar noticed a slight change in her face. "Believe me or not Veronica, but before I took Jack's girl as my prisoner, all I had in the back of my stone dwelling were what vegetables I could find to plant. Nothing more."

"Why would you take Alisia as a prisoner? I thought she was your friend too?" This time the independent young woman was seeing this handsome man in a different lends. "My brother did mention something about me being careful or the beast inside you might come out if you didn't get your way?"

"Veronica, before Jack came into my life, I was a different person than the one you see, and I promise to tell you everything you need to know about me after you tell me something about your life. Life as a child, life as a young girl and what made you decide to be a film director in Hollywood? And did you ever do anything you regret, wished you could undo but know you can only learn by it and live a better life."

"You are asking for a lot, dear friend." She took his hand and started walking down the sweet-smelling path. "My parents had decided to have only one child if their first was a boy, so brother Jack was born and that was supposed to be it. When Jack was four, my parents decided to go away for another romantic trip and left little Jack with his grandparents for a week. Surprise! When they returned, mother was expecting another baby, me!" Veronica laughed along with WarZar.

"That romantic getaway certainly makes me happy Veronica." He squeezed her hand gently, knowing how easily he could crush it.

"I bet you were an active child. Am I right?"

"Right as rain!" She stopped and smiled, remembering Jack's words, WarZar does not understand our modern slang. He grew up in an 1800's world. "Let me rephrase my last statement in case you do not understand, right as rain. This is just an expression for saying absolutely right, since the sight of rain on a dry earth is always a welcome blessing."

"Oh! Right as rain on a parched field!" WarZar began walking again, pointing out various types of roses. "Is that when you got into most of your troubles?"

"How do you know about all my bad decisions WarZar? Jack has never squealed on his little sister before. He has made me own up, I mean, to confess what I had done and just get it out there to avoid more punishment from mom and dad."

"Your faithful brother has not told me anything about your past Veronica, I just have a gift to read people from past experience, that's all." WarZar moved on. "I see yourself in your early teens trying to impress a bunch of troubled youth you buddied up with, by picking up small items and slipping them inside your pockets. Was this something you tried once or twice?"

Believing herself to be a woman of the world, free and independent, Veronica was suddenly feeling vulnerable due to this handsome man being able to read into her shady past. "More like six times, if you must know my failures. I was trying to fit in with this really cool group of kids in school and everything was going great until my sixth attempt to slide a necklace inside my shoulder bag. The store we hit grew suspicious over all their small merchandise getting gone and hired an undercover security guard to find the thieves. Who would have ever suspected a little granny checking out the medicine department, directly across from the jewelry section." The beautiful girl rolled her eyes up dramatically. "I was busted and hauled into the juvenile headquarters. My parents were called in and agreed with my punishment. Two weeks suspension from Graceland Middle while I worked off my sentence cleaning the restrooms in the Norman Department Store and returning my stolen items with a sincere apology." Veronica felt WarZar drop her hand, but was relieved when he draped his arm around her shoulder. She looked up and gave him her beautiful smile. "That was the end of my life of crime. Jack started taking me with him to our church's youth group on Sunday afternoons and that is when I met Johnny and Macy. We became great friends and they helped me break away from those troubled kids." She gave a little laugh. "You might say, I turned my life around, made up for the two weeks missed from school, got a job offer at Norman's as a cashier when I reached fifteen, and the money I made during the three summers working, helped my parents pay for my college courses."

"We all have to learn from our mistakes, although most people have parents who teach them throughout their life, right from wrong." WarZar's eyes were focused straight ahead, knowing he never learned that lesson until he met Jack and Alisia. "All my parents taught me was hate and evil." His dark eyes didn't look down into hers, he would let her finish telling her life story first. "So, you went off to college. Is that when you decided what you wanted to do with your life Veronica?"

"Not right away. I had first thought about being a nurse, but that just seemed to heavy. The long hours waiting on sick people, changing beds and giving shots, just everything in general just didn't seem like me." Seeing a bench nestled inside an arch, she glanced up and motioned to the tranquil setting. "May we sit a while? I get too excited when I speak about my final decision on what career I wanted."

"I would love to take a seat next to such a special young lady." WarZar took her hand and helped her down then joined her, before taking her hand again. "Nursing did not feel exciting enough so you choose acting."

"Not right away, but I never wanted to be on the other side of the camera, being the leading lady in a hit movie. While I was in college, I joined the drama club and that's when I got hooked. I did a few lead roles on our college stage and even got great reviews in the local paper, but I kept watching the person directing our group and I knew that is what I wanted to be, but not for stage, but a movie director. I was accepted at the School of the Arts in Winston-Salem and became the top student in my entire school. Our senior project was to write and produce a short film for a film festival held every year in North Carolina and to my delight, a talent agent from Hollywood, California was there and ask me to come out to Hollywood where he would guarantee me a terrific director's job. Right after college, I told my family and close friends goodbye and headed out to L.A. and the best job I could have ever wanted."

"I bet your family and friends, Johnny and Macy, hated to see you go clear across the country." WarZar knew he had fallen in love with Jack's sister even before he ever met her, but he would not share that information with the woman he loved until he found out how she felt about him. "Did you love Johnny, Veronica?"

"Funny you should ask, dear friend. I loved Johnny and Macy very much, but only as friends." Jack's sister glanced down at her hand, folded lovingly in WarZar's. "I must have hurt Johnny very badly the day he asked me to marry him. I thought, how do you tell your best friend you can't marry them, but I knew before I left, I had no other choice. I knew Macy had always had deep feelings for Johnny, but she could see he only had eyes for me, so I used that approach. I told Johnny I would always love him as a great friend, but I didn't love him as a life mate but there was one very special girl that would like nothing more than to be his loving wife." Thinking back to the happy outcome, Veronica gave a soft laugh. "I had been working in Hollywood for almost six months when I got a call from Macy, asking me to be her maid of honor, so I flew right out and smiled and cried throughout the moving ceremony between my two best friends." She glanced up shyly. "I caught her wedding bouquet, a tradition for the bride to turn her back to the group of available young ladies and toss her wedding flowers back into one girl's lucky hands."

"So, by catching it, did you receive some sort of gift?" WarZar had no clue about human traditions and he knew he had a lot to learn if he were going to marry this modern-day girl.

Veronica couldn't resist her happy laugh. "WarZar, you are the most innocent man I have ever known and I find you so interesting and different, yet so wildly handsome and sexy."

"Sexy? Is this another word to describe my appearance?" he could see her laughter was not intended to make fun of him, but only the knowledge of knowing her date was unlike any other man, due to being sheltered in an old-time world.

"We will tackle what sexy means later friend and as for winning a gift for catching the bride's wedding bouquet, I did not receive a visible gift form the bride, but by catching the flowers, the old myth is, I would be the next single lady to get married." She laughed and looked up to see his serious eyes looking down.

"Did you make those believers in this myth upset when the years past and no wedding bells rang for you?"

"I did think I had made a lot of people disappointed when I

declared I was not interested in marriage and that my job was the only thing I needed to keep me happy." She sighed. "Then I found out the other six singles who had not caught the bouquet, hadn't gotten married either, and the foolish women has blamed me for holding them back." Her eyes caught WarZar's serious ones. "Well, is it my fault those women haven't attracted any men? I've not been around to stand in their way."

"What if you met the right man, Veronica? The man that stole your blocked heart from its prison where you have tucked it safely away." WarZar pulled her up into his arms, his lips inches from hers. "Just suppose such a man has the strong will and ability to make you forget that career and show you his desires and needs so boldly, you find yourself desiring his needs as well! This is what I choose, over and above anything else. To be all man for my woman and give her myself to the fullest. I have never known the love of a woman, for my mighty form was too great to have one, no matter how much I desired one!" Just as Veronica was hoping WarZar would kiss her, he moved away and stood up, pulling her with him. "Let us walk! It is my time to tell you all about what I was before ten-year-old Jack Spencer came inside our forest and changed me into the man you are with today." He took her hand and started down the next section of the large gardens. "My father is a demon, one of Satan's followers, that got thrown from heaven. He made the great and powerful Lucifer angry with him, so for his punishment, the devil trapped Lazar inside the Forbidden Forest to spend the rest of his life. My mother, Carmela Rockford, a cousin to the family who owned this estate, had Lucifer hook her up with Lazar so she could be Queen of her own kingdom. Satan was at her beck and call, if she ever needed a favor. One night, the lustful couple drank one of Carmela's wicked brews and had sex. I was conceived and when I was born, I did not cry like the human people's babies, I screamed out, so loudly it echoed across the mountains." He paused, knowing this next statement might upset the woman he loved, but his story must be told if she was to become his mate. "I was not a human Veronica, I was a hideous beast, a giant standing ten-feet tall, with great horns growing from my head and I walked on hoofs, same as a horse, only having two legs instead of four." WarZar could feel her hand shiver in his. "I understand you feeling frighten and I fear my story only gets worse. I grew up never knowing anything about love or the majestic heavenly God. With a demon as a father and a witch as a

241

mother, I was taught everything involving evil and hate. I was to hate all man and never trust any human. My animal senses alarmed me when a human invaded our forest and got trapped inside, so I would gallop out, screaming my warning, as it echoed through the mountains, to where they waited in fear, a dreadful sense I could also feel. Once captured, I would put them in a trance and turned them into mindless mutes and placed them in our huge rock quarry with the rest of our mindless slaves. If any slaves tried to run away, we would send the snitches after them and they would eat them alive."

"WarZar, did you have no pity for these poor innocent people?" Veronica had slipped her hand free after hearing about the snitches. "What kind of person could do that to another human?"

"A wild beast, trained by his evil father and having ten-times the strength as the evil demon! That kind of beast could and did!" he stared down at her, thinking, a modern-day girl would have to be strong to except him knowing his past. "That is the way I was Veronica, the day I heard your brother get pushed inside the Forbidden Forest. I was resting in my private dwelling place when I heard all the commotion. The rustling of leaves on the moss when his face hit the ground. I knew it would take me a little longer to get to the entrance from Rockford Falls, same name as here, so I did not start screaming until I grew closer, to put fear in what I knew was a young boy. When I arrived where I knew he was, I could not see him, although I could feel him nearby, hiding." The handsome prince thought back. "I threatened Jack and I could hear his heart beating with fear, but I grew weary of his hiding. I knew the girl, we called the good-one, had found him waiting just outside the Old Wagon Road and helped him hide, then eventually get away all together, to her hiding place."

"The girl? Are you referring to Alisia?" Veronica was glad the subject was off the evil snitches, whatever they were. "So, you're saying Alisia was also trapped inside your forest and had found a hiding place so you could not find her."

"At that time, I did not know Alisia had angels helping her. They created a lovely dwelling place for the young seventeen-year-old, safe underground, where she could not be detected by either me or my parents, the only three living in the forest that were capable of sensing an intruder's whereabouts. The same angels helped her leave the forest in spirit form to communicate with Jack when he first arrived at Camp Eagle's Nest. During the scout treasury hunt on

Saylor's Landing, Alisia led ten-year-old Jack to the hiding place of the locket of love, gifted with power from the Almighty God Himself and the aid that helped us escape my evil parents and trapped them in with God's mighty shield, while the Lord removed the one place there by Satan to hold Lazar in." WarZar stopped at the huge water fountain and dripped his fingers down in the water and Veronica noticed how the many goldfish swam over to nuzzle up against his hand.

"The next day I saw Jack for the first time on my return trip to the border. When I galloped up, there stood the young scout with the beautiful blonde-hair young lady, neither showing any fear of me or my unnatural appearance. It was obvious the good one had told her young friend about their ability to keep the evil ones away and the only way we could possess their being was for them to come over to us willingly, on their own." WarZar glanced down, hoping he had not lost all chances with this exciting beautiful young woman. "Jack started talking and the more he talked, the more I wanted to hear what the young genus had to say to me. The very first thing I noticed was how he treated me and I was taken back when he called me friend. Up until then, I hated all humans and I certainly did not need one for a friend. Anybody for that matter! I chose to be alone! To keep everyone, especially my parents, away from my private dwelling place. The time came for Jack to return to the outside so he could grow up, then return to the Forbidden Forest to save the girl he had fallen in love with. Most all humans would have made fun of such a young boy claiming his love for the very beautiful Alisia but not knowing anything about this feeling, I just watched and listened. It was when Alisa made a deal with me to hold her hostage so Jack could get out and return to his scout leader that I realized just how powerful this love really was and suddenly I wanted to be a part of that remarkable gift. I had been trapped inside that dark forest all my life and I wanted to be free from its hold on me. I had never asked to be born and my wicked parents treated me just a little higher than the slaves under me." The tall gentle man stared up at the big house. "When Jack was leaving us, I felt an unusual feeling coming over me and later I realized I was feeling sadness over knowing I would not see Jack for twenty-long-years. I had never shed tears, not even as a baby, but after Jack said I'll be seeing you later, I kept choking back the obvious and after I was alone in my chamber, I whelp for the first time in my miserable life."

243

"My poor daring." Veronica reached up and caressed his face. "You cannot be held responsible for how you were before Jack came into your life. WarZar, when he reached out to you in friendship and love, it was that one thing that had always been missing in your life. I know my brother better than most people, WarZar, and Jack has always been my help in times of trouble. Once Jack becomes your friend, he will always be there for you and his prayers to God always resort in just the right answers when you have a question or a problem. You'll find no better friend than him." She glanced down as she added. "Well, maybe one, the girl who wins your heart and is lucky enough to be your mate for life."

"The girl who wins my heart does not need luck to become my life-long-mate Veronica. All she needs is to except me for who I am, live here at Rockford Falls beside me and most important, love me as much as I love her." WarZar heard the dinner bell chime out. "I know who I want as a mate Veronica, but it must be on my terms. I am and will always be the head of my family, but I will love and cherish my wife for as long as the good Lord permits me to live."

"My friend speaks of me and I respect all your demands and desires dearest friend, but marriage is a very serious step for me and if I can just have a few more days getting to know you WarZar, I will be more certain as to what my answer will be." Veronica gave him a hopeful smile. "I have three more days of my quick getaway before I have to get back to the movie set and restart the filming. Jack made this trip here sound so urgent, I simply gave the crew a five-day vacation and flew out after ordering them to be back Monday morning, bright and early. Darling, in the movie business we are on a tight schedule and a producer expects his next box-office hit to be out on time. There is a lot of money tied up in the movie-making business and every studio is trying to outdo the other so Jack just doesn't understand the urgency in tying up this trip and getting back to keep the movie on track."

"Veronica, I can see you may make this a difficult situation since you hardly know me and you have been a film director ever since you graduated the School of the Arts, but this will have to be your decision to make." WarZar took her hand when the dinner bell rang a second time. "We need to go back before Rollins sends out the snitches. I can see my work is cut out for me, trying to impress you into falling in love with me."

"My wonderful darling, you have already impressed me greatly and my feelings for you are growing deeper." She followed close beside the handsome prince. "If I didn't have feelings for you WarZar, then my choice would be quick and prompt, but I fear this is going to be the hardiest thing I have ever been faced with."

CHAPTER 35

WarZar kept Veronica busy doing things on his new estate. The couple had invited Jack and Alisa to ride out to the Rockford waterfalls, early Saturday morning on horseback and the three friends were taken back at how much the falls resembled the one left behind in the Forbidden Forest.

"So, you're saying the waterfall that hid your estate in the Forbidden Forest looked exactly like this monster?" Speaking loudly over the roar, Veronica strained her neck looking up at the powerful falls. "Jack, how did we never know about this grand landmark so close to the town?"

"The Rockford family walled the town people out in the late 1700's, so after a while the Rockford falls were never mentioned again. Howard knew about the large estate and the mansion itself had been printed in the paper before we moved here, due to an outside photographer having been hired to take a family portrait in 1971. Without the family's knowledge, the man took several photos of the mansion's outside and sold a copy to the Graceland Journal. Howard remembered clipping it out of his parent's newspaper and saving it." Jack gave Alisia a kiss. "That's how he recognized the Rockford Falls mansion in the locket when I assumed it was at WarZar's stone mansion."

"So, you had a stone mansion built in the Forbidden Forest darling and I was picturing more of a rustic lodge with twelve-foot ceilings for your dwelling place." Veronica was surprised someone resembling a beast would have a normal looking home never living on the outside. "You said you never permitted anyone at your estate so I'm sure that was after those many slaves labored on your mansion."

"Sis, when WarZar said he permitted no one, he meant every word of it. Alisia was the first person to step foot on his land and stay inside one of his guest rooms." Jack laughed at his sister's surprised expression. "Not that my big friend ever called the up-stair rooms guest rooms seeing how he kept everyone out, but after I returned, Alisia and I, along with a small group of angels, finally got to see what this big guy built with his own hands."

"WarZar, you built your large home all by yourself? I am impressed." Veronica locked her arms around his neck. "You are quite a remarkable man. It must have taken a very long time to build something that huge all by yourself."

"All I had was time when I left the job site. A lifetime locked inside a large forest with no way out could drive anyone sane, insane without something to keep me busy. It took me several years to complete, but a year inside the eternal forest was nothing compared to the outside world where time marched on." WarZar paused to collect her hands knowing his next statement would be hard for this modern girl to believe. "Veronica, I was 199 years old when I met Jack in 2001 and when he returned 20 years later in 2021, I had turned 219 but had not aged a day."

As Veronica listened with wide-eyes, Alisia stepped up next to her tall friend. "WarZar, you were young compared to me when we finally got to meet Jack." Alisia smiled over at Jack's startled sister. "I was 237 when my dearest Jack returned to the Forbidden Forest, and like your handsome fellow, I was still just 17 years-old but my Jack had turned 30. I know it must be a lot to take in my new sister, but all the truth must be told before you choose a relationship with dear WarZar."

"All this is new for me and if it were someone besides you two, I would really have a hard time believing what you were telling me. The one thing I don't understand is how you lived so many years and never aged a day." Veronica glanced from Alisia to WarZar and knew they had been serious about living so long, yet never aging. "Could you explain how a person can live so long without aging in a place as evil as the Forbidden Forest, same as a believer can maintain eternal youth in heaven?"

"Lucifer was a powerful archangel in heaven, a status that made him and Michael just under the Almighty God. Even though the Lord removed a great deal of the traitor's power before throwing him out of heaven, the mighty angel's power down on earth is greater than all humankind. Lucifer is extremely dangerous and his determination to defeat God makes him our mortal enemy as well." Jack knew the age difference would not come easy for his modern-day sister to understand, so the dedicated brother would try to help her see past reality to what he called a new diversity, once inside the Forbidden Forest. "Remember Lucifer was angry with his demon Lazar for disobeying his command, and in that heated moment, Satan put a curse on Lazar before his angry blast sent him flying into the Forbidden Forest, snapping shut its boundaries forever and the power from Lucifer created eternal life for those of power trapped inside his web, including all the believers."

"Alright Jack, so that explains their eternal youth at such a long age, but now that they are set free of the forest, how can WarZar and Alisia remain youthful?" Jack's sister struggled with ever new thing she found out concerning the interesting handsome man she felt herself falling in love with. "Can a woman 237-years-old give you children, dear brother? Could WarZar make a woman pregnant at his great age?" Jack could not resist his laughter at his sister's dismay. "Jack Spencer, will you tell me what is so funny about this absurd complicated situation you and I are facing? Especially you, big brother, due to the fact that you are already married to this very-elderly, yet youthful looking young lady wrapped in your arms."

"My beautiful sister, please permit me to explain why all your worries over you and I having children with these two-remarkable people are in vain and completely misleading." Jack took his sister over to one of the new benches placed there for the town citizens to enjoy the massive waterfall at a safe distance. "When the three of us stepped out of the forest, Alisia and WarZar vanished. At that moment, I had no clue Jesus had swept them safely away to the garden of Eden."

"Eden? The garden Adam and Eve were banished from for disobeying God's command? The same Eden that was sealed off so no human could ever go inside again? Still guarded this day by an angel with a flaming sword?" Veronica glanced over at the tall handsome stranger who had captivated her heart like no other man had ever been able to penetrate. "Jack, did the tree of life have anything to do with why the Lord took them there?"

"It had everything to do with us being here Veronica." Alisia had walked over with WarZar, gave Jack's sister her beautiful smile before resting down on her husband's lap. The petite blonde smiled up into Jack's eyes when he wrapped his arms securely around her waist. "Veronica, our old bodies could not survive without a miracle from the Lord and our heavenly new bodies would have to wait until we reached God's kingdom. Humans can not touch the beautiful tree of life, but our Lord can and Jesus reached up and took two pieces of fruit off, gave us each the heavenly aroma pear and told us to eat it. Instantly new life poured inside our bodies and we both became a young thirty-year-old, same age as Jack."

"Veronica, I stepped inside that heavenly garden an aged beast, standing ten-feet tall with great horns protruding from my thick-black hair and hoofs instead of feet. I tell you true, dearest woman, the moment I took my first bite from the life-fruit, I could feel the changing process accruing and what I became that miraculous moment is the man you see standing in front of you this day."

"Then my new friends, I must ask you both to forgive my earlier comment concerning children." Veronica gave her brother a big hug. "Jack, you and Alisia may give me as many nieces and nephews as you wish to have. I promise their Aunt Veronica will spoil each one of them." Her alluring eyes looked up at the tall handsome man standing next to her brother. "As for you WarZar, it's pretty obvious you could make any lucky girl a mother for the many offspring you're capable of providing. I do enjoy spoiling other people's cute kids."

"What about you Veronica? Surely you have dreamed of being a mother, then you could spoil your own adorable babies." Jack reached over and patted his sister's head. "I recall all the excitement one little Veronica had when Santa brought her that special baby-doll she asked for one Christmas and how happy she was playing mommy for the entire year." Jack set Alisia off his lap and stood up, then pulled Veronica to her feet before pointing over to his incredible friend, whose attention was on the waterfall. Jack lowered his voice as their eyes were on the owner of the grand estate. "Sis, be honest, haven't you ever wandered just a little bit, what fabulous children you and WarZar could have if you chose marriage over career?"

"This is a subject that has never crossed my mind, Jack baby! I have always been a workaholic, the first one to arrive on the set and the last person to leave the studio. Sweet brother, a career woman does not have time to have babies. Her time is consumed in performance and getting the scene shot perfect the first take. Behind the camera is where I excel dear brother, not behind a baby stroller pushing a cute little kid!"

WarZar had been standing back, taking in Veronica's words. "Then, beautiful lady, you will miss out on the happy things in life." WarZar felt like his dream was turning into a nightmare and this woman he loved would keep running away until she was out of his life for good. "You have told us what you need Veronica, now I will tell you what I want. I want and need a woman who loves me as

249

much as I love her. To love me so much she will give herself to me completely and let go of her past life. A woman who would not have to think twice before she came to me to give me herself." The tall handsome man took her hand and gazed down into her eyes. "You must decide this day, Veronica. You and I have been together for four beautiful days and we have learned many deep secrets between us. Through it all, we have felt something for each other, I know this. I won't lie and tell you whatever you choose will be fine with me dearest one. If you choose to leave and resume your career, my heart will be torn into, completely broken, but I am strong so I will survive and in time find someone to ease the pain of losing you. Veronica, I know what I want. Now you need to find out what you want and when you do dearest one, let me know." WarZar walked away, not looking back.

CHAPTER 36

Jack had knocked on his sister's guest room door and after hearing her soft "come in" he walked in to find her slowly packing her bags.

"Veronica, could I have a word with you before you finish packing?"

With her eyes still cast down on the blue sweater in her hands, she answered. "Jack, please don't try to stop me from catching my plane." Veronica finally glanced up at her serious brother, sadness written on her swollen eyes. "My crew is expecting me to be there tomorrow morning. How can I let them down?"

"How can you let the man you love down sis?" Before she could object, Jack took her trembling hands and pulled her down on the messy bed. "Sweetheart, you have not been crying because you are afraid of upsetting your crew. I have seen the way you and WarZar look at one another. Veronica, you cannot fight love and you sure as heck can't run away from it."

"Alright Jack, it's true, I do have feelings for WarZar." Veronica looked up into her brother's caring eyes. "Oh Jack, I did not come here looking for love and I certainly had no intention to stay. I came because you sounded so desperate and I just couldn't let you down."

"But sis, although you thought you could just pop in to meet a friend of mind then return to your lifestyle, you did find love sweetheart, and not with just any man. You found an incredible, handsome, loving, kind and generous man who is deeply in love with you." Jack lifted his sister's drooping chin. "You are afraid of the sudden change that has happened in your life darling. You have a great assistant working for you and he is capable of stepping in for your absence. You said so yourself on all your many previous holiday visits with the family."

"It's not just my need to return Jack! I worked for years to get where I am now and to give it all up is making me crazy!" Veronica twirled around to face her brother. "Jack, all those years of college, then the years being an assistant to the head director before finally climbing to the head director! This is what I worked and planned for! To have an exciting career, something I have always loved doing! I have never once dreamed of becoming a housewife or a mother!"

"Alright Veronica, I will put it all out there for you, then you can choose the one right for you." Jack Spencer knew his baby sister was struggling with her final decision, so as hard as it would be, he would give her two choices, then leave it for her to decide. "Solution number one: You choose WarZar and have to give up your great career that took years to achieve. Solution number two: You choose your terrific career and remain a single career woman and give up WarZar, the only man you have ever had deep love and devotion for."

"Gee Jack, when you put it that way it puts things into contents and reality sets in." Veronica stood up and walked to the window to gaze down into the garden where she had been with WarZar on the first day there. Had it been four days ago, she thought, when the handsome stranger almost kissed her in the garden below. "Getting my career did take several years Jack, but falling in love with WarZar took only one stroll in that lovely garden below, where he almost kissed me." Veronica gave a soft laugh and closed her eyes still seeing his handsome face drawing closer to hers until their lips were almost touching. "I do believe my beloved was teasing me, knowing I desired his kiss, his lips so close to mine. WarZar pulled away, deep in thought, and all I wanted was to yank the hunk back and give him a fiery kiss."

"WarZar is a rare gentleman, Veronica. He is from a more refine time, when men respected women. He is a gallant, romantic man who would never take advantage of the lady he loved until she truly belonged to him." Jack walked up beside his sister. "If you truly belong to WarZar little sister, go to him now, then he will make both of you happy. Never have I seen a man more in love than my best friend is to my beautiful sister." Jack gave Veronica a brotherly kiss before turning her toward the door. "You will find WarZar in the garden."

Veronica saw the tall handsome man she loved standing at the big fountain with his back turned to her. She stepped up and stopped a short distance from him, admiring his manly figure and strength. WarZar had sensed her behind him and wiped away his fresh tears, then waited for her words.

"Dearest friend, the words you spoke to me have come true." Veronica watched in silence as he turned slowly and gazed down into her eyes. She could feel a rush of butterflies floating around in her stomach and took a deep breath. "WarZar, a very loving man stole my blocked heart from its prison where I have kept it tucked safely away for many years. That wonderful man is you darling. WarZar, I love you far too much to leave your side and here is where I choose to be, if you still want me as much I as I do you."

"Oh yes, Veronica! I have wanted you for a very long time!" WarZar pulled her up into his strong arms and this time he did not pull away when his lips met hers in a long-awaited fiery kiss.

There would be a double wedding to plan and both grooms had a beautiful surprise wedding gift for their happy brides.

CHAPTER 37

Jack had promised his happy sister he would mail off her letter for an immediate resignation from the job she had gladly given up for the man she had fallen in love with. Veronica knew she had a wedding to get ready for and had only one week in which to do it all. The brother and sister's announcement to their parents came as quite a shock but both their mother and father were relieved to see both their children had finally decided to settle down in their hometown. Veronica was happy to know this time it was her getting married so all those single ladies waiting for her to throw the wedding bouquet over her head could finally stop blaming her for their single status.

Since it was going to be a double wedding and knowing Alisia didn't have any relatives alive to choose half the bridesmaids, Veronica decided to just let her and Jack's cute eight-year-old cousin twins, Tracy and Stacy Spencer, toss out rose pedals and their ten-year-old cousin, Jason Spencer, carry a pillow down with both sets of wedding bands lying on top. The beautiful brides would walk side-by-side down the church aisle to where the grooms would be waiting with Howard Spencer, who would perform the ceremony. For their husband's surprise, Alisia and Veronica had chosen a beautiful love song for Alisia to sing during the ceremony while Veronica accompanied her on the piano, another talent the young director had and set aside when she left for Hollywood.

To both Jack and WarZar's dismay, Veronica and Alisia also informed their anxious men they had gotten rooms at the Graceland Hotel for their wedding eve so their bridegrooms could not see them before they walked down the aisle to join them.

The big day finally arrived and Jack and WarZar waited nervously as the pre-wedding march music played. Grace Moravian was overflowing with members from both churches in the small town. Tom Bruster, the wealthy banker had placed the wedding announcement in the local paper where the article gave a small summery of what had happened in the Forbidden Forest to Reverend Jack Spencer and how he had befriended the monster living inside the dangerous forest and became the best of friends to WarZar, the ten-foot beast. Only later did Jack find out that his friend WarZar inherited the old Rockford Falls Estate and his generous heart has opened up the high wall at the Rockford Falls so the town's citizens can once again enjoy the majesty and wonder that the powerful waterfall can display. The article made a big impression and the need to see for themselves the mysterious stranger who once roamed the Forbidden Forest would be getting married to Veronica Spencer, a popular local girl who had made it big in California as a movie director. Jack Spencer was known all over town not only as a great preacher but a perfect catch for any available young lady, and now the need to see this angelic girl that stole his heart at such an early age and at such an unlikely place, as the Forbidden Forest.

The banker had also placed the photo of the massive Rockford Falls mansion on the front page. The newspaper press couldn't keep up with the demand for a copy containing all the information as well as the photo. The entire town of Graceland was in an uproar over the upcoming celebration and every citizen was sending in their request for seating at the wedding ceremony as well as a seat at the reception. By placing people in the balcony and overflow seating wherever possible, the worship committee just did make enough room for all requests. There had been an announcement that the wedding party requested that no gifts be brought, so despite the plea, a table had been set up with a large box for cards and amble room for wedding presents the decorating committee knew would be arriving. As expected, lavishly wrapped wedding gifts filled the white lace tabletop and the large decorated box was fill to the brim with cards with cash or gift cards from the town's antique shops, to purchase suitable items for such an old mansion, where both couples would be living.

The large group grew silent as the familiar strings of the pre-wedding music started and the cute twins walked slowly down the aisle tossing out rose pedals and directly behind them came their brother carrying the pillow, steady and careful, his attention always on the four golden bands riding on top. There was a pause before the wedding march began and the beautiful brides stepped through the back doors both wearing exquisite white flowing gowns. Alisia's long blonde hair flowed in perfect ringlets down to her waist and a cluster of blue flowers were softly attached to one side of her head. Veronica's long chestnut hair was pulled softly around in a long braid and woven throughout with real running cedar, ivy and a rainbow of WarZar's favorite roses. As they watched from the altar, both grooms found it hard to breathe, knowing the woman they loved would soon be theirs forever.

The congregation moved around nervously in the seats when the wedding march came to an end and the brides had not taken one step down the aisle to their anxious grooms. Suddenly feeling nervous, Jack and WarZar exchanged worried glances until they saw Alisia step to one side and lift up a microphone while Veronica sat down at a piano that appeared behind a curtain. The crowd relaxed when Alisia's voice filled the quiet room to the beautiful melody Veronica was playing. A song the girls had written together for their loving grooms called: WE GIVE OURSELVES TO YOU.

After the romantic song was finished, the wedding march once again began and this time both brides walked side-by-side down the rose-pedal floor until they reached the men they loved with all their heart. The brides could hear all the sniffles coming from the crowd and after looking up in their groom's eyes, tears glistened there as well. As the girls had hoped, their song had made an impact on the men they had written them for.

Howard Preston smiled down at Jack and gave him a fatherly pat on the head before giving the other three a big smile. "This day is filled with beautiful surprises my dear friends and that moving love song straight from your bride's hearts is only the first of many." Reverend Preston looked out at the quiet congregation. "I would like to welcome everyone here today and know from the request for seats, most of Graceland are present. Those who could not be here due to jobs like hospital doctors and staff, patients inside those hospitals, the police and firemen on duty, in case there is an emergency and they need to be vigilant. For all those who had hoped to be here but could not, the local television station has set up their camera in the balcony and I am asking all who are present, please stay focused forward and don't get tempted to turned around and wave at Uncle Bob in Utah, or Cousin Janet in Florida, because this camera is strictly for Graceland residents who could not make it in person." Howard smiled up at the camera. "So, welcome all those watching from our community." He glanced down at Veronica before announcing. "I would also like to welcome our special guest, brought here to surprise their boss-lady on her very special day."

Howard chuckled softly when a shocked Veronica twirled around to find her entire Hollywood crew, along with those actors from her current film, seated on the front rows directly behind her.

256

Having placed her attention completely on WarZar when she came forward, she hadn't noticed the familiar faces watching her with happy smiles. As the Hollywood group stood to honor the young woman, they all loved and admired, Veronica felt WarZar take her trembling hands as she let her head fall on his strong chest and smile out at the group she loved dearly. After witnessing how happy they were for her, Veronica felt all the guilt she had had for quitting so abruptly faded away. Her eyes met Jack's as she whispered, "thank you."

Jack returned her smile and shook his head as he nodded toward WarZar. "It was all his idea sis. The man is crazy about you."

Veronica squeezed WarZar's hand lovingly and whispered "Thank you darling. I love you."

"I love you too Veronica baby!" the tall handsome groom gave his bride a wink, then the couple heard Reverend Preston clear his throat before starting the ceremony.

No one inside the large sanctuary could see the invisible spirit standing next to WarZar, tears falling from her eyes as she watched her son say his wedding vows. The silent being marveled at her handsome son's normal male body. WarZar paused, his strong senses picking up the invisible woman standing near him. His eyes fell on the spot where she stood and his words came softly, and with complete love.

"Mother, if your spirit has been brought here, then surely you have been saved." WarZar closed his eyes when he heard his mother whisper next to his ear.

"Yes, my son, the Lord has forgiven me all my sins and soon He will take me up to be with papa and Charlotte." Carmela floated up to kiss her son's cheek, causing the handsome man to lift his hand and gently run his fingers over the place while Veronica watched in amazement at her soon to be husband conversing with someone invisible very close to him. In the background Carmela heard the preacher pronounce them man and wife and knowing the wedding kiss must not be disrupted, Carmela whisper one last phrase. "I'll wait to say my goodbyes dearest WarZar, my beautiful son."

WarZar knew his mother was gone from their presence, but the intelligent giant knew exactly where she would be waiting to say her farewells.

After all the wedding photos had been taken, the married couples found themselves standing front and center in the crowded fellowship hall, glasses raised in a toast. Having everyone to get quiet so the grooms could present their new brides their wedding gifts, both couples had stepped up on a decorated platform. WarZar took Veronica hand and smiled down into her incredible loving eyes.

"My dearest darling Veronica, you gave up the one thing that has made you happy for many years and you set it all aside to prove your deep love and devotion to me. In doing so, you have made me the happiest man alive, of course along with my best friend Jack, who is just as lucky to receive the love of Alisia. Veronica, you gave your brother Jack your letter of resignation to be mailed off immediately to Hollywood, but I took it from him and tore it up."

"Tore it up? WarZar, why would you tear up my letter for resigning?" Veronica looked up sadly, the thoughts of returning to this work so far from the man she needed. "Surely you don't wish for me to return to Hollywood, 2,000 miles away from you."

"No, my dear wife, this will never be permitted. I will never let you return to California ever and be away from your husband." WarZar laughed when she playfully hit him. "I intend to keep you right here at Rockford Falls for as long as I live. My gift to you is: This is where you may continue doing what you enjoy doing, directing films, as soon as your new studio is completed and our extended honeymoon is over. This is the setup: I will allow you to work on certain days but with limited hours." The handsome groom smiled out at the Hollywood staff and actors. "I have purchased the land across from our estate, over two-hundred acres and with the aid of your great crew, the proper size studio and movie lot is already in construction with the layout for your current film. When you are needed at home by your loving husband, your great assistant, Joe Blackford, will fill in for you. Homes are being built on the adjacent tract of land directly across from our grand entrance and I have named it Hollywood Hills, to suit this fine crew and their families."

"WarZar, you are the greatest! I could not possibly love you any more than I do being you have filled up every corner in my heart, my husband." Veronica could not control her tears as she buried her face in his strong chest. "I never doubted your love for me darling, but this truly great surprise only proves your love is pure and lasting."

"Sis, I knew my friend would make you happy. This guy has such a giving heart." Jack turned to Alisia and pulled her over into his arms. "My beautiful bride, my gift to you comes in small packages but I know they will fill my beloved with great joy. I know my girl wishes her mama and papa could have been here to celebrate our beautiful special day, but never doubt they are having a wonderful celebration in heaven watching. Ever since we returned to Graceland, I have been searching on the internet for hard-to-find items in antique stores and I was overjoyed to find the three items I was searching for. I believe these special items will help make your mama and papa feel closer to you." Jack handed his bride the first wrapped package. Alisia opened it carefully and choked up when she saw the old music book dated 1780.

Alisia couldn't stop her tears as she ran her fingers over the old book cover before opening it, where she let out a gasp. "Oh Jack! This is mama's song book! She wrote her name inside on the first page and darling, I know mama's signature anywhere!" she looped her arms around his neck, filled with memories of her mother singing from this very book. "Thank you, my darling!"

"Just seeing how much it means to you is all the thanks I need." Jack reached for the second gift, wrapped in the same old white paper. "Let's see if my girl recognizes this one."

Alisia once again pulled out the old worn book and pulled it to her chest, tears flowing non-stop. "Jack, my dearest husband, I would recognize papa's old Bible anywhere!" She carefully turned the page and wiped her eyes. "See, there is his name, right there where he proudly wrote: Reverend David Solomon, a servant of God!" the beautiful girl buried her face in the old Bible and cried.

Jack lovingly collected his wife in his embrace and spoke softly. "Darling, this last gift was a huge surprise for me to find and I am certain my girl thought it was lost forever." Jack handed Alisia a large painting. It was a portrait of David and Charlotte Solomon standing with their young daughter Alisia. Alisia could only stare at it through blurred vision as the tears pooled up in her eyes. It was the very first time the angelic girl had seen the loving family portrait. "Darling, it appeared the artist hadn't completed your family portrait before your parents had to leave for the Black Forest, so they never got to see it, nor you, precious."

"Jack, I do not know how you managed to track down this painting showing the happy family we were, but until my dying day, my beloved, I will forever be grateful for my wedding surprises!" The beautiful girl could not speak another word because her emotions welled up into a flood of tears and all the wedding guest watching, wept as they clapped for the beautiful moving wedding gifts the grooms had given their brides.

The brides had not been told where their loving husbands were going to take them on their long honeymoon. It was going to be a surprise as well, but one that would prove interesting and different.

CHAPTER 38

The last surprise came at where WarZar and Jack took their new brides on their honeymoon. Alisia and Veronica were happily surprised to find themselves up on Black Mountain, at Saylor's Landing. It was obvious to the petite blonde that the place appeared as if she had stepped through time and was halfway expecting to see Jack and Doris Todd appear at their recently built 1700's cabin that Jack and WarZar had commissioned to be built on the exact spot. More tears came for the beautiful angelic girl when she saw a replica of her papa's church, completely furnished just like it had been when she was there with her parents. When Alisia stepped inside and smelled the same aromas from her past light up her senses, she felt strong emotions as visions of her papa standing behind the pulpit and her mama, standing nearby, singing one of her old familiar songs from the song book in her hand, gave her goosebumps.

"Oh, Jack darling and my dearest friend WarZar, you have made this wedding day even more special by restoring my past for generations to remember."

"And my friend Alisia, this will be our first time staying at Eagle's Nest Lodge instead of watching from the cover of trees in the dark forest." WarZar smiled at his little song bird, knowing each of them had first seen the young Jack Spencer there over twenty-years ago. "I have rented the entire campground for just the four of us. Jack and Alisia will stay at one in, Cabin one and Veronica and I can have his old cabin, next to the woods. I am expecting a visit from my mother before we leave."

"Carmela?" Jack and Alisia said in unison.

"Mother was at our wedding dear ones and by some miracle, she has been saved by the Lord and now she is rejoicing over going to heaven to see your papa and mama."

"Dear friend, if this thing you tell us is true about my half-sister, then I too rejoice in knowing she has finally seen the light and will not be spending eternity in the flames with your father Lazar!" Alisia gave her big friend a hug. "My loving friend, I believe it was your last words to her that touched your mother's heart and soul. I sincerely hope Carmela makes herself known to all of us before she ascends."

"With Carmela's conversion and repentance, I guess that leaves a sex-starved Lazar without his hot wife to share his bed with." Oddly, Jack almost felt sorry for the unfortunate fallen angel she had left behind."

"I guess we shall know how father fared when we see mother, but, until then, I am taking my 'hot' wife to bed and get to know her better, all of her! For the first time since my existence, I shall know how it feels to make love." WarZar's attention was completely on his new bride. "I think I have waited long enough."

Veronica reached for his strong hand. "My darling WarZar, I promise you will not be disappointed." Veronica gave her smiling brother a playful wink. "I know it will be total pleasure for me! See you two lovers later. The best part of the honeymoon is about to happen!"

The couples separated and true to Veronica's words, WarZar had never had such a passionate, fulfilling experience as he did finding out just how making love to the right woman felt.

The next day, the two couples had walked to the exact spot where Jack, Alisia, and WarZar had said their farewells just inside the line of trees before stepping out holding hands. Even though it had been only a couple of weeks since they stepped out, to the three friends it seemed like an eternity. Being her first time on Old Wagon Road, Veronica had a strange feeling looking inside the Forbidden Forest, she suddenly recalled her ten-year-old brother telling her about his frightening experience inside the evil forest before befriending Alisia and finally feeling more at ease in the beast's company. The beast she recalled the excited scout describing standing ten-foot tall with long-thick black hair and two massive horns coming from his head." She glanced at her husband watching her and he gave her a smile as she thought.

"The beast Jack had told me about is the same man I made incredible love to last night until the wee hours of the morning." Veronica returned his sweet smile as she spoke. "It's hard to believe this peaceful looking place could hold such evil." She jumped when a strange woman's voice could be heard.

"My beautiful daughter Veronica, it is very peaceful and tranquil on the spot where I stand." Carmela suddenly appeared with a large group of people waiting behind her, dressed in a variety of clothing. "We have come to this border to wait on the Lord's arrival, then we go to home to heaven."

WarZar stepped up closer and looked out at the familiar and unfamiliar faces surrounding his beautiful mother, all of them dressed in native or period clothing. "Mother, who are all these people with you? When we left the forest, we left only you and father with your small group of servants, some of which stand behind you, but there are hundreds more waiting. Forgive me, but I have never seen the majority of these souls with you, Mother, and it has only been a couple of weeks since we left you."

"No, my son, you could not possibly know the majority of these good souls who wait behind me." Carmela waved her hand across the vast crowd waiting in silence. "These dear souls have been waiting many years, piled up mountain high in the Valley of the Bones. Look closely and you will find many Indians from the Cherokee tribe who either were inside the forest when the devil trapped Lazar inside or they wandered in later, unaware of the invisible trap. You will see ancient settlers waiting with their children, some lifted from the earth where the snitches dragged their bones and buried them. All of these have been wandering souls, trapped inside of decayed bones and the Lord lifted their souls up from their graves." Carmela looked out at Jack. "Those behind me claim they heard words of comfort spoken over their bodies before the Lord's arising. Do you know anything about the one who prayed over their bones in the valley Jack?"

"I remember the day clearly Carmela. The voices they heard a little over two-weeks ago was me and your dear papa." Jack knew Alisia nor WarZar knew nothing about the two ministers' mission before leaving the forest. "We knew no one had given them a proper burial so we felt it was our duty as men of God to give them their last rights and pray that the Lord God would release their wandering spirits and take them home to heaven."

"You and papa are devout Christian men, darling, and I am sure the Lord led you both there before we departed the forest." Alisia squeezed his hand. "Sister, these servants that worked for you, how did they find salvation?"

"They found salvation when after they witnessed the big change in me and I told them about asking the Lord to forgive their sins and just believe that He is the Son of God and that he died for them."

"I recognize all the house workers and gate keepers behind you mother, so who is left with father?"

WarZar couldn't help but feel pity for this fallen angel who could never be forgiven for betraying his creator and God. Lazar had been given that chance in heaven but refused the Lord's offer for forgiveness and was kicked out, his chances forever lost.

"WarZar, my beautiful loving son, Lazar is no longer here, but has returned to his fellow demons. Those closest to Lazar who chose to go with him are few in number. The evil snitches, the razor warts and climbers are no longer a part of this beautiful forest. The only thing left of it is the name. The Lord declared it shall remain the Forbidden Forest, a tranquil-peaceful forest, where anyone who enters will feel safe." Carmela took a step closer to her son and her sister.

"WarZar, the Forbidden Forest belonged to your father and I for many years and it was your home as well darling. I now am sole owner and it is my wish to give the Forbidden Forest as an inheritance to my son and my devoted loving sister Alisia, to share forever with the two you love so dearly. You will find it may look the same in one way but better."

"Then, if it is alright with my co-owner, the Forbidden Forest shall become a mountain resort. A protected park nestled in the Black Mountains of North Carolina." WarZar smile watching Alisia happily agree by nodding her head. "We can transform the palace of Lazar into a mountain lodge, where visitors can come in at last and leave at will."

"We can keep Rockford Falls estate, built by your own powerful hands, for the four of us as our personal mountain retreat!" Jack had grown excited over going back inside the forest. "Now that we don't have to hide from anyone, we can open up the hidden driveway into your estate on either side of the great falls!"

Veronica had been standing back listening and recalling how Lucifer had trapped the demon Lazar inside with the intention of it being there forever, she didn't trust WarZar's mother in knowing all the facts and was nervous about running into WarZar's evil father inside the forest. She pulled her husband to one side and whispered. "WarZar, didn't Lucifer place Lazar inside this forest forever? I, for one, don't feel safe going inside there. Your mother said Lazar had left and went back to other demons. Please tell me how your father escaped both Lucifer's trap and the Lord's outer trap?"

"Sweetheart, Lazar never escaped either trap on his own, but with God, all things are possible." WarZar pulled his pretty wife into his arms. "Your man won't let anything happen to you darling. You know I will forever protect you, but you have nothing to worry about inside our forest, I promise. Before Mother found salvation, God had banished Satan's trap away and replaced it with an even powerful trap, His own. When Carmela found salvation, the Lord decided to put an end to Satan's evil act against his demon and simply sent Lazar back to hell with the one that followed him."

"Then, that is good news for us, but why would the Lord wish to keep Forbidden Forest the name of the new forest if it's now void of evil?"

Carmela heard Veronica statement and called out to her. "Daughter, the Lord chose to keep the name the Forbidden Forest out of respect and in the memory of all the lost lives that accrued under Lazar's evil reign."

"Then we shall erect a permanent sign at the entrance into the forest stating the Lord's words concerning the lives lost inside the Forbidden Forest." Jack moved closer to his wife's sister, a question needing to be asked on his mind. "Carmela, will you share with us what made you decide to give up being queen of the kingdom you wanted so desperately you gave yourself to Lucifer to gain it, then turn to the Lord for salvation? Was it the fear of the eternal fire that awaited you at Jesus return?"

"The eternal fire was frightening, Jack, but that is not my reason for crying out to the Lord to save me from myself and my great sin." Carmela's eyes fell on her son, who stood listening to her reason. Tears filled her eyes as she spoke. "It was because of my son and the words he spoke to me the day he left the forest forever. Jack, I could never speak the word 'love' around Satan or Lazar without severe punishment, but seeing my son about to leave and knowing I would never see his sweet face again, brought back all the memories of him. The little baby I cradled in my arms and sang to, then whispered how his mother loved him in his sleeping ear. Watching him toddle around on his little hooves and grow day by day until he got too old for me to let him know how much his mother loved him. But I did Jack, how I loved my little WarZar. I watched him grow up into a very tall handsome man, strong and brave and it broke my heart knowing how lonely he felt, having no one. There were nights after Lazar made love to me, I would roll over, feeling my tears welling up in my eyes, as I recalled a visit from my boy and how cold he acted toward me. Jack, I loved my son very much, but I never showed him and when I knew he was leaving and I would never see my beautiful boy again, I felt my heart breaking. I knew at that moment the only way I could ever see my son again was to change, to call out to the Lord Jesus and beg His forgiveness. To show me what I needed to do to be saved and go to heaven where I could see WarZar again one day, and my loving papa, the only one who ever showed me love no matter how bad I was." Carmela turned back to Jack. "The Lord did answer my prayer and with his help we found all the souls that had crossed over the forbidden line and had perished either in the stone quarry or by the snitches. I spoke to all the workers and told them about the Lord's salvation. As you might guess, Torren laughed at me before heading to Lazar and reporting my disloyalty. The Lord was waiting for Lazar and Torren and sent them away in a whirlwind."

"Carmela, my sister, I am so happy for you and I know papa is smiling down at his two little girls right now with complete joy in his big heart." Alisia drew as close to her sister as possible, not wishing to disturb the large group's final exit. "Papa never stopped loving you Carmela and neither did I. We never ceased praying for you either and now I can see that little spark of love dear papa planted inside your heart burst into a flame." With tears in both sisters' eyes, Alisia blew Carmela a kiss. "Until we meet in heaven, remember I have always loved you, Carmela. Please tell Papa and Mama I said I love them dearly."

Jack had watched the veil opening after first smelling heaven's sweet aroma drifting down over all of them. He placed his arm around Alisia's shoulders and smiled out at the group and Carmela. "Carmela, my sister, the Lord is waiting to take all of you up."

"Then we go gladly. Goodbye Jack, thank you son for helping WarZar finally find happiness. Knowing my son is happy makes my going easy." Her eyes fell on Alisia. "My beautiful angelic sister, I know the reason you escaped us when you got trapped here, God's angels protected you. I love you Alisia, dearly and I will rejoice with you in heaven." Carmela turned to Veronica. "Veronica, my precious daughter, I regret that I won't be here to spoil my beautiful grandchildren but tell them their grandmother loves them and watches them from heaven. Thank you dear for making my son so incredibly happy. I love you." Fighting her tears, Carmela reached out her hand to WarZar's outstretched one. "WarZar, my beloved boy, mama loves you so very much. Stay as happy as you are right now darling. Goodbye son. I will see you in heaven."

"Mother, I love you! When I get to heaven, I will show you just how much!" WarZar was crying just watching the tears falling down his mother's face. "This is not goodbye mother, that is too final. This is simply, see you soon mama!"

Carmela took the smallest children's hands and with one last smile for her son, stepped out, followed by the rest, all turning to dust and instantly swirling upward to the open veil of heaven. The veil shut with the last soul and WarZar's mother was gone.

CHAPTER 39

WarZar and Jack stepped through the tree line border and immediately heard the sound of many different birds singing high in the treetops. With new excitement, the two friends looked around, their attention falling on all the new residents living in the once evil woods where only vultures and ravens had flown. WarZar spotted a herd of deer grazing peacefully in the open meadow where he had led Jack to and pointed them out to his friend. Jack laughed when the male bald eagle from the neighboring mountain flew over their head and landed in a tall tree on the mountain WarZar had taken him to where they spent the night under the warm bearskin fur. It was as if all the creatures of God knew the forest was safe now from predators and to witness rabbits and squirrels for the very first time, WarZar was speechless. The once Forbidden Forest had now become a haven for all God's creation.

Veronica and Alisia joined their men and watched in wonder as the forest came to life with all the beauty of God's world. Colorful wildflowers had sprung up throughout the forest and the rich smells of cedar and pine could be smelled all around them. A great hawk and its mate flew over, squawking out their welcome and their sound echoed over the hills, valleys and mountain tops, just as the scream from the great beast used to sound.

"Those hawks can give an echoing call my friend, but nothing can match your scary scream that sent chills over everything and everyone inside this forest." Alisia smiled up at WarZar, who glanced down at his new bride to give her his beautiful smile. "Jack is sure to remember the horrifying sound that echoed across the land."

"I shall never forget the first time I heard it." Jack patted his tall friend on the back. "For a brief moment I truly believed the Forbidden Forest was someplace like hell after hearing that heart-stopping scream." Jack chuckled. "Even a frighten woman's screams could not sound close to yours and never as loud."

"Darling, why did you scream so loudly?" Veronica recalled her little brother telling the family about the scary sound of the giant beast. "Was it to frightened people?"

"At first, I started screaming to draw attention. All the subjects were scared of Lazar, but they only saw me as the deformed son, so I was ignored while father and mother got all the attention. I moved out of the palace when I was ten and lived in the cave, where I took you Jack to rest the night before heading for Rockford Falls. No one missed me, until I grew into the ten-foot giant. I had listened to the big cats screaming out at night and watched how the razor warts and climbers hid themselves, frightened of the screams. After practicing a short while, my massive lungs could take it lots of air and my scream grew so loud I drove all the big cats off our mountain and hills. Not only did the razor warts and climbers hide from me, but the evil snitches coward at my approach. All the subjects knew who was the most powerful now and everyone and everything moved out of my way when I walked through." WarZar lifted his shoulders and laughed. "I guess you noticed Jack, I had calmed down a lot when you returned to the forest."

"As a matter of fact, my friend, I believe the one time I remember your great scream was when I was cornered by your parents while I was hiding inside the tree with Amy." Jack smiled down at his sister who had been taking everything in about the man she loved. "My sweet sister, at lease the big guy didn't let out his scream when he had his first fireworks with you."

"I must admit, I came really close to letting my animal emotions come out with such a fantastic feeling!"

WarZar pulled his blushing wife into his strong arms. "Dearest darling, I would never take away your hearing by letting off one of my screams."

"I am very grateful you maintained your gentleman behavior husband." Veronica gave him a beautiful smile. "It does sound too exciting to pass up though, but at a great distance." She pointed to the mountain top. "Like up there, away from the rest of us."

"I would like nothing more than to please my woman but now the forest is filled with pleasant creatures instead of conniving, evil creatures, so I must hold my screams inside." He gave her a kiss. "Besides, I could not possibly stand that far from my lover."

"And I am sure my lovely sister feels the same about being near her man and is only kidding with you, my friend." Jack brought out smiles from the other three, then he looked around, happy to be back. "Dear ones, this is our first day back to what will be our vacation home."

"Jack is absolutely right!" WarZar took his bride's hand. "It is only fitting that my beloved and I spend the night in my old home, Rockford Falls."

"While me and my beautiful Alisia return to our secret hideaway and rekindle our first honeymoon." While looking around, Jack had spotted the huge tree where Alisia had hidden him when he was a ten-year-old scout. It all came flooding back into his mind. How he first heard her sweet voice, then how he saw her appear down the steep steps that led to the underground tunnel, then saw her underground dwelling for the first time. "What do you say Alisia, would you like to return to that romantic place and make new memories there?"

"I would like nothing more, dearest Jack. The angels have been busy preparing the rooms just the way we left them." Alisia laughed softly at Jack's surprised expression. "Surely you must know Brianna and Jason, your guardian, would be along to make sure the rooms are ready for our romantic night." The sweet angelic girl smiled over at WarZar and Veronica. "Both the underground dwellings and WarZar's large mansion have been made ready by a staff of angelic helpers, same as before."

"I would love to receive the heavenly help from angels." Veronica had never been happier than she was in the arms of her handsome prince. "Dearest WarZar, let's go so I can see the home my man built with his own two hands then make love in that oversize bed you used to sleep on."

"It will be my pleasure darling, I assure you." WarZar turned to his friend. "Jack, who knew my entire life would change the day you fell inside my forest, but I shall be grateful for you and your friendship the rest of my life." WarZar gave Jack a brotherly hug. "I feel so lucky your sister loves me Jack. I never thought it possible for me to be loved by anyone, much less someone as beautiful and talented as Veronica."

"Believe me buddy, I can tell just how much my kid sister loves you and believe me WarZar, loving you comes easy." Jack fought back the tears he felt coming. "Howard has always been a great friend to me, but more like a father figure. You are the very best friend I ever had WarZar, the brother I have always wanted and I love you with all my heart."

"I love you as well Jack! You are not just my best friend, but the only friend I have ever had or wanted and it all happened here, in this forest! Jack, I thought I had left the only home I had ever known because I desired freedom and now the Lord has saw fit to give it back, without the feeling of being trapped!"

"You are right WarZar, it did happen here, my friend. The Lord knew this and made it possible for us to have it! To remember and reflect on how we became the best of friends one summer, twenty years ago. This place will always hold the times we shared together and I am proud it shall be forever called. THE FORBIDDEN FOREST!"

AUTHOR'S NOTES

To believe in Jesus Christ puts hope into our heart. To believe He died for all our sins, fills us with his Grace and rewards us with everlasting life.

By following Jack and Alisia's example for being a Christian, start with sincere prayer to the Lord Most High, then our faith can move whatever mountains are standing in our way.

Faith is truly believing without seeing. If you are searching for truth and still feel unsure, then may God's light help your belief.

Jesus said: I am the way, the truth, the life! Jesus is real and He loves each and everyone of us beyond measure. The Lord is waiting outside your heart, knocking. If you open up your heart and let Him come in you will find Jesus Christ as your only hope for Eternal Life.

If you fail to believe and accept His forgiveness, you will find yourself in a place far worse than the Forbidden Forest.

By putting your complete trust in God, you can move those mountains and giants! As followers of Jesus, we must always walk by faith, not by sight!

As human beings, many obstacles and troubles seem impossible for us to manage. But as Christians, our faith has taught us that nothing is impossible for Jesus!

Sweet Peace,
Joan Byrd

www.ingramcontent.com/pod-product-compliance
Lightning Source LLC
Chambersburg PA
CBHW060849250626
47159CB00015B/2869